Poor Choice For A Champion

The Sag

Thanks

Poor Choice For A Champion
Fishbowl Publishing
Published: May 2016
ISBN: 978-0-9954680-2-3
Cover Design: SelfPubBookCovers.com/sigildesigns
Map by: RenFlowerGrapx

This book is dedicated with all my love to Locke. May you too lead the best of lives.

"It's the honesty of these worlds,
ruled by magic and mighty swords
that makes my soul
long for the past."
- Nightwish, *Elvenpath*

"Whether I shall turn out to be the hero of my own life, or whether that station will be held by anybody else, these pages must show."

– Charles Dickens, *David Copperfield*

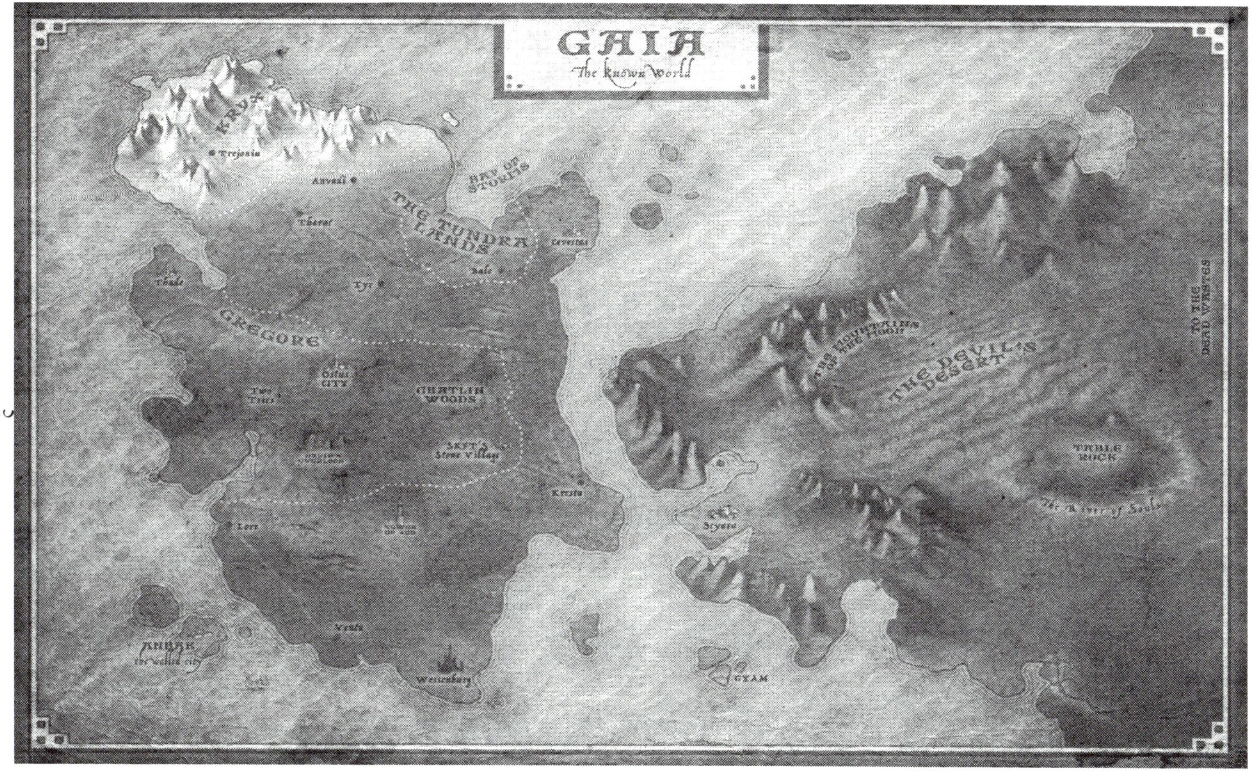
GAIA
The known World
KRUX
BAY OF STORMS
THE TUNDRA LANDS
Tyr
GREGORE
Two Trees
THE MOUNTAINS OF THE MOON
THE DEVIL'S DESERT
TABLE ROCK
The River of Souls
GYAM
TO THE DEAD WASTES

Prologue

To look upon him, the ghost was nothing special. So average and unremarkable was his appearance he could have been any of a thousand men. He was neither tall, nor wide of shoulder, not good looking nor proud of bearing. He wore no finery, just the simple clothes of a farmer. He was, if anything, a rather underwhelming sight. It was not a form he could afford to let others see often.

Hovering upon the balcony of his fortress he stared out over the frozen lands that he commanded. He had not been this troubled in more than five centuries. Out there, below his spire, beneath the glacial mountains and under the ice plains, lay the sunken city of Salgatha where thousands did his bidding out of respect and fear. Yet some had begun to speak against him, muttering whispers of discontent that if not checked would fan the fires of insurrection. He could not blame them. The enemy had routed his army and had killed his corporeal form. It was the worst military defeat in his career. He had been outthought, outmanoeuvred and outclassed. His enemy was a master tactician and inspiring leader and had proved simply too good. Despite his reputation, these things did not make the ghost angry. He rarely experienced anger anymore - he had little time for such an indulgent emotion.

"Come inside," the Ambassador's deep voice rumbled from within his chambers. "Come inside and close that door – I'm freezing."

The ghost did as he was bid. As a spirit he did not need to use doorways but so distracted was his mind that he had opened the large, gilded doors out of habit. He glided inside, willing them shut with his mind.

"Better," grumbled the Ambassador. "You know I hate the cold."

"My apologies," said the ghost, addressing his voice to the shadows where his companion chose to sit. "I have much on my mind."

"Ah, but a king should have much on his mind. Heavy is the head that wears the crown and all that," the Ambassador chuckled, slurping at his wine. The ghost hid his revulsion at his guest's appalling manners. He had long grown used to them. "I don't think I have ever seen you look so weary," the Ambassador continued. "Is it over for you? Has your will left you at last?"

"I don't know," said the ghost. "It is a hard price to pay this time."

"Yes," the voice croaked, undisguised ecstasy in its tone. "The price is beautifully high."

The ghost hovered over his throne for some minutes, staring down at his spectral hands. They had not always belonged to a king. Once they had worked the soil and grown crops. They had ploughed fields and helped birth a child. They had wiped tears from a wife's cheek and bathed an infant. Simple, earthly things had been enough once. The ghost thought back to his beginnings. It was almost impossible to remember who he had been before he started this journey. He thought of all the sacrifices, all of the pain since then - of everything he had given up to become what he was. Did he have it within himself to give more - did he want to give *this* for one last gambit? He could not decide and the dilemma span around and around making him feel weary and wretched.

"I do not know why you torment yourself," the Ambassador spoke. "It has been a long road. You are not going to turn from it now."

The ghost did not reply. Deep down he knew his guest was right. There were some paths that once trodden could never be abandoned.

A knock came from the chamber door and a man entered wearing the dark robes of the inner circle. Pulling back his hood he knelt, bowing his head. "You wished to see me father?"

"Dezzen, my son," said the ghost, gliding towards the young man and bidding him to rise. "We need to discuss our strategy."

"Of course. Things for your resurrection progress favourably," said Dezzen. "Everything will soon be ready."

The ghost waved his hand, showing he was not interested in that line of discussion. "That is all well and good, but we must discuss Athus Glynn. He is the cause of our suffering. But first, take some wine - one of us might as well enjoy it."

Dezzen poured himself a goblet. "Thank you father. What can be done about The Champion?"

The ghost looked at his son fondly; the last of his line and his favourite. No boy had ever made a father prouder. "There is but one thing to do," said the ghost. "Athus is too great both in single combat and in battle. We must use cunning, like in the old days. Without him our enemy will flounder and we will seize our chance."

"What do you have in mind?" Dezzen asked.

The ghost paused for a moment before speaking; trying to place the boy's mother and realising he had forgotten who she was. "I intend to isolate him, to draw his soul into another body and then assassinate him."

The young man's eyes widened. He was no longer a novice and he knew the power needed for such an incantation was vast. "Can it be done?"

"Yes," said the ghost. "It can be done. My blade cut him deep before he slew me; the enchantment is already in his blood. All that is required is a compatible soul and enough power to make the casting."

"You have found a suitable soul?" Dezzen asked.

"I have one in mind, someone who is ideal. They are good but weak, they just need to be steered in the right direction," said the ghost. "They may even come over to us before the end. That is all well in hand. What has troubled me is how to raise the necessary power for the spell. Our allies inform me that it will take no less than the blood of one of the old kings."

"But you are King here father, surely you do not intend to sacrifice yourself?" Dezzen asked.

"You are a loyal son, too loyal I think, and you have learned well," the ghost smiled. "Yet I must confess that I have deceived you on a number of matters. Currently I am a shade and it is written in the old lore, in the deep magics, that no spirit may be a king of men."

Dezzen was his father's son and as such was no fool. The ghost was proud to see he showed no more reaction than the slight dilation of his pupils.

"I do not understand," Dezzen began...

But he did and they both knew it. The young man grabbed for the focus stone he wore around his neck and began to cast a ward, but it was far too little, far too late. The Ambassador's black tentacles snaked out from the darkness, binding the young man tight before slowly dragging him, struggling, towards the shadows.

"You have been a wonderful son," said the ghost parting his hands. "I am sorry your reign was not longer."

Dezzen tried to say something but the tentacle around his neck choked off his words and he disappeared into the dark with little more than a murmur. The sounds that followed were far from pleasant.

The ghost waited until a large belch came from the shadows and the Ambassador spoke. "The deal is made. You will have the power you desire. But this is the last time. My master grows impatient with your lack of progress. Fail again and you will know his displeasure."

The ghost nodded. "Very well."

"I will of course do what I can for you," the Ambassador continued, his tone softening. "But even my voice is unlikely to save you again. It does not carry the power in court it once did."

"Again, my thanks," said the ghost.

"And stop wearing that pathetic visage. That man died over a millennia ago. You are Nemeddes, the King of Death - not some turnip farmer. Your line is now gone and gone forever. There is no reason to keep even a thought of the past alive. Only with us will you live eternal."

The ghost nodded its agreement, its spectral form changing, growing two foot in height, the face becoming sharp and cruelly attractive, the muscles bunching and filling. The simple rags became armour of the darkest night, tipped with drake scale and dragon bone and the humble eyes began to blaze with gold, their black pupils split like a serpent's.

"That is better," the Ambassador said. "That is the Lord of Death I know. Now I must go. I will miss this place and our talks but the situation at home is frightful and my skills are needed. Good luck old friend. To succeed will bring ascension, to fail will bring oblivion. It is that simple now. But then you know that. I hope you have picked the soul carefully you intend to use for this spell."

"Oh I have," said Nemeddes. "I have picked him very carefully indeed."

1.

Leo Kvetch stretched and sighed as he stared up into the blue sky. It was one of those gorgeous days of late summer that seemed to drift on forever, the temperature was just right, the wind refreshing and the hay soft and springy. It was too good a day to break his back building Clayson a new paddock fence. Rolling onto his belly, Leo looked through a gap in the hay pile and watched as his workmates toiled in the far pasture. He should have been back more than half an hour ago but the haystack was so comfortable, the sun so warm and welcoming... and it wasn't as if he hadn't worked *reasonably* hard that morning. Everyone deserved a break from time to time. Yet, even as he justified himself, it was with a grumble and not a little guilt, that he climbed to his feet and dusted the golden straws from his clothes. He winced as he rolled his left shoulder until it ground and cracked, sending a shiver of pain that lanced towards his elbow. None of the others understood of course, they didn't care that he needed to rest his old injury regularly - they just thought him lazy. With a sigh Leo began to trudge back to join the rest of the farmhands.

No one who watched Leo amble back across Clayson's farm could deny that he cut a roguish figure. Rude locks of unkempt, red hair hung down from the brim of his straw hat to be hastily swept behind his ears. His clothes were patched and ill fitting and his bright copper beard was as wild and untamed as a honey badger.

Leo nodded a greeting as he approached his workmates, then picked up some loose planks and began stacking them on the back of the wagon.

"And where the hell have you been?" a voice demanded.

Leo turned and offered Mason an easy smile. "I had to make some repairs to the outhouse in the west pasture. The roof's nearly fallen through."

Another farmhand, Sam, clapped Leo on the back. "Aye, but the only reason that roof is falling through is because you've spent most of the summer basking on it."

"Now that is unfair," said Leo. "I do my bit. I haven't spent all summer lazing on a roof."

"No, he's right," said Mason. "If he'd spent all summer lazing on that roof he wouldn't have had any time to be lazing in bales of hay or lazing around in the barn, or taking the best part of an hour in the privy or an extra half hour for his lunch or floating around the farmhouse trying to work up the courage to speak to Miss Rebecca. Do I need go on?"

Leo's face flushed as Mason's comment was met with laughter from his fellows. "You're going to give me a bad reputation," said Leo, trying to laugh along with the others.

"There's no need for me to help you with that, you do a good enough job on your own," said Mason.

Leo felt a sting of anger and threw a couple more planks onto the back of the wagon before turning back. "Who was it, Mason, who stayed out with you until after dark when you left the north fence open and Thuros got out? And who was it that caught him and got him back? You think Clayson would have been pleased that you nearly lost his best stallion?"

Mason shook his head. "Did I not thank you for it? But you know what, Leo? That was one day! So you pulled your weight for one day, one day all season, so what? You're a nice guy, I've got nothing personal against you, but I'm sick of carrying you – and I'm not the only one. You think the others don't grumble when you disappear? You think because you can tell a joke or two and make a few people laugh that no-one minds that you're workshy and leave us to do the heavy lifting? They might not say it to your face but there's more than a few of us who've had enough."

Leo stood tall for a moment, meeting Mason's eyes before he lowered his gaze and nodded. "You're right, I do slack off too much. I do need to work harder.

It's just this damn shoulder," Leo said, rubbing it for effect. "It slows me down."

"Yeah, yeah," scoffed Mason. "Is this the point when we get to hear, for the thousandth time, about how you were going to be a great wrestler, but you got injured and blah, blah, blah?"

"I *was* going to be a great wrestler!" snapped Leo, then quieter: "I'm just not cut out for manual work."

A few of the men laughed and Mason snorted. "That probably explains why you do so little of it."

With the tools away and the day's work done, the men milled around the farmhouse waiting for Clayson to dismiss them. Leo sat away from the others on an old pallet and felt thoroughly sorry for himself. Mason walked over and sat beside him, noting the beaten down look in Leo's eyes. He let out a low sigh. He had been looking forward to this conversation for some time, but now, seeing the pained, defeated expression on Leo's face, all relish left him. There was no sport in hunting wounded game.

"Look Kvetch, I wanted you to hear this from me, man to man," said Mason. "I didn't want you to think I was going behind your back." Mason paused, giving Leo a chance to speak, but Leo said nothing and just continued staring at the floor. "I've been talking with the men and we've decided we're going to have a word with Clayson about you, on account that you're not pulling your weight. It's nothing personal but we all have families to feed and you're slowing us down."

Leo nodded. "That's fine. I'd probably do the same in your shoes."

"Ok, then," said Mason.

Leo looked tired, his face strained and Mason got the distinct impression that the man was close to tears. Anger faded from him and was replaced with pity. He stood and, in a gesture so unlike him that he shocked himself, put a hand on Leo's shoulder before he walked away.

Leo sat staring into the dirt for a while, then stood and wandered to the paddock fence to watch the horses. He could not explain the weakness in himself or why, as a grown man, he felt close to tears. He did not know why he had not told Mason to shut up or why he hadn't worked an honest day in months. Everything just seemed pointless. He looked at the beauty of the world and could still acknowledge it - how the grass rippled in the wind, how a tiny spider crawled along the fence close to his fingers, how the sky above embraced them all in its boundless blue. He watched the horses bunching by the far gate, such wonderful animals; their flanks shimmering in the sunlight like oil. Carefully, so as not to stare, he watched Clayson's daughter, Rebecca, as she entered the paddock, moving from horse to horse and attaching their food bags. There was such beauty in the world, but it could no longer touch him. At night, he would wonder why anything should exist at all; the pain of life seemed to far outweigh its splendour. If there was nothing, there would be such peace.

"Something's eatin' at you boy," an old voice said from close by.

Leo jumped and turned to see Seabrooke grinning at him toothlessly.

"Give a man some warning before creeping up on him, won't you?" Leo said, grabbing a deep breath.

The old man shuffled closer and leaned his stick against the fence. None of the workers were old enough to remember the time Seabrooke had laboured on the farm. Some said that he had been a young man during the first season, just after Clayson's grandfather had bought the land. Leo was sceptical. By his reckoning, even if Seabrooke had been as young as ten or so at the time, he would now be some years over one hundred. Still, Clayson seemed to believe it, and out of respect for a man who had worked with both his grandfather and father, had allowed Seabrooke to live on at the farm following his retirement. Seabrooke was now positively diminutive and seemed to shrink a little with each passing season, but for someone as crooked and ancient looking as one of the gnarled oaks from The Hollow, he was in fine fettle, walking the paddocks each day and sometimes stopping to eat lunch with the hands.

"I think a whole army could have snuck up on you then, young man, but now I'm here, even these old eyes can see what's got your attention," said Seabrooke with a nod of his head towards Rebecca.

"Something like that," said Leo.

"She's a lovely woman," said Seabrooke. "A shame what happened with her husband."

"It was," said Leo, feeling anger flow through him, pushing back at the melancholy.

Seabrooke chuckled, a strangled, hacking sound like someone having a coughing fit. "That's right, that's right. That's a better look for a man to have in his eyes. Beats that wounded puppy dog expression you've been wearing since coming back from the fields."

"The hell are you talking about?" said Leo.

"Ha!" spat Seabrooke. "You know exactly what I'm talking about. You got something gnawin' at you, boy, didn't I just say? Need to sort that out or it's going to eat you alive."

"Easier said than done," said Leo.

"Most things are, that's why the world's ruled by scholars and diplomats. They're all like a false alarm on the privy, son – all hot air and no follow through," Seabrooke cackled at his own joke. When Leo didn't join in he continued, "Always been easier to say something than to do it - Hell, if that weren't the case, we'd all be kings, wouldn't we?"

"I suppose we would."

"Why am I hearing the rest of the men are putting in a complaint about you?" Seabrooke asked, the hint of an edge to his voice.

Leo shrugged.

"You're just going to take that, like a dog? Damn, if I was even ten years younger I'd thrash a bit of pride back into you," the old man said.

"Maybe you would," said Leo.

"I might look like an old fool, but I've seen a fair bit of the world and I can see you're wasting this life and there are few bigger crimes than that," said Seabrooke. "You need to do something or you're going to drown in this self-pity of yours. There's nothing worse than self-pity, boy, it rots the soul."

"Do you think I want to feel like this?" Leo growled.

"Did you know I used to watch you wrestle, when you were up and coming?" Seabrooke asked. "Saw you win the county finals. What a bout that was!"

"I didn't think anyone remembered that," said Leo.

"You were fierce then. How much older than you was he? Five to ten years I'd bet. He was a bear of a man with shoulders like cannon balls and a chest like a powder keg. I remember it well. You were a slip of a boy and I winced to myself when you squared up. But you schooled him that day. He threw every dirty trick at you, used every ounce of his power. I thought he had you in the second round - I've never seen anyone reverse a move like that. When I saw you escape that hold, then pass his guard, I knew you'd win and he knew it too. You were too good for him, you had too much spirit. I thought, that lad down there, that pale, red-haired lad – he's going to be something, he's going to be a man amongst men. And look at you now. Where the hell did that lad go?"

Leo sniffed and looked away for a moment, running the back of his hand across his face.

Seabrooke leaned in close. "Some men will tell you that there's shame in tears, but not me. God knows I've wept enough of them over the years. I don't know what pain is hiding in you, boy, but I know there's no shame in it. But there's shame in living the way you are, letting life sail past and you not doing anything about it. You got to go find him lad, find that fierce young lad you were. Find whatever went wrong with him and fix it - 'cause you're sinking."

"And how do I do that?" asked Leo.

"By living," said Seabrooke. "You can start by climbing this fence and going to talk to that young lady who you've been lollygagging over for years. She loved you once, why not again? Neither of you are getting any younger."

"And what would she want with a clot like me?" Leo asked.

"I don't know, you're certainly no oil painting, but what have you got to lose?" said Seabrooke with a chuckle. "Seems to me that either nothing changes or everything does. Not bad odds them boy, I can tell you."

Leo allowed himself a small smile. "I suppose when you put it like that," he said, and put his foot onto the first rung of the fence but then the sound of Clayson's bell rang out, holding him in his tracks and signalling the workers to a meeting outside of the farmhouse and Leo stepped back and began to walk towards the farm. "I'll speak to her tomorrow," he said.

Seabrooke watched him go, not hiding the disappointment on his face.

2.

Lindon Clayson was a short, fat man with an honest face and a forehead that extended all the way to his crown. A widower, he lived in the farmhouse with his oldest daughter Rebecca, old Seabrooke and Ansa, their maid. He was, as bosses go, not a bad man to work for, being both prompt with wages and fair with his employees.

Clayson clumped down the wooden farmhouse steps and addressed the workers. "Good work this week, lads," he said, producing a dozen or so envelopes from his back pocket. "Here's your pay, come and get it before I change my mind."

The men filed forward and Clayson doled out to each an envelope. When Leo came to collect his, Clayson kept hold of the packet for a moment until Leo met his eye.

"See me at the end, son," he said before moving on. Leo nodded, waiting while Clayson passed out the last of the slips. "And remember, half twelve start tomorrow, and so help me, any man turning up late or drunk will be looking for another job. Is that understood?"

The men mumbled a half-hearted agreement and began to splinter away into small groups, heading for home or the city or wherever their wage packet called them. Leo alone remained.

Clayson waited for the men to move beyond earshot before turning his attention to Leo. "You know what this is about ?"

"I think so," said Leo.

"Some of your mates think you're not pulling your weight. And it's not the first time I've heard that," Clayson said.

Leo shrugged. "I do my bit Mr. Clayson. I do."

Clayson nodded sagely. "How long you been with me now, son?"

Leo had to think and when the answer came he found himself almost scared by it. "Ten, nearly eleven years."

"Sounds about right. Your uncle asked me to take you on, and I did, as a favour to an old friend. But I was glad I did mind, you worked like a man possessed. I remember saying to Agnes before she passed, the Essence preserve her, that with a few more like Leo Kvetch we could be the biggest ranch this side of Ostus. But I don't hear much about that man anymore. What the hell happened to him?"

In the silence that followed the question, Leo had plenty of answers. That he'd only wanted to work a few seasons while he got his wrestling back on track; that working on the damnable farm had made his shoulder injury worse and ruined his chances; that after a few seasons the awful monotony of it all had got to him; that now the only thing getting him through each day was the thought of his first sip of ale that night; that he felt old and used up before his time; that he could barely sleep a wink and rose each day exhausted; that life seemed pointless. He could have picked any of these, but instead he merely shrugged.

Clayson cleared his throat. "Out of respect for your uncle and deep down because I like you - one more chance Leo. My patience is not inexhaustible. Now get out of here, I'll see you tomorrow. Enjoy the festival."

"Thank you Mr. Clayson," said Leo, and his mood sombre he turned and began the walk home.

The Golden Pear was a little busier than usual by the time Leo arrived, but his favourite spot was still free and he slipped through the crowd to the bar, pleased he had decided to come. He was sure that a night in The Pear would lift his spirits. Venn, the tavern master, greeted him with a curt nod and Leo waited while the large man finished serving a couple of customers before turning his attention to Leo.

Venn was maybe a touch under six foot five, his shoulders round and his chest like the kegs he so effortlessly carried up and down the cellar steps. He was, to Leo's knowledge, the only tavern master in the area who could run his establishment without the need to hire security. No one messed with Venn. A few summers ago he'd taken on a small group of troublemakers single handed and won, earning himself the nickname "the one man gang."

"Usual?" Venn asked.

"Been a tough day," said Leo. "But at least it's payday, I'll take a jug."

Venn raised his eyebrows and fetched the order, placing it on the counter. "Will I be seeing you at the heats for the county team next week?"

"Not sure," said Leo, laying a few coins on the counter. "I'll have to see how my shoulder's doing. I've been seeing Thetius about it, a damn lot of good that seems to be doing."

Venn nodded before being called away by another customer and Leo took his tankard and jug and eased his way across the bar to his favourite seat. The first sip was always the best and Leo tried to savour it. But it passed all too fleetingly and soon the first mugful was gone. After that it was always a blur. The music was pleasant as patrons took turns playing, some singing or playing instruments they'd brought with them. Leo sat drinking and tapping his feet, joining in with the songs he was familiar with. This would be the last time he did this, he promised himself. One last blowout and tomorrow he'd get things back on track. A cynical voice in his head pointed out that he said that every night.

He looked over to where Venn was still serving behind the counter. Maybe he would go down and try out for the county wrestling team. Perhaps he wasn't too old to give it a shot. He'd wrestled Venn once a few years ago and won narrowly. It had been a private match, more like a training session than anything, but he'd bested the bigger man with a combination of tactics and experience that had outfoxed Venn's massive power. To Leo's knowledge he was the only one in the local area to tap the big man. Of course Venn would have improved since then, he wrestled regularly throughout the county now. Leo let the thought go. Tomorrow he'd start training again. One last drinking session tonight he thought to himself again, his mood lifted by the drink, and tomorrow I'll get back on it.

Pushing himself unsteadily to his feet, Leo swayed across to the bar and spilled a few more coins onto the counter. "Another jug when you're ready," he smiled.

Venn eyed him coldly. "One jug is enough for any man. You can hardly stand."

"I can stand perfectly," said Leo, taking his hands away from the bar for a moment as if to prove his point and then quickly grabbing it again.

"I said no," said Venn. "You drink too much. It's getting out of hand." Venn pointed to Leo's belly. "You didn't have that gut a year ago."

Leo scowled. "The hell are you saying?"

"I'm saying that I'm not going to serve you another drop tonight, so go home. And if you want to know more, I'm telling you that you're half a step away from being a drunk. You already look like a vagrant, you want to cut that hair and give your beard a trim. You're turning into a bloody disgrace Kvetch. You need to wise up."

Leo stared at the man, clumsily stuffing his money back into his coin purse. "A fine way to talk to me, that," he snorted and on rubbery legs strode out into the night with as much grace as any drunk ever managed.

It was balmy and close outside and beyond the lights that blazed from the pub windows, there was only darkness. A handful of patrons sat on sturdy tables around the tavern entrance; shadowy figures drinking and smoking and enjoying one of the closing nights of a long summer. Leo felt a sudden gust of wind refresh him and steadying himself only briefly cast himself down the short path towards the track road.

"Well, look who it is," said a voice, as Leo stumbled to support himself on the gatepost.

Leo turned and saw two men rise from a table and walk towards him. At first he had no idea who they were, but as the two men came closer, they were illuminated by light from the pub windows and Leo could make them out clearly.

"Relund, Case, it's good to see you," Leo nodded as way of greeting.

"You're not looking so good Kvetch," Relund spoke, his voice louder than it needed to be. The rest of the people outside turned to watch. Even through the stupor of the drink Leo could tell both men were up for a scrap.

"Yeah, you're not looking so well at all," Case said.

"Looking better than you, Case," Leo grinned. "I wouldn't have thought it possible, but you get uglier every time I see you."

"You shut your mouth Kvetch," Case snarled, glancing to Relund for support.

"Yeah, shut your mouth," Relund menaced, shoving Leo back into the wall.

"Hey, take it easy!" a voice shouted from by the pub door. "Leave the drunk be."

"Hey, I'm not a drunk," said Leo, almost surging past Relund and Case to find out who'd shouted out, but the two men held him firm and it took Leo's ale-addled mind a moment to realise that one was going through his pockets. Leo's hand dropped to where he was keeping his coin purse, but he was a moment too late and he saw Case hold it up with a look of triumph.

"Give that back!" said Leo, snatching at his money, but Case stepped back and threw a punch Leo didn't even know about until it had cannoned off his temple and sent him to one knee.

"Hey! That's enough!" one of the bystanders shouted again, a moment before Leo was knocked flat on his back from another strike. Still with no clear idea exactly what was happening Leo grabbed at something and pulled. He was rewarded as a body landed next to him on the path. He rolled onto it, taking a fierce grip. Whoever he'd coiled around began to struggle and shout and there was a clash of heads between Leo and the man, causing Leo's vision to spin even faster. He felt several blows bounce off him before he was dragged free and he staggered backwards falling onto his rump. He heard shouts, agitated and confusing, coming from all around as people separated him from Case and Relund. A pair of hands took him under the shoulders and levered him up. As he tried to regain his balance he caught a glimpse of Case through the crowd. Case's face was streaked with blood from a cut over his right eye.

"Look what he's done to me," Case shouted, holding a bloodied hand up for all to see.

Calls for calm came from the gathered men and were met with outraged shouts from Relund and Case. In the heat of it, a stranger took Leo aside and began leading him away from the pub. "Look mate, these two are no good, I'd get yourself home if I were you."

"My thoughts exactly," Leo muttered.

"What?" the stranger asked. "By the Essence, how much have you had? Where do you live?"

"Two Trees, just down the lane from the bakers," said Leo.

"Listen mate, I can't understand a damn word you're saying," the man said. "Try to stop slurring and take your time. Where do you live?"

Leo was about to answer when he was tackled to the floor. This time he was dragged roughly up by a furious Case who pulled his fist back to throw a wild punch towards Leo's face. Leo swayed back and Case's fist caught the tip of Leo's beard and not his chin. Off balance, Case stumbled and Leo aimed a kick at the man's backside. It struck, propelling the small frame of Case headlong into the stone fence posts that ringed The Golden Pear. It also sent Leo stumbling the other way to sprawl again in the dirt. This time he managed to right himself. Case however did not. People rallied around the fallen man, then one broke away from them.

"He's killed him! He's killed him!" Relund bellowed.

"He's not killed him, he's just out cold," a voice corrected, but Relund took no notice. Reaching into a pocket he pulled out a skinning knife. The blade caught the light from the pub's windows, gleaming bright, and in that moment it cut through the alcohol in Leo's brain.

Suddenly he was a youth again, the smell of salted meat filling his nostrils. All he could hear was the sound of water slopping onto stone tiles and fingernails clawing, struggling pathetically. A figure loomed towards him, hands covered in blood, its eyes wild and crazed, a glimmering knife like a demon's tooth was raised above its head… "I'm going to gut you like a kipper," a hollow voice rasped in his mind and Leo screamed, covering his eyes.

As suddenly as it had come, the vision left, along with its terrifying smells and sounds. Disorientated, Leo's mind returned to reality and he found himself on his knees outside the tavern. Vaguely he was aware of the warm trickle of urine as his bladder released, soaking the inside of his left leg.

"He's pissed himself, the little fairy," Relund bellowed, advancing.

Leo scrunched his eyes shut, knowing only that, for all the world, he did not want to see that knife again.

"Relund, you dog, don't take another step!" a voice shouted, so deep and powerful that it could only be Venn.

Relund paused for a moment and it saved Leo's life giving him a second he would not otherwise have had. With the spell somehow broken, he scrambled away and began to run. He'd put about ten yards of space between himself and Relund before the man realised, and with a furious cry, began to give chase.

3.

Leo found that sobriety had a way of following closely on the heels of abject terror. With legs that only moments before had ignored the most basic commands, he ran, and ran strongly. Relund followed, shouting threats for the first hundred yards, then going silent and conserving his energy to chase Leo down.

For a little while the dwindling light from the pub and a few outlying homes helped illuminate the gloomy path, then the runners were plunged into the blackness of the moonless night, hurtling along in near complete darkness. Leo held to the path, nearly rolling his ankle on an uneven sod of turf and stumbled, losing speed. Panicked, he glanced back, seeing a vague shape worryingly close. Darting to his left, lungs burning, he veered from the path and crossed the river in wading bounds. Scrambling up the opposite bank he cut into the woods. A loud splash and a curse came from behind him and he knew that Relund had misjudged the bank and fallen. Leo clambered up a small hill and ran on. His breathing was heavy now but he was determined to put as much space between them as he could. The wood closed in, the trees pressing together, and he dodged in and amongst the trunks. Branches slapped at his face whilst roots rose up, trying to grapple him to the floor. Somehow he ran on, and on, and on, until all he could hear was his own breath rasping from his mouth and he stopped, leaned against a tree and listened.

There was no sound of pursuit. The night was still and quiet and it was too dark for anyone to read his tracks. Even so, Leo moved carefully away from where he had stopped, trying to stand on roots and rocks to avoid leaving any sign. When he was satisfied, he sank down amidst some ferns, suddenly exhausted. The ground felt soft as his head came to rest upon it and despite the danger, he fell almost at once into sleep.

He was running again. Running in darkness. Sweat dripped from his face and poured down his body. His legs were racing, desperately trying to get away from something, desperately forging forwards. Ahead of him, somewhere in this shadowy realm, a child's cries echoed, distorted and distressing. There was something behind him he knew; something in the dark that was hunting him. He looked back and saw a vague human figure begin to emerge from the blackness. It piped in like smoke under a doorframe, effortlessly fading into form. It was little more tangible than a shadow at first but the blade it held in its crude right hand, which glimmered like a single, diamond sharp tooth looked real enough.

Terror spread through him and he ran on, and ran on, and ran on. The child's cries continued, more urgent now, but no matter how fast he ran he never seemed to get closer to the child nor further away from the spectral figure with the gleaming blade. Then out of the dark a door appeared, light shining from it like a beacon and without thought he ran through it. At once the dark fell away and he was there again, in that place. He knew what waited for him there. He didn't want to see his plate of tuna fish sandwiches, his favourite, sitting waiting for him on the table. Such a normal thing, innocent and now so perversely out of place. He didn't want to see the carefully folded laundry sitting in its basket, he didn't want to watch her feet struggling, pushing on the slick floorboards. Then stopping.

He turned his back and tried to shut his eyes but they wouldn't close and the dark shape that had been chasing him slunk in from the nothingness behind the door. It had taken on an almost human form now. It grinned. Its mouth spread, opening impossibly wide and its teeth sparkled, and every one, every single one, was a tiny, pearl- handled knife.

"I'm going to gut you like a kipper…" the creature whispered as it lunged. Leo screamed.

He awoke with a muted cry as the nightmare left him and he sat up quickly, feeling exhausted. Dawn light was beginning to pour through the woodland canopy and the morning chorus was in full voice. He squinted and wished the birds would shut up. It felt like someone was banging a drum inside his skull. His head span and he groaned. Groggily he checked his surroundings.

"Where the hell am I?" he whispered, slowly levering himself to his feet. He could remember next to nothing about the night before nor why he was in the middle of the woods. His dreams had been bad again he knew, robbing him of the rest that he needed. He tried to recall what he had dreamt of but, as it was every day, nothing came and he was just left with a sense of terror. Without a drink, he was sometimes too scared to close his eyes at night, knowing that only fear waited for him.

He relieved himself behind a tree then, staggering at first, picked his way through the woods in no particular direction. Likely he'd wandered into The Hollow, the woodland surrounding Two Trees. It was not a particularly large area and he would soon reach the treeline and find his bearings. After a few minutes he came upon a stream and knelt to wash his face and drink. The cold water was sweet and refreshing. He followed the winding tributary for a distance and it was not long until he could hear the river gurgling a little way south. Following his ears he cut towards it and soon broke out of the trees into the morning sunshine. At once he recognised Havecroft's windmill, spinning lazily on the hills in the distance. Set with his bearings, he forded the river and headed for home.

It was still early morning when he got back to his modest cabin. He stripped and washed then prepared himself a breakfast of fried bacon and eggs, buttering his bread with a spoon, before beginning to get ready for work. He was nearly out of the door when he remembered with some excitement that he had the morning off. Nipping back inside, he looked for his coin purse and couldn't find it. He cursed himself; he'd probably left it in The Pear or dropped it on the way home. It wasn't the first time. At least he'd learned never to carry more than he could afford to lose. He filled a spare pouch with a few coins, packed some lunch, and then set off in the direction of Ostus City and the celebrations.

The city was not far, but Leo stopped and caught the carriage anyway, wanting to have as much time as he could in Ostus before he had to return for work. The ride took a little over half an hour and tipping the driver with a copper piece, Leo alighted near the south gate and joined the crowds of people filling the capital's streets. Stalls of every type lined the roads and laughing children played games; darting between the heaving mass of adults. Leo stopped and bought a couple of sweet buns from a vendor, devouring them with relish as he passed amongst the shops and the carnival games.

The revelry was boisterous and at one point a pretty girl rushed out of the crowd and planted a kiss firmly on his lips before running away. Leo's face flushed as red as his beard for a moment, until he realised she was one of many doing the same and had likely mistaken him for an off duty soldier.

Leo could not say he followed politics keenly, but all knew about The War in the North. It had affected every life in the realm. It had hung like a shroud of fear over the country for more than five years. Now, a scant year since the armies of Ostus had won the decisive battle, the rationing of previous years and the constant terror that the armies of Kryx would fight their way south seemed like a distant memory. Although Leo felt the jubilation of his countrymen, the war was, to him at least, somehow abstract. He had heard stories, of course, about battles on the frozen ice-plains and in the treacherous mountain steppes. Kryx was said to be an unforgiving realm. Bards endlessly sang songs about the final battle, where Lord Athus Glynn had dealt a mortal wound to the Kryxian Sorcerer King, Nemeddes. Leo had heard many wonderful tales and they grew taller with each telling. Yet it had all happened so far away. His only contact with it had been through news reports and word of mouth. He himself had never seen a Kryxian and he found it hard to hate what he had never met. He had of course been considered for military service and the shame of his testing still hung with him. There was little place in the army for cowards who were too afraid to even hold their own sword.

A fanfare of trumpets sounded close by and hurriedly, people began dashing down side streets calling excitedly to one another. Leo followed and was soon lost in the crush, being pulled along by a current of human bodies. As the press left the mercantile district, the street became wider and people began to spread out, moving more freely. The road either side of the main thoroughfare was lined with a writhing sea of bodies. He had never seen so many people gathered in one place. Some held banners displaying the King's colours whilst others played drums or pipes. A carnival spirit enveloped the city and excitement spread like wildfire through the masses. In the distance, a small plume of dust rose from the road and Leo knew that this must be the royal party getting closer. The noise of the crowd grew with every passing moment of anticipation.

There was no way to get close to the front now, so Leo took a leaf from others in his position and clambering over a few boxes he shinnied up a drainpipe to a nearby rooftop. As he approached the top a man leaned down and offered him a hand. Leo accepted it and with a nod of thanks took a seat on the crest of the roof with a group of others. The view of the city was beautiful. The morning sun reflected off the white of the buildings and turned the red brown of the roof tiles into majestic amber. The whole of Ostus seemed more vital, more alive than ever before.

On the road the dust cloud grew closer until dark shapes could be seen at the front, flying a banner of white and gold. The people roared, unable to contain the fervour that had built inside them. Leo found himself joining them as the Knights of Fifty Third Cohort galloped past, their mail armour gleaming like star fire in the sunlight. Next came the King's Guard, dressed in their formal black and purple uniforms, their lances held like pillars supporting the very heavens. And then came the King himself, waving from the window of an ornate carriage. Leo could not see the man from where he sat, just an old, gloved hand waving feebly to the crowd. The people's cheers reached a new level as he passed through and flags were waved with greater vigour. Then, when Leo thought the noise could get no louder *they* came into view. Every one of them rode a white horse, unadorned with trappings, apart from a single simple sigil of a golden sun, which fluttered from a pendant around their mount's neck. They were The Sunchasers, the personal unit of Lord Athus. Silver helms and white capes dazzled as they rode by, all eyes to the front, a perfect military unit. They looked invincible and untouchable. At the front of their number, the hero Balthus broke their disciplined stillness, and raised a fist in triumph. The crowd, already at fever pitch, found another notch and went wild. Someone started a chant: "Balthus! Balthus! Balthus!"

The chant spread like a blaze through dry grass and the giant stood up in the saddle of his massive warhorse to acknowledge it. He was, Leo thought, the biggest man he had ever seen, maybe several inches taller than Venn and much broader. His skin was so dark it was like ebony and even from here the raw power of the man was clear. His smile was broad and his gaze felt like it found every person in that crowd and lifted them somehow, inspiring them. He was the sort of man others would follow to hell and back.

Then, The Sunchasers passed, and behind them, drawn on a simple chariot surrounded by a handful of soldiers, stood two people – and the crowd reached euphoria. He did not wear armour, nor carry his legendary lion headed sword. He was not a giant of a man, nor did he play to the crowd. He stood hand in hand with his wife and waved. Even his smile was humble, embarrassed by it all.

Leo had never seen Athus Glynn in the flesh before. He knew him as most knew him, from the stories of the bards and skalds. He was Athus the First Sword of Ostus, he was Athus The Demon Slayer, The Lightbringer, The Undefeated. Most commonly he was just referred to as The Champion. He was the man who had led the final charge on the Kryxian host and who had slain their King in single combat. The noise of the crowd was now like the waves of the sea and Leo felt the primal beat of the celebration deep in his heart.

As the chariot came closer, Leo saw that Athus wore a simple tunic of blue and had chosen not to fly his own banner but the banner of the city itself. He was a man of average height, his body rangy and lean. His hair was short and dark and he was, in many ways, unremarkable. Yet there was, Leo felt, something in the man's stance that set him apart; a readiness underlying an animal grace - a poise that hinted at incredible speed. Then Leo focused on Zarina for the first time and forgot all about The Champion. She wore a dress of white, unadorned apart from a blue gem that sparkled in the sun. Her olive skin was resplendent in the sunlight, her dark hair hanging in shimmering waves. She was a beauty unlike anything he had ever seen. Zarina and Athus were childhood sweethearts and their perfect love story only added to their myth.

Without meaning to, Leo noticed the man driving the chariot and realised immediately that he knew him. It was Cale Gerwood, a lad he had grown up with on the northern coast by Thade. As youths they had wrestled together, played together and been thick as thieves for a time. Cale looked strong, handsome and proud. The emblem of The Sunchasers was embroidered on his tunic. He had done well for himself, Leo thought.

But simultaneously the dark thoughts came - the jealousy and, with it, anger and revulsion for himself. He saw it all again differently, these so called great people, prostrating themselves before a mob of fools. The aged King, barely able to leave his palace while others died for him. The giant Balthus who had ordered plenty to their deaths and whose ego and arrogance still let him play to the crowd. Athus and his beautiful wife, standing there and drinking it all in while all these people called for them, screaming and shouting. How could any man deserve all that? And where was Leo Kvetch – sitting on a roof with the rest of the fools cheering along.

Suddenly the crowd he had felt so much a part of seemed like an alien thing, like a writhing serpent that was crushing what little was left of him and without a word Leo stood, climbed down from the roof and slunk away.

4.

Leo was not completely sure how many goblets of wine he had drunk, nor for how long he had been drinking, when he looked up into the crowd of faces filtering by and recognised the hulking form of Venn. Leo waved but the man acknowledged him only with the slightest nod of the head. Leo thought Venn's look had been disapproving. Angered, he stood, having to stabilise himself briefly on the back of his chair, before throwing a few coins onto the table and pushing out into the sea of people. He shoved himself through the crowd, but quickly realised that there were too many bodies, and although he could see Venn ahead, standing like a tower over those close to him, Leo was unable to catch him.

He flowed with the mob through the streets of Ostus and listened to their sickening talk of wonder at having seen the heroes. A group of pretty girls close by giggled about how handsome Balthus and Athus were and Leo felt his jealousy rise like bile. Why was it that some men had it all - looks, fame, riches, respect and gaggles of women idolising them? Why did no one seem to see what he could do, his potential?

A view down a side street gave Leo a sudden glimpse of the clock tower that rose above the botanical gardens. Nearly noon! Cursing himself, his anger and jealousy forgotten for the moment, he began shoving in earnest, trying to work his way out of the slow stampede. If he could just break free he could make a run through the back city towards the carriage stop. If he was late for work, Clayson would tan his hide for sure. Ignoring the protests around him, he barged through and began to run on wobbly legs through the back streets. Even these were busier than usual and he was forced to duck and weave as best he could. In his tipsy state he crashed into several people, drawing shouts of abuse from two and narrowly avoiding being struck by the walking stick of another. The carriage stop was heaving when he arrived and it took long minutes before his turn came. Even so, according to the driver's watch, he was on the road by ten past the hour, on time to make it back to work… just. Leo sat back in the seat and let out a sigh.

He was a sweaty, out of breath mess having run the last half mile, but he got in through the gates of Clayson's farm two minutes before the bell sounded and collapsed against the fence, sucking in air for all he was worth.

"Good of you to turn up," Mason said. "Cutting it fine aren't you?"

Leo looked up, getting his breathing under control. "Shut up Mason."

"Or what?" Mason asked, his eyes dark.

Leo pushed himself off the fence but his legs throbbed and he felt as weak as a kitten, so he walked away. Mason threw his head back and laughed.

The morning's work passed swiftly and Leo dug in despite the lancing pain in his shoulder and his pounding head. He said not a thing and sweat was pouring from him in waves when the bell that signalled lunch rang out over the pastures.

"Good work this morning, Kvetch," Mason commented. "But one songbird doesn't make a summer."

Leo said nothing, just picked up his pack and put some distance between himself and everyone else. Sinking his tired body down, his back to a tree, he tucked into his dinner, a small block of cheese and a crust of loaf. As he ate, he almost enjoyed letting the melancholy come back. He thought of Cale, riding in the parade. He thought of how he had failed in his wrestling. All the opportunities he'd wasted. How he was a nobody, how he was without pride, without drive or motivation.

"I'm this close to becoming a drunken nobody," he whispered to himself, holding his finger and thumb before his face, an inch apart. He let his hand drop. "What does it matter if I am? What does any of it matter?"

Leo glanced back towards the rest of the farmhands and saw two men approaching them, walking quickly over the fields. One was short and stocky, his bald head bright in the sunlight, the other was tall and wiry, his head dark. Relund and Case. What were they doing here? Then with no warning, fractured and distorted, he remembered parts of the night before, the fight, the chase... the knife.

Immediately, a fear growing in his belly, Leo began to crawl away. If he kept low he might be able to circle around to the old barn and hide before they spotted him. But even as the thought occurred, he saw Mason stand and point in his direction.

Relund looked up and saw him, letting out a cry, and both he and Case broke into a run. Leo rose and began to run away, hearing laughter coming from his workmates. Didn't the idiots know this man had tried to kill him?

Leo ran, but there was nowhere to escape to, only endless fields. He was already tired and it was not long until they were nearly on him and still gaining. He stopped and turned. Case's face was a mess and with a sickening realisation Leo recalled the moment he'd kicked the man head first into a wall.

"I don't want any trouble..." Leo shouted, his voice shrill, but Relund didn't stop and charged straight into him, tumbling them both to the floor. Relund scrabbled quickly up to sit astride of him. This time there was no warm-up, no foreplay or threats. Relund immediately began swinging wildly, aiming to smash his fists through Leo's face and Leo took a shot that glanced across his cheek before bringing up his guard to cover his head, absorbing the other blows. Leo's legs snaked around Relund's and with a roll of his body he reversed their positions so that Relund was now underneath.

At once something hit him in the back of the head and Leo was knocked dazed onto the floor. Arms circled his neck and dragged him up, crushing his throat and Leo felt the world falling away and dwindling into a tiny dot in the distance, like the light at the end of a long tunnel. Old training took over and he tucked his chin down, forcing it in between his attacker's arm and his own throat. If the hold had been applied by a man with even a little skill, the fight would be over, but he was lucky, Case it seemed, had little training.

"I'm going to rip your head off!" Case screamed from behind him. Leo ignored the threat and reached a hand down and grabbed at Case's testicles while simultaneously throwing his other hand up, fingers searching for eyes. Case let out a grunt of pain and the grip loosened for a moment. Leo managed to turn his body, hooking a foot behind Case's, then as the man lost his footing, Leo dropped to one knee, grabbed both of Case's legs and heaved the man upwards and threw him over his shoulder. Case fell heavily, the wind whooshing out of him.

A few cheers went up from the spectators who'd gathered to watch but they were just as loud a second later when Relund's fist connected with Leo's jaw, sending him staggering backwards.

"Don't let him grab you, work him from a distance," Mason's voice came from the ring of men.

Relund took the advice and began circling like a boxer, throwing jabs and half-hearted kicks, wary now of getting too close. Leo dropped into a low wrestler's stance, blood dripping from his nose. Case was bent double and sucking in deep breaths. Soon he would be back in the fight and it didn't look like anyone here felt that two versus one was unfair. Leo knew he had to finish Relund quick. He darted left, then swept right. A jab cannoned off his forehead, snapping his head back, but he ignored it. Leo swept his arms up, bringing them under Relund's and slipped around the back of his opponent taking a master grip. Kicking a leg out and spinning, Leo sat, throwing Relund hard into the dirt and at once rolled on top of the stunned man, taking an arm. He could see Case, still trying to recover, and Leo leaned back into the arm lock, controlling the speed of the technique. Even so Relund let out a scream of pain.

"This is over," said Leo firmly. "Or do you want me to break your arm?"

Case rose, still hurting, and began to approach but Relund shouted him back, his voice panicked.

"All right Kvetch, it's over. Let me go," Relund growled.

"Send Case away first..." Leo began but then stars exploded behind his eyes. He must have been out for a second, because in his next conscious moment he realised he had lost the hold and was prone. He glanced up and saw Mason, holding a stout branch.

"Take your beating like a man, Kvetch," Mason shouted.

Leo heard people arguing, Mason shouting at the top of his voice, but then someone was on him and he was fighting again. This time he was both dizzy and tired, his body slow, his vision blurred. His opponent was on top of him, their knee pressing into his back, pushing his face into the dirt. Punches were clattering into the back of his head and he rolled to face them, taking one straight to his nose which popped and cracked under the impact, but at least he could see his attacker now. Hooking his legs around Relund, he reached up and pulled the man closer to him, robbing him of the range he needed to generate power and tying up his hands. Relund panicked and began to waste energy trying to break free. Leo let one of his hands go, knowing Relund would wind it up for a strike - giving him the perfect opportunity to take a submission hold. This time he would show no mercy.

Then a boot crashed into the side of his head and Leo felt like he'd been cast into a deep, dark pit. Only the tiniest speck of light glimmered at the far end, so far away he felt it might go black forever. Below him the dark seemed welcoming, warm and inviting but he surprised himself and he did not go towards it. Instead he climbed back towards the pain of the light and as he swam closer, it came to embrace him.

He was back in the pasture covering his head. Case was standing close by, lashing vicious kicks at him, but Leo felt no pain, his body was numb. Off to one side Relund was rolling around and screaming in agony, his arm twisted and bent obscenely backwards on itself. Time had no real meaning, everything was happening at once and Leo realised that he must have broken Relund's arm even as he'd been knocked unconscious. He was about to do something about Case, when suddenly the man was dragged out of view. Leo tried to sit up but found he lacked the strength. The clouds passed slowly above and the sky was a calming blue. Vaguely he was aware of Clayson's voice barking orders, then the farm owner was standing above him, an old crossbow held across his chest. He peered at Leo's face for a moment then looked away.

"For the love of the Essence, go fetch Thetius, they've damn well nearly killed him!" Clayson shouted.

Leo heard the comment with extreme detachment and this time, as consciousness left him, there was not even a thought of fight left in him.

5.

For over a week the healer tended Leo's beaten body with an ever-growing sense of concern. Although skilled and able to tend to the outward damage, Thetius began to fear there was a bleed inside Leo's skull. He had seen such things before and they were beyond his abilities to heal. As the days passed he became more and more certain that Leo would never regain consciousness. Not a rich man, Thetius was forced to consider if he could afford to continue to use up his valuable supplies to treat a man who would likely never wake to pay him. He prayed to the Essence and elected to give Leo three more days. His faith was rewarded when, a full eleven days after the fight, Leo finally regained consciousness. After that, with a sense of joy, Thetius cared and nursed Leo back to some semblance of strength. At first, the red-haired farmhand could hardly summon the energy to speak but as the days passed he grew stronger and Thetius knew he would live and recover.

Together the men talked and grew close, often chatting late into the night about all manner of subjects. Leo proved himself good company, despite his periodic swings of melancholy. Steadily he grew strong enough to walk around Thetius' small patch of land and was rapidly regaining his strength. Soon he would be well enough to return home and Thetius conceded he would miss the unaccustomed company.

The healer dried his bony hands on a dishcloth and moved to the table, placing a bowl of soup down carefully. Thetius was a slender man, his hair long, straight and nearly completely white. His kindly face was clean shaven and heavily lined with age but his bright eyes sparkled with intelligence and humour.

"Here, have this, the medicines in it will do you good and it shouldn't taste too bad either," the healer smiled.

Leo mumbled his thanks through swollen lips and slurped the soup from a ladle. It was good.

Thetius moved to a small cabinet and removed two earthenware cups decorated with gold leaf. "My son made these before he left for the army," said the healer.

Leo nodded but said nothing. Everyone in the town knew what had happened to Thetius' son.

"He made these for me as a parting gift. I only use them for special occasions and I believe toasting your last night here certainly qualifies." The healer filled the cups with wine and brought them to the table, setting them down. "To good company," Thetius smiled and raised a toast.

Leo lifted his glass and took a sip. The wine was rich and heady.

"Well my lad," Thetius chuckled, "you truly are built like an ox. Not many men could take a beating like that."

Leo grunted. "It should never have been a beating. Once I'd have dealt with them. I felt so weak during the fight Thetius; weak and slow."

"Well, you're not such a young man anymore Leo, what are you, thirty five now?"

"Thirty four," Leo corrected between mouthfuls. "This is damn good soup, you know."

Thetius grinned. "It should be, it's my mother's own recipe. I'll give you the ingredients for you to take home tomorrow and a tincture of medicine to sprinkle in."

Leo nodded his thanks.

"You say you felt weak and slow but when was the last time you wrestled properly? The last time you trained?" Thetius asked, returning to the subject.

"A long time ago," Leo said. "I kept meaning to get back into it but… it slipped away."

"People are talking about the fight for miles around, singing your virtues. Most men would be proud of that," said Thetius. Leo shrugged. "Anyone can take a beating."

"True," said Thetius, refilling Leo's empty bowl, "but it takes courage to recover from one."

Leo put his head in his hands. "How did I come to this? I'm a grown man and I've never done anything. I was going to do so much. It wasn't meant to be this way."

"Eat your soup and stop moping," Thetius said. "You're not going to win Miss Rebecca by sulking like a child."

Leo snorted but lowered his hands and did as he was told. "How do you even know about that?"

Thetius chuckled. "Everyone knows how you feel about her Leo, everyone sees you gawping at her. I don't know why you don't just go and ask if she'll court you again. Is it because she's divorced?"

"No," said Leo, outraged. "That has nothing to do with it. She did nothing wrong."

"Indeed not, yet most men are not tolerant of that sort of thing in this part of the world. What is it they call her? Used goods?" asked Thetius.

"Aye, and worse," said Leo, the anger in his voice plain.

"Then I suppose you can't be blamed for keeping your distance," said Thetius.

"That has nothing to do with it, damn it!" Leo snapped. "I think she's wonderful. It's just, what do I have to offer her? I had my chance and I threw it away. She does not care for me anymore."

"Really?" Thetius chuckled. "She has visited here three times since you've been ill. Twice when you were unconscious and once only yesterday when you were walking down by the stream."

"She came here?" Leo asked.

"Yes, she has been very concerned for you," said Thetius. "She is a fine, proud woman and it is a terrible shame what has happened to her. I have known her since she was a child and it would do my heart good to see her happy again. You are a good man, Leo Kvetch, and you are no coward, despite what you may think. When you were younger, you two made a good match and I think you could do very well for each other."

"It broke my heart when he married her. I knew he was trouble," said Leo. "I don't know how I let him come between us; I was such a fool. I kept wanting to go to Clayson and ask for her hand, but every time I imagined it, I just saw him saying no." Leo smashed his fist into the table, rocking it. The table shook, causing one of Thetius' priceless earthenware cups to fall and smash on the kitchen floor.

Leo froze. "I'm so sorry," he said, a feeling of horror descending upon him.

He began to push his pained body out of his seat but Thetius stayed him. "There is no use trying to fix that now – it is broken; an accident. It is gone. I will sweep it away and it will be forgotten about." Thetius slowly slid the other cup to the edge of the table so that it sat precariously, half overhanging the edge, then placing a hand on either side of the table began to shake it.

"What are you doing?" Leo shouted, shooting a hand out to save the cup before it too fell and smashed.

"Why did you do that?" Thetius asked.

"You were about to break it," said Leo.

"Too often we spend our time worrying about the dreams that are broken instead of focusing on those that could still be," said Thetius.

"I'm still sorry," said Leo.

"Think nothing of it. It is just a cup, it is not my son."

Later that night, Leo climbed into the small cot where he had slept for the last few weeks. It was homely in the cabin and he would miss Thetius' company.

"How bad do I look?" Leo asked.

The old healer reviewed his patient, observing the broken nose, the puffed-up face which was all blue and black like a patchwork quilt and the half-closed eyes. "Not too bad," Thetius said at last.

"You are a bad liar my friend," said Leo. "I feel like something is broken inside me. My head still aches like a piece has come loose."

"That will pass," said Thetius, "completely normal after a heavy blow to the head. You are tougher than you know, you will heal."

"What about infection?" Leo asked, his eyes betraying his fear.

"I have tended the wounds with all my skill. There will be no infection, and if there is, then I will treat it." Thetius sighed, as if weighing up a decision, then went on. "Earlier this evening you said that things weren't meant to be this way. How were they meant to be Leo? I do not know what dreams you had when you were young, nor if they were stolen from you, or if you lost them. All I know is the now. I see in you a good man, still young, still strong. But I see a pain in you, something that stops you from living.

I think, sometimes when we feel this way, we try to run from the thing that hurts us. It is natural to try to avoid pain, but without pain, we do not grow. This pain will kill you unless you face it. You must go to the centre of it and let it flow in you and through you; otherwise it will haunt you always."

"Seabrooke spoke the same words to me the day before the fight," said Leo.

Thetius spread his hands. "Well there you go."

Leo nodded. "You are both right, I know. But there is something that haunts me. I barely sleep and when I do there is something horrible waiting there and when I wake I can never remember what. It is something to do with my parents I think, how they died. I can't remember."

"What happened to them?" Thetius asked.

"A carriage accident," said Leo. "I was eight."

"I am sorry," said Thetius "but as painful as it is, they are gone, like my son."

Leo sighed. "I have let myself down again and again. I am a terrible coward. I hate myself but cannot change."

"You can change, you just doubt yourself," said Thetius, smiling. "It is the curse of all good people that they doubt themselves. If they did not doubt, they would not be so good. I wish I could simply reach out and take away the pain in you, but we both know this is a pain I cannot reach. As a healer I can treat a fever or splint a broken arm but if the problem is in there," Thetius reached out and tapped Leo's forehead, "well, when the problem is in there, only you can fix it."

"I don't know how," said Leo.

Thetius laughed. "Neither do I my boy, neither do I. But let me tell you a story. Once there was a young man who had made many bad choices. He thought his life was worthless. Like you he felt he had wasted it. One day he felt so wretched and so sick of himself that he went into the woods, away from everyone who cared for him and he strung a rope over a tree branch, looped the noose around his neck and tried to hang himself.

He made a damn meal out of it. He was still dangling from the rope, his neck shredded to ribbons, somewhere between life and death, when an outlaw found him. The outlaw cut the young man down and made sure he was still alive. The outlaw's name was Quarro and he was being pursued for murder. Even so, Quarro stayed with the young man for hours, just talking to him and keeping him company through the night. During that talk, Quarro told the young man something that another man had told him, when he had been young.

He said, nothing of value is ever lost, no matter how hopeless it seemed. When we get lost, he said, we must go back to the beginning. We need to go back in our minds to a place where we can remember everything was possible, before our guilt slipped in. We must recapture our belief in ourselves."

Leo waited for the healer to go on, but Thetius sat back, his story finished.

"Recapture my belief? I do not know if I can do that," said Leo at last.

"Do you know if you can try?" Thetius asked.

Leo rested his head back. "Yes, I think even I can do that. Thank you."

"There is no need to thank me," said Thetius. "I hope you can rise to this challenge."

Suddenly weary beyond words, Leo's eyes began to close. "Thank you for all you've done for me, my friend."

"Think nothing of it," said the healer.

"Thetius, were you the young man in the story?" Leo asked.

Thetius reached a hand up and slowly pulled down the collar of his robe, exposing the scarred flesh that encircled his neck.

After Leo slept the old healer sat for a while and then washed the pots, enjoying the simple sensation of the warm water on his skin. He dried them carefully then moved to his window. He lit a candle and stared into the flame. He had not spoken of Quarro for many years and he had surprised himself when the story had come forth. The outlaw had not been an evil man, but he had been wild and selfish. Quarro had been caught and hung three days after he had saved the young man. The irony of it was not lost on Thetius. Luck, however, had been with Quarro and the rope had snapped. Thetius could still remember the rough jerk that had ripped into his skin, leaving a wound that would scar him always. He had been sentenced to hang again of course, but he had been quick and cunning in those days. The small gaol they placed him in to recover had not held him and he had slain three men in escaping. As he had left the province, he heard news that a man had leapt from the belfry of the town church. Somehow, deep down, he had known it was the lad he'd saved. Something about that realisation had awoken a rich compassion deep within him that he had not even been aware he possessed. The old man smiled. That had been the beginning of the end for Quarro, the thief and brigand, just as it had been the birth pangs of Thetius, the healer.

The old man knelt before the flame and offered a prayer to the Essence, first for his son, then to the memory of Quarro, that he may be forgiven, then for the soul of the young man who had given in to despair and finally for the future of Leo Kvetch.

6.

Summer had passed into autumn when Leo Kvetch stood at the base of Druid's Overlook. He was drunk and miserable. For a few days after returning from Thetius' home, Leo had found a new energy for life. He had decided to make a new start and had worked harder, avoided drink and had even put himself through some training sessions. He had thanked Rebecca for visiting him and even walked with her for a while, at one point nearly telling her how he felt. For a few strange days things seemed as if they were changing. But the feeling, so empowering at first, did not last. Within a fortnight he was back to drinking too much and shirking his duties and his disgust for himself grew to new heights.

The night terrors that haunted him had grown worse and most evenings he was now too afraid to risk sleep. Tonight, as he sat drinking alone, his mind had replayed what Thetius had told him:

"Nothing of value is ever lost, no matter how hopeless it seemed. When we get lost we must go back to the beginning. We need to go back in our minds to a place where we can remember everything was possible, before our guilt slipped in. We must recapture our belief in ourselves."

So Leo stared up through ale-addled eyes at Druid's Overlook and tried to believe. The night was cool but Leo welcomed the chill on his skin. The moon was bright and full, the sky cloudless. Above him the crag loomed, a dark, hunched rise of rock and scree populated only by the odd tree. It was not a treacherous climb, but it was long and difficult. There were few places on the route which called for any real climbing skills but the gradient was extreme in many places, forcing a climber to struggle upwards on hands and knees.

Leo had climbed it when he was sixteen, sneaking from his uncle's house on a night not so different from this. At the summit were the remains of a standing circle that some claimed granted wishes. Leo had battled his way to the top and sat amongst the ruins. He had waited and watched the sun come up and made his wish. Everything had been before him then, he could remember staring into the sun with a feeling that he could do anything. He wondered what that youth would make of the man he had allowed himself to become. He was more than a little drunk, his body sluggish and his vision poor, but without further delay he cast his wine skin aside and began the ascent anyway.

It was harder than Leo remembered; the slopes steeper and the places to rest far less frequent than in his memories. Still he pressed on, trying to ignore the burning pain in his shoulder and the throbbing in his skull. It took him longer than he thought it would to reach the mid-way point and he paused there for a while to catch his breath and loosen his muscles. A familiar part of himself told him this was ridiculous and he should be in bed resting, but tonight he ignored it and once more began to climb. He made his way slowly and carefully, using large rocks and stones or the occasional tree root for purchase. He was fully sober and drenched in sweat by the time he neared the grassy summit and his jerkin clung to his back like damp paper. His legs were weary but he pressed on and the last one hundred foot or so proved easy going.

The ancient circle of stones remained, jutting from the floor like the husks of broken teeth. In the moon-bright night, it was a scene from a fairy tale, magical and otherworldly. Leo walked between the stones and sat in the same spot he had eighteen years ago and let out a satisfied sigh. He would reflect on his life and wait for the sun to rise. Perhaps old Thetius was right; perhaps it was not too late for him. The breeze was pleasant, the stone beneath him smooth and comfortable and the distant sound of water, rushing along the river far below, began to pull at his eyelids.

He sat there, fighting the need for sleep, drifting in and out of a daze. Time passed and his body began to demand rest and even his fear of unknown nightmares could not dissuade it. He felt his head wobble and jerked it upright but at once his eyes began to close again.

"Now is not the time for rest," a voice spoke and Leo nearly jumped out of his skin, his head snapping around.

Beside him, sat a spirit in the shape of a man wearing a long, grey robe. The man's face was strong yet kindly. His eyes were clear and shone with intelligence and honesty and his face had an almost regal quality. Indeed, so tranquil was the being's manner, that apart from the fact it was a phantom, there was nothing truly terrifying about the figure other than his body was made not of flesh but of a light mist, fine enough that Leo could see right through the stranger. The ghost smiled.

Leo stood, his mouth dry, and took two uncertain steps away from the apparition, managing to catch his foot on a loose rock and tumble over onto the dewy grass.

"Do not fear, Leo. I mean you no harm," the man spoke, his voice like the wind amongst reeds.

Leo rose, his heart beating fast. He leaned from side to side, noting how glimmers of light laced through the ghostly form before him, sparkling in the air. "Is this real?" Leo managed to say. "Or is this a part of my nightmares?"

The ghost seemed amused. "It is as real as anything else in this world," he smiled.

"Why are you here, what do you want?" Leo asked.

"When you began this climb you came here to make a wish, did you not?"

"Sort of," said Leo.

"Well, I have come to grant it."

"Who are you?" asked Leo guardedly.

"Does it matter? I once was a man of power and I liked very much to help people like you. Now I am dead and only my spirit remains. Still, I am not without some vestige of my old strength."

"Do you have the power to grant my wish? Do you know what it is?" asked Leo.

"Of course I know what it is. You wish to be a better man. Such a selfless wish, not like most men who desire riches or power or women. It is the selflessness of your wish that has drawn me here."

"Can you make it come true? Really?" Leo asked, swallowing hard.

"Of course," said the ghost, rising from where he sat and gliding closer. "I have long watched this world. Sometimes I see a mortal and I just know that, pushed onto the right track, they could achieve great, great things. I sense that greatness in you. Were it not for a few acts of fate, nothing you had control over, you would already be the great man you so desire to be. You were never meant to be a simple farmhand, Leo. You were made for greater things. If you wish, I will help you achieve that greatness."

Leo nodded. "How can you do that? Don't I have to earn it?"

The spirit laughed. "Oh my boy, you have already earned this prize a thousand times over. I could not wish to give this gift to another."

Leo stared at the ghost. "Are you sure? To me?"

The ghost smiled again, and when he spoke there was such kindness in his voice: "You deserve this, you truly do. I can honestly say that I have never desired to aid someone more."

"What can you do?" Leo asked.

"You have so much anger in you, repressed deep inside. I want to give you an experience that will let you get it all out. I will swap your soul with another for a single night. I will let you experience the life you should have had, then in the morning, with all being well, you will return to your own body, refreshed and invigorated. And then you can rebuild your life."

"Who do you have in mind?" Leo asked.

"Anyone you like, it is your wish and your choice," said the spirit. "Whose life would you like to experience?"

Leo thought for a moment. "I don't know. Clayson is a man respected in the community; I could spend time seeing how he lives. It would be nice to give the orders for once."

The apparition nodded approvingly. "A fine choice. A very safe and steady choice. Well done. It is good when a man knows his limits and does not overreach himself."

"What do you mean?" Leo asked.

"Only that you have the chance of spending one night as anyone in the world and I think it is testament to your fine character that you would select a simple farmer. The last man did not pick so humbly. But then he was cut from a different cloth. He was ambitious, imaginative, daring – you know the sort. They seem impressive at first but they lack that deep quality that is so important. For you Leo, I think you have chosen perfectly. Would you like me to begin the spell?"

"Wait a moment," said Leo. "This other man, who did he choose to be?"

"If you must know he chose a king," the ghost said. "But the king he chose was young and handsome and greatly loved. His wife was an incredible beauty. In many ways even I envied him the night of passion he spent with her. Still, thinking about it, the king in this land is old and weak. I'm not surprised you did not choose him. A shame there is no one like that in this realm."

Leo nodded slowly and thought of the King's feeble hand waving to the crowd out of the window of his carriage. Who would want to spend the night as an infirm, old man? Images of the parade filled Leo's mind and he looked to the ghost.

"I can be literally anyone? Even a hero? Even The Champion? Even Athus Glynn?"

"Yes, of course. I admit I had not thought of him," shrugged the spirit. "I suppose being Athus would be the next best thing to being a king for a night; perhaps better because he would not be bogged down with all the boring trappings of state. And then there is the Lady Zarina..." said the ghost with only a hint of a smile.

Leo found himself blushing. "I think this is a dream," said Leo. "I am asleep on those stones or drunk in a ditch."

"Perhaps. Does it matter?" the spirit asked. "Either it is a pleasant dream and of no consequence or it is real and you have the chance of a lifetime."

Leo nodded. "Then I agree."

"I have to hear you say yes," said the phantom. "It is part of the magic."

"Then yes, I agree," said Leo. "I wish to be a better man, I wish to be Athus Glynn for a night - what do I have to lose?"

The spirit smiled, its mouth splitting like a razor into a broad, satisfied grin. "Leo Kvetch, there is nothing for *you* to lose at all."

7.

There was no grand flash of light or arcane, spidery words yet in the blink of an eye Leo found that he was no longer on the summit of Druid's Overlook. New sensations assailed him from all sides and he found himself in a daze. He felt the stifling warmth of a nearby fire pit and his ears were besieged by the cacophony of noise generated by a hundred different conversations. Before him was a table overflowing with delicious smelling food; a full roasted boar, plates of exotic fruits, sweet cakes, pastries and everything in between. On a stage before him acrobats and dancers, trailing swirls of brightly coloured fabrics, span and somersaulted through the air drawing applause from the packed banquet tables. The people here were no common folk, they were dressed in the finest fashions, the ladies resplendent in bright silk dresses and the men in immaculately tailored formal wear.

Housing all of this was the grandest room Leo had ever seen. The roof was higher than the second storey of The Golden Pear and latticed with beams of glistening wood from which hung the mighty banners of the great houses of Ostus. Chandeliers of glowing crystal swayed with the music and mounted on the stone walls were shields of heraldry. Leo knew that there was only one place this could be, the great hall in Castle Ostus.

A soft hand rested upon his own, squeezing lightly and Leo looked to his left. The Lady Zarina smiled at him. If he had thought her beautiful when he watched the parade it had not done her justice. Now so close to her he found his mouth run dry and the breath race from his body. Zarina turned back to watch the dancers but her hand remained on his and the warmth of it was almost uncomfortable. Leo felt himself begin to sweat.

"Lord Athus, may I refill your cup?" a voice whispered in his ear.

Leo turned slowly, trying to keep calm. It was actually happening, the spirit had done its work. He had wished to be a better man and the spirit had obliged - it had transformed him into The Champion, Athus Glynn. Shock ran through Leo's body as cold as ice and he nodded hastily to the serving girl and held up his chalice. As soon as it was filled he drank deeply. The wine was sweet and heady, easily the finest he had ever tasted. He downed the cup in one and gestured for it to be refilled again. The girl smiled and did as she was bid. Nursing the goblet, Leo turned back to the room, the alcohol taking the edge from his nerves.

The food before him smelt delicious and Leo reached out a hand and picked up a chicken leg. The taste was wonderful, the meat tender and seasoned to perfection. He made short work of it before grabbing another and then turning his attention to a plate of thinly sliced ham. Again the flavour set his taste buds tingling in ecstasy. Never in his life had Leo sampled such food. He washed the meat down with a swig from his goblet, the flavours harmonising into an experience that bordered on the divine. He glanced less shyly towards Zarina. Her eyes were blue, like ice water, a perfect match for the stone in the simple brooch she wore upon her dress. Her nose was soft, her lips full and dark. Her skin was flawless and he could not help himself as his eyes slid down her body, sweeping over the olive skin of her neck, drawn by the simple necklace she wore, to stare at the inviting swell of her breasts.

For tonight, this is my wife, Leo thought, feeling himself blush. This is the woman I will go to bed with. The thought of that had him taking another gulp from his goblet.

The night drew on, the great clock chiming two and then three o'clock. The music played and the dancers danced and Leo ate and drank until he was nearly bursting and the room span in great rushing circles. Guests came to him, bowed low, fawning over him terribly and Leo basked in their praise and adulation. This was the way to live, he thought, as he reached clumsily for a cream cake. It was just out of reach and he knocked his goblet over, spilling wine across the table top. A serving maid rushed forward to clean the mess and moved the plate of cakes closer. He devoured the pastry and settled back in his chair, feeling weary, when a familiar face approached, bowing clumsily, and offering a nervous greeting. It was Clayson.

An aide whispered in Leo's ear: "Lord, this is Mr. Horratio Lindon Clayson, a land owner from Two Trees."

Leo had never truly disliked Clayson. The man had been fair with him over the years but Leo had always been intimidated by the farm owner. In all the time he had courted Rebecca, he had never believed the man had approved of him and as a result Leo had never felt confident enough to ask for his permission for his daughter's hand. Now watching the man squirm and shuffle, Leo resolved to have some fun.

"I know who he is," said Leo, pausing to burp.

"It honours me that you know who I am, Lord," said Clayson. "I own a small farm, my Lord. Stud mainly."

"Well, isn't that wonderful? Was there something you wanted?" Leo asked. Several nearby nobles covered their mouths to hide their amusement.

"No, I, that is to say…" Clayson stuttered.

"Spit it out man," said Leo.

"I have bred two strong, young stallions my Lord. They are fast and spirited. I know your fondness for the beasts and wondered if you might honour me by…"

"I don't think so," said Leo, cutting Clayson off. "You can go now."

Clayson stood for a moment, his face slowly turning red as if slapped. Then, deflated, he bowed and edged away.

Leo found himself laughing, noting how others nearby joined in. It had been fun to put Clayson in his place, yet as he watched the small ranch owner walking away, a pang of guilt hit him. He turned to Zarina with the intention of having her call someone to bring Clayson back, but Zarina was gone.

It took Leo some time to find Athus' bedchamber. The palace was large and he, of course, had never been inside it before. On top of that he was pleasantly drunk, his vision badly blurred and he was having some trouble standing upright. However, with the help of a couple of the King's Guard, he found his way. The room was everything he had imagined. It was high on the palace's east side, large and beautifully furnished. Ribbons of silk hung from the balcony, fluttering in the breeze. Moonlight glistened through the high windows and for a moment Leo stood and stared into the night. Somewhere out there, beyond the city and the woodland, was his own shack. He could not believe this had happened. It seemed little more than a dream.

Then he thought of Zarina and arousal flowed through him. He had but scant hours left to enjoy this. Quickly he stripped and skirted the bed, pausing before a large looking glass. By the Essence he was a majestic sight. His face was handsome, his body toned and powerful; even his manhood was larger. Some men, Leo thought, had all the luck and he turned and admired his new body from every angle.

"Are you quite alright?" Zarina asked.

Leo turned quickly, more than a little embarrassed. "Yes of course."

"You acted disgracefully this evening," she said. Even though the words were harsh, there was no malice or judgement in her voice. "I'm worried about you. I know you dislike public functions but I do not think I have ever seen you drink so much nor be so rude to your guests. You know that you were supposed to move around the tables to thank our supporters and mingle with them. Why did you let them come up to you like that, like you were some sort of messiah?"

Leo tried to think of an answer, but nothing came.

"And you were eating meat too," said Zarina. "You know how I feel about that."

"I'm... I'm sorry," Leo offered, staring at her form beneath her shimmering nightdress. He realised he would say or do anything to climb into that bed with her. His arousal was almost painful.

"You have been through a lot recently and if any man deserves some leeway to let off steam, then you do. You carry much on your shoulders but I never thought to see you behave that way. Now come to bed," she said, holding up the sheets so he could slide in.

Leo did not need asking twice and hurriedly dived into the bed, pushing his body against hers.

"What are you doing?" she asked, her voice icy.

"Don't you want to make love?" Leo asked hopefully.

"No," she said.

"But you're my wife," said Leo.

"Excuse me?" Zarina scoffed. "I'm going to pretend I didn't hear that. Now get dressed and go and find somewhere else to sleep. You might be a great man Athus Glynn, but tonight you're an ugly drunk. NOW GET OUT!"

Bemused Leo found his way to the kitchens and began picking over the leftovers. As was often the case, anger had sobered him up. One night, the spirit had promised him. One night only. Now it was soured. The most beautiful woman in the kingdom, who was *sort* of his wife to boot, had just thrown him out of bed.

"Only I could ruin my own wish," Leo growled to himself, picking up a plate and hurling it into the wall.

In the aftermath of the crash, he glanced at the clock that stood by the far wall. It was nearly half past four. Would this dream end at dawn? It had been going so well, the party had been majestic, but now it was spoiled. A night of bliss he had been promised. He sank down and held his head in his hands. "How can I ruin a night of bliss?" he whispered.

Zarina's words danced in his head. "You acted disgracefully tonight... I do not think I have ever seen you drink so much nor be so rude to your guests… I just never thought I'd see you behave that way… tonight you are an ugly drunk…"

"That's all I am," Leo sobbed. "I'm an ugly drunk. A pathetic, ugly drunk."

Round and round the thoughts danced, driving him mad, pricking his mind like needles. He did not even know the woman, but her words shamed him terribly. Soon they were joined by the familiar voices of despair that inhabited his head.

"You'll never amount to anything… you're a joke… a nothing… a no-one… it would have been better if you'd never been born…"

Leo staggered upright, holding his hands to his ears as if to block out the taunts. On the other side of the room there were pitchers of mead. Drink, though it made nothing better in the long run, was the only thing he knew that stopped the damn voices going around and around. He picked the pitcher up and held it to his lips. Just before he drank a different voice spoke in his mind: his own.

"This is the stuff that ruined your uncle and now you're letting it ruin you."

But he ignored it and tilted the pitcher back, letting the drink rush down his throat and splash down his chin and over his fine clothes. And when he was done he staggered into the corner, sat and began to cry.

8.

Leo awoke with a strangled scream. As always on waking his breathing was ragged and his body laced with sweat. He no longer even tried to remember what he dreamed of and once more, whatever terror it was, had fled leaving him no clue. Blinding morning light burned at his eyes and he rolled his body sluggishly onto his side to escape it. He was exhausted and he buried his head into his soft pillow and wished that, just once, he could have a good night's sleep.

His bladder was irritatingly full, a small blessing he mused. Sometimes the dreams provoked such fear in him that he would wake having wet himself. Normally that only happened when he slept sober and was as good a reason as any to enjoy a nightcap.

Still, the thought of climbing from the soft warmth of the bed to relieve himself was not pleasant. With a sigh he rolled from the bed and limped naked across the room to a small privy. He urinated with a sense of blissful release then stepped back into the bedchamber. He did not recognise it. In fact he could not remember how he got here. The last thing he could recall was… had he been at some sort of party? I have to stop drinking he thought to himself, not for the first time. The blackouts were getting out of hand.

A ticking drew his attention to a clock on the wall. It was nearly noon.

"Great job," he scowled at himself. He had no idea where he was and was already nearly five hours late for work. Clayson would fire him on the spot. He began searching around on the floor for his clothes, preparing his excuses, but could not find them. As he scoured the room, the mass of sheets in the large bed moved. A girl sat up and smiled sleepily at him. She was blonde, young and very beautiful. Leo offered her a nervous, half smile. He had no idea who she was. There was no way he had bedded a girl like that, was there?

"How are you this morning, my Lord?" the girl asked.

Leo was about to respond then stopped. He felt as if he had been hit in the heart with a war hammer. *My Lord?*

He darted to the mirror. His body was lean and strong, with muscle resting on muscle. His hair was short and dark, his face chiselled. His eyes were piercing, his look almost regal. He was Athus. The spell of the drink was washed aside in moments and he remembered it all; the party, the meeting with the spirit on the summit of Druid's Overlook and the deal.

"My Lord, are you unwell?" the girl asked again.

"I don't know," said Leo, hearing his words spoken in Athus' strong voice. Last night that had been exhilarating, but now it was somehow terrifying.

He didn't know whether to laugh or cry. The spirit had said the magic would last only one night. Could it have meant one full day? Twenty-four hours? Something felt very wrong, but then why should he care – he'd gone from being nobody to being the most loved and the most powerful man in the kingdom.

"Why not come back to bed, my Lord?" the girl smiled enchantingly. "It is early, I'm sure you will not be missed for a little longer."

But she was wrong and without warning the door to the room burst open and the huge figure of Balthus rushed inside, virtually ripping the door off its hinges in the process.

"What the hell is going on here?" the dark skinned giant bellowed, taking in the scene with a single, authoritative glance. "Get dressed woman and get the hell out!"

In the flesh, the commander of The Sunchasers made Venn 'the one man gang' look like he needed to eat a few hearty dinners. In fact, Leo had time to think, if Venn was a one man gang, then Balthus was a one-man army. The warrior was unarmed and wore a simple, blue tunic, adorned with the emblem of Royal House. Even so he was an intimidating sight and Leo could only imagine the effect the man would have when dressed in full armour.

The black man's body looked like it was carved from blocks of solid obsidian and as he stood there he looked like a god who had stepped right out of the times of myth. He was so tall he was forced to stoop, even though the ceiling was not low.

The girl in the bed looked nervously between the two men. "Do you wish me to leave, my Lord?" she asked Leo.

"What did I just say?" Balthus raged. "Get out of here you little tart!"

The girl's face turned to thunder. "I am not some tart, I am the niece of Lord Jarl Sebellain!"

Balthus gathered the girl's clothes up and threw them at her. "I don't care if you're Amad El's first born daughter, get the hell out!"

With an indignant sigh the young woman dressed as modestly as she could and hurried from the room.

"What the hell is going on here Athus?" Balthus demanded turning on Leo, his voice like rolling thunder.

Leo's first thought was that they knew. They must have known he was not really Athus and his mind filled with images of torture and imprisonment. But then he reasoned, if they knew, surely they'd send guards, not just one man. He looked at Balthus again. Why would this man need anyone else to back him up? *Gods I have to get out of here*, Leo thought.

He swallowed, nervously. Despite his fear, his mind working fast. "How dare you speak to me like that," he tried.

"Excuse me?" roared Balthus.

"I told you to be quiet, don't talk to The Champion that way," Leo said trying to sound confident.

Balthus snarled and the last thing Leo saw before the floor rose up to meet him was a massive fist flying towards his jaw.

Leo awoke for the second time that day and no more pleasantly than the first. A foul smell was invading his nose and he struggled to get away from it. A firm hand held him still as a spoon was forced into his mouth; the liquid it contained tasting vulgar beyond words. He felt his nose pinched, swallowed without thinking and nearly wretched. He coughed violently for a moment, his eyes streaking. Rubbing them dry, he tried to get a hold of himself. He was in a simple cot in one of the most cluttered, unusual rooms he had ever seen. Papers and scrolls lay everywhere so that there was hardly a view of the floor. Tables were piled high with obscure apparatus, multi-coloured vials and bizarre artefacts. One, closest to him, was strewn with, amongst other things, several animal cadavers. There was not a bare patch of wall in sight, every inch being covered in maps and papers, scrawled with markings and runes Leo had never seen before. From the ceiling hung a large model of a curious machine which swung ominously in the breeze that came from the open sky loft.

Most bizarre of all was a taxidermy of a huge, white bear, bigger than any brown bear Leo had ever seen. The creature dominated the centre of the room, posed standing on its hind legs, its massive paws raised high above its head, a terrifying snarl on its monstrous face.

"Do you like him?" a jovial voice asked. "Thought you might have seen a few of them during the war but from the look on your face, obviously not."

Leo turned toward the man who had spoken. For all the eccentricity of the room, the man himself seemed relatively normal. He was slender, his face sharp but kindly and his eyes were bright with intelligence and perhaps, Leo thought, not a little madness. The man wore a simple robe of blue, tied at his middle with a rawhide belt. It was unadorned with any symbol. His beard and hair, still untouched by grey, were neatly trimmed and his skin bronzed and healthy – the mark of a man who spent plenty of time outdoors. It was obvious to Leo right from this first meeting that this man couldn't keep still for even a moment. It was as if the energy inside him needed to spill out and as he moved around the room he was always tinkering or fiddling with something.

Leo sat up, holding his jaw. "What time is it?"

"One thirty-four and forty eight seconds, Ostus standard time," the man replied instantly, not pausing from where he was closely examining one of the bear's feet with an oversized magnifying glass. "Quite, quite fascinating. I think I shall name him Snowy."

"Very original," Leo groaned, standing up. His back ached terribly and his jaw and head were little better.

"Original?" said the man. "It's not original at all... oh I see, that was sarcasm wasn't it? You know what they say about sarcasm. They say it's the lowest form of wit. Personally I'm not in a position to judge. Sometimes people say they feel sorry for me because I don't understand sarcasm. However, if I had to choose between understanding sarcasm and understanding the celestial movements of the heavenly bodies or the inter-dimensional meta-conditioning of a Prya Shell, I would continue to choose to understand the celestial movements of the heavenly bodies and the inter-dimensional meta-conditioning of a Prya Shell."

"What the hell is a Prya Shell?" Leo asked.

"Another piece of humour. My Lord is in a good mood this morning. This is likely as a result of having sexual relations with a woman other than your wife. I am reliably informed that along with sarcasm, sexual infidelity is something else most people find empowering."

"Who told you that?" Leo asked, watching as his host crawled under a table, producing a tatty, crumpled scroll and examining it closely.

"I have books on these things," said the man. "*Vitaker's Treaties on Normality*, to be specific. I'm sure you remember I'm required to read them... after the incident. Very illuminating. They test me you see, to make sure I'm not mad. Naturally I'm not. They are mad. They just don't understand. Anyway, you should get dressed; we have a council meeting with His Majesty in thirty-four minutes and eighteen seconds.

On average it takes six minutes and twenty-one seconds to walk from here to the council chamber. However, there is a high probability that you will want to talk with either or both Lady Zarina and General Balthus beforehand. I find this irritating as I cannot accurately predict how long these conversations will take."

"I don't think I want to talk to either of them," said Leo, sitting back on the edge of the bed.

The door to the chamber opened and a squat soldier with a serious face saluted. "Lord Athus, Arch-magister Gellen, the council meeting has been brought forward, the King requests you attend at your earliest convenience."

"You may tell him that we will be there in approximately fifteen seconds less than seven minutes," said Gellen.

If this fazed the messenger, he did not show it and the soldier span and turned on his heel.

"I do hate being so imprecise," said the arch-magister, picking up a ridiculous floppy hat and fixing it on his head. "Are you ready?"

Leo nodded, following Gellen from the room. It was nearly two o'clock. The spell is going to wear off soon, he told himself as they walked. If he had met the spirit an hour after midnight he had only to get through a few more hours, then by tomorrow he would be back in his own body. All I have to do is go along with things until then, Leo thought. They don't know I'm not Athus. It's fine, I can deal with it. I'll just keep my mouth shut and it will all be good. How hard can it be?

9.

"So," said the King, his voice still powerful despite his decaying body, "the final vote falls to you Lord Athus. Do we invade the Tundralands now, risking our armies in another war so soon after the last, but potentially striking out this threat before it grows, or do you counsel caution?"

"Er, well, that is to say… it's a tough decision, that one… isn't it? I mean there are pros and cons on each side…" said Leo.

"Yes, yes, and we have heard all of the reports. Now what do you say?" urged the King.

By the Essence, Leo shuddered inwardly, how can I make a decision like this? How am I supposed to know the right thing to do? All eyes were on him and his mind was as blank as fresh snow. A tension began to grow in the room. Leo tried to focus – he had to say something.

Zarina sat on his left, her face impassive. She had already argued against an invasion. Hearing her speak, Leo had been convinced that there should be no war. An invasion meant more bloodshed, more death and directing treasury coin away from pressing needs to the realm such as sanitation and schooling. However, no sooner had she finished speaking against another war, than Zarina had walked calmly to the other side of the chamber and argued equally as articulately for all the merits for war. With her every word she had undermined her own arguments and explained how if the kingdom did not act now, the threat in Tundralands would in time threaten the safety of every man, woman and child in Ostus.

After that other experts had come forth spouting every manner of evidence; some argued for peace, some for war. Leo's head span with it all. There was no right answer. Both sides had equal merit – and now he was being asked to make a decision that could affect the lives of the entire realm.

"Lord Athus, your verdict?" the King pressed.

"I… er, well, that is to say, erm, you don't kill a dog just because you think it might bite you?" Leo tried, remembering something Thetius had once told him.

The King nodded sagely. "Well said, you are right of course. Thank you for your wisdom. For now we have other matters to deal with. There will be no invasion until we have more information."

Leo felt Zarina's hand squeeze his. He glanced at her and she smiled at him. Leo smiled back. Perhaps he had done the right thing.

The hulking form of Balthus stood. "Your majesty, with your leave, we must discuss the final phase of the Kryxian War."

The King waved a hand and nodded. "Go ahead General. I have been interested in hearing your report for some time."

"The people think the war with Kryx is over, but we know better. Athus slew the Lich King Nemeddes, but that only destroyed Nemeddes' physical body. The Lich's power is great and his servants still work their evil. Our spies tell us he has already returned to this world as a spirit. It will not be long before he regains a corporeal form. His plans are moving ahead and the remnants of the Kryxian host have holed up in the frozen city of Salgatha. We must move soon to rout them and seal the entrance to the underworld. If we do not, they will use the Arcana at Salgatha to revive Nemeddes' power and we will be back to square one. It is my belief that we have neither the men nor the resources for another protracted conflict in the north."

The King nodded. "You mean to say that we cannot win another war against the Kryx?"

"It is never impossible to win Sire, however it is not likely. The men are tired of battle and the northlands sap the spirit. We need time to recover," said Balthus.

Zarina stood. "Your majesty, the four of us have discussed this long and hard. We believe our best chance is not in risking open war but rather to take a small force of trusted warriors – the Sunchasers – to Salgatha. Only Athus can seal The Rift, he is the only one who can wield the Star Sword. The men are loyal to him until death; if he commands it they will follow. The land around Salgatha is unpredictable and dangerous, there is not room for an army to manoeuvre, but a small band could pierce their defences, strike deep into the tunnels beneath the glaciers and finish this in one final act. You ordered us back from the North when Athus nearly died, but now we must return, for everyone's sake."

"What are your chances for success?" the King asked.

"Normally I would say we were doomed to failure, Sire," said Balthus, "but with Athus leading us, with his genius for tactics, I'd say we have a great chance of sealing Nemeddes forever in the underworld."

"Do you agree Arch-magister Gellen?" the King asked, turning towards the sprightly mage.

"I predict that we have an eighty nine point four percent chance of sealing the portal to the underworld," said Gellen. "And I estimate that we can achieve this goal within ninety three days, ten hours, thirty two minutes and sixteen seconds – roughly speaking of course."

The King paused and looked over them thoughtfully. "How much this nation owes to you four alone. You have been the foundation of my reign. Athus, The Champion of Ostus, unparalleled with a sword and unmatched in strategy. There is a man like you not even once in a generation. Zarina, the sorceress, the wisest, most loving of people. When things have seemed darkest, your counsel has led us through triumph and trials alike. Balthus, the unbeatable general whose bravery and power are unmatched even in the legends of myth. Gellen, the genius whose contraptions, magic and intelligence find a way when everything seems lost. You are my greatest heroes and I know you and love each of you so well. What is it you are not telling me?"

Zarina looked first at Athus, then Gellen and finally Balthus. "Sire, although we think we have a good chance to close the portal, the likelihood of our return is virtually non existent. The Kryxian host at Salgatha is mighty. We believe that if we strike without warning, we can break through their ranks and enter the tunnels beneath the city. There we can buy Athus enough time to seal The Rift and destroy Nemeddes... but by the time we are finished the whole Kryxian army will descend to block our path to freedom. We will not be able to fight our way clear."

"There is no other way?" the King asked.

"Gellen has evaluated our options, Sire," said Zarina. "He is never wrong about such things. There is no other plan that has nearly as much chance of success."

"I cannot ask you to do this..." said the King.

"You do not need to ask. If Nemeddes returns, we cannot defeat him a second time. He will bring death to every corner of the world, as his master did in the last Scourging. We must stop him. We cannot pass our burden onto future generations. We must act now."

"Spoken as true heroes," said the King. "However, you have remained quiet Athus. What wisdom do you have to offer to all this?"

Leo looked around at the expectant faces gathered about him, then slowly, mechanically even, he took a nub of the flesh on his thigh between finger and thumb and pinched himself. Sadly he did not wake up.

10.

It was nearly seven in the evening when all the matters of council were completed and, the others having personal duties to attend to, Leo found himself alone. A few minutes later he was walking across the castle courtyard heading towards the main gate. The audience with the King had filled him with horror. People had never before looked to him for guidance and leadership, asking him to make decisions with no easy answers – decisions that meant the difference between life and death for others – and now apparently for himself. He was completely out of his depth and desperate to leave the castle. Who knew what burden would be placed on him next?

The day of bliss he'd been promised was more like a nightmare. With every moment he could feel his old life receding into a hazy past that was little more real than a dream. Never before had he longed for the accustomed problems of hating his job, his life and the mildly terrifying realisation that he had become an alcoholic.

A strong hand landed on his shoulder and Leo turned to face a tall, handsome man dressed in the regalia of a knight.

"How are you my Lord? Have you recovered from your injuries?" the man asked.

Leo nodded. "Just about," he said.

"I saw you take the wound my Lord, I'm Sepio from the Fourteenth, helped hold the flank while you slew the arch fiend," the warrior said.

"Good to see you again Sepio," smiled Leo. "Do you think you could fetch me a horse? I have urgent business."

Sepio bowed. "A pleasure my Lord."

It was not an overly long ride through the evening to Druid's Overlook. Tethering his mount to a tree branch Leo dismounted and stretched before he began the climb to the standing stones at the summit.

The climb was much easier in Athus' strong body, the power of the arms and of the core, coupled with the heightened fitness, made easy work of the crag and Leo reached the top having hardly broken a sweat.

Wasting no time he moved to the ancient rocks and walked amongst them.

"Hello?" he called feeling foolish. "Spirit, are you here?"

His calls were answered only by the sounds of the wind whistling through the tall stones.

Leo called again and again but there was nothing, no reply and no sign of the ghostly guardian. He moved to the stone he had sat on when the spectre had appeared and tried to recreate the same series of events that had summoned the apparition. Still there was nothing.

He sat still and tried to think. His mind raced and he could find no clarity. With luck he had only to wait here until after midnight and the spell would be undone. Then he heard footsteps behind him and he span.

Balthus nodded to him, having to stoop his giant form to pass beneath an archway of stone. Without a word he sat down beside Leo and stared into the distance of the night sky. Unsure of what to do, his stomach tight, Leo said nothing. He tried to hide how intimidated he felt by the presence of the massive warrior.

"What are you doing here, my friend? This is an unholy place," Balthus said at last.

"I just needed to get away and think," said Leo.

"You have not been yourself these last few days," said Balthus.

"I do not feel myself," said Leo weakly.

"I have never known you lose your cool my friend. Never seen you crack under pressure. You always hold your nerve, you always have a plan. This is what separates us. What has always separated us. I am a great fighter, but I have no gift for strategy, unlike you. And I cannot keep my head," Balthus chuckled.

"When I fight, I am like fire, all passion and instinct. You are like ice, disciplined and clinical. It is all those books on swordplay and tactics you read. All those damn pages full of spidery words – I have tried to read them, but the sentences just spin around and around in my mind and won't go in. Now give me my battle axe, point me at a foe and I know what to do. That is easy. I do not envy you the burdens you hold on your shoulders. I would not be able to make the decisions you make, either in the heat of battle nor in the council chamber – but then that is what makes you The Champion, the hero of Ostus."

Leo looked into Balthus' proud eyes. "I do not feel much like a hero today."

"You do not have that luxury. I see the cracks starting to show in you. The wound you suffered was grave and I know the aftermath of his magic lingers in you. But you do not have my permission to fall apart until after we defeat the Lich. When that is done, you can rest. We need you Athus, the whole kingdom needs you. You have chosen a poor time to begin to doubt yourself. Now come on, enough of this, let's head back."

Balthus stood and silently Leo followed him. They clambered down from the Overlook and were again on flat ground and nearly at the horses when Balthus found the body. It had been left just off the trail, hidden in the long grass. Leo realised he must have walked within a few yards of it only an hour before.

"Poor bastard," Balthus commented, turning the body over. "He's been ripped to pieces."

The body was torn, with ragged gashes from its neck to its navel. The man's intestines hung from a wound in his stomach. One arm was severed at the elbow.

"What does that to a man?" Leo asked, his voice sounding far away even to himself.

"Damned if I know," said Balthus. "A bear maybe? Could be something more dangerous, this is a place of old magic. We should leave the body here;

Gellen will want to examine it. Mad old fool will probably be furious I touched it at all."

Leo nodded. Although the body was grotesquely mauled the face was intact, almost, Leo would think later, as if whatever had done this had somehow known he would see it. Despite the awful violence that had been done to it, the bushy red beard and long, copper hair were untouched and although it was now sunken and discoloured there was no doubt that it was his real face, his real body.

He did not wretch nor panic, indeed he found himself strangely calm and somehow momentarily beyond terror as he looked down at his own corpse and its green eyes twinkled back at him in the moonlight.

The pair rode back to the palace mainly in silence. Leo's mind had begun to race. He had many faults but he was not a stupid man and one thought pulsed again and again with disquieting power. If he had been sent into the body of Athus Glynn, was it not possible that Athus could have been placed in his body? And if he had, was it possible that something had been waiting for Athus at those standing stones? Something that had ripped him apart and killed him? Something that knew it could not reach him inside the palace, surrounded by his friends and allies? Something that knew it could not best him in his own powerful body – something that had killed the world's greatest hero, alone, in an old, flabby body that was weary and exhausted. Leo felt bile crawling up inside him, like ants crawling inside their nest.

Balthus' voice drew him from his thoughts as they arrived at the palace gates. "I never knew a love between man and woman like that between yourself and Zarina. Such a pure love. I never thought that you, the great and honourable Athus, would betray her. Don't get me wrong, I do not judge. I love my Jaina with all my heart and I have strayed enough times. Temptation is all around." Balthus' hand grabbed Leo's wrist and although the man's voice stayed soft, the grip was like a vice. "I have followed you my whole life. I always thought you were a better man than this - than me. That is why I chose to follow you. Do not make me regret my choice now."

Even through the strangeness and madness of it all, of the spell, of seeing his own dead body, of the disquieting thoughts that Athus had been led into a trap and even though Balthus was not his friend, nor Zarina really his wife, the words stung and Leo knew shame.

In silence the two stabled their horses and entered the castle. Before they parted Balthus again spoke.

"You have taken on much and I do not resent you having some freedom. Now go home, put last night behind you; we are all allowed to make a mistake once in a while. Go make love to your wife, calm your nerves and sleep. And when you wake, wake as the man I know you are - the best of men."

With that the giant turned and walked away towards his chambers.

Leo waited alone in the great library of the palace until after three o'clock but in his heart he knew nothing would happen. He knew that he had been tricked and was almost certain he had caused the death of Athus Glynn. He felt trapped and alone in a way that, until that moment, he had never experienced.

Not knowing what to do, Leo eventually let himself into Lord Athus and Zarina's bedchamber. Worry had rendered him close to exhaustion. Outside, the sun sat like liquid gold in the troughs of the hills, promising a dawn that was not far away. Leo heard movement from the bed and glanced to see Zarina raise herself onto an elbow. She smiled at him in the gloom. It was a look he had never been the recipient of whilst in his own skin and he found himself suddenly close to tears. It was a look that spoke of an enduring, deep love.

"I'm sorry for my behaviour," he found himself stuttering.

"Put it from your mind. We're all allowed to slip from time to time," she said, her voice heavy with sleep. "Come to bed."

"I'm sorry it's so late - well early," he murmured. "I didn't mean to be so long."

"You're here now," she said softly, lying back. "That is all that matters."

Disrobing, Leo slid in beside her, feeling her warmth as she cuddled against him. "Are you alright my love?" she asked.

"I'm fine," said Leo, feeling anything but.

"Do not worry about tomorrow's combat," she whispered; her voice soft and on the cusp of sleep. "I know how you get but you have fought a hundred duels like this one. He is just a brute, you are the finest sword in the land."

Leo waited for a moment and was about to ask more but her breathing had deepened and she was asleep again, nestled under his arm. Now a Lord, in bed with a beautiful sorceress, in a fine room atop of a mighty citadel, Leo found himself more lost than ever.

11.

Leo stood still while the squires fussed and attended to him. It seemed easier that way. What could he do? This nightmare just got worse and worse. He had considered telling Zarina everything that morning, but even as he had tried to speak the words, his throat had tightened as he imagined her kind face turning dark and angry. After all, he was responsible for killing her love, the great hero Athus. They would torture him and execute him for sure. He deserved no less. So he had stayed silent and she had prepared him breakfast, tried to soothe his nerves and taken his quietness to be apprehension over this duel, this trial by combat that he would soon be fighting.

He had slept not a wink the night before and his eyes were itchy and tired when Balthus had collected him and taken him to the arena. Here he had been massaged, oiled, then dressed in cloth, then leather and now the heavy plate was being strapped into place by a team of aspirants. The formality of the servants was lucky because Leo had not a clue how to don a piece of armour and he watched with detached wonder at the dexterity of the squires as they tightened each strap and fixing. He could think of no solutions, no way to change what had happened and no way to avert the course he was sealed upon. It had been but a few hours and yet his own life, his true life as Leo Kvetch, felt as far away as the sun itself.

As the helm was slowly lowered onto his head a chill of claustrophobia flowed through him and his vision was reduced to a small slit through the metal visor. He felt a blade pressed into one hand. His fingers tightened on the hilt even as his mind recoiled and he was sure to hold it low, pointing at the floor. For the first time he was glad of the helmet.

"As long as I don't look at it, I'll be ok," he whispered to himself. But how could he fight a duel when he was terrified of his own sword?

There was no time to think much about it because the large, wooden doors before him were opened and the bright sunshine blazed in. The crowd went wild, cheering for their hero and, feeling like an actor in a play following a script, Leo was led by a team of squires out into the arena.

He stumbled unsteadily, unused to the weight of the armour and found it hard to walk across the sandy floor. It was a hot, dry day and on top of the extra weight, the heat of the layers was already sapping at his strength. If it had not been for Athus' strong body he would have been ready to collapse before he'd even reached the centre of the stadium. The crowd's shouts clamoured and reverberated through the metal suit, the sounds distorted, almost as if he were underwater. A large man entered from the opposite end, strolling across the sand. He was bald and dressed in the ragged furs of the Eldwei Tribe. A large bone piercing was punched through his nose and he carried a blackwood club with a spike driven through one end. Leo stared through the narrow slit in his visor and for the first time some of the unreality of it all fell away in the face of survival instinct.

He had to fight this man? The tribal looked wild and half crazed; his eyes like fire. There was no fear in him that Leo could see. The warrior was powerful looking, not huge like Venn the tavern master and nowhere near the size of Balthus, yet fearsome enough. He looked strong of shoulder and although grey streaked his long, matted beard, he was far from an old man. The way he hefted the club told of familiarity with the weapon.

Suddenly the crowd cheered and it took Leo a moment to turn to see that Balthus had appeared, striding over the sand like he owned it. He walked to stand beside the warriors and raised his arm. There was immediate quiet.

"This combat has been approved by the Law Sages and it has been ratified by His Majesty," Balthus proclaimed, his voice booming out across the stadium. "Morvus Gern, of the Eldwei Tribe, has been accused of murder and rape. A jury of his peers was unable to reach a verdict, and instead of waiting for a re-trial, Morvus has called for trial by combat, as is his right. If any here know of new evidence then let them speak now."

The huge arena, so boisterous before, was spookily silent. Leo could even hear the wind picking up grains of sand and throwing them against his armoured greaves.

"Then let this combat decide what is right and what is just. This contest will continue until one man dies, yields or is unable to continue, for it is well known that no man who is false can stand against one who is true." Balthus threw his arms high, "May the Lady's judgement burn bright this day!"

The crowd exploded with fervour and Balthus nodded to Leo before backing away, turning, and marching from the sands.

Leo found himself swallowing in a dry throat. Then a bugle sounded and all hell broke loose.

It was clear, Leo realised later whilst he was recovering from his wounds, that Morvus Gern had expected to die quickly in that contest. Perhaps the idea of a rapid, honourable death at the hands of a master swordsman was preferable for a man like Gern than decades of rotting in a dungeon. Whatever the case, the tribal spent little time weighing him up and instead charged in like a madman, perhaps seeking to force his opponent to strike a killing blow. Had Gern, as he thought, been fighting the most dangerous swordsman in the realm, his life might have been ended swiftly. However, he was not, he was fighting a cowardly, half terrified ranch hand with virtually no experience in armed combat.

Even Leo, during one of those timeless moments that only seem to happen in the heat of some action, had to admit that the surprised look on Morvus Gern's face when his first clumsy blow smashed into Leo's left pauldron and sent 'The Champion' staggering, was priceless. Gern struck again, this time his ugly face was half turned away and distorted. Both his eyes were screwed shut in anticipation of a killing repost that never came. Instead, Leo was struck once more and this time was knocked to his knees, pain screaming through his left arm. The crowd booed, perhaps thinking Gern had attacked before the bugle had fully sounded. Leo righted himself in time to be struck again, the blow staggering him backwards, but this time he kept his feet. He swung out with his own sword, more an act of self preservation than a real attempt to do harm and Gern stepped easily clear of the blade.

Leo had a chance to steady himself, a moment to feel the dampness of the sweat soaking his back and a moment to watch as Gern's whole body language changed. Like a starving wolf who smells fresh quarry on the wind, Gern seemed to bristle and his eyes began to sparkle. And Leo knew why; Gern had realised that he could win.

The next strike very nearly killed Leo. The club crashed into his head and the spike driven through it actually punched through the helmet, missing Leo's eye by less than an inch and drawing a ragged cut across his forehead that spilled salty blood into his eyes and down his face. Gern pulled at his club, which was stuck fast to the helm and with a mighty scream, pulled it free, ripping the helmet from Leo in the process. Light and blood filled Leo's eyes and he stumbled backwards, his legs going from under him, his sword flying from his grip and landing somewhere behind him as he fell onto his back. He heard both the sigh of terror that came from the crowd, like air being drawn sharply from bellows and then Gern's heavy footfalls approaching.

Leo struggled but he was like a tortoise unable to right itself. His vision was obscured by his own blood and he wasn't sure exactly where the tribal was. His mind was filled with images of the raised club smashing down to dash his skull to pulp and his brain leaking onto the hot sand. Then Leo heard something else – Athus' voice coming from his own mouth, screaming, "I yield! I yield! I yield!" over and over again like a crazed chant.

Even amidst his terror he could acknowledge that he sounded truly pathetic. He began to lash out, flailing like a madman, and when his foot connected with something his words just became screams as every beat of his quickened heart heralded the moment of his death.

In those seconds, facing certain death, he realised that he had never wanted to live so much. He was suddenly so grateful for his little cabin and his simple job and the feeling of grass against his feet or the sound of a bird calling to its fellows and he would have given anything to just be sitting before his fire in his home. He was still screaming like a babe but did not care and then he felt strong hands on him lifting him up and was aware that, still howling in terror, he was being carried from the arena.

12.

Limply, he allowed them to remove his armour and tend to his wounds. Gellen came and administered another of his foul tasting concoctions and Leo swallowed it without resistance. A squire cleaned and stitched the wound to his head and another fastened him a sling for his damaged arm. No one spoke. He lay back and smooth sheets covered him and a soft mattress was below him. His body felt snug, a deep sleepiness invading every muscle and his thoughts were warm and fuzzy.

As Gellen's medicine worked on him, numbing his senses, he became aware of low voices, echoing slightly in the heavy air and he had to strain to hear them, able to catch only snatches.

"What are we going to do?... The man's a wreck .... Gone mad," came a babble of distorted speech. Leo opened his eyes and found his vision was now as blurry as his senses. He saw a cluster of people standing close together beneath a tall window. He tried to focus but the more he strained the more the figures merged into one mass that his eyes could not separate. Even their voices seemed slow and distorted, sometimes deep and heavy, other times high and whimsical. He knew the people were talking about him but he felt so removed from the world it was like listening to people talk about another person.

"He's finished ... Did you hear him screaming out?... Pathetic... And the people ... the people heard it. Gods..."

Turning his head he suddenly became aware that someone was sitting over him. Even through the drugs he could recognise Zarina's face and even the worry on it.

She soothed his head and smiled. "Get well my love," she whispered again and again.

Leo tried to speak to her, found he could not and even as he willed his mouth to work he felt his mind recede from the room, felt himself sinking deeper into the softness of the bed, sudden terror gripping at him as the darkness flowed towards him - and then he slept.

His dream was pleasant at first. He was walking down a wide boulevard in a city of gleaming white stone. The sun was bright and families ate picnics beneath the shade of trees crowned with purple blossoms. Clear water pulsed from a fountain in the middle of the alabaster square and Leo paused to splash his face. Catching a view of his reflection in the water, Leo saw he was himself again, his red beard and hair restored. Happily he strolled on. The giant Balthus passed him, walking hand in hand with a beautiful, raven haired woman. A child sat on his shoulders, joyfully shaking a toy rattle. Balthus waved cheerily and smiled a greeting that Leo returned. Some paces behind him, a long procession of women followed the General. Some in the line looked happy whilst others wept. Leo noticed that some carried dark-skinned children.

Leo walked on. In a small grove of neatly kept flowers and trees, just off the main street, he caught sight of Zarina. The sorceress was not dressed in her usual bright garbs but rather all in black, a dark veil obscuring her face. She stood over a simple grave and even from this distance he could see she was weeping brokenly. A tightness seized Leo's throat and he hurried past, leaving her to grieve alone.

Suddenly he caught sight of Rebecca. She was moving amongst a group of beggars, handing out coins and food. Instead of the rugged farm clothes she normally sported, she was wearing a dress of sparkling blue that immodestly displayed her figure. Her dark hair was held up with a circlet of silver, set with sapphires, and the sight of her took Leo's breath away. She glanced up as Leo approached and smiled. Rebecca handed him some bread and he found himself moving from one hooded person to the next, offering aid. The people accepted it graciously and his heart filled with the pleasure of charity. Then a hand grabbed at his wrist.

Leo looked down to see bony fingers clutching at him like writhing maggots. The man who had seized him looked out from the darkness of his hooded robe. His face was almost white and painfully sunken, the eyes rimmed with blood and glazed with cataracts. Leo knew it like it was his own, because in a way it now was, it was the face of Athus Glynn, The Champion. The man's strength had gone, his princely appearance ravaged by the grave. Glynn was a skeletal leper and as the hood fell back, Leo gasped, wrenching his arm free. Glynn's head was bald and covered in festering lesions that leaked a sickly puss.

"Help me..." croaked the man. "Help me..."

But Leo did not want to help him, he did not want to be even near the man and he turned and ran as fast as he could. He ran and ran and ran - out of the city gates, into the woods and onwards. The night descended as he ran and then everything was gone, the land, the sky, the stars – there was just nothingness.

And he was still running, running in darkness. Sweat was coursing down his body, dripping from his face and stinging his eyes. His heart smashed inside his chest and he knew it was there, somewhere behind him, something unknowable and evil and he dared not stop. The cries would start soon he knew, the broken cries of the child sobbing. Barely had the thought come to him than the cries began, grating inside him like nails across slate. He looked back and saw the dark figure begin to emerge, peeling itself out of the nothingness, the shining tooth-like blade forming in its hand. Terror spread through him and he ran on and ran on and ran deeper into this nowhere place. The child's cries were all around now and he put his hands to his ears and screamed but it did nothing to quiet the noise.

Then out of the dark a door appeared, light shining from it like a beacon and, without thought, he ran through it and the dark fell away and he was there again, in that kitchen. He knew what waited for him there. He didn't want to see his plate of tuna fish sandwiches. He didn't want to see the carefully folded laundry. He didn't want to watch her feet struggling, pushing on the slick floorboards. Then stopping.

He turned his back and tried to shut his eyes but they wouldn't close and the dark shape that had been chasing him slunk in from the nothingness behind the door. It took on an almost human form and then grinned. Leo stared puzzled for a moment. Something wasn't right. The face was usually a shadow lined with tiny pearl- handled knives for teeth, but this face was different and crudely human. It was like an artist's sketch yet to be filled out and instead of lunging at him and ending the dream, it merely stood and grinned.

"It's you," Leo gasped. "The spirit from the standing stones, the one that cast the spell."

The spirit smiled, its face for the first time forming into something concrete, at first the kind looking face it had worn on Druid's Overlook but then suddenly it became long and haughty. The man grew in height, his eyes flashing unnaturally golden, bright with intelligence and malice. When the spirit smiled Leo saw that his teeth were filed to points.

"Indeed I am," it said in a rich, jovial voice. "I am the Necromancer Nemeddes, the Lich King of Kryx, Lord of Death."

"What do you want with me?" asked Leo, his voice trembling, trying to ignore the sounds of struggle behind him and the splashing water slopping against the wooden floor.

"I came to thank you of course," the Lich smiled, and Leo noticed with disquiet that the man's pupils were dark gashes like those of a snake.

"I don't understand," Leo said, his whole body shaking, his lip trembling. He heard fingernails ripping at wood, gauging through it as she desperately tried to save herself.

"I know you don't," said the Lich. "You are a simple man; that is why I chose you. The Champion was the only one who could halt my return, he is the only one who could wield the sword of star metal that can seal The Underworld. Now, thanks to you, he is dead and a weak, pathetic fool inhabits his body. I could never have killed him without you Leo. He was too strong, too skilful, too powerful and too courageous. But you let me bring him away from all that protected him, his allies, his

friends – that damnable white witch he loved so much. The kill was sweet, his soul tasted... divine."

"I didn't want any of this," said Leo weakly.

"Yes you did," smiled the Lich. "You wanted it with all your heart. You wanted to be someone important, you wanted to be a hero; you thought you deserved all that. You have done well, I am proud of you Leo. You have behaved beyond my wildest expectations. When they find out what you have done they will kill you of course, but do not fear, for when I return and bring this world to its knees, I will make sure you have a place of honour at my feet. I always have room for the worthless at my table. I will drink the world dry, Leo, and I will leave you until last, so you can see what you have done."

"Leave me be!" Leo screamed.

"As you wish," Nemeddes said. "But first turn and look upon the sight that you loath most."

Leo resisted but the Lich span a finger and Leo felt himself jerked around to watch again as his father drowned his mother in a bucket of water on the kitchen floor. She struggled and tore at the floorboards until her fingernails were torn away. She thrashed one last time and then was still. Leo watched as his father removed a small pearl-handled knife from his pocket, then drew it across her throat, bleaching the water a deep red.

His father looked up at him and slowly stood and pointed that awful knife with its gleaming handle directly at Leo. As he advanced, he seemed to grow in size with each step until he towered impossibly high above Leo, his voice deep and menacing.

"Don't you tell no one what you seen, you useless sprat," the colossus bellowed. "If you do..." and he leaned forward bringing the terrifying blade with its glittering point up to Leo's eyes. "If you do... I'll gut you like a kipper." Leo stood and stared at the pearl handle of the knife and how the oil shimmered along it. Then he turned and ran, his father chasing.

"I should have killed you when I had the chance, sprat!" the giant called. "I should have drowned you when you popped out!" And Leo ran and ran and ran, through the night, through the woods and onwards and

onwards back into the city and through the streets and then, just as he thought his heart would fail, he saw Rebecca, still helping the poor. He ran to her for help but as soon as he approached the beggars rose up around her, changing into grotesque monsters and their taloned hands, each tipped with a tiny pearl-handled knife, ripped at her, tearing her apart. Leo had time only to scream before they turned and fell upon him.

13.

Leo awoke with a piercing cry and sat bolt upright breathing heavily. The bed was drenched in sweat and his heart was racing. Zarina smiled at him from where she sat close at hand and her presence calmed him a little. Softly, with a movement of infinite kindness, she reached out and gently soothed his head.

"How are you feeling?" she asked.

Leo could not answer and drew in several deep breaths before resting back and allowing his head to flop onto the pillow. Most of his nightmare, as always, was obscured to him but he remembered the Lich King's words and threats. He tried to sit up but his body ached.

"Easy," she smiled. "You have been asleep for hours and you are bruised from head to toe. You took quite a beating. Rest now. You are unwell, but we will make sure the best physicians attend you."

He nodded, looking at her closely, and he could see she was close to tears. "I'm sorry for the distress I've caused you," he mumbled.

She said nothing, just bent and kissed his brow and continued stroking his hair. Leo found the silence between them and the intensity of the way she looked at him unsettling. For a moment he again considered confessing everything, but the Lich's voice came to his mind and with it the threats of pain and torture. Cowardice got the better of him and he remained silent. She lingered, just sitting with him and not knowing what to do, he closed his eyes and feigned sleep. Surprisingly it came once more and when he awoke, thrashing and screaming in terror, the bright sunshine had given way to darkness. Zarina still sat by his bedside, her face a mask of worry. His heart melted for her and he wished with all his being he could do something to cheer her.

He craned his neck towards her and managed a smile. "Do not worry, everything will be alright," he said, although he felt like nothing could be further from the truth. But it seemed to be the sort of thing a hero might say.

"What is it that terrifies you so when you sleep?" she asked.

"I don't know," said Leo, relieved this was not something he had to lie about.

Zarina nodded and Leo could tell that she had been crying.

"Who is Rebecca?" she asked softly. "You called for her from your dreams."

"Did I?" asked Leo, the question taking him by surprise. He thought of the farm girl, so plain compared to the woman before him, but it was like a veil was lifted and he realised the depth of his feelings for her. For a moment the intensity of the revelation struck him dumb. He swallowed. "She was someone I knew once," he said. "It feels like another lifetime now."

Zarina nodded. "I know you are in pain, but my heart has been troubled. If there is something you need to tell me, now is the time." She looked at him, her blue eyes so open and vulnerable. Leo gulped remembering his conversation with Balthus and the infidelity he'd committed that wasn't really an infidelity – by all the gods this was already too complicated.

"I have nothing to tell you," he said and smiled.

She nodded and rose, kissed his head and gently stroked his cheek. "You need to rest and there are many matters of state to attend to," she said. "I will be back within the hour."

"Ok," he smiled back.

She nodded; sadly he thought, then walked slowly from the room and shut the door behind her.

Leo closed his eyes and tried to think but he had little time to himself as a moment later he heard the door open again. He looked up to see the little magister Gellen enter, offering him a curt nod. The man sat with an awkward precision and said nothing for a few moments, rocking slightly in the chair as if in deep thought. Leo did not know the man well but in the brief moments he had been around Gellen, the man had reminded Leo of someone he had once known called

Jeg. Jeg had been introduced to Leo as an idiot savant; which he had been informed by Jeg's sister, not unkindly, meant that a person was a genius trapped inside the body of an idiot. Jeg could hardly have been trusted to sit on the toilet the right way nor go out alone, he could not understand humour or jest and often held conversations with himself. He would have frequent episodes where he could not control his temper and would charge off in a rage and take everything said literally, which had led to a lot of problems when Leo had once asked him not to lose his head. Jeg had paled in fear and it had taken his sister several months of gentle persuasion before Jeg had believed her that he could not simply 'lose his head'. All that aside however, he was capable, with unerring precision, to work out any sum asked of him, calculate complex mathematical equations and could remember nearly everything he had ever heard.

"Are you a savant?" Leo asked of Gellen, just to break the silence.

"Some call it that," said Gellen. "I do not like the term. Most savants are people who have memorised a large volume of facts, usually through studying or observing worldly phenomena. They are then able to repeat this information. Naturally this ability is of limited use. I do not learn facts, I understand them. People think there are those who are intelligent because they can recite the work and knowledge of others. This is a fallacy. Intelligence is defined by discovery."

"I knew a man who was a savant," said Leo, largely ignoring the thrust of Gellen's words before telling Gellen what he knew about Jeg.

Gellen listened intently, nodded, then ignoring the line of conversation simply said: "You are not Athus Glynn."

Leo's blood ran cold. "What are you talking about?"

"I can read any known language including fourteen that I have invented myself," said Gellen. "Reading the micro movements of a human face is much simpler. It is obvious to me that you are not Athus Glynn. It has been since the moment you awoke in my laboratory."

"Now wait a minute..." Leo began.

"There really is no need for you to speak," said Gellen. "I have already predicted with over ninety nine per cent accuracy what you will say. People often criticise my conversation skills; however it is a difficult task to talk to people. It is not easy being vastly more intelligent than everyone around you. I tend to find that as soon as a conversation begins I know everything a person will say on the subject. This means it is far more efficient for me to not speak to them as I already know in advance what they will say."

"Well, what am I supposed to say to that?"

"I knew you'd say that," said Gellen.

"Good for you," said Leo, as he slowly levered himself onto his elbows.

"And that too," said Gellen. "However, we are at an impasse. Everyone believes that you have suffered some sort of mental breakdown due to the pressures of your station; but this is not the case. I would know if that was the case. It is not. You are not Athus Glynn. You look like him and sound like him but there the similarities end. Do you want to know how I'm so sure?"

"Because you're so clever?" said Leo, swinging his legs out of the bed and wincing.

"I know because Athus Glynn is the one person I have ever met who is closest in intelligence to myself. Unusually, I could not always predict his conversational patterns. He could surprise me. He even beat me at Shaddak once, certainly the happiest day of my life. I have never been beaten before or since. Yet I can predict your every move with pin point accuracy."

"I see, so what am I planning now?" Leo asked.

"You are planning on hitting me over the head with the candlestick on your bedside table and then trying to make a run for it," said Gellen.

"Not necessarily," said Leo, withdrawing his hand from where it was already creeping towards the candlestick.

"There is no need for violence; I am not going to stop you. No one will believe me if I tell them," said Gellen. "People tend to take the truth with a pinch of salt, especially when it comes from someone most consider mad."

"Then why are you here?" Leo asked.

"I have come to tell you that despite your fears that you will be punished for telling the truth, Lady Zarina will not let harm come to you. You should confess to her and tell her what you know. It is obvious that you are far too inept to be a servant of Nemeddes."

Nemeddes. Leo shivered at the name and remembered afresh the Lich appearing in his dream. "The Lich." Leo said. "Who is he?"

"A king who sold himself to the dark arts for power," said Gellen. "He rose a thousand years ago from the ash of the last Scourging when his master Zallandex was destroyed by the hero Amad El. Nemeddes has long grown his power in secret but Athus Glynn led an army against him and killed his mortal form."

"So he's dead?"

"For a necromancer, death is merely inconvenient," said Gellen. "We did half a job. His soul lives on in the Ether and waits to inhabit a new body. It is possible to close the 'portal'," said Gellen, making a sign in the air with both index and middle finger like bobbing bunny ears. "Then we can seal the 'underworld' with the 'magic sword'."

"Why do you keep doing that with your hands?" asked Leo.

"Because it all comes down to quantum physics and the relativity of time and space," said Gellen. "However, others seem quite incapable of grasping even the simplest concepts when it comes to extra-dimensional theorem no matter how many times I explain it. So it is easier to talk in terms of 'magic'."

"Which all means?" Leo asked.

"That a powerful, cruel leader will ride forward with a Kryxian host and an army of monstrous beasts not of this world and will destroy and conquer. Only Athus had any real chance to avert that but you are not Athus."

"Are you saying I have doomed the world?" Leo asked.

"Very probably," said Gellen.

"What should I do? I haven't known what to do since it all began," Leo protested.

"You should begin by telling the truth to Zarina; then maybe we can achieve something," said Gellen.

Leo nodded. "If you promise I'll be safe, then I will and happily."

But Gellen ignored him and rose suddenly out of his seat. "It would be best now for you to hide under the bed."

"Why?" asked Leo.

"Krylla are coming," said Gellen.

"What the hell are Krylla?" Leo snapped.

The temperature in the room dropped and Leo felt himself begin to shiver. The hairs on his body stood on end and a primitive fear gnawed at his heart. He rose in panic, his breath steaming the air before him. The door to the room shattered inward with an ear-splitting crash. A monster darted through impossibly quickly, its body made of gleaming, black chitin. Four powerful, armoured legs supported its upper frame that was encased in a cuirass of dark metal. It had four upper limbs; two mantis like arms which extended from its chest and two large, muscular limbs that ended in claws. Its head was small and sported mandibles like some enormous ant and its eyes were dull, inhuman orbs. It emitted a series of clicks and sidled to its left, making room for one of its fellows to join it in the chamber.

Gellen had done nothing to prepare himself but stood with an air of indifference as the creatures continued to communicate in their strange, grating language.

"If I were you, I would run," Gellen advised.

Leo was not sure to whom the magister was speaking, the monsters or himself, but thought it best to take no chances. The window to his right was open and he dashed for it and scrambled quickly onto the sill. One of the monsters let out a high pitched squeal and leapt after him but there was a sudden crack and a flash of light and the creature was hurled against the wall. Leo glanced back, seeing the beast right itself and turn its attention to Gellen. He did not tarry to see what happened next and leapt to the floor below, tucking and rolling to cushion the impact. Then, the pain of his wounds forgotten, he was running across a small courtyard and running, and running...

14.

Leo sucked in deep breaths as he walked. Like in any city, there were places in Ostus that never slept. Being surrounded by people had seemed to be the safest option so he had dashed as quickly as he could to the centre of the Sapphire Mile, a row of taverns, bars and inns that took up the whole south quarter of the city. The streets were well lit but Leo found his eyes searching the shadows just beyond the reach of the torches, unable to stop himself wondering what lurked just out of sight. In his mind's eye he kept seeing the butchered corpse of his real body. He was in no doubt that the chitinous creatures he'd just escaped from had been responsible, tearing at their prey with their saw-like forearms, massive pincers and vicious mandibles. He had no intention of making himself an easy target.

He had stolen a riding coat as he had fled the palace. His collar was pulled high and his hood was up but he was still fearful of being recognised. Nemeddes, this Lich King - who knew what other resources he had to draw on? Leo had seen enough of life to know that not all monsters had dripping fangs and claws. He walked for some time following the flow of people in a circle through the streets and trying to think. He had to do something. Things were trying to kill him, the world was in danger but no matter how many times he went through it, his mind could barely accept what had happened to him and he had no idea what to do. He fell into simply wishing that none of this had happened, alternately consoling himself on his bad luck then berating himself for his stupidity.

His thoughts swirled, all jumbled and tumbling together, until out of nowhere a moment of clarity dawned. He realised, with a wry smile, that he had spent a huge amount of his life wishing things had been different for him. He had always felt he was destined for something more and had daydreamed constantly about the mistakes he'd made and about the wrongs others had done to him that had held him back. All his life, deep down he'd wished for one thing – purpose.

"I got my wish," he whispered to himself in a moment that was both terribly depressing and somehow euphoric. "Now I have to step up to the mark. I have to do something."

But what? He decided to keep things simple. To begin with he needed more information.

Decision made, Leo pushed through the crowd, keeping his head down and his hood well forward and headed for The Wyrd. He knew very little about magic but there were plenty in the city that did. He needed to find out more about what had been done to him - that was a start at least. Perhaps there was even a way to reverse the spell.

The Wyrd was located close to the docks and was not one of the most pleasant parts of the city. Funding to complete the area had been swallowed up by the war and many of the white, stone walls were left only half finished giving the area a patchwork, dishevelled look. The prices of the homes had still been too much for the common folk to afford, even in their half finished state and the trade class had moved in and bought up the whole area. The region had become the working hub for magisters, sorcerers, witches and hedge mages. For the right price people consulted the Ether on love, life and the future. Others traded in common or garden variety magical trinkets and spells. There were even rumours some conversed with darker powers.

Leo had never cared for the place and had visited only a handful of times. He wandered the streets, keeping to the shadows so as not to be recognised, bypassing potion sellers and witchdoctors until he saw a brightly coloured tent pitched outside a large house. The sign read: "Madam Skillattus - expert diviner, fortune teller, healer and scryer – Consultation free, services from one gold piece."

Leo's knowledge was hazy on such things, but as far as he was aware, if you had an object with some unknown magical properties, you paid to have someone to scry it for you and they would discover what manner of spell had been cast on it. If that was the case with objects, then perhaps it was the same with people?

Being one of the more expensive establishments on the row, there was little in the way of a queue and after only a few minutes of waiting a bald headed man lifted up the tent flap and gestured for Leo to enter.

After a brief discussion on payment, Leo was directed into the house and led through a series of corridors to a small room only furnished with a round table. An old hag of a woman, who managed to alleviate not even a single stereotype about witches, sat at the table and gestured for Leo to join her.

"Cross my palm with gold," she said as way of greeting.

"I thought the consultation was free," said Leo.

"I'm sure The Champion of Ostus can afford it," the witch smiled, displaying rows of broken, crooked teeth.

Leo nodded, removing the silver bracelet Athus wore on his left wrist. "I think this will suffice, Madam Skillattus."

The woman snatched out her hand like a starving crow pecking at a fresh eyeball and grabbed the bracelet. "I am not Skillattus, she is busy. I am Rhea. What is it you want to know my Lord?"

With as much skill as he could muster and leaving out information he did not think was essential or might do himself harm, such as his real identity and the involvement of the Lich King, Leo summarised the scenario he was in as best he could. Rhea sat completely motionless throughout and waited for him to finish.

"What you speak of is called Soul Swapping," said the witch. "It is a powerful magic to be sure – and rare. Not all souls are the same you see. For a soul swap to be successful both souls must be compatible, which is rare enough in its own right, and both individuals must be bound by a spell of blood. The spell itself is actually quite straightforward, a novice could cast it, but the connection the magister needs to have to the

Ether is profound. There are few these days with that sort of power. "

"Can these spells be undone?" Leo asked.

"To reverse a spell of that magnitude, great power is needed, but it can be done," Rhea spoke. "A fraction of any spell remains inside those who are the target. All it would take is for a magister of sufficient skill to reform and recreate the spell, then reverse it, returning each of the people soul swapped."

"Could you do it?" Leo asked.

Rhea shrugged. "Perhaps. Skillattus certainly could. First let me see if I can sense the spell."

The witch leaned forward, gently pressing the fingers of each hand against either side of Leo's head. The crone closed her eyes and began to hum softly to herself. For Leo there was no sensation at all, save one of mild discomfort at being so close to an old woman whose stale breath puffed against his face.

"Yes," said the witch nearly at once. "I can sense the fragment of the soul swap spell. It has been elegantly cast, masterfully even."

"Can you reverse it?" Leo pressed.

"Perhaps. Naturally I would need to work with the other soul involved also," said the witch, her voice distracted. "This is very strange, I'm detecting another spell fragment, much deeper and harder to find. Are you aware of any other magics cast on you, charms, hexes, that sort of thing?"

"No," said Leo.

"Peculiar. This is very unusual," Rhea droned. "You have a mnemonic spell in place."

"What is that?" Leo asked.

"A memory spell. A powerful one too, but poorly cast."

"I don't know anything about that," said Leo.

"That's why it's a memory spell," the crone said as if talking to a child "As for the soul swap, return here with the other person involved and I should be able to reverse the casting."

"Can the spell be reversed if one of the people involved is dead?" Leo asked.

"Let me have a closer look at this Mnemonic Barrier," the witch said ignoring him. "I'm going to close in on it a little. It's fractured and leaking and... quite aggressive..." the witch grimaced. "A powerful protection on this, nothing I can't handle but, just going to back off it a little." Suddenly the witch began to scream in pain.

"Are you hurt?" Leo asked.

With a jerk the woman broke away from him and staggered backwards crashing into the wall and upsetting the small table. Leo watched in horror as her hands clutched at her face. Her eyes began to fill with darkness as he looked, then with a final, piercing scream the witch fell to the floor. He stood and moved to her but her body was already cold. She was stone dead.

A moment later the door flew open and another old crone with blazing white hair entered.

"What is going on in here? What have you done?"

"I didn't do anything, I don't know anything about it," said Leo. "She just collapsed."

"Stay where you are," the woman commanded, moving to the fallen witch and placing her hand on her brow. Her face furrowed, her eyes flicking rapidly in her head. Then she looked up, furious.

"How dare you bring this to my home!" she screamed and at once two large minders appeared and seized Leo.

Roughly he was dragged through the back of the house and unceremoniously ejected through the rear door to be thrown into the street behind. Skillattus' face appeared at a window, pale and afraid.

"Please help me!" Leo shouted to her.

She surprised him by opening the window. "Whoever you are, I want no part of it," she said. "A being of colossal evil stalks you."

"Please, it is Nemeddes – help me," Leo begged.

"No it is not the Lord of Kryx. There is something darker in you than that," the witch replied.

"I must reverse this spell," Leo called, climbing to his feet.

"What did Rhea tell you?" Skillattus asked.

"She said I was soul swapped," said Leo. "But the other person is dead."

"If that is true the only way to break this spell now would be to find a grand master of time magic, someone who could send you back to before the soul swap," said the witch. "However, there hasn't been such a person on Gaia for more than a thousand years."

Leo pressed: "But there must be a way."

"They are said to have had a temple to the east at Table Rock, beyond the desert, but everyone who knows anything about these matters knows it was destroyed during the final days of the last Scourging." The witch's voice softened. "But if there is hope for a fool such as you, then you might start looking there. Now do not darken this doorway again."

15.

With no clear plan of action Leo made his way towards the city gates. Reason dictated that he could not remain here. One of two things must have happened by now; either the body of the arch-magister Gellen would have been found, in which case people from the castle would be searching for Athus and, presumably - what had Gellen called those beasts, the Krylla? – would be hunting him too.

On the other hand Gellen may have somehow defeated the two monsters, in which case he would report Leo's cowardly escape and the guards would be out in force searching for him. Leo was not optimistic about how long he could outrun his pursuers. He was a farmhand with no training and no special skills – what chance did he have against monsters and professional warriors? A part of him put forward a case for giving up and getting drunk; what was the point in resisting? However, the coward in him pointed out that if he was caught he could no longer see an outcome that didn't involve a painful death and that at least kept him moving.

He actually got further than he thought he would and even managed to slip past two patrols before, in the early hours of the morning some way south of the city, he was chased down by a group of warriors on horseback. Even in the darkness he could make out the sun banners that hung from their horses' necks. He had been caught by the Sunchasers – Athus' personal guard. For a moment all he could see were the tips of a dozen spears levelled at him, then the horses parted and Zarina and Balthus dismounted from the rear of the party and approached. The giant walked behind the woman, dwarfing her.

"Where are you going?" Zarina asked, her voice cold. "We have been looking for you all night."

"Er, I'm on a secret mission," said Leo, hopefully, fully aware that his luck had run out hours ago. "It's for the good of everyone. Sorry I couldn't tell you about it."

"Were you on a secret mission when you bedded Lord Jarl's niece?" she asked, her voice like a whip. "Was that for the greater good too?"

"That was ... complicated," said Leo, feeling shame despite the circumstances. "I didn't mean to hurt you."

"Well you have hurt me," she said sadly. "We swore to each other. I sacrificed so much to love you - you know what I gave up."

"I'm sorry," he said meekly, with no idea of what she was talking about.

"Gellen could have been killed. Why did you run?" Balthus rumbled, his anger barely held in check.

Leo had no answer; he knew Athus would never abandon a friend. "He lives?" he asked instead.

"Yes," said Zarina, placing a calming hand on Balthus' arm. "You need to come with us."

"I don't know if that is a good idea," said Leo. "I have something I need to do."

"Where are you planning to go?" Balthus snapped.

"I'm going to deal with Nemeddes," Leo bluffed.

"So you're planning to go to the Arcana in Salgatha, alone?" Zarina asked.

"Yes, I'm the only one who can do this, right?" Leo said, trying to sound confident.

"We were going to take five hundred men," Balthus pointed out.

"Not to mention that the Arcana lies to the north and you are heading south," Zarina observed.

"Well, isn't the first rule of war to be unpredictable?" Leo offered.

Zarina let out a brief laugh but there was no mirth to it. "When we first met I gave you something, what was it?"

Leo stalled. "We don't have time for this..."

"What was it?" she asked, her voice fierce.

Leo thought for a moment and then pointed to the chain of silver he wore around his neck. "This of course," he said.

Zarina smiled and for a moment he was relieved. "Seize him," she commanded. "He is an imposter."

It would be fair to say that Leo Kvetch was not a stoic. He had of course heard many tales from bards of heroes during his life and in many of these the characters resisted torture and laughed at pain even in the face of certain death. Leo had always privately wondered why the heroes in those stories didn't just tell their captors everything to begin with. After all, if there was even a chance it was going to mitigate the horror they were certain to endure it seemed worth it.

After being dragged into a dungeon and locked in a cell, Leo's panicked mind quickly convinced him he was now faced with this very situation. When the door opened and Zarina, Balthus and a wounded but very much alive Gellen appeared, Leo, close to weeping, told them everything he knew without prompting. How he had met the spirit by the stones and his actions afterwards and how he thought he would return to his own body. He watched them carefully as he told them that he believed that Athus was dead, murdered by Nemeddes. The three glanced at each other but made no comment. When he had finished they left him again, closing the door behind them.

Leo sat in dread waiting for them to return, his thoughts filled with visions of torture and execution. He had no idea how much time had passed when the lock clicked and the door swung open.

Zarina entered, closing the door behind her. Taking a wooden chair from by the wall she moved so she was close to him.

"Are you here to kill me?" Leo asked.

Zarina shook her head, her face grave. "No, not even to judge you."

Leo nodded. "I do not blame you for hating me. I'm so sorry for what I've done," he blurted. "I didn't mean to do all this. I didn't know it was Nemeddes and he said it would only be for one night - you have to believe me."

"I do not hate and that you did not mean it is something I suppose. However, the man I loved most in the world is dead and our enemy, the Arch Lich, has once again gained the upper hand. You are partly responsible for those things."

"I know," said Leo. "I don't know how to make it better. I don't know what to do. I never know what to do."

"But you were trying to do something; I think that is important," Zarina said softly. "Why were you heading south?"

Leo told her what Skillattus had told him about a temple at Table Rock. "I didn't really have any options and I didn't expect to get there. I don't know anything about these things. I don't know what I was thinking. Everything I do just brings pain to people."

"Even if it was foolhardy, that was a long and perilous journey you intended to take," she said. "And I find it very interesting that the Temple of Time should be mentioned," said Zarina. "Are you aware that the Temple was said to be destroyed during the last Scourging?"

Leo nodded. "The witch told me so."

"There is a prophesy you see, in the Book of Shadows - an unholy tome written by Nemeddes' former master, Zallandex - that prophesises that the Temple will return just before the end of this world."

"To save it?" Leo asked.

Zarina shook her head. "That is not the usual interpretation. The servants of Nemeddes believe the Temple's return signals their ultimate victory."

"That doesn't sound great," Leo observed.

Zarina ignored him. "Even though Athus slew Nemeddes in the flesh and we defeated the Kryxian armies, the Arch Lich's power grows. Soon he will unleash his undead host and try to consume the world in darkness. We have spent months debating a course of action to avert this. At best the plan was… precarious. Now just as we were set on course and about to make our move, the game has shifted once more. Seemingly our greatest asset, Athus Glynn, has been removed from play and we have you instead, a farmhand from Two Trees." Leo did not know what to say and remained silent. At length Zarina continued. "I am and always have been a woman of faith. Sometimes when things seem darkest, that is when The Essence works its greatest magic."

"What does that mean?" Leo asked.

"I suppose we will see," she said, standing and opening the door.

Balthus entered and moved to stand over Leo. "I can't say I'm happy about this, worm," the giant growled. "You have Zarina to thank for your worthless life. If it were me I would crush your skull right now." With that the warrior untied Leo's binds and hoisted him effortlessly over his shoulder. "If you struggle I have permission to beat you senseless. So by all means, struggle."

Leo decided it was in his best interests to remain still.

16.

The four of them rode for hours through the dawn and into the day. No one spoke and Leo had neither the courage nor the inclination to ask where they were taking him. The fear of torture had given way and was replaced with a familiar sense of melancholy and shame. Zarina rode out in front, leading them, Gellen rode a few lengths ahead of him and Balthus' large mount rumbled behind.

At length Zarina led them into a copse of trees and stopped. The group dismounted and Leo, bone weary, caught his foot on his stirrup, stumbled and fell. Balthus snorted in contempt and muttered something under his breath. Leo got to his feet and felt useless as, without words, the three companions began constructing a camp. Firewood was gathered, Zarina tended the tired mounts and Gellen began to cook. Leo sat on a rock and waited.

"Come, join us," Zarina gestured when the food was ready. Leo approached and warily sat between her and Gellen.

"A capital meal this," Gellen commented. "It contains all the requisite proteins and nutrients a body needs to remain in tip top condition."

"What is it?" Leo asked.

"A broth made from a fungus. It is very good for you," said Zarina offering Leo a bowl.

Leo accepted but his eyes moved to where Balthus was heartily tucking into a bacon sandwich. Leo felt his stomach rumble.

"Couldn't I have what he's having?" he enquired, gesturing to where more cuts of bacon sizzled in the pan.

"Athus did not eat meat and had not for years. Therefore it is better for his body to keep his diet as similar as we can," Zarina explained.

Leo nodded and looked down into the greenish broth. Delicately he raised his ladle and tried a bit. It was not pleasant.

"There is no point saying you do not like it," Gellen said, "that is just in your head. Athus used to enjoy this meal and so his body and taste receptors are perfectly attuned to it."

"He's right," said Zarina. "Today's ride has made you weary, but Athus could ride all day and night and show no fatigue. It is not your body which is lacking, it is your mind."

"I am not a hero," said Leo indignantly. "I am nobody; a farmhand and a poor one at that."

"You are not a nobody," said Zarina. "There is only one of you in all creation."

"One too many," Leo mumbled under his breath.

Zarina gently placed her hand on his. "You should never say that Leo," she said.

"Your ancestors would weep if they could hear you," Balthus scoffed. "After all they did to give you life. You throw it back in their face when you say that."

"I doubt my ancestors care very much at all," said Leo; a sudden steel to his voice.

Zarina squeezed his hand. "You are in a lot of pain. I am sorry for your suffering."

"Why do you say these words to me?" Leo shouted at her. "Why show kindness? I've ruined everything, not just my own life this time but everyone's life."

"That is the past now. You need to decide what to do with your future," she said, and with that stood and carried her meal to the edge of camp.

"Personally, I'm less understanding," the dark-skinned giant rumbled. "I would have cut open your cowardly belly and pinned you to a tree for the wolves." Then he stood and moved to join Zarina.

Gellen stood also. "Where are you going?" Leo asked.

"To join them," he replied. "It is their way. When a man is melancholy they leave him to his thoughts. Having never been melancholy I do not understand it but I like to try to fit in with these things, I have books about it."

Leo stared into the fire until the last of the day's sun faded into dusk.

It was some hours past sundown when Zarina re-joined him. "You should get some rest Leo; the days ahead will be long and hard."

"The truth is I do not rest well at the best of times," said Leo. "And I am even more uneasy when I do not know where I am going."

"As crazy as it sounds," Zarina smiled, "we follow your plan. We are going to search out the Temple of Time."

"By the gods, even I can tell you it's a fool's mission; one born of desperation and stupidity," said Leo.

"Desperate times are when faith is required most," said Zarina. "A slim chance is better than none."

"Is this really the best hope there is? It is a children's story surely?"

She shrugged. "Without Athus, we cannot go north against Nemeddes. The Lich knows this; he has done his work well. Soon he will galvanise his armies and strike south. We do not have the men to hold him. He will roll over Tharat and the Western Tribes will not slow him. If he has his way he will usher in an age of blood and death."

"The Scourging," said Leo, suppressing a shudder.

"Just so."

"Then I have really doomed us all."

"Balthus and Gellen think so," Zarina smiled, "but they do not believe as I do."

"I do not know how faith can save us," said Leo. "And if it can I have little to offer."

"Have you heard the tale of Perhaps?" Zarina asked. Leo shook his head and she continued; her voice soft and enchanting. "There was a rancher who lived across the sea. He bred horses. One day his prize stallion bolted from the field and raced off across the moors. The men searched for it all day but the horse could not be found. When they returned one of the men approached the rancher and said: "That horse would have made you a fortune. It's terrible bad luck what has happened."

"Perhaps," said the rancher.

The next day the horse returned from the moors and brought six fine new horses with it.

"That is incredible!" said one of the workers. "You are the luckiest man I know."

"Perhaps," said the rancher.

That afternoon the rancher's son tried to break in one of the new mounts but he was thrown and broke his ankle.

"Your son was your best worker, he'll be out of action all season," said one of the men. "What a terrible thing to happen."

"Perhaps," said the rancher.

"That very evening an officer from the army arrived in the town to conscript the young men to fight overseas.

"If your son had not broken his ankle, he would have been enlisted," said one of the townsmen bitterly. "You are so lucky."

"Perhaps," said the rancher.

"I get it," said Leo, "a pleasant tale but how is it relevant?"

"Because, if this misfortune had not happened, we would never have considered the Temple of Time. We would have followed Athus' plan. Perhaps that would have led us to ruin. Perhaps, this new plan will work out for the best. The ways of the Essence are unknowable Leo. The only constant in this world is change. Things have changed, Athus is gone; the old plan is gone. We must embrace what remains."

Leo was not truly asleep but dozing when he heard a sound to his left. Rolling to his side he looked into the trees and listened. Perhaps a fox or deer was close to their camp. He heard nothing and his eyes were closing once more when he saw a shadow move against the dark brush. Sitting up Leo rubbed at his eyes, unsure if what he had seen was real or imagined, but when a bush parted and a man dressed in dark leather ran from the trees, a long knife raised above his head, he knew it was all too real. Leo's eyes focused on the blade and he began to scream, scrabbling backwards away from the weapon. Then in a blink the man was down, punched from his feet as a shaft of golden light hammered into his chest.

Leo turned to see Zarina unleash two more bolts of magic into the undergrowth, drawing a scream of pain with the second. Two more men burst forward, racing towards the priestess, but Balthus appeared, shoulder charging one and smashing his double headed axe into the other, nearly cutting the man in half. The downed man tried to rise but Gellen casually hurled a flaming missile from his fingertips that buried into the man's left eye. There was more movement beyond the perimeter of the camp and Leo, regaining command of his legs, rose and began to back away. Three more men leapt forward, seeking to isolate Gellen, their curved knives held like dark talons. For a moment Leo thought of running to Gellen's aid. There was a cooking pot close by, he could use it as a makeshift weapon. Then one of the knives once more glinted in the firelight and he screamed again, turned and ran, and ran, and ran into darkness.

The woods swallowed him up and he dodged between the trees, staggering over roots and slipping on loose stones. Leo ran until he could hear nothing but his own footfalls and then knelt down, resting his back against a tree trunk. He let out a long slow breath.

A twig snapped and he glanced up to see a dark, robed shape step from the shadows, a crooked knife raised. Then somehow Balthus was there. He hit the man like a sledgehammer, tackling him to the floor and wrestling the knife from him in one easy movement before stabbing it down into the man's neck.

"Stupid worm," snarled the warrior climbing to his feet. "The safest place for you is with us."

Leo could not have resisted if he had wanted to as the giant dragged him back to the camp. The floor of the clearing was littered with half a dozen corpses and

Zarina and Gellen had readied the horses. Balthus dragged Leo to his and roughly tethered his hands to the pommel of his saddle. "We lose you, worm, we lose everything. Try not to make it more difficult for me to keep you alive," Balthus growled, moving off to examine a vicious cut across his bicep.

"That looks pretty bad," Leo said. "Is that going to be ok?"

"Just a scratch, worm, don't worry about it."

"Are you alright Leo?" Zarina asked approaching.

"I am sorry," said Leo, the shame stinging his eyes. "My guts just turn to water… I have no courage."

"Courage is just a tool, like a blacksmith's hammer or an artist's brush. It must be maintained, looked after carefully. Sometimes it must be renewed. Like any tool you cannot put it away in a dark closet for years and expect it will be in good condition when you need it. You were attacked by men set to kill you, you are not a warrior; it was natural to run."

"I could have helped you," said Leo. "I thought about it."

"You could," she smiled, "and if you had you would likely have died. We need you alive. If you die too there is no hope even with time magic. At this point the universe needed someone who would run. Perhaps that is why the Essence chose you."

"Because I am a coward?" Leo asked.

"Because you were the right person for the moment," said Zarina. "Can you ride?"

Leo nodded and Zarina mounted her horse.

Balthus pulled his horse alongside Zarina. "All my life I have followed you and Athus my Lady. If you say the worm must live, let it be so, but I fear the future. We were poised to win, Athus' plan was sound. Now we are on the brink once again."

"The universe tests us, that is all," Zarina smiled, looking to where Leo sat in his saddle looking pathetic. "I do not know why the Essence chose him for this, but it has a reason."

"Your belief that this worm was chosen for a reason is all well and good," said Balthus - "If it was the Essence which truly chose him and not the Lich."

17.

Although Zarina tried to keep them off the main roads and away from people, it had always been unlikely they could slip away from Ostus without being noticed. On the morning after the attack at their camp they were spotted by a group of washerwomen as they forded a stream near Ghatlin Woods. The news obviously travelled quickly and a crowd of onlookers were out in force at the crossroads close to the village of Sket's Stone.

"We should just ride past," urged Balthus as they approached. "Every delay is against us."

"People will talk more if we just thunder by," said Zarina. "We must stop. We can little afford panic in the realm."

"I calculate little probability that Nemeddes has agents in this area," said Gellen. "In fact there is only around a two point four percent chance that..."

"We get the idea," snapped Balthus as he reined in his horse. "And you," he growled, looking at Leo, "say as little as possible."

They slowed their horses to a stop before the assembled folk and a young woman came forward and curtsied. "Wise mother," she said, addressing Zarina, "surely it must be the will of the Essence that you have come to Sket's Stone today."

"Why do you say that, child?" Zarina asked.

"Today is my sister's wedding day and only last night the priest who was to wed her fell ill. We have been in a panic all morning but when we heard news that you rode this way my Lady, we just knew everything would be all right. My sister wondered humbly if you might lead the proceedings?"

Zarina smiled. "Of course child, it would be an honour."

"The Essence provides," the girl said, bowing her head.

"Indeed it does," Zarina replied.

"We don't have time for this silly brat's wedding," Balthus hissed.

Zarina turned and, still smiling, shot Balthus a look of such authority that the big man fell silent without further protest. Zarina turned back to the people. "Please lead the way to your village."

"I still don't see why we're doing this," Balthus groaned.

"We are doing it because it is right to do it," Zarina said as she adjusted her robes.

"There are more important things afoot than this country tart's wedding," snapped Balthus.

Leo winced and shot a look at Gellen who was fiddling with some salves that were on the window ledge of the elder's house. Either the mage did not register Leo's look, had not noticed the unusual hostility between Zarina and Balthus, or quite possibly did not care to become involved in the argument. In any event he did not react in any way.

"It is important not to forget the small things when a large matter arises," said Zarina. "In fact it is important to pay extra attention to the details of everyday life. This is an important day for this village. Perhaps the Essence desires our presence here."

Balthus shook his head, opened his mouth to speak, thought better of it and stormed out.

Zarina turned to Leo. "What do you think?"

"Does it matter?" Leo asked.

"Of course it matters," said Zarina.

"You might as well marry them then, how long can it take?" Leo shrugged.

The answer was a lot longer than Leo imagined.

Although the people of Sket's Stone were not rich, the wedding was as grand and formal an affair as common folk could muster. Leo, in his guise as Athus, was placed in a position of honour and was even called on to place the sacred wreath that symbolised the unity of marriage on the altar.

Zarina presided over the proceedings masterfully and with practised ease, drawing reverence, laughter, solemn silence and joy from the congregation as needed. The couple themselves were young and happy but as the ceremony drew on Leo could not help but think of Rebecca's simple wedding and how he had stood and watched, his heart bleeding in his chest. Dark thoughts began to circle in his mind and he was glad when the bride and groom led the congregation outside to the sunshine of the village green. Leo was dragged along by the crowd and placed at the head of a large table. A pitcher of mead was slapped down before him and without thought he downed it, enjoying the taste. It had been his first drink in too long. Festivities began all around, games for children and adults to play and watch. Leo looked on as a strongman began performing, hoisting massive weights above his head as if they were nothing and defeating whole teams of men at tug-of-war.

Games of Shaddak were set up around the tables and Leo watched as Gellen was drawn over at once and moved from game to game, scrutinising each move. Meanwhile Balthus sauntered over to watch the strongman in action. Children played Casta near the chapel, running over the ground, chasing the pigskin ball and tackling each other with enthusiasm. The mood was full and happy but Leo felt none of it and turned back to his drink.

"You have had enough," said Zarina sitting beside him and leaning in as a wife might whisper into her husband's ear. "Athus was not a man prone to drink; his body will not deal with it well."

"Well, my body needs it," Leo said.

"Perhaps it does, but then this is not your body. Any addiction you have is just in your mind now," Zarina said.

"I'm not addicted," said Leo, not believing his own words. "It just helps me."

"What does it help you to do?" Zarina asked. "It does not seem like it helps you to be happy. Perhaps you should see what life is like without drinking for a while and then decide how helpful it is. I do not want you to make a scene, so make this your last sip."

With that she stood and left. Leo took another deep swill and then pushed the tankard away, scared at how great the temptation was to pick it up again. After a moment the need he felt began to anger him and he left the table and wandered amongst the festivities. People bowed to him as he passed and he returned an uncomfortable nod each time.

He found Gellen engrossed in a Shaddak contest against not one but three different opponents. The magister moved between the separate boards placing his stones with confidence. It was not a game Leo knew much about but he was impressed at the speed with which Gellen defeated all three men, drawing a ripple of applause from those watching. The boards were reset and Gellen quickly demolished his opponents once more before, with a flourish, playing the best of the three men whilst blindfolded. The atmosphere that settled as the match was played was electrifying and Leo watched in amazement as Gellen won with surety.

"How did you do that?" Leo asked as the game finished. "You couldn't even see where he was placing his pieces."

"I had ample time to observe his play in the two games before," Gellen said. "His understanding of the game is rather limited. It was no great challenge to predict his moves."

Leo was going to ask more, but a flow of people caught his attention and he turned to see Balthus step into the middle of the green and inspect some of the strongman's weights, a crowd rapidly gathering around him. Leo hurried to join them.

The strongman was probably a foot smaller than Balthus but was built of solid muscle, easily a match for the giant warrior. The strongman's shoulders were huge as was the width of his chest and the muscles of his trapezius had to be seen to be believed. The strongman gestured to a pair of kettlebells, then picking one up tossed it high into the air and caught it, drawing a murmur of appreciation from the growing crowd. Balthus mirrored the action and Leo fancied threw the weight higher, but he fumbled the catch and the kettlebell buried itself in the ground with a thud.

With a smug smile the strongman gestured to a heavy bar, then moved to it and lifted it above his head with one arm. The crowd erupted in applause. This time Balthus made no mistake and mirrored the strength feat with apparent ease. The strongman looked on impressed then gestured towards two large blocks of stone with iron handles set inside them. This time however Balthus shook his head and instead pointed to the large tug-of-war rope that lay at the centre of the green. The strongman looked unsure but before he could speak the crowd caught on to Balthus' challenge and a roar of approval went up.

Without words the two powerful men walked to the rope and took an end each, fixed their feet and began to pull. The contest that followed was an amazing spectacle and Leo was nearly deafened by the crowd's screaming and cheering. At first neither man budged an inch and they seemed completely evenly matched but slowly Balthus began to get pulled forward, inch by murderous inch. Leo watched as the titanic warrior was dragged closer and closer towards the mark that would signal his defeat. The strongman's power seemed so vast, his pull so inexorable, there seemed no way Balthus could regain the ground he had lost.

"He's going to lose," Leo said to Gellen and Zarina who had joined him.

"No he is not," said Gellen. "Balthus is a master at this game."

"He's awfully close to being pulled over the line," Leo pointed out.

"True, but then you don't lose by almost being pulled over the line," said Gellen. "That strongman will end up on his face in the dirt in, let us say, forty five seconds."

Leo would have quizzed the man more but the wizard was already wandering away.

"The truth is that it is taking their man a lot more energy to pull Balthus forward than it is costing

Balthus to offer resistance," said Zarina. "When Balthus is a yard away from the line he will begin to pull back. Tired and sensing victory their strongman will give it everything he has to claim the last yard. Balthus is still fresh and will resist him, their man will burn himself out trying to win and then Balthus will drag him around with ease."

Leo did not respond and could not help smiling as, like a prophecy unfolding before him, he watched as Balthus' slide towards defeat slowed then stopped. The strongman issued a cry and gave his all to move Balthus those last few feet, but the giant warrior would not budge. Then, flexing his massive arms, Balthus bent his legs and leapt backwards, dragging the strongman from his feet. Exhausted, the man was unable to even hold onto the rope and crashed to the floor in a heap, defeated. Balthus raised his arms in triumph and not even looking tired, accepted the applause of the watching spectators.

The day faded into evening and the townsfolk gathered around fires telling stories and playing instruments. The mood was light and carefree but Leo found his thoughts once more darkening.

"What is it that troubles you about this occasion?" Zarina asked him. "I can sense your unhappiness a mile away."

"I do not care for weddings," said Leo.

"And why is that? Do you not rejoice in seeing people united in love?" she asked.

"I loved a woman and she married another," said Leo. "I attended the wedding and it broke my heart. Now unless you are trying to spur me back to drink I would prefer we spoke no more about it."

"I am sorry for you but if she chose another you must respect that," said Zarina.

"The punch line is I know she would have wed me," said Leo. "I just never had the courage to ask. I doubted her father would accept me; he wanted a better match for her. Things got... complicated. I was a fool as usual."

Zarina patted his hand. "This is Rebecca, the woman you call to in your dreams?"

Leo nodded. "Do I really call her name?"

"Every night," said Zarina.

"She is no longer married," said Leo. "I never liked the man, although I suppose much of that was jealousy. She was with his child but the baby did not make it to term. He blamed her and divorced her. How could anyone do that?"

"Some people make poor choices or are guided by fear," said Zarina. "It is not for us to judge. Have you spoken to Rebecca of your feelings?"

"No," said Leo. "I always meant to but I could never imagine her receiving my words favourably. Strangely since this misadventure began it is all I can think about."

Zarina smiled. "After all this is over perhaps it is something you can remedy?"

"A far off hope," Leo replied.

"Do not rely on hope Leo, hope does not exist. It is just a word for daydreaming about pleasant things. Rely on right action and courage in the moment," Zarina advised.

Suddenly a rock crashed into the fire before them scattering flame and ash. Leo fell back with a squawk but Zarina did not flinch.

"How dare you! How dare you!" a deep voice rumbled.

Everyone at the fire turned to see the town's strongman, somewhat the worse for drink, pointing at Balthus. "You tricked me, you made a fool out of me!"

"Seydar, sit down!" one of the townsfolk urged.

"I will not," the strongman glared. "I will teach him a lesson."

"There is no need for this Seydar," said Balthus rising. "It was a fair contest and you did well. Go and walk off your anger and your drink."

"You think you're so mighty? I could crush you like an insect you cheating coward," Seydar threatened.

"Then do it," said Balthus, walking to the man with his hands behind his back and presenting his chin.

"I will show you I am no coward and give you a free strike. Take it if you dare."

Seydar scoffed. "Another trick of the great general?"

"I give you my word I will not flinch," said Balthus. "Knock me down, unless you are all talk."

With a roar Seydar swung his huge fist in a murderous arc; smashing it into Balthus' face. Balthus' head snapped to one side but his feet did not give an inch. Seydar stepped back not believing what he was seeing.

"Is that all?" Balthus asked as if nothing had happened then stepped in and drove a powerful punch of his own deep into the strongman's belly, bringing the man to his knees and doubling him over.

As apologetic members of the village helped carry Seydar away, Balthus sat down next to Zarina and Leo.

"You have a nasty cut under your eye," Zarina pointed out.

"A scratch, nothing more," said Balthus.

Leo nodded in wonder. "I can't believe you let that man punch you, he's built like a castle wall."

Balthus shrugged. "My belly is full and I am a little drunk. No doubt that man was a strong fighter. I did not feel like a full bout so I let him give me his best punch. After that failed to knock me out his spirit left him and he tumbled easily."

"You made it look like it was nothing, didn't it hurt?" Leo asked.

"Of course it hurt, nearly took my bloody head off," said Balthus, "but he's not to know that is he? Now pass me that wine skin worm, I can feel a headache coming on."

18.

The four companions rode south, keeping to the back country, for over a week. Balthus was consistently hostile, keeping Leo close by and within sight at all times. Gellen and Zarina showed Leo genuine warmth and were happy to converse with the ranch hand on many subjects. Leo was not sure which approach he was more comfortable with but mostly he was just relieved that they had not been attacked again.

"No one appears to be following us," Balthus announced one morning after scanning their back trail for long moments.

"There is no need," said Gellen. "It is a long way to Table Rock and the Temple ruins."

"I am surprised he sent those warriors. He must have known they could not best you," said Leo.

"Shut up, worm!" growled Balthus. "When we want your opinion we'll give it to you."

"You are right Leo," said Gellen. "He sent them hoping to panic you into running. Isolated you are an easy kill."

"And you played into his hands once more," Balthus said.

"But I'm not Athus; I'm no threat to anyone. Hasn't he already won? Why would he want to kill me?" Leo asked.

"Am I talking to a brick wall? Silence!" Balthus roared.

"Calm yourself," said Zarina. "Leo raises an interesting point. That Nemeddes seeks Leo's death is a ray of hope. It shows that our plan has merit."

"Indeed. Logically, if Nemeddes seeks Leo's death then it follows Leo must be of some concern to him," Gellen said.

"And yet he does not attack again," said Balthus.

"He does not need to waste resources chasing us. He knows where we are going," Gellen pointed out. "He will position his minions ahead of us. He knows we must cross the Corvus Channel."

"I have never been to sea," said Leo.

"Quiet, worm," snapped Balthus. "No one cares."

Zarina rolled her eyes at Balthus' impatience. "Come, we will not get our answers here."

They slowed the pace that afternoon, allowing the horses a well earned respite. Gellen, Zarina and Balthus had drawn close together and were talking about logistics and travel plans. Leo had listened for the first few minutes but had quickly become bored. He had not been this far from the capital for more than a decade and the slow pace and a soft breeze were quite pleasant. The wild flowers in the grass verge were a beautiful multi-coloured sea. Leo watched as a bee thrummed lazily between them, intent on its business. His mind turned to Rebecca. He wondered if she would think of him. Did she know he still loved her, did she know he even still lived? What would she think of this terrible adventure he was on?

Suddenly a light caught Leo's eye and he glanced to where Athus' sword was bound to Balthus' saddlebag. The sword was pulsing faintly.

"Excuse me..." Leo began.

"Be quiet, we're trying to talk," snapped Balthus.

"I think you should see this," Leo said. "The sword, Athus' sword... it's glowing..."

"What?" said Zarina, her piercing, sapphire eyes locking on the sword.

Leo continued to watch as the weapon began to pulse more and more quickly, golden light swelling and pooling around the lion head on the handle. Suddenly the sword broke free of its binding and raced, hilt first, towards Leo. The sight of the blade coming towards him caused Leo to panic and he quickly dismounted, hiding behind his horse. Peering around his mount he was shocked to see the blade hovering towards him, bobbing lightly in the air as if floating on the breeze.

"What does it want?" Leo shrieked, trying not to look at the glowing blade.

"Take it Leo," said Zarina, her voice stern. "Something wicked is coming..."

But Leo had no interest in taking the sword. Covering his eyes he turned his back on it, but the blade floated around him, the hilt nuzzling his hand like a loyal hound.

Then a smell overrode the sweetness of the flowers, a smell of rot and decay. Leo uncovered his eyes and saw the flowers by the roadside begin to wilt and fade, their rich colours peeling away as their stalks withered and died. A smoke began to rise from the ground, seeping amongst the trees and flowers, so thick it was like black mist. Leo stepped away from it as it quickly swirled into a shadowy, humanoid form, taking the appearance of a young woman, its face a mask of anguish and pain. It gusted forward on a chill current, one of its limbs reaching for Leo.

"Don't let it touch you!" Balthus screamed jerking Leo away from it, then darting forward and swinging his axe in a merciless arc. The weapon passed right through the shade and the creature shrieked with laughter and moved forward with speed. Balthus dived to his left, narrowly avoiding its outstretched arm. The shade screeched again but ignored the giant and moved once more towards Leo.

"Take the sword, use it!" Zarina urged.

Leo looked at the thing closing in on him and then the blade. He tried to push the sword away and the phantom, seeing his disdain for the weapon, cackled a laugh and sped forward with more confidence.

On instinct Leo ducked and rolled, scrabbling through the legs of his mount to get away from the clutching fingers. The horse reared as he dodged through and he turned to see the phantom snatch at the animal. At its touch the horse broke apart into flakes of ash, like petrified wood, and the ghoulish hag seemed to grow in size, moving more quickly towards him. Again the Star Sword nuzzled at his hand but Leo could not bring himself to grab it.

"You are a disappointing enemy," the creature hissed. "Your soul is weak."

"Keep away from him!" Zarina exclaimed, stepping in front of Leo.

"What will you do, child of the light? Kill me with love?" the spirit mocked.

"Do not pretend you are not afraid," said Zarina. "The dark fears the light as much as the opposite is true."

The shade howled again. "The light is weak. Darkness is eternal - ever present. The darkness has always been there. We simply wait for the light to fade to nothing."

"You do not understand," Zarina said. "The light and dark are one."

"We are nothing like you!" spat the shade. "You talk of compassion and kindness, they are lies, you know nothing of pain. But you will. Let us see if the light burns as brightly in your self-righteous eyes when Nemeddes takes you as his woman."

"A cheap threat," said Zarina.

"It is no threat, priestess. He will squeeze the light slowly from you until you are one of us – like him." The creature laughed, pointing to where Leo stood terrified. "Let us take him, we will replace his fear with hate and make him strong."

"He is not for you," said Zarina. "His fate is not yet decided. Now leave this place."

"Or what?"

"Or I will fill you with so much light that the darkness in you will fall away forever."

"Such a thing is not possible," the spirit mocked, but Leo noticed that it drew back several feet. "Now give us Kvetch, he belongs with us."

"No I don't!" shouted Leo. "I don't want anything to do with you!"

Again the shade shrieked its callous laughter. "You are one of us. I feel the despair in you, the loathing and the pain. Do not be their puppet. Come with me, Nemeddes will reward you. Do you want to be weak forever?"

"Enough!" snapped Zarina stepping forward and grabbing the shade's hand. Light coursed down the priestess' arm, flowing into the apparition. The creature screamed, trying to break free but Zarina held her firm. As Leo watched, light pulsed from Zarina's hand, flowing and filling the shade, washing away the inky darkness like fresh water washing away soot.

In moments the dark shade was gone and a being floated before them, glowing with golden energy.

"Thank you," the spirit called, crystal tears flowing down her cheeks. Then it began rising upward, "Thank you…" it called once more before it vanished. Leo stood staring at the sky dumfounded. It was some long moments later before he realised that Zarina had collapsed.

"Is she going to be all right?" Leo asked, looking at Zarina's pale face.

"She will be well," said Gellen. "She merely needs, I would estimate, three point two five hours of recovery time."

"No thanks to you, worm," growled Balthus. "All you had to do was use the sword."

"I don't know how to use a sword, let alone a magic one," Leo snapped. "Anyway, you could have used it."

"No he cannot," said Zarina, opening her eyes. "The sword is bound to Athus."

"Then why did it fly to me?" Leo asked.

"A good question," said Zarina, "but I need rest. Please stop your bickering." With that she closed her eyes and drifted off to sleep. With a huff Balthus rose and stalked away from their camp.

Gellen smiled at Leo. "Would you like a game of Shaddak?"

"I don't know how to play," said Leo.

"Then truly it is a great day," said Gellen, "for I am a great teacher."

The magister rooted in his knapsack and produced a small board and two bags, one containing black stones and the other white.

"When you become good enough we will play on the full board," said Gellen. "For now, we will play in just one quarter."

"What do I do, put a stone down?" Leo asked, placing a piece on the board.

"Yes but never put one there," said Gellen. "Let me show you..."

Two hours later Leo had barely more understanding of what he was doing than when he began, however the magister had provided pleasant company and Leo had always enjoyed games. Gellen was explaining the pros and cons of a particular move when Zarina yawned and rose herself up onto her elbows. Balthus, who had been honing his axe nearby, stood up at once and moved to her side, helping her to sit up.

She smiled and then the colour again fell from her face. At first Leo thought she would faint but then looked to where her gaze was focused. A figure, tall and strong, stood at the edge of the camp. The man was dressed in dark armour with a golden tunic. His helmet was burnished gold with two large spikes pointing upwards carved like the horns of a goat.

"What do you want?" Zarina asked. And Leo heard fear in her voice.

"I wondered if I might join your fire for a while," said the man already approaching.

"Stay back," snapped Balthus.

The figure moved forward, his handsome face smiling. Leo saw the wood smoke pass right through him. "Is it another shade?" he asked.

"No," said Gellen. "It is a projection."

"Of Nemeddes?" Leo asked, swallowing hard.

"How astute he is," Nemeddes noted before sitting on a rock beside the fire. "How are you priestess, has your strength returned?"

"I am strong enough," said Zarina.

"Well, that is good. Let me get to business. I know you will not hand him over straight away, but think on this: the sooner you deliver this imposter to me, the easier it will be for all involved."

"You know I will never do that," said Zarina.

"Oh, I was not talking to you, my dear," smiled Nemeddes. "I wouldn't expect such behaviour from you. But you Gellen, you are a man of enviable intelligence. You must see that by prolonging this, you will incur my anger. That will mean more suffering, more problems."

"Yes, I agree," said Gellen.

"And Balthus – you hate him. I feel it in you."

"What I feel for him is nothing compared to my loathing of you," Balthus said and spat into the fire.

"Well, just see how you feel when the worm lets you down again and again," said Nemeddes. "My master destroyed the Temple of Time in the last Scourging, it cannot help you. Besides," the Lich laughed, "it is written in the Book of Shadows that the reappearance of the Temple is the harbinger of the end of times for this world."

"Then why are you trying to dissuade us?" Zarina asked.

"I am not trying to dissuade you. I am negotiating with you," said Nemeddes. "This is about expediency. I have already won; I want to tie up the loose ends economically. You should all consider it. Despite what you think of me, I am capable of mercy. There are worse fates than torture and death. I could spare you those – if you let me."

"You are a fool," said Zarina. "For all your power you do not understand the unity of the light and the dark."

"Oh please, save me your sentimental philosophies. I understand that the light is fading and the darkness is rising. It is our time soon, your kind has ruled for too long. Already my armies are on the move. We have crushed Anvadi. We will roll over the Tundralands next."

"That is not possible," said Balthus. "You would not move before Athus was taken from us. You are weeks away from Anvadi."

"Yes, that is why I gave the order to move my forces weeks ago, before I even enlisted this foolish farmhand. Listen, I will make you a pledge; I will not attack you or cause you grief - if you come to me. When you do I will treat you all well. But if you try to cross the Corvus Channel, I will make each of you suffer in ways only I can imagine. And believe me, my imagination for such things is very good indeed." With that Nemeddes rose. "Have a pleasant evening," he said, sauntering into the shadows and vanishing.

"He was not what I expected," said Leo.

"Why? Has he convinced you to give yourself up?" Balthus asked. "I'll take watch tonight; I do not trust the cur's words."

"Maybe I could take the watch, you need rest too," said Leo.

Balthus threw his head back and laughed. "I would rather trust our safety to the Lich than to you," he said as he wandered to the tree line.

"That was kind of you Leo," said Zarina. "Why don't you take joint watch tonight?"

19.

Leo was kicked roughly from his nightmares and sat up mumbling to himself. The light of the morning sun dazzled him and he shielded his eyes as he looked up to see Balthus standing above him, his face mocking.

"Good job, worm," the giant quipped before walking away.

Leo cursed himself for falling asleep. He could not even remember the time when sleep had pressed itself upon him.

He hurried to rise and gather his things but Zarina joined him, placing a hand on his arm.

"Do not be angry with yourself. Yesterday was a stressful day. You were more tired than you know."

"That is not the point," said Leo. "I said I would stand watch and I failed."

"Then do not let the shame of that make you angry, let it make you determined that it will never happen again," said the sorceress. "But that is not what I wanted to speak to you of. I have questions."

"I will answer if I can," Leo offered.

"Why did you fear the sword when it came to you?"

Leo parted his hands. "That, I cannot answer. For as long as I can remember I have been terrified of swords or knives. It is like a deep fear that grabs me – I am powerless against it."

"We are never powerless against our fears. But tell me, look to where Balthus chops wood for the fire."

Leo did as he was bidden, watching with no small degree of awe the strength and power of the warrior as he arced the mighty axe through the air, each time a perfect strike.

"Balthus is one of the greatest warriors of his generation," said Zarina. "His axe has killed countless men. Do you feel the same fear watching that?"

"No," said Leo.

"What of this?"

Leo looked down and saw Zarina had produced a small skinning knife from her belt. At once his eyes widened and his breathing quickened and he fell backwards. "No…" he whispered, childlike, shaking his head from side to side.

Zarina advanced. "What do you find so terrifying about…"

But Leo could not answer, his eyes rolled back in his head and with a scream he collapsed in a faint.

"What by all the stars is wrong with him now?" Balthus demanded.

"I do not know," said Zarina, her face troubled. "But it is no small thing. There is a deep fear in him, so deep he does not even know the cause of it."

"Repression," said Gellen. "Interesting and dangerous too. The subconscious keeps secrets better than any spy."

"And this is a time where we need as few secrets as possible," Zarina mused. The priestess knelt, placing her hands on Leo's brow. "See how he tosses and turns. He told me he does not rest easy. I think he is brave to put it so lightly."

"A first from him," Balthus muttered.

"It is hard to judge another's courage," Zarina observed. "Who knows the depth of the terror he faces in his dreams."

"I do not advise your current course of action," said Gellen. "You need longer to recover after yesterday's exertions."

"Perhaps," said Zarina. "But if I could just know what ails him – and discover if it is connected with Nemeddes…"

"You must do what you think best," said Gellen.

With that Zarina nodded and closed her eyes. She drifted slowly into Leo's outer mind, felt with sadness the anguish and shame that he carried with him each day, the utter dislike of himself. She pushed deeper and images and feelings of such power washed over her, the face of a woman, a name chanted again and again in a sorrowful dirge – Rebecca. She felt Leo's anger at himself, his loathing, but also in there, so pure she felt tears welling, she felt the love he held for this woman, not sullied, nor overly sexualised by lust, just a perfect, giving love. And for the first time, shining through all the dust and decay, the loathing and pity, Zarina felt the power of Leo's soul in that love. The strength of that drew her deeper. Then she heard a sound, a child crying, and she saw an image of a doorway. Instinctively she moved towards it sensing the pain and anguish that lay behind it yet as she approached, a black mass began to seep forward. A shadow took shape, a monstrous creature of tentacles and barbed hooks that blotted out what light there was. It slashed at Zarina and she held up her hand lancing a line of blazing light into the creature. The tentacle fizzled and died and the being screamed in rage, growing and growing. More of its tentacles lashed at her and again Zarina drew the darkness out of them... but for every one she purified, two more grew in their place. One snaked around her ankle, another around her wrist. She tried to break free, but the creature pulled her closer. Zarina felt herself begin to scream, felt her other leg seized and saw the monstrous darkness part and rows and rows of teeth form - and each tooth was a tiny, pearl-handled knife. She fought with all her strength, sending blasts of her power at the creature but now they deflected off its obsidian hide with no more effect than a pebble hurled against a fortress wall.

Zarina fought again and with horror realised that whatever this mental guardian was, it was beyond her. It was going to draw her in and devour her... then a blast of fire struck the creature, and it howled. She felt its grip loosen for a moment and with a titanic effort pulled herself free. Gellen's astral form grabbed her hand, flying them away from it, soaring back to the softer thoughts of Rebecca... and beyond to safety.

"A close call," the arch mage spoke into her mind.

Zarina was too weary to respond and re-joined with her body.

"Have you seen this stool?" Gellen exclaimed excitedly. "Isn't it fascinating?"

"For the love of the gods man, put that down!" Balthus snapped.

"But don't you see how wonderful it is. This excrement partially proves my theory pertaining to how plant life diversifies and reproduces through the spread of their seeds by animals..."

Balthus slapped the wizard's hand sending the faeces flying into the woods. "Will you concentrate on the matter in hand?"

"I have already solved the matter at hand," said Gellen.

"Then what is going on?"

"Leo has a powerful mnemonic spell fragment in his mind. Someone has put it there with the intention that no one can undo it."

"Nemeddes?"

"Well that is speculation," said Gellen.

"But possibly?"

"Anything is possible."

Leo sat by the fire and listened to the two talking. Things just seemed to go from bad to worse. Now Zarina was injured again and once more he blamed himself. Zarina had informed them all that what she needed was rest, but she had looked beyond exhaustion and Balthus was clearly worried. She would be unable to ride today, maybe not even tomorrow.

"It is my fault," Leo heard himself say.

"Oh shut up, I'm tired of your melancholy mutterings," Balthus snapped.

"Besides," said Gellen, "you were in a swoon, there was nothing you could do."

"But this is my fault," said Leo. "I went to see a fortune teller in Ostus. She went into my mind, like Zarina did, and it killed her..."

"You knew you had this... evil... in you and you said nothing?" Balthus roared, grabbing Leo by the neck and hoisting him into the air. Leo struggled but striking Balthus' arm was like trying to break an oaken beam.

Leo tried to speak but could only gurgle and felt himself slipping towards unconsciousness when Balthus hurled him to the floor. "Maybe it will not be so hard to take up the Lich's offer," the giant admitted striding away.

"This is not wise," said Gellen. "We need you here."

"I need some time to myself," snapped Balthus saddling his horse. "I will return by morning."

"Where is he going?" Leo croaked, holding his neck.

"To the town we passed last night. It is his way when things are bad." Gellen came and helped Leo up. "There there, my boy. Don't worry about him, he doesn't mean what he says."

"Things just keep getting worse," said Leo.

"Perhaps," said Gellen with a wink.

Leo smiled. "I thought you did not understand humour?"

"I do not. But I calculated a high probability that answering *perhaps,* now Zarina has told her *story,* would lift your spirits based on recent data I have collated on your character and behaviours."

"You speak like no one I have ever known," said Leo. "And yet you always show me kindness. Thank you."

"People think I do not understand other humans," said Gellen. "In some ways that is true, in other ways I understand them better than any other person alive."

"How can that be so?"

"Most people surround themselves with falseness," said Gellen. "They pretend this or pretend that, or act this way or that way - something I have never understood. I used to have a habit of running by the lake in Ostus each morning. Everyday I would pass the kennel master walking his hounds. Every day, out of etiquette, I would say "Good morning." Every day he would reply with something similar. On one particularly fine day I greeted him with my normal address only for him to reply: "What's good about it?"

I mentioned this to Zarina in one of our sessions – she helps me understand the ways of people. She told me that the man's wife had run away with another man. But I still do not know what that had to do with the morning – it was as beautiful as ever.

Of course, intellectually, I now understand his response but I do not accept it as a valid comment."

"He was upset because all he could think about was his wife," said Leo.

"That is why I do not understand pain very well. Why could he not simply think about any number of other things?" Gellen asked.

"It's not that easy," said Leo. "Sometimes thoughts come unbidden."

"Yes, for others it does seem to be that way – as in your case," said Gellen. "I find it hard to understand why you cannot simply control your thoughts as I can. But I am told this simple skill is exceedingly rare. Athus could do it, as can Zarina, although they were not born with the ability as I was, but acquired it through practise. In summation and to conclude my story, I visited the kennel master and told him I was sorry for what had happened and if I could help, I would, within reason."

"That was kind," said Leo.

"I did not do it to be kind," said Gellen. "I still do not understand why people get upset and melancholy about everyday events. But that does not mean I do not have compassion for them. Now let us play Shaddak!"

"Really, now?"

"What better time is there?" Gellen asked.

Leo looked to where Zarina was sleeping. "I suppose."

"Ahh, that is good," said Gellen setting up the board. "Zarina does not like to play and Balthus is incapable of playing well – but you show promise. Where were we?"

"You don't remember?"

"Of course I do, I have eidetic memory. I merely want to know what you have absorbed."

"You were telling me about how, if I place a stone, I should not leave it unsupported," said Leo.

"Just so," said Gellen with a wide smile. "Let us continue."

The two played for several hours. Zarina slept and Balthus did not return. Abruptly Gellen stood and yawned, stretching his arms and legs.

"If you are tired, please sleep," Leo offered. "I will take watch."

Gellen nodded and withdrew to his bedroll. Leo moved to the edge of camp as he had observed the others do on many occasions and concealed himself where he had a good view in all directions. The night was long and quiet but this time he did not fall asleep.

20.

"That is completely unacceptable," Balthus raged. "I refuse."

"You have a better idea?" Zarina asked. "If you do, let us hear it."

Balthus chewed his lip for a long moment then spat onto the floor. "You know damn well I don't have a better idea. But this… this is humiliating. Degrading."

Leo turned from the debate and looked down the sloping grasslands towards the river city of Kresta, nestled on the banks of the Corvus Channel. The city was not built out of the white stones from which Ostus had been constructed, but an earthy red brick. Smoke rose from the roofs of houses and a steady procession of carts and horses filed through the gates and along the mill lined road that led north to Cevestas and south to Wessenburg.

To Leo the whole of Kresta felt ominous and dark. He did not see why they had to ride into it at all; certainly as he had suggested there were other places to cross the Corvus.

But Zarina had explained to him that their trip had not gone unnoticed. The Lord of the City would know where they were and if they passed by without paying their respects, he may grow uneasy. Besides, the liege of Kresta, Lord Yellund, was an ally to Ostus and had fought bravely in Kryx. He was a trusted and honoured friend and Zarina was sure that, if he were asked, he would aid them and be able to slow the Lich's forces.

The debate now was how to enter the city. They had only three horses after the wraith had slain Leo's mount. The obvious choice, Zarina had suggested, was for Leo to ride Balthus' mighty warhorse while the giant led it as Athus' trusty shield bearer. Gellen and Zarina both were concerned that any other arrangement would draw suspicion.

"You know we cannot just sneak through the city," Zarina reasoned. "Lord Yellund's scouts will already have spotted us."

"But to lead him in like he's some sort of hero..." Balthus grumbled. "It just doesn't sit right."

"In outward appearance he is still Athus," said Zarina. "Yellund is a friend, we must pay our respects – you know what he is like for etiquette and ceremony. Would you have Athus Glynn ride into Kresta on the back of your horse, holding onto you like you're his father?"

"Athus would not have thought it shameful," said Balthus.

"No, he would not. He would have seen the funny side," Zarina admitted.

"He would have understood why it must be done however," said Gellen. "The people will already have heard about the incident in the arena and his defeat. Athus must appear strong here, like the hero they believe in. If he does not seem like the man they look up to – well, panic spreads quicker than fire."

"I understand all that," snapped Balthus. "And I know we must find out if the Lich was bluffing about taking Anvadi. Look, I'll do it but I don't like it." Balthus turned to Leo. "And if you give me one smug look after this is done, I will wring your neck myself."

Leo could not have imagined what was to follow. He had ridden before Gellen and Zarina, Balthus leading his horse, while the people of Kresta cheered wildly as they passed. Being the epicentre of that frenzy had not been pleasant and despite the positivity of the crowd Leo had been glad of the cohort of Krestan warriors who had escorted them. A few times Zarina had prompted him to raise his arm in a wave and he had obliged, hearing the crowd explode to new levels of rapture. Yet there had been a knot in his stomach the whole ride and he had not enjoyed it. Such attention seemed unnatural, almost perverse. By the stars, he knew well enough he did not deserve a moment's praise.

Once inside Lord Yellund's fortress it had not been any better. A tense but dignified meal had been provided where Leo had tried to follow Zarina's lead with the impenetrable etiquette of seven courses and what seemed to be hundreds of pieces of silverware. There was a knife for this, a fork for that and a spoon for the other. It had taken all his courage to even hold a table knife and even this had left him in a terrible sweat. Leo would not have minded entirely if the food hadn't been so ghastly. During the meal, conversation had been light, but after the Lord and his advisors withdrew to a small antechamber. Here the talk had become more frank. Yellund's scouts confirmed that Nemeddes had indeed overrun Anvadi and was said to now be two days march outside of Bale, capital of the Tundralands. Zarina explained the reasons for their need to cross the Corvus Channel to search for the Temple of Time, but omitted the facts about Athus and Leo's soul swap. Leo said as little as possible, adding his agreement when it felt safe and deflecting any direct questions where possible, but even that had felt too much. Yellund for his part had been an agreeable host and had promised to loan them his fastest ship to cross the Corvus. They would be on their way by the light of dawn.

Now Leo lay on the divan in the fine guest quarters and fought the need to sleep. Zarina had retired to the bedroom hours ago and Balthus and Gellen had their own rooms further down the hall. Leo realised it was the first time he had spent alone for weeks. Even while in the saddle, if he allowed himself to think for a moment about how crazy all this was, it was enough to drive him mad. Alone in the unnatural quiet of this fortress, it was too much.

Levering himself up he pulled on his tunic and leggings and let himself out of the apartment. The corridor outside was deserted and feeling like a child sneaking from his room, Leo crept towards the stairs. He wandered the empty palace for some time, perhaps an hour or more. There were many exquisite sets of armour, rich tapestries and beautiful paintings to look at in the candlelit halls and Leo moved amongst them with pleasure.

If he had been a seasoned adventurer or used to the standard protocol of the running of a fortress, Leo might have found the lack of activity in the halls and galleries unusual. There were no servants running chores or cleaning, no sentries on patrol, no guards posted where guards should be posted. But Leo was not used to these things and so the thought that something was out of place did not occur to him until he returned to his chambers.

Letting himself in quietly he closed the door and moved to a small table and began to pour himself a goblet of wine. As he watched the dark red liquid spill into the cup he realised that he hadn't drunk in weeks. Not only that – he had no desire to. Putting the cup down he picked up another and poured himself some water instead. It was as he moved back towards his makeshift bed that the hairs on the back of his neck began to rise. With the strangest feeling Leo slowly turned. Standing by the balcony door, which up to a moment ago was closed, stood a man dressed all in black, his face covered by a dark mask. The two stared at each other for a moment.

Leo was reminded of his duel in the arena with the barbarian Morvus Gern. This assassin could have rushed forward and slain him in a heartbeat – but it did not know it faced Leo Kvetch, it thought it faced Athus Glynn, who even unarmed was not an opponent to take lightly.

Slowly the assassin unclipped a crossbow from his back and brought it to bear. An instinctive part of Leo told him that, as soon as he moved, things were going to get out of hand quickly. He tightened his grip on his goblet and decided he would throw himself to his left at the last moment. Slowly the assassin's bow rose until the bolt tip was aimed squarely at Leo's heart. Leo stared at the man's gloved hand, waiting for the twitch that would signal the shot was loose.

Then the doors to the bedchamber burst open and Zarina swarmed out, her white robes billowing in the draught from the balcony. Spectral light blazed from her hands, striking the crossbow and blasting it into the wall. The assassin recoiled and drew a pair of small axes. He hurled one at Leo who threw himself to his left and rolled on the hard, mosaic floor. The axe thudded into the wall behind. A war cry sounded and the doors to the room burst open and two more assassins entered, each carrying a pair of hand axes. Leo scrambled to his feet and away from them, but the nearest crossed the ground between them in two easy bounds and spinning like a dervish, aimed a double strike at Leo's head. A moment before they hit, a stream of golden light punched the attacker from his feet. The other in the doorway took a step forward, gesturing to the assassin by the window. Leo glanced to Zarina, waiting for another blast of her magic, but the priestess appeared pale and tired and Leo realised she had not recovered from her ordeals on the road. He looked back to see the assassin by the door pull an arm back to hurl an axe, but a moment later the figure was careened from his feet as the fully armoured form of Balthus shoulder-charged him, sending the assassin crashing into the wall. The man bounced back, dazed and staggering and Balthus put an end to him with a vicious sweep of his axe.

"Get away from her!" Balthus screamed and Leo jerked his head to see the remaining assassin making a dart for Zarina who had sagged, exhausted and defenceless, against the far wall. Balthus threw himself into a sprint but it was obvious he was not going to make it in time.

Something ignited in Leo at that moment, some deep power he had thought long forgotten. Without a thought, he took two steps and dived, hitting the assassin low and hard. Even as they flew through the air Leo snaked his leg around the man, tangling him. Both men crashed onto the floor, Leo on top. Old wrestling training, long neglected but still deeply rooted, took over and the farmhand coiled around the assassin's weapon arm, taking it in a strong hold. With a powerful thrust of his hips and an arch of his back he snapped the man's arm before regaining his feet. The assassin screamed and rolled onto his side before Balthus' axe smashed through his ribs and he moved no more.

"Where the hell did you learn to do that?" Balthus growled.

Leo ignored him. "Check your side, you're bleeding."

Balthus glanced down nonchalantly at the wound. "Nothing but a scratch."

Gellen backed into the room, his hands up defensively. Leo could see the air crackling just beyond the magister's fingertips, forming a protective bubble over the doorway. When it was in place he turned to the others.

"I have let you down," said Gellen. "I should have anticipated this."

"You can't predict everything Gellen," said Balthus. "Can we get out of here?"

"There is no point in leaving," a voice came from the doorway. The companions turned to see Lord Yellund standing just beyond the crackling barrier, flanked by two of his personal guard. "It is over."

Zarina tried to rise but fell back and Leo moved to her and offered his arm. She smiled, took it and with his help regained her feet.

"And when did the Great Ingurd Yellund, Lord of Kresta and Master of the Corvus bend his knee to the Arch Fiend?" Balthus snapped.

"When I saw sense," said Yellund. "We tried, the Essence knows we tried. We threw everything at him and he still lives. And now his armies ride forth. They have conquered Anvadi and Tharat. Next will be Bale, then Tyr. Ostus will be next. Then what? Should I let Kresta fall too? Will mighty Wessenburg stand alone against him? Nemeddes has won."

"What did he offer you?" Zarina asked.

"When you are dead, he will return my sons and my wife to me," said Yellund. "And he will spare Kresta."

"He is full of lies Yellund," said Leo. "I know that better than any."

"Ah yes, the farmhand speaks," Yellund scoffed. "Nemeddes came to me tonight in my dreams. A shame he did not appear to me before I briefed my warriors. It would have been simpler just to rush him."

Zarina smiled. "The Essence provides."

"Forget the Essence, its time is over," said Yellund. "Nemeddes is the true power in this world now. Athus Glynn is dead and a coward wears his face. I will make this known in the world. There will be nowhere left for you to hide. This truly is your last chance Leo Kvetch. Hand yourself in now and he will forgive you but try to resist him a moment more and your death will be unbearable."

Leo laughed. "I found life unbearable. That is how I got into this mess in the first place. I'm tired of taking the easy way out. For once in my life I'm taking some responsibility so my answer is, and be sure when you speak to the ugly whore son that you get this right, tell him I'll make this as hard for him as I can and ... he can kiss my spotty arse."

"Ha!" boomed Balthus. "The worm shows its teeth! Gellen, are you ready?"

"Just a moment more," said the mage.

"You fools!" Yellund raged, turning to his men. "Destroy this barrier! Rip it down!"

A blue robed magister appeared, sending searing energy into Gellen's magic field, but the shield did not so much as flinch.

"What's wrong with you?!" Yellund raged. "I said rip it down!"

"But my Lord, I cannot," said the magister.

"You cannot? I have seen you destroy such things a hundred times," said Yellund.

"My Lord, that field was placed by Erasmus Gellen, not some hedgemage. If I had a week, a month, a year… I do not know."

"You are better than this Sanctimus," Gellen said looking up from his incantations and addressing the magister beyond the barrier. "Your master has lost his mind. As my final action in my capacity as head of the Council of Magi, you are free of your vow to him."

Leo watched as a look of understanding passed between the two magisters; then the blue robed wizard bowed low to Gellen and vanished.

"Treachery!" screamed Yellund. "If we cannot destroy the barrier- smash this wall down."

"I am ready," said Gellen. "Forgive me for the delay. Teleportation is a subject where it is better to be safe than sorry. Join hands please."

The four companions did so and a white light began to envelop them.

"You will not win!" Yellund screamed. "You cannot! You are fools. And you Kvetch, you coward, you cur, you have picked a pretty time to grow a spine! I know all about you! Nemeddes knows all about you – he's been in your mind. Will you be as brash when he brings you Rebecca's broken, tormented body...?"

But then the light swelled and covered them, leaving behind Yellund's screaming voice.

21.

Leo gripped the starboard rail tightly as the fishing boat rolled through the choppy waters. He felt sick and tried to fight off another wave of nausea. It was better above deck where the sea air was fresh and cool. In the cabins below the sensation became unbearable.

They had brokered passage on the small craft, paying the captain a king's ransom for what should have cost but a handful of coins. Now they had been at sea for two days. It would be another day before they reached Scyara on the eastern shore of the Corvus. For Leo it could not come soon enough. A couple of fish leapt from the water not thirty feet away, seeming to glide above the waves for a moment before returning to the surf. Leo watched with awe, for a moment his sickness forgotten.

"A magnificent sight," said Balthus, joining him at the rail.

"Indeed," said Leo trying not to sound like a man whose insides were attempting to squirm their way up his neck and out of his mouth. "I have never been at sea before," he admitted.

Balthus grunted and offered Leo a drink from his flask. "Whisky, from Wessenburg."

Leo glanced at the big man. "I better not," he said.

"Oh of course, my apologies," said the giant, sounding uncomfortable for a moment. "I forgot."

"It is nothing," said Leo.

Balthus nodded and stared deep out over the ocean. "It's not natural this," he said. "Makes a man's head spin to think of all that water beneath him. I much prefer to have my feet on solid ground."

"I have to agree with you," said Leo. "But it does not seem to bother them," he said, gesturing to where two of the crew moved through the rigging.

Balthus looked, his eyes lingering on a tall, rangy woman with knotted auburn hair. "Yes, people of the sea those. Spend more time afloat than on land."

"Back at the keep, how in all that confusion did you get your armour on so quickly?" Leo asked changing the subject.

Balthus chuckled. "Because I never slept. I was ready all night. Call it a warrior's hunch. That whole place smelled wrong to me as soon as we entered. I might not have magic like the others, but I can read a man more often than not. Yellund was a pale reflection of the man I fought with in Kryx."

"I suppose the Lich deceived him, like it did me," said Leo.

"Oh no, Yellund's crime was far worse. He knew it was Nemeddes giving the orders, you did not. I have not been particularly kind to you Kvetch, but I do not think you would willingly have bowed your knee to the Arch Fiend, even if he had offered you all the jewels in heaven."

"Whether I knew it was him or not I bowed for far less," said Leo.

Balthus shrugged. "You are not without courage, you showed that at Yellund's keep. Where did you learn to fight like that?"

"When I was a young man I trained in Sarono's Wrestling Stable. I hoped to enter the tourneys and fight professionally but..." Leo trailed off about to blame his shoulder injury, then for the first time in his life admitted the truth... "I lost focus, I didn't train hard enough."

Balthus nodded. "That is a well respected stable and the quality of your movement at the keep shows you have a high level of skill."

"I was surprised I even remembered that move," said Leo. "I'm not sure I could repeat it now."

"Ahh! That is the eye of the warrior," said Balthus. "The right action arriving spontaneously at the right moment."

"So," said Leo with a smile. "I am not a worm anymore?"

Balthus grinned. "Perhaps there is some more bite to you, a grass snake maybe?"

Leo laughed. "I'll take that as a compliment."

Balthus' face grew serious and he rested a hand on Leo's shoulder. "You saved her life. I will always respect you for that."

It was without doubt one of the proudest moments of Leo's life hearing the mighty warrior's praise but it was tinged with a great realisation for, in that moment, Leo realised that Balthus was in love with Zarina. A wave of empathy washed over him. The great warrior loved the wife of his best friend. It was a love Balthus could never, would never admit to, a lonely love that isolated him from his own wife, from his friends, a constant itch that burned. Leo knew it well for he had felt the same when he saw Rebecca taken to the chapel by another man.

The thought was broken as the ship rocked again and Leo found himself on the verge of throwing up.

"By the stars man, you look awful," said Balthus. "Why did you not say that you were seasick?"

"I didn't want to make a fuss," said Leo. "None of you are complaining about it."

Balthus laughed. "That is because we have been taking Gellen's remedy since we set sail. Come on, I'll take you to the mage."

Balthus moved over the rocking deck sipping on his flask. The giant opened the door that led below deck and held it as Leo passed through and waited for Balthus to follow, but the tall warrior did not. His eyes had landed on the lithe form of the female deckhand who smiled coyly at the warrior before moving toward the rear of the ship.

"I'll catch up with you later," said Balthus walking after her. Leo watched him go then descended into the rocking bowels of the ship.

Entering their shared bunkhouse, Leo found Gellen swinging in his hammock, his nose in a book.

The mage looked up and smiled warmly as Leo approached. "A game of Shaddak?" he offered at once.

Leo shook his head. "Balthus tells me you have some remedy for this sickness."

"Oh yes, a compound that soothes the stomach and calms the body," said Gellen. "I don't care for it myself, but then I seem unaffected by this motion anxiety."

"I just want something that will make me not want to hurl my guts out," said Leo.

"Well, quite," said the magister fishing in his pack and retrieving a biscuit. "It is laced with a pleasant concoction that will take effect as you digest it. I have read that blueberries are good for your memory too, although," Gellen gave a dramatic pause, "I can't remember where I read that."

"Was that a joke?" Leo asked accepting the biscuit.

"Yes. It was. What did you make of it?"

"Not bad," said Leo. "I think you're getting the hang of it. Perhaps you could change the tone of your voice when you get to the punch line."

"I would. Indeed when Balthus helped me with the joke he suggested exactly the same thing."

"When I feel better I'll help you with it," said Leo as the ship rocked violently to one side. "Perhaps Balthus will too, he seems in fine spirits."

"Well, if you mean that he is inebriated that is only because he is terrified of the sea," said Gellen. "Balthus was nearly drowned as a child. He is drunk most of the time and no doubt copulating as often as possible with the sailor Ymarra."

"Balthus is afraid?" asked Leo as the boat rocked once more. "I didn't think he was afraid of anything."

"Everyone is afraid of something," said Gellen. "Fear is a normal human survival mechanism."

"What are you afraid of Gellen?" Leo asked.

"Mental deterioration. Naturally people fear to lose what they value most. Normally this appears to be family or friends, however I have no family and have long accepted that my friends, due to their adventurous lifestyles, will likely die long before they reach old age."

"You have no family, no parents or siblings?" Leo asked.

"None left alive," said Gellen. "I do not know who my mother was. My father was a diplomat from Anbak. He considered me an embarrassment and tried to have me killed. I was saved from that eventuality by one of my father's retainers, a man named Osric. Although he was not an educated man I learned much from him. We had a great many adventures until he grew old and senile. He still lives but has no idea who I am."

"I'm sorry," said Leo.

"Why would you be sorry?" Gellen asked. "They are just facts. It is I who should be sorry for my inability to teleport us further. No matter how many times I revisit the equations I am unable to improve on my calculations."

"Your spell saved our lives Gellen," Leo pointed out.

"Indeed. But it would have been pleasant to move us closer to our goal."

"I'm sure even moving us a small distance is challenging enough," said Leo.

"There is no such thing as teleporting a small distance," said the mage. "Even if I was to try to move you what you perceive as an inch, what you must realise is that our planet is constantly spinning whilst orbiting our sun, which in turn is orbiting a larger cosmic body, which in turn is orbiting another cosmic body in a universe that is not stationary but contracting at exponential speed. Even the smallest teleportation spell traverses colossal distances through three dimensional space and time and the calculations for such a thing are quite remarkably complex."

"I'm not sure I'm following," Leo admitted.

Gellen nodded. "It matters not. Yet I concede that I find it impossible to find credibility in the idea of a Temple of Time which is capable of not only teleporting vast physical distances but is also reputed to leap along different time lines. The calculations involved in such a thing would be as far beyond me as infinitesimal calculus is beyond an ant."

"Or me, I would expect," Leo said. "But who knows, perhaps someone has worked it out."

"Doubtful," said Gellen. "I have a theory as to how it could work but I cannot marry it to any solid mathematics. Highly frustrating."

Leo went to answer but the boat rolled again and he took a deep breath instead.

"Curious," commented Gellen, rising. "That movement of the ship was highly unusual. Naturally I could be mistaken..." the magister trailed off as a scream sounded above deck and the ship lurched again. At once Gellen was moving and Leo followed as the agile mage charged above deck.

By the time Leo arrived on the main deck the ship was tilted dangerously in the water. It took no time to see the cause. Four large, bloated tentacles had emerged from the sea and were pulling at the port rail. Waves were beginning to lap over the deck.

"Cut that monster loose or it will pull us down!" the ship's captain shouted, raising a cutlass above his head.

Balthus joined him, axe in hand, and the two attacked the rubbery, white limbs. The captain's sabre barely scratched the beast but Balthus' axe chopped clean through. Whatever manner of creature that was attacking them screamed, a high pitched wail of pain that left Leo covering his ears. At once the tentacles released and the ship rolled back onto an even keel, throwing him from his feet. Balthus too lost his footing and stumbled over the rail, grabbing at it with one hand. The deck hand, Ymarra, rushed to him and helped haul him back on board but as she did the beast rose from the water, one of its tentacles swiping across the deck, shattering the main mast and smashing the woman from her feet with such force that she bounced across the decking twice and slammed into some crates. From the broken way her body landed it was obvious that she was dead. Balthus screamed a battle cry, brandishing his axe, but the monster had disappeared beneath the waves once more.

Leo looked around wide-eyed, glad to see Zarina standing calmly by his side.

"What manner of creature is that?" he asked, hoping to keep the fear from his voice.

"No creature at all," said Zarina gravely. "That is a Zullifskag, an elder daemon. I did not know Nemeddes had the power to command one."

"What do we do if it comes back?" Leo asked.

"I do not know," said Zarina. "It is beyond my skill to banish it but perhaps the way will become clear when..."

But her words were interrupted as the boat groaned in pain as its timbers were once more attacked and Leo watched in horror as a crack appeared and split through the deck half way between the prow and the stern. Four huge, white tentacles broke through the middle of the ship sending all on board staggering. Leo grabbed frantically at the ship's rail as the boat tilted in the water as the monster pulled the prow below the waves, completely submerging the figurehead. The deck now elevated, Leo began to slide and turned his head looking to where he could see the white, ghostlike maw of the daemon; a circular pit of concentric rings of teeth waiting just below the waves. The ship's captain slid down the deck towards that horrific mouth and Leo grabbed at him, the jerk as he stopped the man's sliding descent nearly jarring him loose. The captain nodded his thanks but a moment later one of the Zullifskag's barbed limbs eviscerated him, cutting him in two. The man died without a scream and Leo released the cadaver, watching with dread fascination as it slipped into the beast's waiting mouth.

Shocked and panicked Leo began to drag himself up the rail, using it like a ladder, desperate to get clear of the creature. He saw Zarina holding on to what was left of the mast, one arm wrapped around it while she fired bolts of liquid gold into the tentacle closest to her, turning the blubbery white flesh black with every strike. The creature once more let go of the ship and sank beneath the water.

Free from the beast's hold, the ship began to right itself, but the damage was too great and the rolling sea finished what the monster had begun, quickly pulling the boat into two parts. For a moment each levelled out before they both began to sink. Leo climbed to his feet looking to the others for guidance. Balthus was on the other part of the ship which was now beginning to drift away from the section that Leo, Zarina and Gellen stood upon. The giant surged into a run and leapt the mounting gap, narrowly making it. The warrior was wild eyed and desperate looking as he landed and Leo remembered that Gellen had told him Balthus was terrified of water.

There was no time to regroup and come up with a plan. With a splash that showered them all, the daemon appeared again, this time close to the stern, its tentacles grabbing the ship and speeding its journey beneath the waves. All four of them stumbled, tumbling down the steep incline towards the gaping ringed mouth that waited just below the tide. Leo rolled twice before, in a moment that was part luck and part instinct, his hand grabbed at a loop of rope and he found himself dangling mere feet from the water. He looked up to see Balthus had secured himself on the rail and was supporting Zarina while again she fired bursts of her magic that seared into the fiend, flash boiling the seawater as it lanced home. Leo began to pull himself away from the monster but as he did it rose up, its head breaking the surface for the first time. He looked at its putrid skin and fought his revulsion at the vile smell that came from its mouth. A dense cluster of red eyes, mounted on its crown, regarded him with ancient intelligence and as he looked at them the image of Nemeddes' haughty face formed in each one. The creature slowly brought a tentacle down and held it before Leo's eyes and Leo was shocked to see Gellen held tightly inside its coils. The mage's face was contorted in agony as the mighty limb squeezed him. Leo heard bones pop and snap and Gellen screamed. Slowly and with infinite malice the monster flipped the mage high into the air and Leo caught one last look at the magister before he fell into the rings of death that was the Zullifskag's mouth. The monster closed its maw once with a definitive crunch and Leo screamed in anguish as Nemeddes' laugh rolled out over the empty sea like thunder.

22.

In the moments after Erasmus Gellen's death Leo was seized first by shock then by a righteous fury that began to flow through every sinew of his being. He stared at the Zullifskag as it gripped what was left of the deteriorating ship, casually rocking it from side to side, hoping to dislodge any of the remaining survivors. Leo glanced quickly to where Zarina and Balthus clung higher up the deck which was now little more than a deadly slide leading into the monster's waiting mouth.

There was, Leo realised, no way out of this. The ship was broken and sinking and the creature could afford to wait until the boat sank, then pick them out of the water at its leisure. Suddenly in Leo's mind bloomed the image of Athus' sword, forming with crystal clarity. The thought was so urgent and immediate it blocked out all else, even his normal revulsion for such weapons. His anger outweighed his fear of the blade many times over and he heard it calling to him. For a second he had a vision of it, strapped to Balthus' pack, sinking into the dark of the sea. With no idea if it would work he urged it to come to him and moments later, with a crash of timber, the sword exploded upwards through the deck, the lion hilt throwing itself into his waiting hand. His fingers closed around it and the blade blazed with golden light. Leo almost saw himself from the outside as, with a bellowing cry, he released the rope he was holding and leapt towards the elder daemon, jumping over its mouth to land on the island of rubbery flesh that was its head. He nearly staggered, but he righted himself and drove the Star Sword downward, skewering it deep into the beast. The Zullifskag rewarded him with a high-pitched scream of anger and rage. It began to raise a tentacle to dislodge him, but letting out a war cry, Leo swung the Star Sword, the blade chopping through the meaty limb as easily as he might pass his hand through a fountain of water. The beast screamed again, the sea beginning to foam as it began to dive. Leo plunged

Athus' blade downwards striking blow after blow with the sword until the creature was beyond reach and he was left bobbing in the freezing waters.

"Quickly!" he heard Balthus shout and looked to see the giant hurl a coil of rope towards him.

Leo grabbed at it and Balthus hauled him up the incline of the smashed vessel.

"We must get off this ship," said Zarina, her voice as calm as ever. She pointed to where several wooden pallets had floated free of the hull. "The daemon is going to drag this boat down."

"How far are we from land?" Leo asked.

"Not as close as I'd like," said Zarina. "But Scyara Bluffs cannot be too far east."

"It's not like we have a great deal of options," pointed out Balthus.

"The pallets are not far, we can swim for them," said Leo.

Balthus and Zarina exchanged a glance. "Balthus cannot swim," said the priestess.

Leo nodded and struggled up the deck and passed the Star Sword to Zarina then tied a rope firmly around his middle. "I'll swim out to them and bring one back. I can't do much, but I swim well enough."

"You have done plenty this day," said Zarina. "Be careful, I will distract the beast if it returns."

Leo nodded, turned and dived into the water, swimming hard for the pallets. There was little point in wondering if a tentacle would grab him and drag him under or if the sea would send a wave to smash him off course, he just swam strongly and focused on each stroke, trying to ignore the cold that gripped at his muscles and the fear in his heart. It took less than a minute for him to reach the pallet and he secured the rope to it before turning and swimming back towards the ship. Of the Zullifskag there was no sign.

The return swim was exhausting, but he made it and called to the others to leap onto the raft. Zarina jumped first, splashing into the icy water and Leo, kneeling on the pallet, ducked below the waves to grab her and haul her on board. As he did, he saw a blur of movement far below, inky blood wisping from its missing limbs as it circled.

"It's coming," he said. "We need to hurry."

Balthus stood above them holding the rail of the sinking ship. The warrior's eyes were wide with terror. "I can't do it!" he bellowed. "My legs won't do it."

"Jump!" Zarina called. "It's coming back!"

"I can't!" he shouted again.

"You've got seconds!" Leo shouted. "Jump, I'll grab you."

"I don't need help from a damn worm!" Balthus raged but still could not bring himself to leap.

Leo stood up and began prancing around on the pallet. "I'm a worm? Ha! You're the worm you pathetic coward. I've never seen anyone look so useless, standing up there like a child. What is the great general Balthus going to do next, cry like a babe?"

With a mighty roar Balthus leapt, landing in the water a foot away. Zarina and Leo grabbed at him, pulling the massive man on board with difficulty. Balthus scrambled onto the floating salvage and immediately grabbed Leo by the throat.

"What were you saying you cur!?" he roared.

"Let him go, he only said it to make you jump you big fool!" Zarina snapped.

Shamefaced, Balthus let go of his grip and Leo fell to his knees coughing and spluttering.

"Apologies," Balthus said gruffly.

"Think nothing of it," Leo wheezed, scooping some driftwood from the water and using it as a barge pole to push them away from the main body of the ship.

No sooner had he done so than the Zullifskag burst upwards, dealing one half of the ruined boat a final, fatal blow and shattering it into pieces. The wave the monster made was enough to push the raft out and away, carried on the crest of the surf.

The three companions watched as, in a rage, the massive daemon fell upon the other half of the ship, thrashing at it with its massive arms.

"Will it follow us?" Leo asked.

"Yes," said Zarina. "But if we are lucky the current will pull us towards shore before it realises we are no longer aboard.

"If it comes back…" Leo began.

Zarina nodded. There was no point in stating the obvious. If it came back they were all dead.

What followed were the most tense hours of Leo's life. None of them spoke as the raft slowly drifted towards the rocky coastline. With each passing moment Leo expected to see sign of the behemoth rising from the sea, but it did not and it was with a sense of unreality that, shivering and stunned, Leo and the others waded the last few metres onto the stony shore.

Balthus fell to his knees and kissed the red earth, laughing like a man gone mad. After a moment he turned to them both.

"Look at me, laughing like a fool when Gellen has lost his life." The giant sighed and stood offering Leo his hand. "Forgive me for what I did, fear brings hasty action. I know what you did for me."

Leo shook the man's hand noticing the large, ragged cut the barbs of the Zullifskag had torn down Balthus' arm. "You never have to apologise to me Balthus. I understand better than most about fear. And you better check your arm - looks nasty."

Balthus glanced at the wound. "No more than a scratch. We must find fire and shelter."

"Come," said Zarina gently taking their hands. "Before that we must say our farewells to Gellen. She turned them both so that all three stared out over the water towards the setting sun. She looked at Balthus and then Leo before facing the waters, addressing her words to the sea and to the sky.

"In our hearts it seems a great light has gone out, lost into darkness and pain. This morning we walked with a man of honour, compassion, kindness and bravery. We will never walk with him again in this lifetime. Never again will we enjoy the sound of his voice or the pleasure of his company. Tonight we are left feeling only the empty space our friend left behind.

But all is not as it seems, for nothing of value can ever truly be lost. Our friend has just returned to the beginning, to the Essence of all things, he has fulfilled his duty in this life, he has brought love and kindness to those around him, he has brought laughter and tears, joy and sorrow. He lived a good life and was true to himself. For him the wheel has turned once more and we must go on holding the lessons he taught us in our hearts. His time as we know it is over, but he will not be forgotten in our lifetimes because we will carry the flame of his memory deep within us. So to the universe I say this: one of your sons has died this day but let me tell you that he has done you proud with his life. Welcome him with open arms as you would embrace a dear friend after a long journey."

Listening to Zarina's words, Leo found himself begin to cry.

That night they camped in a shallow cave high above the beach. They had managed to salvage next to nothing of their supplies save what they were fortunate enough to be carrying during the attack. After stitching his wound, Balthus caught some crabs from a rock pool for himself and Leo, while Zarina picked berries along the coastal cliff top. They ate in silence, the mood was sombre, and for the first time Leo felt a sense of inevitable failure hanging over them. He wondered how many adventures the four of them had been on over the years and could not guess at the pain they felt having now lost another of their number.

Balthus had said nothing since the beach and sat nursing his axe, using dry sand to try to clean the salt water from the weapon's pores.

"What changed your mind with the sword?" Zarina asked.

"I do not know," said Leo, absently poking the fire with a stick. "Anger perhaps overtook my fear. I have never been able to hold one before."

"Can you hold it now?" Zarina asked.

Leo held out his hand and the Star Sword flew from where it rested to sit in his palm. The blade was now a dull silver. "It is not pleasant to look at it, but for some reason the terror I felt for these weapons is gone."

"I saw that terror," said Zarina. "On the road I looked into your mind. The fear and anger there nearly consumed me."

"I do not know what causes it," said Leo. "Every night I have nightmares but on waking I cannot remember them. I sense they have something to do with a sword or a knife, but it is beyond me to remember why."

"There are two powerful spells at work in you," said Zarina. "Nemeddes' soul swap obviously, but someone else has played with your memory. If the second spell could be dispelled then you would be able to remember."

"What could have happened to me that would be so bad I would need that?" Leo asked. "Would I even want to remember it?"

"It is a funny thing in life," said Balthus without looking up. "A man is often called to face their worst fears. Better to face them on your own terms if you can."

"Can you remove the spell?" Leo asked Zarina.

Zarina shook her head. "No. It is protected by a powerful ward. That was what nearly destroyed me. But there are those more powerful than I; I am no expert with the magic of dreams and memory. Perhaps another could help."

"Well," said Leo. "I suppose we will see." Even he could hear the fatigue in his voice.

"Do not despair," said Zarina. "There is yet hope."

"There seems precious little to me," Leo admitted. "But I am game to travel on."

Zarina smiled. "The Star Sword is not linked to anyone by body you know, it is a soul link. There are few who can wield such weapons. The odds that you, who were supposedly randomly chosen by the Lich would have this ability, is unbelievable."

"What are you suggesting?" Leo asked.

"It is easy to see things as pairs; up and down, love and hate, light and dark. But all are one Leo. The universe thrives on balance. When someone loses another gains, when something is lost another thing is found. The Lich wove his plan with care; he intended to doom this world and he could have chosen anyone for his scheme, but for this role he chose Leo Kvetch. Now Leo Kvetch has saved Balthus' life. He has saved my life. He has shown courage he did not know he possessed. He has shown he can wield a weapon forged of star metal from the great beyond. We are not beaten yet, the Essence guides our steps."

"But if the Lich can command creatures like that sea monster, if he can throw enemies like that at us, honestly, is there truly hope?" Leo asked.

Zarina smiled. "While there is life there is hope, and for now at least, we are still alive."

23.

It took them a little over a week to arrive in the desert city of Scyara and with the last of their funds Zarina purchased them lodgings close to the Northgate. Balthus had sent word for an ally to meet them who would lead them outwards across the Devil's Desert towards Table Rock and the last known location of the Temple of Time. Yet days had passed without response. Neither Balthus or Zarina knew the way ahead and the group could not decide how to proceed, save for a general agreement that they needed to keep a low profile following Yellund's treachery. If Balthus' man did not come forward soon they would be forced to enter the city to search out a different guide.

The only small consolation had been that the enforced rest had been welcome and had allowed the companions to recoup some energy. There had also been no sign of threat from Nemeddes since the treacherous crossing, but on the fourth day of their stay in the city, Zarina overheard news as to why. The great city of Tyr had fallen. The rumours said Nemeddes himself had been the one to lead the charge. Now nothing stood between the Lich's forces and Ostus.

The news struck each of them a hammer blow but none of them spoke about it. Leo's mind of course turned to Rebecca. He hoped she was planning her escape before the Kryxian army descended on the land. Had Yellund's threat been truthful? Would Nemeddes seek to harm her to punish him? He hoped with every ounce of his being that this would not be the case.

The news had come early in the morning and Leo was surprised when Balthus arrived at his door, training swords in hand. The warrior had been teaching Leo to fight and although Leo was still wary of the blades, he had been working hard.

"Do you still want to train today?" Leo asked. "I thought maybe after what we learned about Tyr... I know you had friends there..."

Balthus nodded. "Good friends. All the more reason to train," he said. "Come on."

For the next hour or so Balthus pushed Leo through a series of drills in the courtyard, mostly working on his footwork and starting positions. The intensity of the workout coupled with the day's growing heat had Leo dripping with sweat in minutes. Still Balthus pushed him further.

"Keep your elbows flexed!" the general barked. "You can't extend into a thrust if you begin with your arms already outstretched! And stop using your right hand so much; right hand is steering, left hand is power!"

Leo wiped sweat from his brow and tried again.

"You twitch your foot before every step!" said Balthus. "You might as well send a brass band out in front of you to announce you're going to attack. And how many times have I told you to bring your left hand to the crown of your head before cutting?"

"Many times..." said Leo, gulping in air.

"Then do it!" screamed Balthus.

Training went on like this for another half an hour before the large warrior called a break and threw Leo a skin of water. Gratefully Leo accepted it and slumped down in the shade.

Balthus sat beside him. "Not bad," he said then rooted in his pocket and dumped Gellen's Shaddak board into Leo's lap. "Found this amongst what was left of our supplies. He made this himself you know; carved the box and the board. Always wanted for me to learn to play but I never had the patience. It's a bit warped from the sea, doesn't close right anymore, but I figured he might have wanted you to have it. You seemed to enjoy playing it with him."

"Thank you," said Leo, genuinely touched.

"It's nothing," said Balthus, rising and walking inside. "Take some rest, we start again in twenty minutes."

Zarina approached from where she had been sitting watching.

"He is growing fond of you," she said, sitting beside Leo.

"Fond of me? Balthus?"

"Yes, of course. You have shown him the thing he values most - courage. On the boat, well, I have rarely seen bravery like when you leapt onto the beast's head. He is also grateful for when you protected me."

"I was terrified both times," said Leo.

"Courage, despite what some say, is not the absence of fear. Courage is taking action even though it terrifies you. Athus was Balthus' best friend. He mourns for his loss and of course, every time he sees you it reminds him of that. But despite this he is a good man. He is warming to you Leo. He sees as I do that you are a far better man than you give yourself credit for."

"You have all been so good to me," said Leo. "I will come with you to the end, face whatever we must face. I will not leave you or abandon you. I swear it with what little honour I have."

She smiled. "I believe you Leo. But be careful of making promises that you cannot guarantee to keep."

That afternoon, still with no word from Balthus' contact, the three had no choice but to enter the city. The northern district was a maze of merchants and bazaars, but in a square close to the eastern wall rows upon rows of tents were erected, each offering competitive scouting fees.

"There are so many. Which do we choose?" Leo asked.

"And which do we trust?" added Balthus.

Suddenly a man pushed through the crowd and bowed to Leo. "My Lord, I knew it was you. I am Arrif. I serve the noble house Cataran. Is there some assistance you need? My master has sent me to invite you to his palace."

Leo glanced to Zarina and saw her almost imperceptibly shake her head.

"That is kind," said Leo, "but we have everything in hand."

"Is that so? Why then are you hundreds of leagues away from your home when every report suggests that soon it will be besieged?" Arrif asked, losing his deference.

"I suppose that is my affair," said Leo. "Now if you have no further business with us, I suggest you move along."

"Lord Cataran will hear of this," said the young man. "Your refusal of his offer of kindness is an insult. My master will not be pleased."

Balthus grabbed the man by the neck. "If we have already insulted him, perhaps I should snap your neck like a twig. That way you will not be able to tell him of this insult and he may continue to be unoffended."

"No, that will not be necessary," the man gurgled. "I merely meant..."

"We have had dealings enough with House Cataran," said Zarina. "I remember during my engagement to my Lord Athus, your master desired Athus to marry his cousin. He sent me a dress. Inside was a needle coated with venom from the Ablak Spider. I did not care for the dress and gave it to a friend. The needle pricked her and she lay close to death for two weeks before she recovered. My husband and I have not forgotten your master's hospitality."

"My Lady," the man wheezed, struggling to speak through Balthus' grip. "I do not know of what you speak."

Balthus hurled the man into a wall. "Get out of here, worm!"

Arrif's face was like thunder but he turned and hurried away.

"I'd say that meeting is going to cause us some trouble," said Leo. "I think we need to find a guide - and fast."

"Indeed," said Zarina, "but which one?"

They looked across the square at the heaving tents. Balthus pointed to a large, embossed one of fine silks flying a flag of a crescent moon. It was appointed by six tough looking men dressed in desert garb. "Looks as good as any."

"I'm not sure," said Leo. "I think that is a better bet." Leo pointed to an empty stall, coarsely woven together, of animal hide. Next to it a small, squat woman in soiled clothes was stacking supplies.

"Are you joking?" Balthus asked.

"No," said Leo. "Think about it. They're tradespeople. If they're so good, why are six of them still at the stall. If they were the best guides wouldn't they be out working, not looking for work? She's not looking for work because she doesn't need to, it comes to her."

"Or she's lazy," said Balthus, "or incompetent."

"Perhaps," said Leo.

Zarina smiled. "Let Leo choose," she said.

"As you wish," said Balthus. "But if this ends badly it's not my responsibility."

Leo walked to the stall and greeted the woman. She turned and nodded at him. She was young, her face was fair even though it was marked with the lines of hard living. She cocked her head at Leo, weighing him up, her deep green eyes permanently slitted from exposure to the desert sun.

"We need a guide," Leo said.

"I don't accept criminals," the woman said returning to her duties.

"What do you mean?" Leo asked. "We're not..."

"Don't waste my time, I saw you arguing with Arrif, Catalan's man. If I take you it'll be the branding iron for me."

"We are not criminals but you are right we are hunted. We need help. We need to go into the eastern desert and we desperately need a guide – today."

The woman turned and looked Leo up and down. "What can you pay?"

"Two, maybe three hundred rupees," Leo said. "And a dagger made from Ostian steel with a ruby set in the hilt – very fine."

"Pah!" the woman scoffed, "probably fake. Do you know how dangerous the Devil's Desert is? I've never been offered so little."

"That is all we have," said Leo.

"Why do you want to go?" she asked.

Leo pointed to Zarina. That woman is my cousin. She is a servant from Kresta. A city lord forced himself upon her one night. She is pregnant with the child and has fled across the Corvus. Even now he pursues her. He killed her husband, her brothers. He is determined to kill her and the child to prevent a scandal. We are her last hope. We must outrun him, for if he catches her, her life will be worse than death..."

The woman threw her head back and laughed loudly. "By all the sand and stars are you a bad liar."

"Alright," said Leo, losing patience. "I am a farmhand from a small village. My soul has been cast into the body of a great hero, the only man who can save the world. I need to get to the Temple of Time at Table Rock to travel through time and stop the events that led to this spell being cast on me in the first place. We are hunted by an evil necromancer and if he catches me he will kill me and doom us all to a world of eternal torment and darkness."

"Your first lie was better," said the woman "but I am, as it happens, heading east within a few hours, plus I hate the Catarans and enjoyed seeing your friend nearly choke the life out of Arrif. Five hundred rupees, that bracelet and a night with the giant and you've got yourselves a deal. What do you say?"

"I think that can be arranged," said Leo.

24.

They sold what equipment they could part with to raise the extra funds and were on their way within the hour. Their guide introduced herself as Samla, making sure to make her large, green eyes twinkle when she shook Balthus' hand. Balthus grumbled theatrically about his part of the deal but as they camped their first night in the desert he went behind some dunes with their guide willingly enough and did not return until daybreak.

The second day saw them riding their mounts along a rocky pass leading into the mountains. As they rode Zarina pointed behind them as from the city streams of mounted soldiers rode forward like ants swarming from a nest. The horsemen formed into groups and with the blast of a trumpet headed off towards all four compass points.

"You are certainly popular people to know," Samla commented.

"Yes," said Leo. "Wherever we go we make a whole bunch of new friends who all want to kill us."

Samla snorted what might have been a laugh and rode on.

They camped high in the mountains that evening and although the deal they had struck with their guide had been paid in full, Balthus obviously felt she had undervalued her services and disappeared with her into a cave a little further up the trail. Occasionally sounds of their pleasure would carry on the wind to reach where Leo rested, making him uncomfortable. He wondered abstractedly whether Balthus thought of his wife at these moments, or did he picture Zarina beneath him? Did he feel any guilt at all? Balthus was, he decided, as irrepressible as the sea or the breeze. He was so full of life that it could not be contained and his alertness, his intrinsic thrill of being wherever he was and doing whatever he was doing spilled out of him and empowered those nearby. You could no more think badly of him for his actions than you could curse the sun for rising, or the grass for growing.

Leo looked to where Zarina lay on her side resting. In many ways she was the perfect woman, kind, intelligent, wise and beautiful. When he had seen her in the parade and later at the banquet, he could not deny he had desired her greatly but in knowing her, somehow something was missing. He had grown to love her in a way he had not thought possible. He knew he would do anything for her, but despite her obvious beauty his love was not sexual. He could admit that Rebecca was plain next to the sorceress, but the desire he felt for Rebecca was so intense, so right. He longed to see the rancher's daughter once more, to tell her he had loved her every day since they had parted, to beg her forgiveness for not having the courage to ask her to wed. To hold her, to kiss her, to make love with her; he realised he would give nearly anything for that. He sensed his thoughts growing melancholy but it was somehow different. Through his actions in the last weeks he was not simply overwhelmed. He had proved to himself he had courage, he was not weak. He pushed the thoughts back by simply deciding they would have no power over him. He would no longer be a prisoner to the mistakes he had made in the past.

Taking the Shaddak board from his pack he laid it on a rock and opened it, placing the pieces and allowing himself to pretend that, rather than playing against himself, he was playing Gellen. He remembered the man's voice, the surety of his hand as he placed a stone upon the board. When he made a mistake he imagined the mage correcting him, discussing his error. The game filled a pleasant hour and Leo packed the board away and lay back to rest. "Whatever fears come to me in the night, let them come," he whispered to himself and closed his eyes.

The next day they passed out onto a rocky plain, keeping to the shade offered by the mountains above. They made good progress and saw not a soul until an hour before midday. On a lower trail than the one they followed a young boy was lashed to a tree with rope. Two soldiers, outriders of Catalan by their purple sashes, took turns striking the lad. Four or five others sat nearby drinking and playing dice.

"They must have ridden through the night," said Samla. "Eager to catch you aren't they?"

"I would say so," said Balthus stopping his horse.

"Why do you stop?" Samla asked.

"I'm not going to let them continue doing that, am I?" said Balthus, gesturing towards the boy.

"Do not be stupid. Those men are dangerous. They call themselves the Unlawful. They are not mere scouts of the city but hard men chosen from the best of the local clans."

"But they might kill him," said Leo. "He's just a boy."

"A boy, yes - but from the Gkari clan. They practise black magics. Better to leave him be. Good riddance."

"Well I for one am not going to stand by and let him die," said Balthus, dismounting and readying his axe. The warrior ignored further talk and began climbing down the embankment towards the men below.

For a second Leo was unsure what to do, so abrupt was Balthus' departure, but he drew the Star Sword, slipped from his saddle and followed. Zarina watched him closely but said nothing.

By the time Leo reached the top of the embankment Balthus was more than half way down, bounding towards the soldiers in agile, powerful strides. Leo made to follow but almost immediately slipped and tumbled head over heels, passing Balthus at some speed and rolling to a halt at the bottom of the slope, the wind knocked from him.

The men at the bottom began to laugh, putting aside their game to stand and ready their weapons. Their smiles faded as the massive form of Balthus joined Leo at the bottom, his axe held casually over one shoulder.

"Very stealthy," Balthus observed as he pulled Leo to his feet. "Now be quiet and follow my lead. Oh, and the basics I've been showing you, forget them. A novice is always better fighting on instinct. If you try to remember a technique it will get you killed. Do what comes naturally."

"Are you two finished talking?" one of the men a head taller than the others smirked.

"You should hope we are not," said Balthus turning to face him. "Because when I stop talking I'm going to start killing and I'm going to kill you first."

The man curled his lip. "Strong words if you have sand to back them up."

"I think you know well enough that I have more sand than this whole desert," said Balthus. "If you all walk away now and turn the boy free, we will leave it at that. But if you do not, none of you will see another evening."

The man laughed. "We are not going anywhere, you think your size and words scare us, we are..." but then he was cut silent as Balthus hurled his hunting knife into the man's eye and he dropped and said no more.

The others, not short on courage, roared and rushed forward. Balthus stepped to meet them, a cut from his axe smashing one from his feet. Another of the men skewered a cut at his side, but the big man swayed away and slammed the haft of his axe into the man's chest sending him flying.

Leo darted forward with a lunge of his own, which his opponent parried, and Leo immediately followed up with a vertical slash towards the scout's head. The man had plenty of time to raise his sword to block, but the Star Sword cut through the inferior metal of the man's sabre and plunged into his neck. The man fell. A second warrior came in with a lancing strike that Leo barely avoided, feeling the blade rake against his ribs. He slashed the Star Sword wildly, forcing the man to jump backwards. Behind his opponent Leo saw Balthus down another then round on a fresh enemy. The man facing Leo tried a more cautious thrust and

Leo noticed as he did that he moved his left foot a half pace forward before attacking. The next time the man shuffled his foot Leo dived and pierced the man through the chest. Pulling his sword free he was in time to watch Balthus take the head of the last man.

The tall warrior retrieved his knife and moved to the post the boy was tied to before cutting him free. The youth ran off without a word. Balthus returned to Leo and clapped him on the back, offering him his water canteen. "A thirsty business killing," Balthus commented.

Leo took a deep swig and nodded.

"Ever killed a man before?" Balthus asked.

Leo shook his head.

Balthus nodded. "You did well. Take no glory in it for that is the path that leads you to dark places. Some repress it and it leads to nightmares. You need no more of those. Just accept it for what it was. These men were dangerous; they would have killed that lad and that is all we know. We gave them a chance to walk away and they did not take it."

Leo nodded, unable to stop looking at the men he had killed.

"Come," said Balthus. "Let us keep moving."

The two warriors struggled up the dry scree and back to the horses. Samla looked at Balthus with undisguised lust. "You just slew four Unlawful as if it were nothing."

"It was nothing," said Balthus, stowing his axe and climbing into the saddle.

"We should wed," Samla insisted. "If a boy takes root in me he would be a war chief like no other."

"Did she really just say that?" Leo whispered to Zarina.

The sorceress smiled. "Their culture is very different from ours. This is a hard land, life is short; there is little time for being coy. Are you well after the combat?" she asked.

"I don't know," said Leo. "I have never killed anyone before."

"I meant your wound," said Zarina with a smile.

"Leo looked down at his side. It was not a deep cut but now attention was drawn to it he felt it sting and throb. "It's just a scratch," he said.

"Then we need to ride, a new enemy hunts us." Zarina pointed back down the trail to where three tiny cones of swirling air were billowing across the desert.

"What are they?" Leo asked.

"They are Nazzaka," said Zarina. "Air daemons."

At that word Samla jerked her head, her sharp eyes scanning where Zarina pointed. "We must ride and ride fast," she said. "Dust daemons are quick, but we are not far from my village, our shamani can repel them."

With that she heeled her mount and Balthus, Zarina and Leo gave chase. They rode hard and their mounts were nearing exhaustion when Samla led them down a narrow trail. Leo had seen no sign of these Nazzaka, these air daemons, since they had raced off but he had no reason to doubt they were close. As they rounded a corner, Samla's village came into sight and as it did, two of the daemons appeared behind them. The creatures swept over the dry land in a plume of dark, swirling smoke, crested the top of the trail and began bearing down on the riders with frightening speed.

"Hurry!" Samla urged, slapping her mount's flank. "We must make it past the banners!"

The last hundred yards was dicey at best. Leo looked back and saw the swirling dust closing in. Inside it there was something... inhuman... but impossible to distinguish, a writhing in the mass of air and sand. The four horses streaked past the banners that signalled the outskirts of the village and the daemons raced on, then struck a wall of crackling light. Each howled, and drifted away in soft plumes of smoke.

"That wasn't so bad," said Leo catching his breath. "Are we safe?"

"They will wait in the rocks for you to leave and run you down in moments," said Samla, "but while you remain here, yes you are safe."

25.

The commotion in the village caused by their arrival was short lived and the organisation of the tribespeople was something to behold. In moments, hunters armed with bows flanked them whilst shamans ran to the barrier checking it for damage. Samla called to her people in her own tongue and led Balthus, Zarina and Leo to a large yurt in the centre of the camp, gesturing for them to enter. Inside, an ancient woman sat in a throne of polished bones with neither guards nor servants to attend her.

As the three entered Zarina bowed low. "Old Mother, I pay my respects to those who have gone before," said Zarina. Leo took her cue and bowed also. Balthus nodded his head in the briefest of acknowledgments.

"Come close children," the old woman said, her voice as thin as reed paper. "Let us talk. My barrier will hold back the evil."

The three approached and the old woman smiled and looked at Leo with white, cataract covered eyes. "So you are the soul stealer?" she said.

"I wouldn't say I stole it," said Leo. "It was more of a swap."

The Old Mother laughed. "Who knows yet whether you were chosen for good or for ill - but at least you have a sense of humour."

"We are sorry for bringing this darkness here, Old Mother," said Zarina.

"Do not think on it child," the woman said. "Always the darkness seeks a way to reach me here, either through its daemons or men from Scyara."

"I fear Scyara sides with the Lich," said Zarina.

"Indeed it does," said the Old Mother. "That city has courted with dark powers since its first stones were laid. The land here has never recovered from the last Scourging. The darkness runs deep in the sands. I had, I must confess, accepted the coming darkness and now three heroes arrive seeking a forgotten temple. Truly the Essence provides."

"Does the Temple still stand?" Leo asked.

"The truth is that I do not know," said the woman. "No one goes to Table Rock now, it is encased in darkness. The Temple of Time was at the epicentre of the final battle of the last Scourging where Amad El turned the tide and destroyed the archfiend Zallandex. Nemeddes was but an apprentice then, he witnessed the death of his master. It is said he wept tears of blood when Zallandex was slain."

"Is there no way to reach the Temple then?" Leo asked.

"There is always a way," smiled the Old Mother. "It is said even slaying Zallandex was not enough and as the great Amad El delivered the death blow others were at work. The forces of light were still badly outmatched and even without their Lord the darkness was close to victory. A spell was cast sealing what was left of the Daemon horde in the River of Souls; an eddy of displaced time that circles Table Rock endlessly."

"How can we pass through?" Balthus asked.

"Two paths stretch before you. Your weapons will be useless inside the River. What dwells there is ancient and vile: only Zarina's light and the Star Sword can aid you. To walk the River is likely death for any mortal. Are you ready for that test child?" the Old Mother asked of Zarina.

"As ready as I can be," Zarina replied simply.

"And our other option?" asked Balthus.

"There is another route, deep beneath the earth. A series of ancient tunnels lead under the River of Souls. But that place holds an evil of its own. The path is dark and dangerous, but the creatures there bleed and die like any other," said the Old Mother.

"Our main problem is that we are still many miles from Table Rock," said Zarina. "We have lost a dear friend and without his skill will have to make the journey over land. Can you help us?"

"Of course," said the Old Mother. "I have stood against the darkness since the beginning. I will lend my power again now. Now go and rest, gather your strength for what is to come."

That night Leo sat alone and gazed at the stars. Zarina was in deep consultation with the Old Mother and Balthus was no doubt with Samla once more. He looked up at the sky, watched the clouds billow far above and tried to find some rest but even as he did, his mind would not clear. A shadow moved into his vision and Leo knew at once who it was. He summoned the Star Sword, yet as Nemeddes sat beside him, Leo noticed the sword blade did not glow. The Lich was not truly present.

"What do you want?" Leo asked, sheathing the blade.

"Just to talk," said Nemeddes.

"Then do it and leave me be," said Leo. "I doubt there is much I wish to hear from you."

Nemeddes laughed, tugging at his neat beard. "If only I had seen what sort of man you were under all that grime," said the Lich. "I would have saved myself a lot of trouble. It seems I chose poorly."

"Thank you, I suppose," said Leo.

"But that aside, this is all futile Leo. I misjudged you. But where are you running to really? The Temple of Time? I was there you know; I saw what happened to it. Despite what that colossal fool Amad El intended, it was struck by a beam of magic the like of which this world has not seen before or since. It was vaporised, completely destroyed - erased from all existence. After all of your efforts you will find nothing more than an empty patch of dirt and some broken foundations. There will be no saviour in sight, no magic temple, no last ditch throw of the dice. You will be surrounded, isolated and alone."

"If the Temple is gone why does it say in your own holy book that it will return?" asked Leo.

"A good point," Nemeddes conceded. The Lich stood and stared up into the heavens, for a moment looking all too weary and human. "It is all in how you interpret the ancient language of the Book of Shadows. The Book speaks of places of great power in our world, places where the fabric of space and time grow thin.

Table Rock is such a place and its magic goes deep into the core of Gaia. Since humans first had the ability to build, someone has built something on Table Rock. People are drawn to its power like insects to flame.

"When I rule I will build my cathedral there and tap into that power. It will be a new temple in my own image and, the darkness willing, I will travel between the worlds and through time and space to seek new places as yet unknown to me. That is what the Temple of Time once did, you know. It was home to a group of people called Wanderers or World Striders, individuals who moved from world to world as we might sail across an ocean. The Temple of Time will return symbolically I suppose, but it will be my temple. The old home of the World Striders is lost."

"I do not pretend to understand the mysteries of the past or future, all I know is how I feel right now," said Leo. "What is it you want? Is it for me to just give up? You're not really negotiating from a point of strength there, I can tell you; you've tried to kill me again and again. I'm hardly likely to trust you."

"That is true," Nemeddes chuckled. "The truth is that commanding my forces takes considerable time and attention and I greatly underestimated you. Pursuing you has proven draining. You should be proud of how thin you have stretched me. I am not, despite what people say, prone to hubris. I am not so conceited to think I know everything or consider myself invincible. I am not so arrogant that I cannot admit there is a chance, no matter how slim, that you could somehow best me. I don't want to take any chances. Tomorrow I will go into battle once again. A part of me is afraid. I am not a monster, Leo. I have friends amongst my order. Even the great Nemeddes, the Arch Fiend, knows sadness when they suffer and die. I want my concentration solely on the battle, not worrying about you and your plans. Is that not understandable?"

Leo found the Lich's words all too understandable and did not reply.

"I see something in you Leo," Nemeddes continued. "These people, Zarina and Balthus, they are not your friends, not really; no more than I am. We are merely different sides of the same coin. Tonight you sit on that coin edge, an important piece in a game that is not your own. Remember that the biggest mistakes you have made in your life stem from never seizing the initiative. Look how you let Rebecca wed another. This is no different. You need to start thinking about what *you* are going to achieve out of this. You do not wish to serve me and that is fine - but do not blindly serve the light and think that it is any different. It is still slavery. Currently all the light is offering you for your service is a humiliating and painful death. I can offer you so much more. I could see to it that you have a land of your own; women, riches, eternal life; not just for you, but for a large group of people. Imagine it - a pocket of land a thousand leagues in every direction. You could live a life of bliss there with Rebecca, your friends, anyone you wished. You would never even know I ruled this world. You could be the man who brokered a deal that saved the lives of thousands. You can come out of this a real hero. Just leave this village, come to me, let us sit down face to face and discuss this like men."

Leo sat for a moment before he looked into the Lich's golden eyes. "You must think I just fell right off the turnip truck," said Leo. "You want me to walk out of here? Walk out of here so you can rip me to pieces?"

Nemeddes laughed but there was suddenly no mirth in his voice. In a second his whole manner changed and he seemed to grow with each word that he spoke.

"I see you distrust me, perhaps that is fair, so let me change tack. This is your last chance to offer supplication. The next time we speak I will be far less reasonable. Tomorrow you will receive grave news. I will come to you again in the days that follow, only this time I will hold her in my arms. You know of whom I speak; that sweet rancher's daughter you crave. I will do unspeakable things to her Leo. And I will catch you and I will make you watch me do them until you beg to carve your own eyes out of your skull. Do not doubt me," the Lich finished, his voice like that of an angry god.

Leo swallowed in a dry throat and pushed away his fear, finding anger of his own. "I think if you could do that, you'd be doing it right now," said Leo. "I have never had an enemy before, Nemeddes; not a real one. You are my first, but I swear to you if I can find a way to defeat you - I will. And then you can go to hell, or whatever place a thing like you goes to when it finally dies, knowing that you were sent there not by some great warrior or sorcerer - by a cowardly ranch hand from Two Trees. Now get out of my sight."

Nemeddes curled his lip into a snarl and vanished into the air.

Leo gulped, sucking in a deep breath and wiped the sweat from his brow. He tried to stop his hands from shaking but found he was unable.

"Well said," a voice came from behind him. Leo span to see the Old Mother standing in the shadows.

"How long have you been there?" he asked.

"Long enough to see you deny temptation and push away your fear," said the Old Mother. "Zarina is meditating. I thought we could speak alone for a while."

Leo nodded. "Of course."

The old woman made herself comfortable on a rock, spreading a shawl over her knee and looked intently at Leo. "Zarina tells me there is a spell in your mind; a memory spell and it is guarded by a powerful defence."

"So I have been told," said Leo.

"Come here, let me see it."

"I cannot do that as much as I long to know what is wrong with me. The spell has already claimed one life and nearly destroyed Zarina too," said Leo.

"Do you know what I am, Leo Kvetch?" the Old Mother asked, without a hint of arrogance to her voice.

"A witch?"

"Some have called me that," the Old Mother smiled. "I am a dream walker. Gellen was a master of alteration, Zarina studies the spiritual realm but for me the dream world is my specialism. And here we are, surrounded by evil and a soul stealer arrives whose dreams are masked to him. It seems only right that I should look into your mind, if you will let me."

"Is it not just coincidence?"

"I do not believe in coincidence anymore, I have lived too long," said the Old Mother. "Coincidence is just a pattern we cannot yet see."

"It scares me that I have this thing in my mind," said Leo.

"Then let me look," said the Old Mother, "I will not approach it, just observe."

Leo nodded his consent and lay down. The Old Mother moved to sit by his head and placed her bony hands on his temples.

"Yes," she said. "I feel it at once. There is a spell repressing your memory. The spell has not been cast well. It is breaking down and leaks into your dreams, poisoning them. Had a master of mnemonic magic cast the enchantment this would not have happened. Likely it was some amateur or apprentice."

"But why would I have something like this in my head? Who would do that to me?" asked Leo.

"Who knows, perhaps you asked for it to be done to yourself," said the Old Mother. "Perhaps you saw something or did something you longed to forget."

"What of the ward guarding it, the counter spell?" Leo asked.

The Old Mother chuckled. "In this Zarina is wrong. There is no spell protecting the seal."

"Then what nearly consumed her, what killed the witch who tried?"

"You did Leo. Your own angst and hate and pain protects the spell. You are terrified of remembering and that force lashes out at any who draw near to the barrier. If you can face that fear, it will be undone," the Old Mother spoke.

Leo's heart sank. "Are you saying I killed that poor old woman?"

"Not intentionally, but the psychic power you have amassed to repress your memories and protect the mnemonic spell did. I will help you dissolve the seal, but you must protect me while I do, you must allow me through."

"If something goes wrong, do not risk yourself," said Leo,

"In every brave act there is risk," said the Old Mother. "Now relax, I am going to begin."

26.

He was running again. Running in darkness. Sweat poured down his body, dripped from his face and soaked him but he ran on. His legs were racing, desperately trying to get away from something, desperately forging forwards. Somewhere ahead a child's cries echoed in this shadowy realm. And there was something behind him, somewhere in the dark. Something vicious. He looked back and saw a dark figure begin to emerge, fading into a form as black as coal - apart from the knife it held in its right hand which glimmered like a single, diamond sharp tooth. Terror spread through him and he ran on, and ran on, and ran on. But this time a light appeared close by and its power flowed into him and suddenly the thing that followed him was not so monstrous. He stopped and looked in amazement as the nightmare creature faded away to be replaced by a shaggy, toothless hound. The beast growled half-heartedly at him then wandered away into the blackness.

The child's cries continued though, more urgent now. He moved towards them but he never seemed to get closer to the child. Then out of the dark a door appeared, light shining from it like a beacon and without thought he passed through it. At once the dark fell away and he was there again, in that kitchen. He knew what waited for him there. He didn't want to see his plate of tuna fish sandwiches, his favourite, sitting waiting for him on the side. Such a normal thing, innocent and now so perversely out of place. He didn't want to see the carefully folded laundry sitting innocently on the table, he didn't want to watch her feet struggling, pushing on the slick floorboards. Then stopping.

He longed to turn his back and shut his eyes but somehow this time he had the strength to look upon what he loathed. Leo watched again as his father held his mother's head in a bucket of water on the kitchen floor. She struggled and clawed at the floorboards until her fingernails were torn away. She thrashed one last time and then was still. Leo watched as his father drew a small pearl- handled knife from his pocket, then slid it across her throat, turning the water a deep red.

His father looked up at him and slowly stood and pointed that awful knife with its gleaming handle directly at Leo. As he advanced, the man seemed to grow in size with each step until he towered, high above Leo, his voice deep and menacing.

"Don't you tell no one what you seen you useless sprat," the colossus bellowed. "If you do..." and he leaned forward bringing the terrifying blade with its glittering point up to Leo's eyes. "If you do... I'll gut you like a kipper." Leo stood and stared at the pearl handle of the knife and how the oil shimmered along it. Then he turned and ran, his father chasing.

"I should have killed you when I had the chance, sprat!" the giant called. "I should have drowned you when you popped out!" And Leo ran and ran and ran, and ran and screamed.

And this time, when he woke he remembered everything.

As Leo awoke from *that* dream, cradled on the lap of the Old Mother, his cries of pain and anguish echoed around the camp, chilling all who heard them and then, almost at once, he fell back and slept again, reliving the nightmare once more.

He awoke alone in a small yurt, feeling confused and afraid. He dressed quickly and as he took his first steps with his memory restored, he had slipped into a state he had never experienced before. It was not like depression or melancholy nor apathy; he knew those well. It was not even akin to shock or fear; it was something almost divine. Zarina, Balthus and Samla came to talk to him. He listened to them but said nothing. He was perfectly aware; he could hear their words but felt no need to respond. Balthus took his mood for weakness and struck him a blow that knocked him to the floor. Leo merely stood back up and made no comment.

His mind was too busy to communicate, replaying again and again a sight that had been repressed inside him for nearly thirty years. His parents had not died in a carriage accident. His father had murdered his mother. His father had been a vile, terrifying figure of a man who was cruel at the best of times. He had been hung for it; Leo had even watched the noose snap tight around his neck. Now the jigsaw of memory had returned, it seemed ridiculous to even entertain the possibility he had forgotten all he had witnessed and experienced.

He had been eight years old; his father was drunk again and angry. He had struck Leo with the back of his hand and Leo had run outside and hidden in the crawlspace in the barn, behind the hayloft. His father did not know of it. It had been the one safe place of his childhood. Over time he had decorated the small, tight space with things of meaning to him: a blanket he had slept in as a baby, a brush that belonged to his mother, a colourful stone he had found on the beach one happy summer. He had buried his face into the blanket and tried to keep very still. He could hear his father raving and shouting inside the house, his every outburst bringing fresh pangs of fear.

Then he had heard the sound of the front door, his mother's voice calling for him. She had been so kind, so loving. She was a bright beacon in his mind as he remembered her, how she gathered him up, swinging him in her arms as she sang to him as she took him from the bath. He remembered helping her with the chores, playing with her in the wheat fields, a thousand different memories of her that had been stolen were now returned.

That night, from the hayloft, he heard his father shouting again. He had heard his mother scream back and they had argued – then abruptly, nothing. It was the nothing that had eventually scared him enough to move. Shouting and screaming he was used to – but not quiet. Not silence. He had crept from the crawlspace, slunk across the yard and gone to the house and there the eight year old boy had stood and watched his father drown his mother in a bucket of shallow water in the middle of their kitchen and when he was done drag a tiny pearl-handled knife across her throat.

Leo could now remember the scene with awful clarity. His father, so strong, so terrifyingly large, scowling as he did the deed and then advancing on him, threatening him, pointing that terrible knife at his eye until the young Leo had turned and fled. He could remember running to his uncle, beating his fists on the man's door, dragging him from his bed. He could remember being there when the officers of the watch seized his father. He could remember now the months of anguish, of his constant crying, unable to sleep, too afraid to go out, too afraid to talk, to play. He could remember how his uncle had taken him to the witch, how she had placed her hands upon him for four pieces of silver and shut out the memories as best she could.

And suddenly, after replaying all these events again and again, his mind had finally accepted it all and he had sat down and wept unashamedly and innocently like a child. He had stumbled back to his yurt and had thrown himself on his bedroll, exhausted from grief. In moments he had drifted to sleep but this time, for the first time since he was eight years of age, there were no nightmares.

Leo jerked upright and screamed. Balthus stood above him holding an empty pitcher of water. "Rise and shine," he said.

Leo stood, grinning despite the soaking. He had enjoyed the most restful sleep he could imagine, totally free of fear. He stretched.

"I feel incredible," he said. "I must thank the Old Mother. She has cured me."

Balthus placed a training sword in his hand. "Soon we must leave this place. Only the Star Sword can harm those dust devils, so let us practise."

For an hour Balthus sparred with Leo, helping him improve. Leo marvelled at the big man's skill and could not land a blow upon the General no matter what he tried.

"There is a saying, you may have heard it," said Balthus. "The best swordsman in Ostus fears the worst."

Leo shook his head.

"They say that because the journey of the sword is a long one. A warrior learns in a set way, learns set attacks, ripostes, parries and stances. In time this creates a complete fighter but it has the limitation that it makes a warrior predictable. For example, after a centreline parry, most fighters respond with a riposte to the head or chest, like this," said Balthus, knocking Leo's weapon to one side and wrapping him on the side of the head with his training sword.

"Now if you know that is how a fighter has been trained, you can anticipate it and counter easily. It sounds ridiculous but warriors get so used to fighting in these systems that without realising it they fight to rhythms and patterns even they do not see. Athus was a master at spotting that, it made him great. He was a truly unpredictable fighter, never once moving in the same way. I could never best him."

"I still don't understand," Leo admitted.

Balthus pursed his lip thinking of how to rephrase his tuition. "A novice sets fear into the heart of even a seasoned fighter because a novice is unpredictable. They may not be good, but they are erratic. Sometimes this is more effective than being skilled. For example, they may risk everything on a crazy lunge as you did when we fought those Unlawful," said Balthus.

"It worked," Leo nodded. "Also I noticed my opponent shifted his feet each time before attacking."

"Impressive you had such awareness in your first skirmish," Balthus said. "And you are right, your reckless lunge did work. Only a fool would attempt such a move. It took your opponent by surprise but left you completely open. No seasoned swordsman would risk it all like that when fighting superior numbers."

"What are you saying? That because I am a novice, it gives me an edge?" Leo asked.

"No sadly. You have improved," said Balthus. "Now you are beginning to fight with technique. In time you might make a fine swordsman, but for now you are a liability."

"Not a great boost to my confidence," Leo observed.

Balthus did not reply, his attention taken as Zarina joined them. Her face was grave.

"Ostus has fallen," she said, then turned and walked away.

"As I was saying," said Balthus as if he had not heard, "you are a liability. We have a few hours to teach you something of use."

"Did you not just hear her?" said Leo, the colour fallen from his face. "Nemeddes has taken Ostus."

"I heard," said Balthus. "What can we do about it? Sit and worry? I am a good general Leo, not great like Athus, I am merely good. A good general creates a plan and then holds to it no matter what. He does not change his tactics; the battle is won or lost before it is fought. Doubt creeps in easily if you let it, and nothing destroys an army faster than an abrupt change of plan. The way of the warrior is to choose a path of action and see it through. Success or failure may come - you may be branded a hero or a fool. That is for historians and scholars to argue over. Those who do not have the courage to make their mark on the world love to comment on those who do. But the spirit does not grow through watching or worrying, it grows through acting. A warrior makes a choice based on the best information and advice they have to hand and then we see it through to the end, no matter what."

"I do not know if I could live like that," said Leo.

"You have already proven several times that you can, now let us continue your training."

Balthus continued to push Leo for nearly two more hours until the sweat was falling from Leo in waves. When Balthus sensed his student could not go on, he called a halt.

"You take a rest, I will be indisposed for a while," Balthus said.

"You seem quite taken with her," Leo observed as the man walked away.

Balthus shrugged. "She is a strong woman and I find the sex clears my head. You are not Athus and Zarina is not your wife, she would not object to you finding a woman here. It will ease your nerves."

"I don't think that's appropriate," said Leo.

"As you say," said Balthus, heading off in search of Samla.

27.

In Balthus' absence Leo went in search of the Old Mother, but instead found Zarina sitting alone in her yurt. The priestess looked tired and withdrawn and was holding the blue brooch she often wore on her robes.

"Are you alright?" Leo asked.

Zarina smiled sadly at him and nodded. "Your eye looks bad," she said.

"Yes," said Leo, holding his hand to the puffy bruise. "Balthus caught it in training. An accident that is all."

"Where is he?" Zarina asked.

"With Samla I think," said Leo.

She smiled. "He is afraid and upset Leo, the sex takes his mind off it. He is scared for his wife and children and for his friends in Ostus. Do not judge him."

"I wasn't..." said Leo.

"Of course you were," said Zarina. "It is only natural. The Old Mother tells me she has dissolved the mnemonic spell."

Leo nodded and told her of how the Old Mother had come to him and of the memories she had awakened.

Zarina listened quietly. "I am sorry for the pain you have lived with," she said when he had finished.

"I am well enough now," he said. "It is I who am worried about you. Seeing this face every day and it not being the man you love. It must be hard for you."

Zarina looked down, thumbing at the gem in her hands. "It has been hard," she admitted.

"Was that stone a gift from Athus?" Leo asked.

"Yes," said Zarina, her voice almost cracking. Leo's heart bled to see her like that. "We were sixteen when we first met. Life was simpler then and it was a beautiful time. I loved him from the first moment we met. We were at Gyam, far south of here, on a long, sandy beach. No one knew us. There were a few stalls selling trinkets and odds and ends. At one you could pay a copper piece to throw three balls at a coconut shy. Athus paid and knocked two down and missed the last. He was disappointed because if he had knocked down all three he would have won us a boat trip. For two hits I got to pick a prize. I chose this little bit of blue glass." Zarina smiled, staring at it. "It's worthless really; they wash up on the beach at Gyam every day. We agreed it was perfect because our love was not about money or riches. He told me he would happily wed me and live our lives on that beach fishing in the sea and making necklaces from shells. He looked into my eyes..." Zarina went on, tears beginning to run down her cheeks... "he looked into my eyes and he promised me that no matter what happened we would always be together to face the future. He promised me that when things were darkest he would be with me... he never broke a promise to me until now."

Leo moved to her then and said nothing, just held her while she cried. In time she pushed herself free and stood, wiping her eyes.

"Thank you for talking with me," said Leo.

She smiled. "Thank you for listening."

"If there is anything I can do, please let me know," Leo offered. "You are so strong. Everyone relies on you and on your plan to get us to the Temple of Time even though you had no part in the wrongdoing that created this crisis."

"You are partly right," she said. "I do feel the weight of it on my shoulders. As to whose wrongdoing it is, well that's irrelevant. If there is serious danger one cannot say it is not my fault, it's nothing to do with me. A good person must put themselves forward, it is not enough to simply step back and be content that you yourself have caused no wrong. We all affect each other in this world on the subtlest and most gross levels."

"I am beginning to understand that," said Leo.

"As for this being my plan, well, I don't want to scare you Leo, but it is not. This plan is yours. I would not even have thought of it. It was your idea to travel to the Temple of Time. It was your idea not to take an army but to go it alone. I merely chose to side with you."

Leo stared blankly for a moment. "I didn't think of it like that. I do not even know if there will be anything at the Temple when we get there."

"Nor I," she smiled. "Now if you'll excuse me, I must give my strength to the barrier. The Zullifskag has returned and the process is tiring."

Leo's face paled. "How can it return, wasn't it confined to the sea?"

"It is a being of old power, Leo. It can change its shape as it wishes. It is angry and seeks revenge. It is hunting us now. Get some rest. We leave soon," said Zarina.

At the midnight hour the companions stood with their horses inside a complex design the Old Mother had drawn into the sand. Leo was surprised to see Samla join them.

"I have made a decision this day," the Old Mother spoke. "To leave our village now is death. Nazzaka daemons wait in the hills and a Zullifskag hunts in the air. I will transport you across the desert, to the stone circle near Thule. There, with the Essence's help, you can pass through the Valley of the Moon and gain entrance to Table Rock."

"Will that lead us beneath the River of Souls?" Balthus asked.

The River encircles Table Rock on the surface and permeates the shallow tunnels, but a path is known to our scouts, a deep tunnel that leads under the river. The route is dangerous and seldom travelled," said the Old Mother.

"I cannot allow this," said Zarina. "The power of such a transportation spell is too much. You will not be able to maintain the spirit barrier and keep the village safe."

"And what will that avail us if there is a new Scourging?" the Old Mother asked. "It is not your place to advise me child. I was old before you walked this earth."

"My apologies," said Zarina and said no more.

"Samla will guide you. You must ride swift and hard. Are you ready?" the Old Mother asked.

They nodded that they were and Leo stepped forward and abruptly put his arms around the old woman. "Thank you for what you did for me, and for your sacrifice," he said.

"Shoo! Get off me," said the woman not unkindly. She then leaned in close and whispered. "You have become a good man Leo Kvetch, but now you must be brave," she warned. "Your testing is not yet over."

Leo stepped back to join the others and the four of them stood while the Old Mother cast her spell, then in a blink of an eye the village was gone and they stood in a stone circle high upon a rocky peak.

"Follow me," said Samla. "The open land here is treacherous. We must make it to the Valley of the Moon as quickly as we can. The route there is dangerous for those who do not know it and it will slow down any who follow. Any who are human anyway."

The ride to The Valley was electrifying, speeding down rocky passes and racing around the sheer bends of the cliffs before sprinting the horses over patches of open land. They did not speak or slow, but followed Samla, and there was not a sign of pursuit until close to dawn when a piercing shriek ripped through the skies and Zarina had them take refuge in a shallow cave.

A moment later a monstrous white form, like a giant albino bat, circled above screeching in the sky, then broke off for the east.

"By the stars," said Balthus. "That thing will take some killing."

"Such a thing may be beyond us," said Zarina. "If we can, let us avoid it."

"That gets my vote," said Leo, looking with fear as the Zullifskag disappeared out of view.

"The Valley of the Moon is not far," said Samla. "That creature cannot follow us through there, the caves and passages are too narrow."

Satisfied the Zullifskag was hunting elsewhere they left the cave and followed Samla to The Valley, heeling their horses inside without a pause. Soon the route was too narrow to ride and they dismounted, leading the animals through the caves.

The narrow tunnels were dark and tight. Balthus lit his torch and led the way, following Samla's directions whilst Leo took up the rear. After an hour or more of slow going, the way opened up into a larger chasm.

"We must be careful here," Samla urged. "Our sounds can be carried through the tunnels. If enemies are close outside they may hear us."

The companions moved as silently as they could but whether they were not quiet enough or it was just bad luck two Nazzaka dust devils swirled into the chamber and sped towards them. As they neared, the eddying air current slowed and faded and from each a daemon sprang out, shaped like huge hounds with hides of black bone. Zarina sent golden light crashing into one, knocking it back, and Leo drew the Star Sword and leapt to meet the other. His timing was out by half a beat and his strike sailed over the creature's head. It pounced for him and he rolled to one side, a massive paw raking his shoulder. Balthus' axe was no use against the creatures, but he hammered at them anyway, even though the weapon bounced feebly from their ebony hides.

Leo swiped the Star Sword at one again, this time catching the devil's forepaw. The creature howled and leapt backwards. In that moment Zarina fired an arc of golden flame that blasted the daemon to pieces. Leo turned and saw Balthus' axe knocked from his hand. He leapt between the creature and the unarmed warrior just as it was about to hurl itself on the giant. The daemon snarled and Leo lunged forward, skewering the Star Sword into its side. The beast let out a roar and Leo twisted the blade before wrenching it free and the daemon fell to the sand and turned to dust.

Balthus grimaced as he recovered his axe.

"Are you hurt?" Leo asked.

"A scratch, nothing more," said Balthus. "You fought well. It would have had me if not for you. That is the second time you have saved my life."

"I hope we're not keeping score," said Leo. "I fear I am well behind in that game."

"That is true," Balthus said with a grin.

They moved through the rest of the tunnels which slowly wound upwards back to the surface and met with no further resistance.

"How far?" asked Zarina.

"We must cross the open sand here. It is not a long ride, but we are exposed. After that there is a short trip through more tunnels to the edge of the River of Souls. Then we must head north for half a day," said Samla, urging her mount forward.

As they rode across the dunes the sun began to rise, throwing its light on a huge, flat mountain of brick red in the distance.

"Is that it?" asked Leo.

"It is," said Zarina. "That is Table Rock."

"So close I feel like I can touch it," Leo said.

Then a dark shape passed before the sun and for a moment blotted out the light of the dawn. A huge shriek filled the sky, echoing off the nearby mountains, and suddenly Table Rock felt very far away indeed.

The four riders spurred their mounts on as the Zullifskag began to dive, shrieking its rage and anger at the mortals who had defied it. It flew over them, seeing the entrance to the cave network they were heading towards, and landed before the narrow opening, its monstrous weight throwing up sand in all directions. The four companions pulled their horses up sharply. The Zullifskag turned and roared at them, changing form before their eyes, its wings receding into its pale, white body. As they did, the legs gained in power and strength and the daemon took on the aspect of a giant, ghastly bear that even whilst stood on all fours was some fifteen metres high.

"What do we do?" Leo called, feeling panic welling inside hm.

"When you are unsure… attack!" Balthus boomed, drawing his axe and standing up in his saddle and offering a war cry as he charged at the beast.

28.

As Balthus raced off towards the daemon, Leo looked to Zarina who nodded and they all joined his charge. Samla drew her bow, controlling her steed with her strong legs and loosed shaft after shaft at the monster. Most of her arrows bounced from the creature's hide but two pierced the flesh, one by its throat and one by its left eye. Zarina urged her mount forward and brought her hands together, her whole body glowing like star fire, as she lanced a beam of golden power at the Zullifskag, striking it in the chest. The beast screamed and sagged and Balthus rode beneath its forelegs, hacking his axe into its belly. Again the beast roared and it was Leo's turn to strike a blow. The Star Sword gleamed with golden light and he sliced it deeply into the Zullifskag's right foreleg, biting bone.

The monster growled and locked its flaming eyes onto Leo and opened its mouth. With a snarl it breathed forth a cone of darkness that crackled through the air like a lightning bolt. Leo held up the Star Sword before him and the dark wave split around the blade for a moment before he was torn from the saddle by the impact. He spilled over the desert surface, the sword flying from his hand. It took him precious moments to recover his bearing and climb again to his feet. As he did the Zullifskag charged towards him ignoring the others. Leo reached his hand out and willed the sword to return to him. He saw the blade lift from beneath the desert sand and begin to fly towards him, but the daemon saw it too. One of its taloned forelegs slashed out, shimmering with dark energy, and raked at the sword while it was in flight. Leo screamed as the Star Sword shattered into fragments sending chunks of flaming metal flying like shrapnel to bite deep into the sandy dunes.

The Zullifskag roared in triumph then howled in pain as Zarina blasted it again. Samla loosed two more shafts, more carefully this time, aimed for the daemon's eyes but neither shot hit the mark, both bouncing from the creature's skull. Leo raced to where the sword had landed. Only the lion hilt and the tiniest sliver of blade remained intact and when he held it, the weapon no longer glowed. In his hand the sword felt dull and heavy- ordinary. Leo looked up and saw Balthus swiped by the creature's tail and sent spinning to the floor. Then the beast looked to Zarina, firing lines of dark energy from its mouth. Zarina countered with a blazing light of her own and Leo watched as the light and dark met in streams of liquid magic, showering sparks onto the desert floor.

First Zarina's light seemed to be pushing the Zullifskag's magic back but then the priestess screamed with effort and the dark began to drive her back. The daemon cackled and soon the darkness had nearly won. Leo brandished all that was left of the Star Sword and raced towards the creature holding the ruined blade aloft.

"Zarina! Light the sword!" he screamed.

She glanced to him and nodded and with a final effort sent a bolt of light magic that struck the fractured blade. Leo leapt, holding the sword in a reverse grip, and stabbed it high into the Zullifskag's neck and wrenched downwards opening a deep, ragged cut that leaked a sickly, dark ooze. The daemon screamed and thrashed from side to side, forgetting its duel with Zarina, who struck it a mighty blow with her magic. As she did, Balthus leapt up, nimbly pulling himself onto its back, before mounting its head. With a shout he swung his axe in a murderous arc and buried the weapon into the monster's right eye.

Roaring in pain and partly blinded, the Zullifskag swiped blindly at the giant warrior, catching him with a vicious blow with its forepaw. Balthus was hurled from its back and landed hard, struggling to rise. Leo dragged the star fragment clear and rolled directly under the beast's neck and drove the failing weapon upwards into its jugular. The creature gurgled, thrashed once more then fell to the sand, nearly crushing Leo in the process. The beast let out two long, deep breaths then drew quiet.

In the aftermath and silence that followed the four looked at each other in shock trying to compose themselves.

"Come," said Zarina. "Let us get to shelter. Others will come."

Both Leo's and Balthus' horses had bolted and it was a tiring slog for both of them to reach the safety and shade of the cliffs where Samla and Zarina waited. It was with some shock that Leo looked back at one point and saw that Balthus was some metres behind him. He dropped back to help the warrior, but Balthus shooed him away.

"Just need to catch my breath," the giant gasped, his voice ragged. Leo tried not to look concerned at the blood spilling from the warrior's side.

Leo ran ahead to tell Zarina when, still some one hundred metres behind, Balthus let out a cry and collapsed. Together they managed to lift the General's massive form onto the back of Samla's horse and carry him into the shade.

Bringing him down from the saddle as gently as they could Zarina checked his wound and looked at Leo gravely. "The daemon's claws have cut deep."

"Can you heal him?" Leo asked, moving to kneel beside Balthus. "We have supplies don't we? Herbs? Medicine?"

Balthus caught Leo's arm in an iron grip. "I'm dying Leo, let it be."

"No, no you're not," said Leo. "Nothing can kill you. It's just a scratch, right?"

Zarina shook her head sadly. "The wound is deep and infected with darkness. He does not have long."

"Bring me my axe," Balthus said, his voice still firm and Leo realised they had left the weapon in the desert where the giant had fallen. Leo ran to it, tears beginning to blur his vision. It took him frustrating moments to find it and he struggled to carry the mighty weapon back to where Balthus lay.

The giant was still when Leo returned and for a terrible moment Leo thought he had slipped away.

Then Balthus spoke, his voice pitiably weak. "Do you have it?"

"I have it," said Leo pressing it in the warrior's hands.

Balthus closed his fingers about the haft and pulled the weapon to his chest. "You should go now. I need a little rest then I will make my stand and fight off whatever comes. Buy you some time."

"What are you talking about, we're not going to leave you!" Leo said, the anguish in his voice evident.

Zarina placed a gentle hand on Leo's and whispered in his ear. "He cannot rise, he has no strength. Do not rob him of his pride. He does not want us to see him like this."

Leo nodded, choking back tears as he looked at the fear in Balthus' eyes and was surprised when Balthus took his hand in the warrior's grip.

"Thank you for being my friend," said Leo.

"Thank you for being mine," said Balthus. The giant managed one last chuckle. "In the end it was an honour," he said.

The two men nodded and Leo rose and turned away so the proud man would not see his tears.

Zarina knelt by Balthus then, kissing his brow. "You are as true and good a friend as anyone could ever wish for. There is nothing for a man who has lived as fully as you to fear in what comes now." Then she stood and walked away.

Samla said nothing, exchanging one last look with the great warrior before turning her back and following the others.

Leo was in shock as they squeezed through the rocky canyons, leading their remaining two horses behind them. He found himself constantly scanning their back trail, childishly hoping to see Balthus risen and striding after them, somehow recovered.

"The cave entrance is not far," said Samla. "We will make it."

"No, we will not," said Zarina. "I fear that without Balthus we cannot fight our way through the tunnels - and the enemy draws near."

"What do you mean?" asked Leo. "Nothing is following us."

Samla scoffed. "She is right. Look again: the high pass to the right."

Leo scanned upwards and first saw nothing, but then a shadow darted from one patch of darkness to another.

"Krylla," said Zarina, "and plenty of them. They have been following for some time."

Leo shivered. He remembered the insectoid monstrosities well from when they had tried to trap him as he recovered from his fight in the arena. He remembered with shame how he had fled. That all seemed such a long time ago now.

"What can we do?" Leo asked.

"There is only one chance now," said Zarina. "We must walk the River of Souls."

"Isn't that like walking into the lion's den?" Leo asked. "The Old Mother said that the River was death for any mortal."

"She only said that because no mortal has ever walked through it and lived," said Zarina.

"Well that's comforting," Leo said.

"It is a place where people face their worst nightmares," said Samla.

"You see?" Leo urged Zarina. "How can we contend with that? We don't even have the Star Sword."

The priestess stopped and turned slowly, her face unusually cold and distant. "My worst nightmares have already come true. The love of my life has died alone and I could not help him. My two best friends have been slain and my greatest enemy has sacked my home and the whole world is falling into ruin. Whatever lies inside the River, it cannot be as bad as that."

Leo's words stuck in his mouth and he did not know what to say. Zarina continued. "And you now know what your worst nightmare is, you have remembered it. We are uniquely placed to be the first to pass through the River and live. Even through suffering the Essence provides."

But for the first time Leo felt that even Zarina did not truly believe her own words.

"I do not know if I can face my nightmare again," said Leo.

"Perhaps you will not need to. I have walked other dark places before," said Zarina. "I was alone then, never protecting others, but I can supply us with some protection."

"Can the Krylla follow us?" Leo asked.

"I hope they do. When Amad El defeated Zallandex at the last Scourging he cast a powerful spell that trapped much of the Lich's army in a prison of time, exiling them to torment. Zallandex did not have the power left to counter the spell and abandoned his servants. Because of this the creatures trapped in the time barrier blame Zallandex for deserting them. They are mad, lost and deprived and they lash out at everything, especially minions of the dark who they consider traitors," said Zarina.

"The enemy of your enemy…" said Samla.

"Is still our enemy!" Leo finished

"Yes," smiled Zarina. "But with the Essence with us, the daemons in the River will attack the Krylla first and give us enough time to slip through."

Leo fell silent. He had no arguments against the plan, after all what alternative was there now? Even so the idea of walking into a realm filled with daemons sent pangs of terror racing up and down his spine.

Samla led them on before stopping abruptly, pointing to a series of rocks painted blue on one side. "Our people have marked the edge of the barrier; it is not good to wander in by accident. A few hundred feet beyond is the River of Souls."

Zarina turned to Leo. "I have told you what I think, but if you still wish to attempt the other path, we can."

"Why are you asking me?" said Leo. "I know less than you."

"We have spoken of this already," said Zarina. "This is your plan, it always has been. Now we are close to the end, one way or another. I think we should pass through the River but I leave it to you. Do we risk the open desert again and the tunnels under the earth or take this route? It is your choice."

"I am not the one to decide something like this," Leo protested.

"That is the old you talking," said Zarina. "They are not the words of the man I have seen you become. By the stars, you just slew a Zullifskag."

"It was luck," said Leo. "Just luck. It was distracted."

"Perhaps. But was all of it just luck?" said Zarina. "Was it luck when you saved my life? Is it luck that you have stood with courage when most would have run? Is it luck that you were picked for this and despite Nemeddes' best efforts that you have made it this far?

I am not omniscient Leo. Perhaps for you the universe is just pure chaos and chance – but then perhaps it is not. Perhaps for you it is time to believe in something a little more. Either way, you must make a choice."

Leo took a deep breath. "You are right, we cannot defend ourselves in the desert; Balthus is gone, the Star Sword is gone. We cannot outrun what pursues us for long either. So I agree with you, we will take the River of Souls."

"Then let us hurry," said Zarina. "Stay close to me."

"This is as far as I go," said Samla. "I will not go in there."

"What of the Krylla?" asked Leo.

"I will take my chances in the caves. I am not easy prey," said the scout. "The Essence go with you."

"We must stick together," said Leo. "Tell her, Zarina."

But Samla was already walking away.

"She has made her choice," said Zarina. "Let us finish this."

29.

Zarina moved a few feet beyond the blue painted rocks and sat down. "I need a little time to prepare," she said.

"Should we find cover?" Leo asked.

The priestess shook her head. "I will prepare here, that way if we need to we can run into the River if we are pursued."

Leo nodded and sat beside her. "I am sorry about Balthus. I can't believe he's gone, he seemed invincible."

"I know," Zarina smiled. "The amount of times Athus would tell me about how reckless Balthus was. Athus thought it a miracle the man was still alive. Apparently, once, he charged alone into a half century of Kryxian berserkers. Athus gave chase of course with the Sunchasers, but Balthus stood alone for over a minute completely surrounded. When Athus arrived Balthus was latticed in cuts over his whole body. Athus called for a healer and Balthus stopped him at once."

Leo grinned from ear to ear. "Did he say it?"

"Yes," smiled Zarina, making her voice as deep and rough as she could: "I don't need a healer, it's just a scratch."

Leo laughed and the mood lifted a little. "A shame Samla did not come with us."

"It does not matter," said Zarina. "Either we will fail and the world will fall to Nemeddes, or we will succeed and this world will cease to be."

"What do you mean?" Leo asked shocked. "I thought we were fighting to save it."

"In a way, yes. If we can get you to the Temple then you will be able to go back to the time before Athus was killed, before you made your pact. The Lich would not have dared move his armies south while Athus lived. Nemeddes fears Athus terribly. The whole series of events that have occurred from then to now, well they will simply not have happened."

"And what of this world, now?" Leo asked. "What of all the people? They can't surely just disappear?" Leo asked.

"This will never have happened. They will not die, not disappear, they never will have been - this world will be replaced," Zarina corrected. "Replaced with a world where Nemeddes is not on the brink of victory."

"What will happen to us?" Leo asked.

"We will have to cross that bridge when we come to it," said Zarina. "Now I need some quiet while I focus my strength."

As they journeyed into the River of Souls at first there was little change. The air was perhaps slightly denser but other than that they could have been anywhere in the desert. As they moved deeper though, it became evident that this was a place of magic. Leo's jaw dropped when he glanced to his right and saw a ghostly phalanx of armed soldiers rushing up the dunes. The men were clearly shouting to each other but Leo could hear no sound.

"Try to pay it no mind," said Zarina. "You are seeing fragments from the battle that ended the last Scourging. They cannot see us; they are just ghosts, like the light that burns in your eyes after staring at the sun."

Leo nodded in awe as a host of cavalry charged past them, their spectral pennants rippling even though there was no breeze.

"Stay close to me," said Zarina, creating a bubble of light around them. "We are passing the point of ghosts and entering an area of danger. Do not step outside of the light, no matter what occurs."

The sorceress led on and the landscape began to falter and change with every footfall, becoming something alien and out of time. The yellow sand darkened to ash and now all around the ghostly battle raged. Daemons and warriors threw themselves at each other locked for all eternity in a battle that had ended more than a thousand years before.

"This was where the forces of the Sapphire King failed," said Zarina, leading them through the carnage. She pointed ahead to where a line of cavalry were routed and scores of daemons chased them down, falling on them with murderous rage. "The light would have receded then if not for Amad El."

"Who was he?" Leo asked, glancing about as if hoping to get a view of the great hero.

"Like all legends, no one truly knows," Zarina spoke. "A sorcerer, most likely, but some tales say he was a warrior also. Some say as the line broke he fought his way to Zallandex and cut him down. Others say that he cast the spell that trapped the Daemon horde in the River of Souls. It is doubtful anyone knows the complete truth."

"When Nemeddes came to me at Samla's village, he seemed to know," said Leo. "But then, wasn't he supposed to be here?"

"Yes," said Zarina. "Nemeddes watched the fall of his master Zallandex the Invincible. It seems he has learned nothing from what he witnessed."

"Zallandex the Invincible?" Leo asked. "How do you defeat someone called that?"

"With difficulty," said Zarina, guiding them up another dune. "But Amad El found a way. Be careful now," the priestess said pointing ahead.

Leo looked to where she indicated, seeing a series of huge chasms pockmarking the ground. The way that lay between them was narrow and dangerous.

"So far so good," Leo said as the two of them began to pick their way over the uneven ground.

"Do not speak so soon," said Zarina. "So far we have seen only the ghosts of those who died in here. Daemons do not age and die as men do, some of them will still live."

Almost on cue Leo heard a screech and looked upwards to see dark shapes, like huge bats circling above and howling like banshees.

"Ignore them," said Zarina. "Stay close to me, my faith shield will hold them back."

Even as she spoke several of the bat-like daemons dived at them, hitting the protective aura of energy Zarina was projecting. The creatures, horrible things with large, leathery wings and vicious, serrated hind legs and tails, screamed as they hit the barrier, before flying upwards again calling to one another. Zarina took a deep breath and pushed on.

The daemons continued to circle above, more cautious now and the companions made it to the top of a small rise.

"There it is!" said Leo pointing. Ahead was the majestic site of Table Rock and at the top stood a temple of alabaster and ebony crowned with gold.

"Yes," said Zarina. "The Temple of Time."

Leo looked to her alarmed at how weary her voice was. "Are you alright?"

"It is more fatiguing than I imagined," she admitted.

Leo moved to her and looped her arm around his neck. "Come on," he said. "We are nearly there."

They made it across two more rises before the flying daemons chanced a second attack. Like moths to a flame they swooped down, smashing into Zarina's golden barrier. They were immediately repelled and sent flying back into the dark heavens, but Zarina grunted with exhaustion every time the barrier was struck. Then, perhaps sensing her weariness, the winged creatures swooped down en masse, droves of them all hammering into the barrier. The sorceress screamed out in anguish, trickles of blood running from her nose and mouth – but the shield held.

Leo scooped the priestess into his arms and began to run but even as he did he knew it was too far. The shield would not survive another attack like that. Then, with a chittering screech, another threat crested a dune to their left and in a formation that must have numbered at least one hundred, a legion of Krylla scuttled forward.

Leo pushed his legs harder, staggering in the loose sand. He watched the Krylla come on, their four insect-like legs skimming over the blackened earth faster than any man could hope to run. His legs were burning now and they were gaining fast.

Above, the bat daemons howled again, afraid their prey was being stolen and they dived at the Krylla, smashing into their ordered charge, hacking and slashing with their serrated tails and powerful hind legs. The Krylla fought back, scything at their swooping kin with their pincers and claws. As Leo struggled on, holding Zarina tightly, another wave of the bat creatures attacked the faith shield which pulsed now with only a fraction of its previous vibrancy. One landed on top of the shield itself, scrabbling on its surface. Leo heard its flesh sizzle and the daemon howled but did not fly away. It lashed out at the field, scratching it with its claws and then lifted its tail and drove it downwards. The shield cracked and shattered like glass, shards of golden light flying in all directions, scattering the monsters closest by. Leo was punched from his feet. He rose, struggling to reach the fallen body of Zarina, but a choking black swarm of energy flowed into his mouth when he tried to breathe and where there should have been air there was only darkness. Falling to his knees he crawled towards Zarina but suddenly he could not see and his strength left him and choking, he collapsed.

Zarina rolled to her back as a bat daemon screeched out of the sky towards her. She blasted a bolt of light into it and it shrieked and wheeled away. She heard Leo convulsing nearby, choking on the unholy air and with a mighty surge of strength reformed the faith shield about them.

The battle outside raged on, the Krylla and the bats locked in a titanic struggle, the ground heaped with corpses from both sides. But the bats had the advantage of numbers and for a moment it looked like they would win. Then, with fear gnawing at her, she saw a Krylla Alpha appear on a nearby ridge. With a cry it led another contingent of its fellows to strike into the bats, shattering their formation. Zarina watched the massive Krylla, larger by a foot than any of its companions, as it decapitated two of the bats and with a mighty leap, bounded onto another, snapping it in two.

A cry of terror rose up from the remaining bats and the rest of them took off, flying high and away. The Krylla finished off any wounded and led by their Alpha began sidling up the hill towards Zarina. The priestess gathered Leo to her, put his head on her lap and softly soothed his hair. "Come on Leo," she whispered. "We have come so far, do not give up now."

But Leo did not respond, just shook as he was lost to his own nightmares.

The Krylla advanced, surrounding the faith shield. The Alpha approached and held his head to the edge of the light. It was different from the others, not just larger but its face was somehow more humanoid. Its outer jaws slid back and Zarina shivered as they revealed a human mouth, somehow hideously placed below the daemon's monstrous head. Two clusters of beady, red eyes stared at Zarina intently.

"This is the dying of the light, witch..." it hissed with its perverse human lips. As it spoke it scraped one large chitinous claw along the barrier. Sparks flew. "You do not have the power to protect yourself from us for long. We will wait. We have all the time in the world."

Zarina stared defiantly at the beast, but lacked the strength to reply.

30.

He was running again. Running in darkness. Sweat poured down his body and dripped from his face but he ran on. His legs were racing, desperately trying to get away from something, desperately forging forwards. Ahead of him, somewhere always ahead, a child's cries echoed in this shadowy realm and then...

Then the shouting started again suddenly and he pushed his face deep into his blanket, his hand tightening around the pebble his mother had taken from the sea and painted for him. He said his prayers. If he said them just right sometimes the shouting would stop. But only if he said them just so and only if he squeezed the pebble just right and only if he pushed his head into his blanket in just the right way.

And then the shouting did stop. Normally this made Leo feel happy but tonight Leo felt no joy. Because it never stopped like that. Not abruptly. It petered off, diminished, shrank – but it never just stopped.

He finished praying and sat up, a strange sense of fear he could not consciously identify in his heart. Suddenly an image of his mother filled his mind. It was strange. Even though he had only seen her that afternoon, he longed to see her, almost as though he hadn't set eyes on her for years. His legs and back itched from the belt marks, from the beatings and he suddenly felt very confused and alone. He knew he was a bad boy, a worthless boy, and a little mummy's cry baby - his father had said so many times - but he needed to see his mother so badly it pushed past his fear and despite knowing that when he came out he would be beaten again. He just needed to see her.

He sat still for some moments gathering his courage to him before he began to move. Carefully he left the crawl space and crept down the stairs from the hayloft. He reached the bottom and still there was silence from the house. Carefully he tiptoed across the cobbles in the yard. The sun had completely gone down and the only light shone from the open kitchen doorway ahead. He was still some thirty metres away when he heard the snarl, his heart leaping in his chest. His father, drunk again, had left Zack off his lead. The old hound growled again somewhere in the darkness and Leo began to run towards the light from the open door. He heard the dog's paws on the cobbles behind him as he ran on in the darkness. Zack was an old thing now and slow, but it stank and Leo was terrified of it. He could hear his father's mocking voice telling him one day he would let old Zack have some fun with him and rag him around before it had Leo for its tea.

He raced on with fear of what was before him and what was behind. Every second he waited for a gummy bite to his heels as he closed in on the doorway. Its light shone like a beacon and without thought he ran through it, slamming the door behind him.

The kitchen was almost normal, warm and homely. It was his mother's place, his father rarely came here. A plate of tuna fish sandwiches sat on the side – his supper. Next to them sat the carefully folded laundry. He loved the smell of it when it was fresh. It smelled of her clothes. But there was another sight that took all his attention. His father was standing over his mother, pushing her head into a bucket of water. She struggled with all her strength, clawing at the floorboards with her hands and pushing with her feet and slipping on the slick boards.

His father looked up from his work and snarled as the kitchen door slammed shut. His large hands brought forth a knife and Leo watched with dread fascination as the pearl handle glistened as he held it above his head.

Pain wracked every inch of Zarina's body. She bit her lips, holding the barrier in place while the Krylla paced around casually striking it with their talons and claws. Blood flowed from her nose with the exertion of maintaining the barrier and large cracks began to spread around the surface of the faith shield.

"Careful," their leader hissed. "Don't break it; let her suffer a little longer. She knows what waits for her when her strength fails. She is nearly spent."

Zarina screamed in pain as the Alpha stabbed his claw into the shield again, sending waves of dark energy pulsing into the decaying barrier.

"Your pain is delicious to me child of light," it said as it scored down the barrier again with its talons.

This time it was too much and with an anguished sob both Zarina and the barrier collapsed. The Krylla leader did not rush forwards but slowly watched, allowing his minions to scuttle nearer and poke at Zarina with their sharp claws, slicing and scratching her skin whilst they chittered to each other. Zarina pushed herself up to all fours and tried to stand but the Alpha stepped forward and caught her neck in one of its powerful pincers, dragging her up to stare into its insectoid eyes.

The Krylla around her chittered excitedly as their leader's long, leathery tongue flickered against her face. The stench of it was foul and she tried not to wretch. She felt one of its bladed forelegs trace its way up her thigh and stop at her side, the point pressing into her flesh, then with infinite cruelty the beast held her in place and slowly, fraction by agonising fraction, eased the blade into her, breaking her skin and sliding it deep beneath her ribs.

Zarina let out a tormented scream, tasting blood in her throat, and as she did so the beast thrust forth its tongue, stabbing it into her mouth. All around its fellow creatures showed their amusement. It held her there for a long moment, enjoying her humiliation, before it hurled her to the floor. Blood seeped freely from the open wound in her flank and sank into the black earth.

"No good deed goes unpunished," it hissed at her. "And you have done so many. And here you are, at the end, alone in darkness. What a reward for your years of purity. Breaking you is going to be the honour of my life, witch. Do you have any last words before I begin?"

Zarina's hand slipped into a pocket of her robe and fastened tight around the blue brooch Athus had won for her. Seeing her movement, the monster seized her hand in its pincer and drew it forth. The brooch spilled from her grip onto the black sand at the creature's feet.

Zarina looked at the brooch, and pushing back tears looked into the mass of tiny red dots that were the Krylla's eyes. "I forgive you for what you will do," she said. "You know no better."

The beast threw back its head and laughed, its fellows joining in with their chittering cries. "How noble of you! We will see how long that spirit lasts when you finally accept you are alone and abandoned."

Zarina's head sank and she felt all hope leave her. Her eyes blurred with tears as she looked to the blue brooch lying between the monster's feet. She waited for the creature to move, accidently crushing it to fragments.

The Krylla followed her gaze. "Welcome to your darkest hour, witch. Trinkets will not save you now."

"But I will," came a powerful voice.

The leader span around and Zarina looked up. The rest of the daemons nervously turned to face the newcomer. Then Zarina saw them relax, as only one spirit approached.

"Leave this woman alone and go," the spirit commanded.

"Or what?" cackled the leader. At that moment the spirit hurled a spectral knife that punched through the Alpha Krylla's mass of eyes and laid the beast low. The others jumped, scattering like startled cats, and the ghost casually walked forward and retrieved his blade from the fallen brute. "Is that a clear enough answer?" the spirit asked the others.

A Krylla circled and quickly tried to skewer Zarina's saviour but the man sidestepped and parried the thrust with ease before cutting the daemon down. "Obviously not," he commented.

The others fell back then and the man moved to Zarina.

"At first I didn't recognise you," she said, tears streaming down her face freely.

"Did you think I would abandon you my love," the spirit said, picking up the blue brooch and pressing it into Zarina's hand. "I promised you I would always be there."

"I didn't know what to think," Zarina cried, throwing her arms around him. The spirit of Athus held her tight and for the first time since his passing she allowed herself to grieve, her body shaking with emotion. He said nothing but placed his spectral hand to her side and she felt healing energy flow into the wound, feeling her pain lessen even as she saw him diminish.

"I do not have long," he said in answer to her unspoken question. "Your wound is grave. We will be together soon in any event."

She nodded, allowing him to steady her while he scooped up Leo, slinging him over one shoulder. "Come let us move to somewhere easier to defend," said Athus.

Another Krylla flew at the swordsman, thinking him unable to defend whilst bearing Leo, but Athus parried the beast's talon and cut its head clean off with a precise counter cut. Now, more wary, the other daemons fell back allowing Athus to lead Zarina onwards towards the grand steps that led to Table Rock. When they reached the foot of the steps he lowered Leo to the floor and helped Zarina sit.

"Am I right in saying he cannot leave here like this?" Athus asked, gesturing to Leo.

"His soul must awaken or it will remain trapped here," Zarina confirmed.

Athus re-drew his long knife and looked out over the growing sea of daemons appearing before them. "Can we help him?"

"The problem is deep within himself. He will either conquer whatever torments him, or remain trapped where he is forever," said Zarina.

"He will overcome it," said Athus. "He is a good man."

Zarina nodded. "Yes, he is."

Four daemons flew forward and Athus danced amongst them, slaying them in seconds. Again the others fell back, but new monsters were joining their ranks with every moment. "Let us just hope he does not take too long," Athus observed.

31.

Leo stood helpless while his father held his mother's head below the water, that dreaded knife still clutched above his head.

"Watch what happens when people speak back to me!" his father growled.

Leo felt emotions attacking him from all sides, dragging him downwards... fear... terror... weakness... why didn't he do something? He felt himself lose control of his bladder, felt shame and despair. He covered his eyes with his hands and peeking through the gaps, as if in slow motion, his father brought the knife down, down, down towards his mother's neck.

Suddenly a strange thought hit the eight year old boy, his hands... they were not a child's hands. He took them from his eyes and saw they were large and lined with use. A man's hands. The memory fractured and he was drawn back and away from himself. He saw his childlike body from the outside as the boy he had been stood cowering and afraid. But no longer was the boy alone.

Leo Kvetch, the man, was now in the room behind the boy. In an instant Leo surged forward pushing his father back, sending him tumbling and pulled his mother from the water. She coughed and spluttered and he held her to him, putting himself between his father, his childish self and his mother. She looked at him and somehow knowing who he was, smiled.

"I am sorry I didn't stop him," Leo said, tears bursting from his eyes.

"You were just a boy," his mother said, stroking his face. "There is nothing to forgive."

Leo glanced to where the boy stood; his tufty, red hair shaggy and ridiculous. "You are not me," Leo said aloud. "You are not me; you are like a younger brother ... a son."

Then, compassion filling him, Leo moved to the lad, still holding his mother tightly and touched the boy on the shoulder. The boy looked afraid but Leo smiled kindly at him. "It's ok," said Leo. "You do not need to be afraid. I am here now."

"Get away from them you waste of space!" his father's voice snarled.

Leo turned towards the memory of the man who had tormented him both in life and death for so many years. His eyes went to the knife in his father's hand, the knife he had seen held before him in every unremembered nightmare. He relived hearing his father threaten to gut him, to cut pieces off him, to feed him to the dog. For the last time, for a split second Leo felt fear looking on that man holding that knife – then his fear fell away forever.

Through his adult eyes the man before him was not the man he remembered. He was not powerful and strong, but greasy and tired looking. He was not some giant monster, but a full head shorter than Leo had become, his arms spindly and weak; his gut full and lazy. And the knife... nothing but a simple, kitchen knife with a shiny handle.

"I said get away from them you pathetic mistake!" his father howled again, curling his lip in a way he thought must look threatening.

Leo felt the boy grab onto his leg and cling there in terror. Gently Leo patted the boy's hands and detached him before stepping away from his mother.

"Get away from them!" his father howled, desperation in his voice.

"I do not think so," said Leo. "The time of you giving orders here is over."

"What? What did you say to me?" his father raged.

"You heard me, your power over me is gone and your time is at an end," said Leo.

"I'll gut you like a fish..." his father threatened.

"Then do it if you can," challenged Leo. "Or just stand and make your cowardly threats. There is no longer a place in me for your poison to enter."

"You good for nothing, I won't take you talking to me like this!" his father screamed - but he took a step back.

"I love you father," said Leo. "All boys love their fathers, even the fathers who don't deserve it. I wish you had been a better man. I wish you had been the father I wanted, but I forgive you, you were afraid and alone and scared, I understand that now. I forgive you for your weakness."

"I was not weak! Don't you dare say that to me!" his father spat, almost shrinking at the words.

Leo stepped forward and reached out with his hands, seeing them begin to glow with golden light. "I forgive you," Leo repeated. "I forgive you."

"Stop saying that!" the old man screamed, flinching away.

Leo took two quick steps and took hold of his father, embracing him. "I forgive you," he said, taking his father's head and kissing his brow. "Rest now and find the peace in death you could not find in life."

A look of shock passed over his father's face, then with a spark of blazing energy the knife in his hand began to dissolve. Soon the light spread up his father's arms and into his body then with a flash he was gone.

Leo moved to his mother. She was so beautiful, her red hair hanging in shimmering waves.

"My brave boy," she said with a soft smile. "My brave boy, I'm so proud of you. Look how strong you have become."

Leo embraced her, tears running freely down his face. "I miss you so much," he sobbed. "I love you so much."

"I love you too my son," she whispered. "I will always love you."

The roof of the small house ripped open and light blazed in bathing everything in its radiance as the dream began to break down.

"I don't want to go," Leo screamed to her. "I want to stay here with you."

"You must go Leo, you have to."

"I don't want to be without you again," he cried.

"Silly boy," she smiled, wiping his tears. "You will never be without me."

With that his mother's form splintered into a honeycomb of blinding segments that broke outwards into golden particles and flowed inside Leo.

The walls of the house were torn away and a rushing, deafening wind began to erase the edges of the dream. In moments the farmhouse was nearly gone. Leo looked around for the boy but he was not there. Leo knew instinctively where he would run and rushed across what was left of the yard. Sprinting into the barn he raced up the steps towards the hayloft and the crawl space.

"Leave me alone!" the boy shouted, his head peering out of the small gap in the back wall.

Leo made to reply but as he did half the barn was torn away, leaving what was left floating in the blackness of nothing. Leo span in space holding onto what was left of the stairs and watched as the hayloft began to drift away from him.

"Take my hand!" Leo shouted, leaning out into the void, his fingers outstretched.

"Why should I?" the boy asked. "Who are you?"

"I am the man you will become," Leo replied. "Now jump, I will catch you."

"I can't do it, I'm scared," the boy wailed.

Another gust tore through the dream world, nearly blowing Leo into the growing abyss. All that was left of their home now was a fragment of spinning stairs and a tiny portion of the hayloft.

"You can do it!" Leo called. "I believe in you! You have it in you to be the best of men, but you must face your fear and jump now!"

"Why are you here, why are you doing this?" the boy shrieked as the space between them began to grow.

"Because I love you, Leo, because I love you so much," the adult called. "Jump now and I will catch you - I promise."

The boy nodded and climbing to his feet ran and leapt screaming into the void. Leo pushed himself from the stairs and they met, Leo grabbing the lad and they both tumbled together, spinning through nothingness.

Leo looked at the boy and grinned. "You're safe now, you're with me and no one will ever hurt you again." The boy smiled with joy and nodded. For a moment, both of them drifted alone and at peace in the emptiness and then each began to glow and merge into a single ball of golden light and then... Leo woke up.

Leo opened his eyes to look on Zarina's tired and worried face.

"I did it," he said dreamily. "I stopped him and I saved them all."

She smiled and stroked his hair. "Well done Leo. We knew you would."

"We?" Leo asked sitting up.

Zarina pointed. At the base of the steps stood the ghost of a man. He was tall and lean. His back was to them and in one hand he held a long, spectral knife. At his feet lay at least two score of daemon corpses. Leo knew who it was in an instant.

"Athus..." Leo whispered. "He's here."

"Yes," said Zarina proudly, the love in her voice evident. "When things were darkest, he came just like he promised he always would."

Leo watched as Athus countered the next attack, dispatching another daemon before turning. "Ah you're awake. Really, I would love to do this all day but if you could find it in yourself to hurry..."

Leo arose at once, seeing for the first time the blood on Zarina's robes and helping her to rise.

"Are you well?" he asked alarmed.

Her face told him what he dreaded. "I have enough strength to finish this adventure," she said. "But I will need your help to climb the stairs."

"Of course," said Leo.

Athus joined them and Leo found himself staring in the face of the man he had heard so much about.

"I don't know what to say..." Leo began.

"There is nothing that needs to be said," replied Athus and the spirit offered his hand. Leo took it in the warrior's grip.

"You have done well, Leo Kvetch. Now you must see this through," The Champion said.

Leo nodded and Athus leaned in and kissed Zarina tenderly. "We will be together soon my Lady," he said. "Forever."

A deafening roar came from behind them and they all turned. A huge daemon was approaching, swelled with the power from this dark place. It was twice the size of the Zullifskag Leo had helped slay.

A grim smile spread across Athus' face and for the first time he drew his own Star Sword. Even in its spectral form it shone like a beacon of light far brighter than ever it had when Leo had held it.

"At last, a worthy opponent," Athus said walking to meet the monstrosity, and the tide of daemons at the base of the steps fell back before him in fear and awe.

"Before you go... what is it like?" Zarina called after him.

He turned then and smiled. "It is everything you have ever hoped my love. And so much more."

Then the hero Athus Glynn turned back and the sea of monsters closed about him.

32.

It was a slow climb up the stone steps towards the Temple and Zarina grunted in pain with every footfall. Leo supported her and together they passed to the edge of the River of Souls, the sand losing its blackened colour and becoming golden once more. Within a few steps the river fell away completely and the steps were no longer definable, just old hunks of rock, jagged and weathered by the ages. Together they struggled on, Zarina weakening with every moment.

"Just a little further," he said. "When we get to the Temple they will be able to heal you."

Zarina smiled and nodded but did not reply.

Leo's heart had sunk before they even reached the summit. It had been obvious for some time that the towering Temple of black, white and gold was not there. What they had seen from the bottom of the steps had been no more than a mirage, the Temple preserved as it had looked a thousand years ago. Yet he had hoped that something remained in their time, he had been sure that some remnant would be there, hidden from their view, some ruin… something… anything.

Both of them were exhausted when they reached the top and Leo helped Zarina to sit on the highest step, then trying to control his emotions he began scouring the surface of Table Rock. He looked calmly for several minutes hoping to find some secret door or hidden fissure but there was nothing; nothing but rubble, scorched stones and the howling wind.

Dejected he moved back to Zarina and sat beside her. "There is nothing here," he sighed. "Nothing."

Zarina did not reply and he followed her gaze to the horizon. In the distance the sky was darkening, the blue being invaded by streams of inky blackness.

"What is that?" he asked.

"The Scourging," she said. "It has begun."

They sat in silence and watched as the darkness spread into the sky, rushing towards them. Beneath them at the foot of the Temple steps Krylla began to march out of the River of Souls and scuttle upwards.

"Where is The Temple, why is it not here?" Leo asked. "I had started to believe."

"It is not here because it is not here," she said.

"What do you mean? Has this all been for nothing?"

She slapped him then, hard, and Leo looked at her shocked. "What was that for?"

"Because when we first met you did not know better. Now such a question is beneath you. Even if all falls to darkness, how can you ask that? Look at the man you have become. How can any of this have been for nothing?" Zarina asked.

"A whole world for me to become a better man? That is too high a price," said Leo.

"Is it?" Zarina mused. "I do not know. But after all that has happened, how is it you still have so little faith?"

Leo gestured to the darkening sky that was eating up the blue of the heavens. "Does that not answer enough? And they are coming," he said frustrated, pointing down the steps to where the Krylla were slowly and confidently making their ascent. "Nemeddes is coming. The world is ending and you... you are dying ... and I don't know what to do."

Zarina pointed to where the sun's light was fighting a losing battle against the growing darkness. "Does the light yet remain?"

"Yes, but it is shrinking," said Leo.

"Then we are not yet out of time," said Zarina.

"But what do we do?" Leo urged.

"Nothing," said Zarina, her voice far away. "We have done our work and done it well. For now just sit, just be still. Feel the life in your lungs. Feel the rock beneath you. Feel the tingling in your fingertips, feel the hairs on your head touched by the breeze, feel that *aliveness* deep within you. There is no more to be done."

"But..." he began, but the priestess waved him into silence.

"Are you still so self absorbed and conceited to think that the universe needs *you* to do a single thing? Perhaps, if you try, you can accept the possibility that at this very moment the universe does not need Leo Kvetch to do anything on its behalf."

Leo sat for a few moments shaking his head. "I can't accept that."

"This is time magic Leo, and there is a time for everything, for being ahead and for being behind, for working and for resting, for doing and for non-doing, for living and for dying." Zarina smiled. "Be still, it will come. The Essence provides."

Leo sat with the priestess and watched the growing dark in silence in what must have been the longest, most present moments of his life. And then, almost as if Zarina's faith had willed it, with a brief flash of light The Temple appeared not thirty foot from where they sat.

Leo leapt to his feet. "It's here!"

"Yes," Zarina smiled. "Now go and do what you must."

Leo ran over the rocky ground to where the huge fortress now stood, heading for the large, gilded doors. He was ten foot away when the shadow of Nemeddes appeared before him.

"You are just a shadow," Leo said but found himself ground to a halt nonetheless.

"That is true," Nemeddes replied. "But I still have a voice."

Leo took a wide berth around the Lich's apparition and walked to the doors of the Temple of Time.

"Do not be hasty Leo," the Lich smiled. "Let us talk a while. Would you like Zarina? It is obvious you care deeply for her."

"I don't want anything from you," said Leo, mounting the first step before the entrance.

"There must be something you want," Nemeddes offered, his voice like that of an old, caring friend. "Tell me Leo and it's yours."

Leo knocked on the wooden doors.

"I have Rebecca, Leo. I will drown her in front of you if you do not stop!" Nemeddes roared.

"You do not have her," said Leo without looking around. "If you did you would prove it."

"No, you are right, it was a lie," the Lich spoke, forcing some levity back into his voice. "They were hasty words. I will give you anything you desire, just name it. There must be something. There is always something."

"I don't want anything from anyone anymore," said Leo. "Everything I need I have always possessed."

"My servants will be here soon and they will feast on your marrow," Nemeddes snarled and then disappeared.

A moment later the doors to The Temple opened and a lone mage stood in the doorway wearing robes of deep ochre. He was young, his head tightly shorn and he smiled warmly. "Welcome Leo Kvetch. We are glad you could make it. Are you ready?"

"Nearly," said Leo. "I just need to go back and bring my friend."

The mage shook his head. "I'm afraid it has long been arranged that only you will travel with us."

"But..." Leo began.

"Do you understand the rudimentary practicalities of time and space travel?" the mage asked.

"No," snapped Leo.

"There is little point explaining them now. You and you alone will travel. That is the deal that was struck," the mage said.

"And who made this deal?" Leo demanded.

"That is none of your concern," said the mage. "Now these doors are going to close in a little over one minute. If you have goodbyes, now is the time."

Leo raced back over the ground to Zarina, noting as he sank down close to her how much nearer the Scourging had come. Soon only a tiny portion of blue sky would remain over Table Rock.

Leo glanced down the steps. "Why have the Krylla stopped?"

"They are waiting for Nemeddes," said Zarina.

"He is coming here?" Leo asked.

"He will be using all his power to arrive here and stop you. You must not delay," she warned.

"But, they won't take you…" Leo said.

"I knew they would not. This is my world. Another Zarina waits in yours. You are the key to this Leo, not me."

"But I promised I would never leave you," he said.

"And I warned you not to make promises that you might not be able to keep," she said, holding a hand to his cheek. "You are a good friend but you must leave me Leo, you know that. If you do not, Nemeddes will win - the darkness will win. It is my time. I will face the darkening of this world. But do not despair for if you go, you will re-write time itself. This place will simply cease to be. There will be no pain." Zarina held out the blue brooch Athus had won for her. "Take this to the Zarina in your world, tell her of our adventure. See the same mistakes are not repeated."

"Thank you for all you have done for me," said Leo, taking the brooch and kissing her cheek. "Thank you for everything."

"I did nothing. You did it all for yourself. Now go!" she urged.

Turning with a strange sense of coldness Leo ran back over Table Rock to the Temple of Time.

"Are you ready?" the mage asked.

"Yes," said Leo.

"Then come inside, we don't have all day," the young man grinned, chuckling at his own joke. "A little time travel humour for you there."

"It is my experience that mages should avoid jokes," Leo said more sharply than he intended. "My friend is out there alone, facing death and darkness."

"Possibly from your perspective," said the mage, resting a hand on Leo's shoulder and drawing him into a side passage just as another group entered the small entrance chamber. "Now can we please vacate the area, others need to use it. Follow me."

"Who are you?" Leo asked as he walked with the mage through the maze like corridors of the Temple.

"No one of consequence," said the mage.

"You must have a name," Leo pressed, but the mage ignored him, leading him at a dizzying pace through the fortress.

At every turn the walls were decorated with murals and scenes of battles and heroes sculpted into the very stone and Leo watched in amazement as the living rock shifted and changed before his eyes. He tried to ask his guide what he was seeing but the man continued to ignore him and Leo was hurriedly swept down another series of corridors. As they passed an intersection, Leo's jaw dropped as two beings of pure light drifted by.

"Did you think only humans would operate a temple of time and space?" the mage asked, looking amused. "I was simply chosen because we are the same race."

"I didn't know what to expect," Leo admitted. "I only ever met one man who seemed to understand space and time."

"Ah yes, Master Erasmus Gellen," the mage said and something in the way he spoke made Leo stare at the man carefully.

"Do you know of him?" Leo asked.

"Naturally, everyone here knows Master Gellen," the mage replied.

"But... he is dead. Or does he live?" Leo asked. "Is that even possible?"

"Nothing is impossible," the mage replied, pulling up sharp before a simple, wooden door. "We have arrived. Please enter this room."

"I have a favour to ask..." Leo began.

"Yes, we already know - very noble. It has actually already been taken care of," said the mage. "So if you could please hurry..."

"But I haven't asked it yet," said Leo.

"Not this time, no," smiled the mage. "Now we're very busy here, do you think yours is the only world we have to save this morning?"

Before Leo could respond he found himself firmly pushed through the door into a small, empty room.

Almost at once, burning white light began to engulf everything and for just a moment, the tiniest moment, Leo got a glimpse of it all in its indescribable beauty.

33.

As with the first time, when he had been soul swapped into Athus' body, there was no great fanfare or flashing lights. There was no sense of nausea or displacement. He was simply back. The sun shone down warmly over Clayson's farm and his shirt was damp with sweat from that morning's toil. His lunch was by his side and next to it lay Zarina's blue brooch. He picked it up and stood, feeling his way back into his body, sensing its weakness compared to the one he had inhabited until recently.

"Just another thing I will have to rectify now that I am home," he said to himself and stared at his hands as if they were not his own. Slowly he reached up to feel his bushy, red beard.

Leo glanced towards where the other farmhands were finishing their lunch and saw two men approaching the group, walking quickly over the fields. One was short and stocky, his bald head bright in the sunlight, the other was tall and wiry, his head dark. It took a second for him to place them: Relund and Case. He was back at the moment before his beating. Leo pocketed the brooch and strode towards the coming men.

"You, Kvetch!" Relund shouted. "We have business with you!"

"I apologise to you both for our argument and your injuries, but you were partly to blame," said Leo. "Now you should leave and we will talk about this later."

"We will talk about it now!" said Relund.

"Yeah, we'll talk about it now, Kvetch," Case sneered.

"As you wish," said Leo, immediately dropping to one knee and hoisting Case over his shoulder and throwing him hard into the ground, knocking the wind from him. Leo retained the man's arm, holding it in a wicked lock.

"Let him go or I'll knock your bloody block off," Relund threatened.

Still holding onto Case, who struggled and cursed on the ground, unable to stand, Leo presented his chin. "Why don't you give it your best shot, Relund. This one's on me."

Relund's eyes narrowed as he balled a fist and threw a punch at Leo. The shot crashed into Leo's cheek and the watching men let out a mutual groan at the impact - which quickly turned to murmurs of appreciation as Leo barely flinched.

"That the best you have?" Leo asked, releasing his hold on Case and stepping forward to drive a punch of his own deep into Relund's gut. The man staggered back before falling to his knees and doubling over, unable to rise.

"Get him out of here, Case," Leo said rounding on the smaller man. "And don't bother me while I'm at work again."

Case curled his lip but said nothing as he moved to his friend and helped him limp away.

"That was a hell of a shot to take," said Mason. "You've got a nasty cut under your eye."

"Nothing but a scratch," said Leo.

Leo worked hard through the afternoon until his body was near exhaustion and sweat soaked his clothes. As the bell sounded to end the day's labours Leo wiped his brow and breathed deeply.

"A good shift today," said Mason. "What's got into you?"

Leo said nothing and took another deep breath before getting back to work.

Mason stared at him. "Have you gone mad? We're done for today."

"I'm going to finish this up," said Leo. "I'll see you tomorrow."

Mason snorted and turned before filing away with the other hands.

For two more hours Leo toiled until the job was done and the sun was beginning to sink into a darkening sky. He stretched his tired body, feeling it ache in a way it had not done in too long. The sky above was dark blue now, soon it would be black. As he looked at it he could not help but think of Zarina and the sky over Table Rock. How must she have felt knowing her sky would never see another dawn? Laying down his tools he pulled off his shirt, wringing it out.

"I'm not in the habit of paying out overtime if that's what you're after," said Clayson, joining Leo by the newly constructed fence.

"I do not seek extra pay," said Leo. "I owe you a great deal of overtime Mr. Clayson, on account of all the times I have slacked off and shirked my duties. But I assure you, I will work overtime every night and be here all the earlier each morning until I am convinced I have paid you back in full."

Clayson nodded, inspecting the fence. "This is good, sturdy work, Leo. What happened to your eye?"

"Nothing worth talking about," said Leo. "But there is something I would very much like to ask you..."

Leo returned home via a neighbour's house, borrowing a razor and scissors. It had been a long time since he had kept either in his cottage. He bathed and shaved, neatening his beard and hair before dressing in his best clothes. His heart was aflutter as he approached Clayson's farmhouse and knocked on the door.

Clayson answered, his face a picture. "What happened to the beard, lad, gust of wind?"

"Something like that," Leo smiled.

"Don't make me regret this," Clayson said. "In truth, if you had asked even yesterday I would have refused, but there is something in your eyes that tells me something has changed in you Leo."

"A great deal has changed. I have wasted too much of my life," said Leo.

"Then you may ask her," said Clayson.

The walk up the stairs and across the landing to Rebecca's room was one of the most exhilarating, nervous, sickening and wonderful things Leo had ever done. He paused before her door, took a deep breath and then knocked.

"Come in," Rebecca called from inside.

Leo opened the door. She sat on a chair by the window reading a book and the look of genuine warmth and surprise on her face to see him there tugged at his heart.

"I was wondering, if you have not eaten, if you might like to have some dinner with me? We could go to the carnival for a while afterwards?" Leo offered.

Rebecca smiled broadly. "I would like that very much," she said.

They stopped at a small restaurant on the outskirts of the city and enjoyed a pleasant meal and afterwards Leo took Rebecca's hand as they walked amongst the celebrations and carnival stalls. As they talked and laughed with one another it was as if no time had passed at all. The years they had been apart fell away and they discovered that they were as at ease with each other as they ever had been. They tried their hands at fairground games of luck and skill and as they made their way down the main boulevard towards the square, Rebecca slipped her arm through Leo's and rested her head on his shoulder and Leo found himself blushing.

Ostus City's main plaza was filled with all manner of attractions, from exotic animals, incredible dancers to a huge ferris wheel that almost rivalled the height of the great clock of the botanical gardens. For now though the entertainments were forgotten as the people lined the thoroughfare hoping for a glimpse of the great heroes in the evening parade.

The crowd was excited and cheering wildly by the time the Sunchasers filed past. This parade was more sedate than the one that had charged into the city earlier but it was still a grand spectacle. Leo remembered sitting on a roof and watching as Athus, Zarina and Balthus had entered the city. He had to keep reminding himself that in this world that had only been this morning. As the troops marched their horses in a slow, stately procession, Leo found it both wonderful and painful to see Balthus leading them, waving to crowds and clearly relishing their cheers. A part of him wanted to run out and greet the big man, but he knew of course, that this Balthus did not know him.

After the Sunchasers came Athus and Zarina, walking and shaking hands with the people in the crowd. Zarina passed not a few feet from where Rebecca and Leo were stood. Suddenly the priestess stopped and stared intently into the crowd, her eyes falling on Leo.

"Come forward," she said and Leo found himself pressed to the barriers by those around him.

Zarina looked at him for a moment. "Do I know you?" she asked, her expression strange.

Leo smiled. "No, my Lady, we have not met."

Zarina nodded, her face unconvinced, but she moved on nonetheless and Leo drew back into the crowd, taking Rebecca by the hand and leading her to the big wheel.

They boarded a carriage and climbed high above the city, watching the tail end of the parade from the air. The stillness of the ride was pleasant after the bustle of being on the street.

"I can't believe Lady Zarina called you forward. What did she say to you?" asked Rebecca.

"She thought she knew me," said Leo. "Perhaps she mistook me for someone else."

"She is so beautiful," said Rebecca.

Leo produced a wild flower he had picked for her and kept in a napkin. Gently he pinned it to her dress. "But not as beautiful as you."

"Oh please," Rebecca laughed, rolling her eyes. But she did not object as he leaned in slowly and kissed her lips.

They kissed gently until their carriage stopped at the highest point and they stared out over the city.

"What has happened to you, Leo?" she asked.

"I woke up," he smiled and kissed her again.

The next evening Leo sat in an antechamber in Ostus Palace and waited. His body ached from another hard day at work and the hour was drawing late. Each time the doors to his left opened he would rise excitedly, only for it to be another servant who paid him no heed at all.

When finally the doors opened and Athus, Zarina, Balthus and Gellen entered he could not help himself grinning and he had to resist the urge to greet them as friends.

"We are told," said Athus, "that you have waited here for nearly six hours and refuse to leave unless you see Lady Zarina personally. Normally we would not grant such a request but my Lady decided she would make an exception. What is it you have to say?"

"You were at the parade last night," said Zarina, not waiting for Leo to respond. "There is something unusual about you."

Leo nodded. "I have a story so magical and wondrous that you might all think me insane but my tale is crucial to the safety of the realm."

"By the stars, I told you he would be a madman," scoffed Balthus. "Let me throw him out and be done with it."

"Madness is a relative condition," spoke Gellen.

"Don't start with all that again," the giant sighed. "I've told you before, if you need to read books on how to act like you're normal, you're not qualified to give an opinion on what madness is."

"That's a very transitory position," Gellen countered.

"Gentlemen," said Athus softly. "This is not the time or the place."

Leo grinned from ear to ear. "I've missed you all very much."

Zarina's eyes narrowed. "What is your meaning?"

Leo slowly reached into his pocket and removed the blue brooch, seeing the shock in Zarina's eyes as her hand moved to grab the one attached to her robes.

"Where did you get that?" Zarina asked.

"As I said," Leo smiled. "It is a magical and wondrous story."

Epilogue

Zarina watched as the doors to the Temple of Time closed and Leo disappeared inside. Her strength was fading as fast as the light in the sky. Only a tiny pool of blue light remained directly above her now, the last glimpse of the sky this world would ever see. Her robes were soaked with blood, her breathing was shallow and uneven and a feeling of dark loneliness had settled upon her. There was no escape this time, no last minute reprieve. She was alone, surrounded by enemies and measuring her life in minutes.

The darkness continued to race onwards devouring everything it touched and the Krylla waited a mere few feet before her, shuffling and chittering with glee. She pushed despair back and hoped that Leo would be successful and the world would cease to be before Nemeddes found her.

A noise came from behind her and she turned her head, surprised to see the doors to The Temple open once more. An old man stepped out and walked towards her. Despite his obviously advanced years and that his hair and beard were long and white; he still wore a mail shirt and carried a war hammer over powerful shoulders. His gait was that of a confident warrior and as he approached, the milling Krylla grew nervous and fell back a little. Although Zarina had never set eyes on this man before, she knew at once who he was and smiled warmly.

As the warrior stood beside her, a flash of light came from The Temple then it disappeared.

"I promised I would not leave you," the man said. "I keep my promises."

Zarina smiled. "Did it work?"

"It worked," he replied, loosening his strong shoulders and swinging the weapon masterfully. As he did the metal of the war hammer began to glow, pulsing a gentle, golden light.

"You have a Star Weapon?" she commented, with only the slightest raise of an eyebrow.

"Yes," said the man. "You gave me this after the siege at Trejonin on the eve of our final battle against the Lich. I was strong then, my hair still as red as fire. Not like the old man who stands before you."

"You were with us?" she smiled.

"Aye, I was. I fought shoulder to shoulder with Balthus. He fought... bravely. I was there when he passed," the man said sadly. "Died saving my life. Even Gellen's magic could not save him."

"And Athus, my champion?" Zarina pressed.

"Oh, he lives still, as do you. He led the charge that day, we would have faltered without him. He, as you know, is a man amongst men."

"I long to see him again," Zarina admitted.

"You live a long, happy life in my world - are still living. You and Athus have a child, a daughter. She has become a great woman."

"Really?" asked Zarina, tears in her eyes. "We did not think..."

He smiled. "Yes. She is friends with my daughters. They are truly people to walk the mountains with."

"A strange phrase, I have not heard it before," Zarina admitted.

"I read it in a book by a great story teller," the man said. "It has always stuck with me."

Only the tiniest pinprick of blue remained in the heavens now and the warrior's war hammer was glowing brightly. A dark form appeared on the horizon, so massive and grotesque it could only be Nemeddes in his true and terrible form. The twisted creature moved towards them with terrible speed and they both tracked its approach.

"Help me," Zarina urged and the man lent her his arm, pulling her to her feet. The pain in her side was extreme, but it did not matter. This was the end.

The old warrior locked his gaze onto the nearing archfiend and widened his stance. Planting his feet solidly he held the golden hammer expertly at the ready.

Zarina willed waves of golden energy into her hands, using the last of her strength to charge her body with divine light. All around the Krylla began to chitter and hiss their excitement, sensing the closeness of their lord. Whether Nemeddes would reach them before this world ceased to be, neither of the heroes could tell.

"You have lived a good life then, Leo Kvetch?" Zarina shouted over the growing noise of the beasts.

"Oh yes, the very best of lives," he replied.

Author's Acknowledgements

Firstly I want to say a big thanks to you, whoever you may be, for reading this story – I really hope you found something to enjoy within it.

I also need to say a huge thanks to my mum, my mother-in-law and my lovely wife for all the hard work they put into proof reading this book and all the encouragement they gave me while I was writing it. Naturally any mistakes that are left are totally down to them.

And one last thing - if you did enjoy this story then please help me out if you can. Get in touch, drop me a line - let me know what you thought. Promoting an indie book is pretty hard so if you could pop a review online, like my Facebook page, follow me on Twitter, check out my site – well that would all be great. And, whether it's me or someone else, do keep supporting indie writers, artists, musicians – whatever it may be. Because when you do, it really means a lot to us.

See you space cowpokes,

Sam, Lancashire 2016

www.samgoodings.com
Find Sam Goodings on Facebook
or Twitter @samsdg01

20065105R00139

Printed in Great Britain
by Amazon

STOP!

A tutti quelli che si sono fermati. Per poi ripartire.
- PIERDOMENICO E ANDREA

Un sentitissimo grazie a tutto il team con cui ho fatto questo bellissimo viaggio.
Grazie a Chiara, Andrea e Pierdomenico, agli amici di scuola e a Mattia, senza i quali quest'avventura non sarebbe stata così bella.
- SUSANNA

Andrea Canobbio - Pierdomenico Baccalario - Susanna Mariani
Stop!

viale Andrea Doria 7, 20124 Milano
www.editriceilcastoro.it
info@editriceilcastoro.it

Da un'idea di Book on a Tree
www.bookonatree.com

Impaginazione e lettering: Maria Letizia Mirabella

ISBN 979-12-5533-093-6

ANDREA
CANOBBIO

PIERDOMENICO
BACCALARIO

SUSANNA
MARIANI

STOP!

il castoro

MUOVITI, CLOUD!
ACC...!
ARRIVO!

LIVELLO 1
SHOOT 'EM UP
FACCIAMO TARDI!
DATTI UNA MOSSA...!

AVETE RAGIONE, RAGAZZI!... SONO PIÙ LENTO DI UN 1530!
UN CHE...?
... IL REGISTRATORE DEL COMMODORE 64!
TESTONE! PENSI SEMPRE AL TUO VIDEOGIOCO, EH?
A PROPOSITO, L'HAI FINITO?
MA SCHERZI? DEVO ANCORA DISE-GNARE ALMENO METÀ DEI LIVELLI.
DOVRESTI FARTI AIUTARE DA QUALCUNO.
DICI? E DA CHI?
RRRIIIIIING!

BUONGIORNO!
BUONGIORNO!
BUONGIORNO!
'GIORNO!
ALESSANDRO MANZONI BLA BLA BLA
LA PROVVIDENZA BLABLA BLA
BILL
CLOUD!
CHE C'È?
CHE STAI COMBINANDO?
GLOM!...

PERCHÉ NON CHIEDI A LUI?
AL PIRATA?
MA SEI PAZZO?
È INARRIVABILE! MI TERRORIZZA IL SOLO PENSIERO DI ANDARCI A PARLARE...
GUARDA CHE È UN TIPO ALLA MANO. HAI DEI SOLDI?
SÌ, PERCHÉ?
DAMMELI E VEDRAI.
E POI È GIÀ PIUTTOSTO IMPEGNATO CON LA SUA "ATTIVITÀ"... FIGURATI SE HA TEMPO PER ME!
GIÀ!

SEMBRA ANCHE SIMPATICO, NON UNO A CUI PIACCIONO I VIDEOGIOCHI.
SE LO DICI TU.
SCOMMETTO CHE CI FA DEI BEI SOLDI, A COPIARLI E RIVENDERLI A MEZZA SCUOLA. TU CHE DICI?
UN SACCO DI SOLDI.
NON LASCIA NIENTE AL CASO. LE NOVITÀ COSTANO IL DOPPIO. MA SE NE COMPRI TRE, TI FA LO SCONTO.
E COME HAI DETTO CHE SI CHIAMA?
BUCK SO
BUCK, COME IL CANE.
QUANTO? HAI SPESO TUTTO? MA È UN LADRO!
DI SICURO! MA VEDRAI, APPENA ARRIVI A CASA.

GOONIES
HA SPROTETTO IKARI WARRIORS ALLA PERFEZIONE... E CI HA MONTATO LA SUA INTRO.
BUCK SOFTWARE
LA MUSICHETTA È UNA FIGATA!
FACCIAMO MERENDA?
AH AH! TI HANNO SPARATO!

L'INTRO! LA MUSICA! ACCIDENTI A LUI! IO, L'UNICA COSA CHE SO FARE, È DISEGNARE MOSTRI.
PENSA A STUDIARE!
FACCIAMO IL PUNTO DELLA SITUAZIONE.
OKAY.
CLOUD KING
HO QUASI DISEGNATO TUTTO UN VIDEOGIOCO...
MHM-MHM!
E HO ANCHE IL TITOLO!
CLOUD KING
SAI CHE ROBA. SI CHIAMA COME IL TUO SOPRANNOME.
E ALLORA?
MA DI INTRO E MUSICA NIENTE: NON SAPREI DA CHE PARTE INIZIARE.
E ALLORA FATTI AIUTARE.
CHE ABBIA RAGIONE?

FATTI SOTTO, CLOUD!
EHI! BUCK!
DICI A ME?
SÌ, TU. IO CONOSCO IL VIDEOGIOCO PIÙ FIGO DEL MONDO. VUOI PROVARLO?
MA SENTI IL PRIMINO!
HO DIECI MINUTI PRIMA DELLA CAMPANELLA.
FATTELI BASTARE.

ALLORA, DI CHE SI TRATTA?
NON CI PUOI ARRIVARE.
SEI UN PIRATA?
NAAH!
SONO UNO CHE LI DISEGNA.
DISEGNI COSA, SCUSA?

SPARATUTTO.
WOW. E CHE TIPO DI SPARATUTTO?
SCORRIMENTO VERTICALE.
SCROLLING AUTOMATICO O A SPINTA?
AUTOMATICO.
BUCK, TI SBRIGHI?
E HA ANCHE UN NOME, QUESTO VIDEOGIOCO?
CLOUD KING.
COME LA TUA MAGLIETTA?

EHM...
GIÀ. NIENTE MALE, EH?
È LA COSA PIÙ BRUTTA CHE ABBIA MAI VISTO.
CLOUD
SCHERZO! CLOUD KING, HAI DETTO?
QUANDO È USCITO?
VERAMENTE NON LO HO ANCORA PROPRIO FINITO...
AH!

MA È LO SPARATUTTO DEFINITIVO!
COME NO.
PROVARE PER CREDERE.
PROVIAMO, ALLORA. COSA FAI OGGI POMERIGGIO?
COSA FACCIO?
DOMANI HO IL COMPITO IN CLASSE.
AH, PECCATO! MAGARI CI DAVO UN'OCCHIATA.
ASPETTA! ASPETTA! PERCHÉ NO? VEDIAMOCI!
BENE, ALLORA, TI ASPETTO DA ME. LO SAI DOVE ABITO?

LIVELLO 2
CLOUD KING

???
!!!
COM'È CHE TI CHIAMI, BELLO? EH? FIDO? FALKOR?
DRAGOMIRO! QUI!

TU DEVI ESSERE IL NUOVO AMICO DI BUCK. E VEDO CHE HAI GIÀ INCONTRATO DRAGOMIRO.
IL MIO POVERO, POVERO, LEVRIERO.
COSA VUOLE DA TE QUESTO RAGAZZO? COSA?
UUUUUUUH!
LO FACCIAMO ENTRARE? DAI! ANDIAMO.

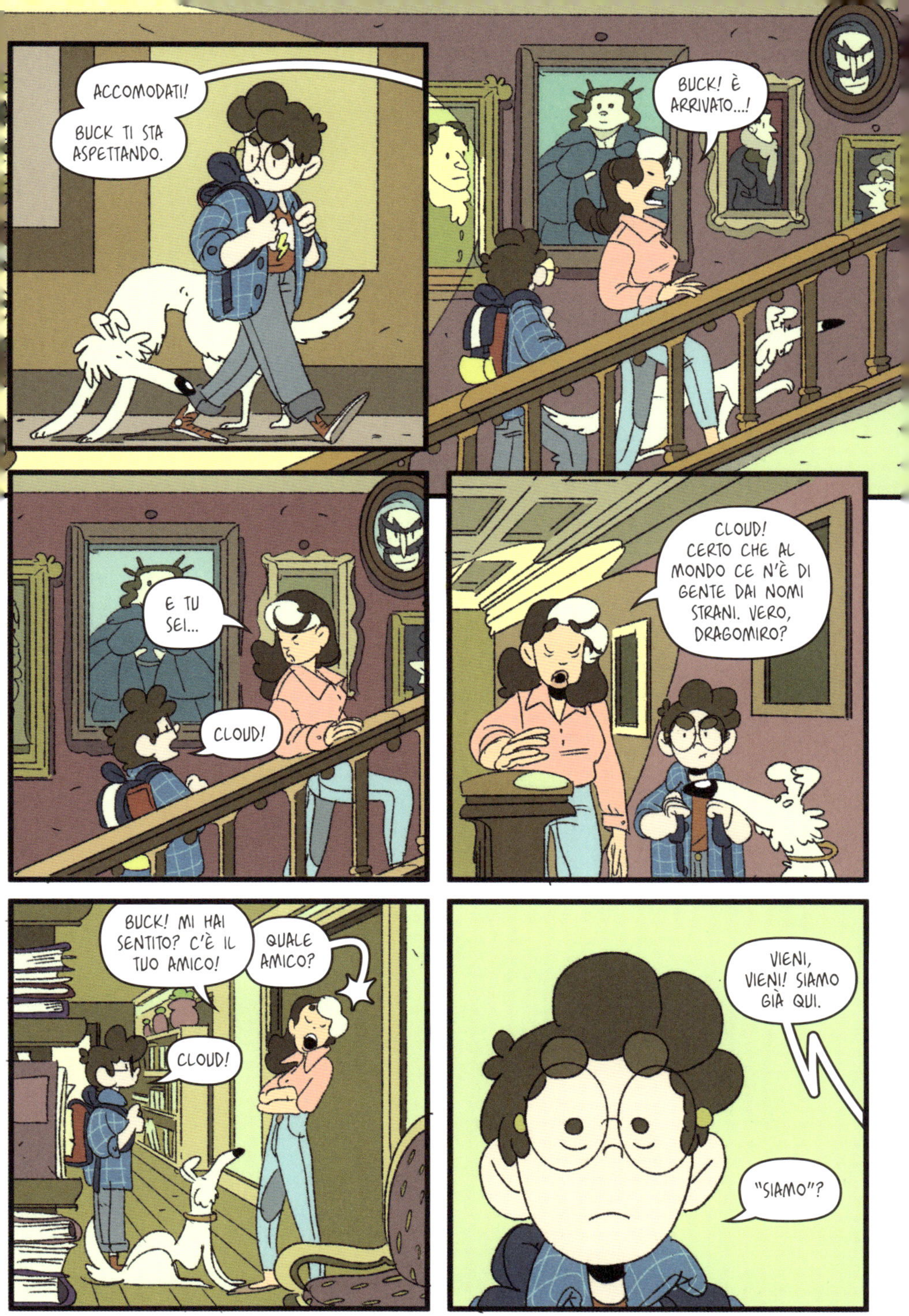
ACCOMODATI!
BUCK TI STA ASPETTANDO.
BUCK! È ARRIVATO...!
E TU SEI...
CLOUD!
CLOUD! CERTO CHE AL MONDO CE N'È DI GENTE DAI NOMI STRANI. VERO, DRAGOMIRO?
BUCK! MI HAI SENTITO? C'È IL TUO AMICO!
QUALE AMICO?
CLOUD!
VIENI, VIENI! SIAMO GIÀ QUI.
"SIAMO"?

CIAO CLOUD! LUI È OLLIE.
CIAO. SEI QUELLO DELLO SPARATUTTO?
KICK OFF
CE L'HO QUI DENTRO!
OOPS!
COLPO DI TACCO!
TO'! ANCHE MEGLIO DI MANCINI!
BRIIIM... BREEEKZZZ... VRCCZZZ...
LA SOLITA MEZZ'ORA PER CARICARE, EH?
NELL'ATTESA, PERCHÉ NON FACCIAMO DUE TIRI?
DUE TIRI...?
DAI! VIENI, CLOUD?

PASSA, PASSA!

VAI, CLOUD, È TUA!
VADO!

VHAM

CAAAAIIIII!
BUCK!!!
CRACK
SCUSATE! SCUSATE! NON VOLEVO TIRARE COSÌ FORTE, MA...
ZITTO E SCAPPA!
PANT! PANT!
UNA COSA È SICURA, IL MIO FUTURO NON SARÀ NEL CALCIO.
È QUELLO CHE MI DICONO SEMPRE ANCHE I MIEI GENITORI.
???
VIA LIBERA! ANDIAMO!

ECCO, NON L'HO DEL TUTTO FINITO... È SOLO LA PRIMA VERSIONE.
ZITTO E FAMMI GIOCARE.
AHAHA! BESTIACCE!
CAVOLO, CLOUD, QUESTA ROBA SPACCA.
AH, BE'... GRAZIE TANTE!
MA PENSA UN PO', IL PRIMINO.
CAVOLO...
GLI STA PIACENDO!

NIENTE DA DIRE, CI SAI FARE. OLLIE?
CONFERMO. E TIRA ANCHE DELLE CANNONATE NIENTE MALE.
VI HO DETTO CHE NON...
PERCHÉ NON CI FAI UN DISEGNO PER LA BUCK SOFTWARE? TI ANDREBBE?
CERTO CHE MI ANDREBBE.
SE CE LO FAI PER DOMANI, LO METTIAMO SU KICK OFF.
IL GIOCO DI CALCIO?
IL GIOCO DEFINITIVO.
PER DOMANI?
BUCK!
OH, NO! CI HA BECCATI.
TI HA BECCATO, NOI CE NE ANDIAMO!
DOBBIAMO ANDARE! C'È UN LEVRIERO DA SALVARE!
UN ALTRO?
VUOI UN PASSAGGIO?
BELLA IDEA!
VROOOM!
BRUTTA, BRUTTISSIMA IDEA.

TESORO! LA CENA È QUASI PRONTA.
???
STASERA NON MANGIO, MAMMA! TE L'HO DETTO!
SGRUNT!
ANCORA DIECI MINUTI!...
TESORO, È PRONTA...
MAMMA, TI HO DETTO CHE NON MANGIO!
... LA COLAZIONE.

TUTTO BENE?
HAI DORMITO IN UN CASSONETTO?
MAGARI! SAREBBE STATO MEGLIO...
OH, BRAVO. CE L'HAI FATTA.
TSK! UNA BAZZECOLA!
NON GLI HO NEMMENO CHIESTO COME È ANDATA CON IL LEVRIERO DA SALVARE...
CICERONE, BLA BLA BLA
... E PERCHÉ AVEVA QUEI GRAFFI?
BOH? CHI SE NE IMPORTA...
ZZZ

GREMLINS
È USCITO! È USCITO KICK OFF!
MA A TE FANNO SCHIFO I GIOCHI DI CALCIO!
SONO FAMOSO!
GUARDA!
GUARDO COSA?
BUCK GAMES PRESENTA
KICK OFF!
disegnato da Cloud
QUELLA L'HO FATTA IO! C'È IL MIO NOME!
MA DOVE?
QUI! IN FONDO, NELL'ANGOLINO!
MA ALMENO TI SEI FATTO PAGARE?
ZITTO. E GIOCA!

LIVELLO 3
SOURCE CODE
SAI COSA? DOVREMMO FARE UN VIDEOGIOCO PER AMIGA.
PER AMIGA?

PENSACI, CLOUD. OLLIE È UN GENIO. IO FACCIO LE MUSICHE. TU DISEGNI. COSA CI MANCA?
NON SAPREI: UN'AMIGA?
"L'AMIGA, LA LEGGENDA FORGIATA DA JAY MINER NEI FUOCHI DI SANTA CLARA, IN CALIFORNIA, ALL'INSAPUTA DI QUELLI DELLA SILICON VALLEY..."
MA È CARISSIMA!
QUELLO NON È UN PROBLEMA.
IL PROBLEMA È UN ALTRO: CI MANCA IL PROGRAMMATORE. MA FORSE OLLIE NE CONOSCE UNO.
CHI?
UN TIZIO DI RIVERE, UNA SPECIE DI PAESE A OTTO CHILOMETRI DA QUI. MA IN MOTO, CON OLLIE...
NO.
"NO" COSA?
MI VA BENE TUTTO. L'AMIGA, RIVERE, OTTO CHILOMETRI. MA IN MOTO CON OLLIE NO.

GLI POSSIAMO PROPORRE CLOUD KING: IL GIOCO DI RUOLO!
E BLACK RAGE!
SWORD QUEST!
SHRIEEEEK!
PATATIS!
SOLAR WINDER!
DAI QUA!
OTTIMO LAVORO!
BLACK RAGE SPACCA, MA CI VORREBBE UNA LOTTATRICE FEMMINA.
E COME? NON SO DISEGNARE LE RAGAZZE.

PANE & DOLCI
DOVE SIAMO FINITI?
RIVERE
NON RIESCO A CREDERE CHE QUI PUÒ ABITARE UNO CHE SA PROGRAMMARE UN VIDEOGIOCO.
CE L'AVETE FATTA, FINALMENTE!
SICURO?
È DENTRO CHE CI ASPETTA.
VENITE AVANTI, LENTAMENTE.

OLÁ, OLLIE.
OLÁ, TISTAR. ECCO QUELLI DI CUI TI HO PARLATO.

POF

EHM, PIACERE...
SGRUNT.

OKAY. SPARATE L'IDEA.
UN VIDEOGIOCO PER AMIGA.
BAH! NON CE L'HO L'AMIGA: COSTA TROPPO.
LE COMPRO IO PER TUTTI.
E DA DOVE TI SALTANO FUORI I SOLDI?
TU NON CI PENSARE.
SOLO: C'È SPAZIO DA TE?
PERCHÉ, DA TE NO?
HA LA MAMMA SVITATA!
E DA TE?
SOLO NEL POLLAIO. SE VOLETE PROGRAMMARE COI POLLI...
NON GUARDATE ME! HO UN FRATELLO ROMPISCATOLE.
E TU CHI SEI, MICROBO?

LUI È IL GRAFICO.
ART-DIRECTOR. IO DECIDO IL MOOD.
E TU, ALLORA, CHE FAI?
E IL MICROBO LAVORA.
CAPITO.
E CHE GIOCO VORRESTE FARE?
UN GIOCO DI RUOLO TIPO ZELDA...
... UN PICCHIADURO ALLA STREET FIGHTER!
ZELDA MI FA SCHIFO. STREET FIGHTER NON FUNZIONA... NON AVETE UN GIOCO DIVERSO?
SÌ CHE CE L'ABBIAMO.

LA NOSTRA VERA IDEA È QUESTA, GIUSTO, BUCK?
CLOUD
MA CERTO! QUESTA È L'IDEONA.
QUESTA È UNA PALLA.
MA È UNA PALLA CHE NON STA MAI FERMA.
CLOUD
QUANDO PARTE, NON LA FERMI PIÙ.
E COSA FA?
VA CONTRO IL MURO E POI RIMBALZA INDIETRO.
QUANDO LE COLPISCI LA PRIMA VOLTA, SI SVEGLIANO.
E CI SONO ALTRE PALLE. ADDOR-MENTATE.
MA SE LE COLPISCI DI NUOVO, SI INCAZZANO.
E MUORI.
E POI CI SONO GLI OSTACOLI.
BARRIERE ELETTRICHE, TELETRASPORTI, NEMICI.
E I BONUS.
COME SE PIOVESSERO.

HA UN NOME, QUESTA ROBA?
COFF!
COFF!
STOP!
"STOP!"?
MI PIACE.

OKAY, SE NE PUÒ PARLARE.
VENITE CON ME.
LÌ DENTRO? COS'È QUELLA ROBA?
È IL RIFUGIO ANTIATOMICO DI MIO NONNO.
FIGATA!
MA CERTO, CHE DOMANDA STUPIDA: OVVIO, CHE È UN RIFUGIO ANTIATOMICO...
CLOUD
OUCH! COSA HO DETTO? MA NON CREDERAI CHE...
E QUINDI, ABBIAMO UNA SEDE DOVE STARE?
CI RESTA SOLO DA CONVINCERE UNA PERSONA.

VROOOOOM!
CIAO NIPOTE.

SONO AMICI MIEI, NONNO.
MA QUELLO NON È IL FIGLIO DI PIPPO?
SONO IO, SÌ.
BUONO, QUELLO.
SPOMF
DA QUANDO IN QUA FRATERNIZZI CON IL NEMICO?
?
POI TE LA SPIEGO.
ALLORA, SPUTA IL ROSPO. CHE VOLETE, TUTTI QUANTI?
VORREMMO USARE IL RIFUGIO ANTIATOMICO.
SCORDATELO.
PER FARE COSA?
ПРАВДА
CI ARRIVA ANCORA LA CORRENTE?

LIVELLO 4
UNDERGROUND EMPIRE

RAGAZZI? È SUCCESSO ANCORA!
AL MIO TRE. UNO, DUE E...
SBRAANG!
NONNO!!!
LONTANI DALLA PORTA!
SBA-DADAGANGANG!
ECCO FATTO! BASTAVA SOLO UN PO' DI INCORAGGIA-MENTO!

C'È DI TUTTO QUI DENTRO!
PER FORZA! TUTTO PUÒ SERVIRE, IN CASO DI GUERRA NUCLEARE.
QUESTO DOVE VA?
NEL GARAGE, CON LE ALTRE COSE DELLA PALESTRA.
E QUESTI?
ERANO QUELLI DELL'INTERCITY. MIO NONNO HA FATTO IL FERROVIERE...
CRASH!
PUAH! VEDI LA ROBA DELLE FERROVIE? NON DURA VENT'ANNI.

APRIII!
ARGH!
CHIUUUDI!
UFF.
ABBIAMO FINITO?
QUASI. CI SERVE UN LOGO!
CLOUD
NIENTE MALE! MA PRIMA, PENSIAMO ALL'ATTREZZATURA.

POSSIAMO PRENDERLO, MAMMA?
UHM... PER COSA TI SERVE?
PRESTO, PRESTO!
ACCIDENTI SE PESA!
SST...!
GUARDA LÀ, MAMMA, CHE BELLE PETUNIE!
IL PAVIMENTO È UN PO' SPOGLIO, NON TROVATE...?
PRESTO, PRESTO!

UNDERGROUND
EMPIRE
È ARRIVATO.
VROOOM!
CAVOLO, BUCK! SEI STATO DI PAROLA. MA COME HAI FATTO?
EH EH! NON LO SAPRETE MAI!
ANCORA NON RIESCO A CREDERCI...
CREDICI, MICROBO. È TUTTO VERO.

SIGNORI... COMINCIA LO SPETTACOLO!
CLAP
CLAP

CLAP
CLAP
CLAP
CLAP
CLAP
CLAP
CLAP
LIVELLO 5
SAVED GAME

E QUESTO CHE CAVOLO È?
È UN MOUSE.
UN MOUSE?
VEDI? LO MUOVI E QUELLO SI MUOVE SULLO SCHERMO.
E QUANDO FINISCI IL TAVOLO?
LO SOLLEVI.
TUTTO IL TAVOLO?
SOLLEVI IL MOUSE.
WOW! CHI L'AVREBBE MAI DETTO?
E QUESTI?
FORTE! SONO PICCOLI.
ME LO LEVI DI TORNO? PER FAVORE.

VIENI A VEDERE LA TUA POSTAZIONE, CLOUD. E TIENITI FORTE...
HO UN MOUSE TUTTO PER ME?
CERTO! E HAI ANCHE L'ULTIMA VERSIONE DEL DELUXE PAINT.
CHE SAREBBE?
IL MIGLIOR PROGRAMMA DI DISEGNO DEL MONDO!
CHE COLORI!
NON È POSSIBILE.
MA QUANTI SONO?
SESSANTAQUATTRO.
E... POSSO USARLI TUTTI?
TUTTI QUELLI CHE VUOI!
!
E ORA SENTI QUESTA...

!!!
CHE ROBA È? HANNO RESUSCITATO WAGNER?
HAI SENTITO COME SPACCA?
ALTROCHÉ!
TIC TAC TAC TIC TIC
E ADESSO GUARDA, METTO IL DISCHETTO... E IN UN ATTIMO...
TIC TIC TAC TAC TIC
CRUNCH
VRRRR
SI FA PER DIRE, MA...
SE TU SUONI UNA NOTA SULLA TASTIERA... **SUONA, OLLIE!**
TAC TAC TIC TIC
... LA NOTA ARRIVA QUI.
GRANDE! QUINDI SIAMO A POSTO.
GIUSTO?
SBAGLIATO.
TIC

NON SI PUÒ LAVORARE COSÌ.
RILASSATI. STAVAMO SOLO PROVANDO LA TASTIERA.
NON È LA TASTIERA.
NON TI PIACE IL LOGO?
NO, GUARDATE QUI.
IO ACCENDO.
SCRIVO, OKAY? E COSA SUCCEDE?
TIC
TAC
TIC
TIC
TAC
SHELL KICKSTART AMIGADOS ROM WORKBENCH SALVATAGGIO DISCHETTO.
IPNOTICO!
OGNI VOLTA DEVO SALVARE SU UN DISCHETTO DIVERSO, VEDI? PIPPO 1, PIPPO 2, PIPPO 3...
VEDO, VEDO...
E QUINDI?
E QUINDI CI MANCA L'HARD DISK.
E LEI CHI È?

HO LA SENSAZIONE DI AVERLA GIÀ VISTA...
MA DOVE?
FORSE AL CINEMA?
ECCO CHI È! LA RAGAZZA DI PRIMA!
SE VOLETE CARICARE E AGGIORNARE I DATI DI UN VIDEOGIOCO SENZA UN HARD DISK, DIVENTERETE VECCHI.
LEI SÌ CHE NE SA!
HA RAGIONE.
HA RAGIONE SÌ, CASPITA...
POSSO FARE UNA DOMANDA STUPIDA?
NO!

UN HARD DISK È UN DISCO FISSO SU CUI SI POSSONO LEGGERE E SALVARE GRANDI QUANTITÀ DI DATI IN MODO SICURO...
PRATICAMENTE INDISTRUTTIBILE.
SI AGGANCIA QUI E NON LO LEVI PIÙ.
ED È VELOCISSIMO!
PECCATO CHE ADESSO NON CE LI ABBIAMO I SOLDI PER UN HARD DISK. COSTA COME UN'ALTRA AMIGA.
E ALLORA SCORDATEVI IL GIOCO.
OPPURE, TROVATE QUALCUNO CHE CE L'HA GIÀ.

COME NO... E CHI? TU, MAGARI?
NO.
CAVOLO, PECCATO. ERA UN GRAN BEL LOGO.
NON RIESCO A CREDERCI! ABBIAMO GIÀ FINITO PRIMA DI INIZIARE? E... PER COSA? UN... UN...
MA... VOI COME ANDATE IN MATE-MATICA?
MALE. PERCHÉ?
STAI PARLANDO CON LA CAMPIONES-SA REGIONALE DI MATEMATICA.
SIETE MAI ANDATI A RIPETIZIONE DA VALENTI?
QUELLO CON LA CASA CHE PUZZA DI GATTO?
LUI!
MIO NONNO DICE CHE È UN SERVO DEL CAPITALISMO.
VUOI DIRE CHE QUEL VECCHIO PROF DI MATEMATICA HA UN HARD DISK?
?
NO, MA SUO FIGLIO VITO... SÌ.
AGGANCIATE VITO, E AVRETE IL VOSTRO HARD DISK.
GRANDE! HAI APPENA SALVATO L'UNDERGROUND EMPIRE DALLA SUA PRIMA, GRANDE, CRISI.

CIAO!
CIAO!
VROOOM
BE', ALLORA, CIAO, EHM...?
PANE & DOLC
LALLI, PER GLI AMICI. PER I NEMICI, INVECE, LORELAI.
... LALLI?
CLOOOUD? TI MUOVI?
QUESTO PARTE!

LIVELLO 6
POWER-UP

BRAVO, RAGAZZO!
PUNTUALE COME UN OROLOGIO.
ACCOMODATI!
VIENI, VIENI! NON BADARE A GREEBO, È UN GIOCHERELLONE.
AHIA!
MIA FIGLIA! CAMPIONESSA NAZIONALE JUNIORES DI SLALOM SPECIALE E SLALOM GIGANTE.
MEOW!
DI LÀ INVECE C'È MIO FIGLIO, CHE È UN GENIO DEL COMPUTER!
TAC
TAC
TAC
PERFETTO! ALLORA IO ANDREI...
MA DOVE VAI? SIEDITI LÌ. VEDIAMO DOV'È IL PROBLEMA...
GUARDI, IO...
ALLORA, PER PRIMA COSA, QUALCHE ESERCIZIO SUGLI INSIEMI DISGIUNTI...
VERAMENTE...
HIISSS!

STRANO! NON HAI FATTO NEMMENO UN ERRORE. MA ALLORA, DOV'È IL PROBLEMA?
HO PROVATO A DIRGLIELO! IO VADO BENE IN MATEMATICA!
NON SOPRAVVALUTARTI, SCIUTTO! TUO PADRE MI HA DETTO CHE SEI UN TESTONE.
NON SONO SCIUTTO! SONO CANOBBIO! E SONO QUI PER VEDERE SUO FIGLIO!
SIAMO UN GRUPPO DI GIOVANI SVILUPPATORI INDIPENDENTI, TUTTI DEL PAESE. STIAMO PROGRAMMANDO UN VIDEOGIOCO, E...
COSA?!?
MEOW?
MA MIO FIGLIO LO SA?
EH NO, ERO VENUTO APPOSTA PER PARLARGLIENE...
E PERCHÉ NON L'HAI DETTO PRIMA? ANDIAMO!
VITO, STAI LAVORANDO?
UHM? SÌ, PAPÀ. MA ENTRA PURE.

LO SAPEVI CHE STANNO PROGRAMMANDO UN VIDEOGIOCO?
AH, SÌ, ME L'HA DETTO IERI AL TELEFONO.
VITO È UN PROGRAMMATORE.
OTTIMA SCELTA! I COMPUTER SONO IL LAVORO DEL FUTURO!
ECCOLO!
È LA STESSA COSA CHE DICO IO. LA STESSA SPICCICATA. NON È VERO, VITO?
MMM... GIÀ.
ALLORA VI LASCIO SOLI! CHISSÀ QUANTE NE AVETE, DA RACCONTARVI.
INFATTI! AH AH!

CLACK!
SCUSA PER MIO PADRE.
R-TYPE
SE NON È TUO PADRE.
E DI COSA? SEMBRA SIMPATICO.
VOGLIO DIRE, NON SONO TANTI I GRANDI CHE NE SANNO QUALCOSA DI VIDEOGIOCHI, NO?
...
E VA BENE! È IL MOMENTO DI RICORRERE ALLE MANIERE FORTI.
SEMBRANO DANNATAMENTE VELOCI. DEVI STARE A SINISTRA.
COME NO? VUOI PROVARE?
OH, NON SAPREI! NON CI HO MAI GIOCATO.

GIORNI PRIMA...
STAI A SINISTRA! A SINISTRA!
CI STO PROVANDO!
IL POD ROSSO! PRENDI IL POD ROSSO!
BOOM!
YKES!
AAAAAH!
DOVEVI PRENDERE IL POD ROSSO.
RICOMINCIAMO! DI NUOVO!
NOOO...! MA PERCHÉ?
PERCHÉ È IL GIOCO PREFERITO DI VITO. SE VUOI CONVINCERLO CHE SEI UN FIGO, NON C'È NIENTE DI MEGLIO CHE FINIRGLI IL LIVELLO SOTTO IL NASO.
E VA BENE!
PRONTO? VIA!

BEAM
8900
HI-

174500

EHI! MA COME HAI FATTO A PRENDERE IL POD ROSSO?
TSK!
UNA BAZZECOLA.
R-TYPE È BELLISSIMO, MA NOI PENSIAMO DI FARE UN GIOCO MIGLIORE...
R-TYPE II? EH, ORMAI È TARDI. L'HANNO GIÀ FATTO.
NO, INTENDO DIRE, UN GIOCO COMPLETAMENTE DIVERSO. ORIGINALE... UN GIOCO TUTTO NOSTRO, DA PROGETTARE DA ZERO!
E PERCHÉ MAI? CE NE SONO MIGLIAIA GIÀ FATTI.
BUCK
BLA BLA
OLLIE
BLA BLA
GRAFICA
BLA BLA
MUSICA
HARD DISK
BLA BLA
LALLI
BLA BLA
BLA BLA
PROGRAMMATORE
E POI, CON I VIDEOGIOCHI SI CONOSCONO UN SACCO DI RAGAZZE.
DAVVERO?
ANDIAMO, FIGLIOLO!
MEEEOW!
È RIMASTO LÌ DIETRO TUTTO IL TEMPO AD ASCOLTARCI?!

FIGURIAMOCI! MONITOR NUOVI CHE NON ROVINANO GLI OCCHI E UNA STAMPANTE. È IL MINIMO CHE POTESSI FARE!
I VIDEOGIOCHI SONO IL MERCATO DEL FUTURO! SOLO L'ANNO SCORSO, HANNO FATTURATO 354 MILIARDI DI LIRE!
LA SOLA NINTENDO HA UN GIRO DI 4 MILA MILIARDI L'ANNO! HA CHIUSO IL MESE SCORSO CON UN BILANCIO LORDO DI 1000 MILIARDI, E IN BORSA NE CAPITALIZZA...
... E NON APPENA IL SUPER FAMICON APPRODERÀ NEGLI STATI UNITI A SETTEMBRE AVRANNO LA LORO CONSOLE A 16 BIT E...
SGRUNT!
QUESTO PUÒ TORNARE DOV'ERA!
ORA SÌ CHE SI FA DAVVERO SUL SERIO.

TIC TAC
TAC TIC
TIC
MA... LUI NON LAVORA MAI?
È UN PATTO TRA LORO DUE. TISTAR PUÒ USARE IL SUO HARD DISK, E VITO PUÒ GIOCARE QUANTO VUOLE, SENZA NESSUNO CHE GLI ROMPA LE PALLE.
RAGAZZO, CHE STAI FA-CENDO?
PREGO?
ПРАВДА
LO SAI CHI È QUESTO?
È ALEXEY PAJITNOV. IL CREATORE DI TETRIS.
AH! IL GIOCO PER GAME BOY!

ESATTO, IL PIÙ GRANDE VIDEOGIOCO DEL PIANETA. LO STANNO METTENDO NEI COMODINI DEGLI ALBERGHI AL POSTO DELLA BIBBIA.
MMM...
E CHI L'HA PROGRAMMATO? TE LO DICO IO! UN RUSSO, L'HA PROGRAMMATO. UNO DI NOI!
MA LEI NON È RUSSO.
NON SONO RUSSO? MA COME TI PERMETTI, RAGAZZINO?
BAM!
E VOI DATEVI DA FARE, CON QUESTI GIOCHINI. E MAGARI, UN GIORNO ANCHE VOI SARETE IN PRIMA PAGINA SULLA PRAVDA.
... OPPURE, IN SIBERIA!
TIC TAC TAC TAC
TIC TAC TIC TIC
TIC TIC
TAC
TIC TAC

LIVELLO 7
GAMEPLAY
AHIMÈ, POVERO STOP!

CREDEVAMO DI AVER DEFINITO IL PROGETTO E DI DOVERLO SOLO REALIZZARE...
PERCHÉ POVERO, SCUSA?
RISPONDITI DA SOLO. CHE GIOCO VOGLIAMO FARE?
CHE DOMANDA! UN GIOCO DI PALLINE!
QUESTO LO SO. MA IN PRATICA...?
MA CI SCONTRAMMO CON L'ATAVICA INCOMUNICABILITÀ TRA CREATIVI E PROGRAMMATORI.
QUESTA SI MUOVE, NON SI FERMA MAI...
... E QUANDO ARRIVA AL BORDO, C'È UNO SCROLLING MULTIDI-REZIONALE!
LO SCROLLING NON SI PUÒ FARE.
MA PERCHÉ NOOOOO?
ARRIVAMMO A UN COMPROMESSO...
LO FACCIAMO A SCHERMO FISSO, COME VOLETE VOI. MA CI PREPARATE UN EDITOR DI LIVELLI. NOI PENSIAMO AL GAMEPLAY, ALLA GRAFICA E AL SONORO. E VOI NON CI METTETE IL BECCO!
AFFARE FATTO...
ABBIAMO FATTO UNA MAPPA CONCETTUALE CON I CORDINI COLORATI, COME I VERI CREATIVI.
MMMH! MMMH!

ANDAVAMO AL RIFUGIO OGNI FINE SETTIMANA. E CI STAVAMO FINO A TARDI.
LA SAMP ESPUGNA SAN SIRO! GOAL DI VIALLI! INTER-SAMPDORIA 0-2.
LA DOMENICA SARÀ SEMPRE COSÌ?
SÌ.
ANDIAMO AL PUB?
TISTAR, NOI ANDIAMO... LASCIAMO APERTO?
LAVORA COME UN MATTO.
TIC
TAC
TAC TIC
TIC
SECONDO ME, GIOCA A ELITE. CE L'HAI PRESENTE, ELITE? QUELLO DEI LIBRI DI FREDERIK POHL.
NO, LAVORA DURO, TI DICO.
MALEDETTI IMPERIALI! NON AVRETE MAI IL MIO CARICO!
COSA FAI?
GLI STRAORDINARI.

A VOLTE LO STRESS CI GIOCAVA BRUTTI SCHERZI...
COLORARE TUTTI I BONUS ENTRO FINE MESE? MA È IMPOSSIBILE!
ALLORA VEDI DI SPICCIARTI.
I MERCANTI DELLO SPAZIO
MA INSOMMA, OLLIE, CHIEDIGLI SCUSA!
PERCHÉ?
SENNÒ, COSA FAI? FAI LEGGERE ANCHE A ME UN LIBRO PALLOSO?
DIAMOCI UNA CALMATA, VA BENE? OLLIE, CHE HAI? TI HA MORSO UN SERPENTE?
QUELLI DELLA SAMP MI HANNO CHIESTO DI ANDARE A FARE UN PROVINO, E MIO PAPÀ...
PROVINO, EH? TO', QUESTO È IL PASTONE PER LE GALLINE.
MI SPIACE...
DAI, ANDIAMO A GIOCARE A PALLONE.
CORAGGIO, OLLIE: SIAMO NOI!
SNIFF... GIOCARE?

NIENTE CHE NON POTESSIMO RISOLVERE...
DASAEV!
CORTINA D'ACCIAIO!
... TUTTI INSIEME.
EHI! STAI QUASI IMPARANDO.
CI PROVO!
PROGRAM-MATORI CONTRO CREATIVI? AH! VI STRACCIAMO.
QUESTO LO VEDREMO...!
ROBA DA MATTI! OLLIE POTREBBE DIVENTARE UN CAMPIONE... SE NON FOSSE NATO DOVE È NATO...
CHE INTENDI DIRE?
I GRANDI SONO STRANI. TI TAGLIANO LE ALI OGNI VOLTA CHE PROVI A USARLE.
MA TU SEI UNA NUVOLA, NON È VERO, BOGGAN?

PANG
SUPER PANG
PUYO PUYO
ATOMINO
CHE SONO?
GIOCHI DI PALLINE!
?
DOBBIAMO VEDERE COME SONO FATTI GLI ALTRI VIDEO-GIOCHI SIMILI AL NOSTRO, OKAY?
VEDI COME MUOVONO LORO GLI SPRITE?
TE LO PUOI SOGNARE.
SECONDO ME, CI MANCA ANCORA QUALCOSA...
C'È POSTA PER VOI...
KICK OFF 2
!!!
!!!
GIOCHI DI CALCIO... *PUAH!*
MA PORC...!
IL GOLLONZO!
FORTE! LA PALLA SI MUOVE SENZA RIMANERE ATTACCATA AI PIEDI DEI CALCIATORI.

PASSA!
CROSSA!
TIRO DA TRENTA METRI!
HO TROVATO!
ANCHE IN **STOP!**, LA PALLA DEVE ANDARE PER CONTO SUO.
PER FARLE CAMBIARE DIREZIONE, VAI SU O GIÙ, E SOLO DOPO NELLA DIREZIONE OPPOSTA.
SI PUÒ FARE.

CLOUD, CHE COMBINI?
LASCIA PERDERE, GEPPO, NON TE LO DIRÀ! NON PARLA PIÙ CON I SUOI VECCHI AMICI.
Polifemo
DISEGNO I BONUS PER IL LIVELLO MITOLOGICO DI STOP!
CHE ROBA È?
IL VIDEOGIOCO DELL'UNDERGROUND EMPIRE!
ALLORA FAI IL LIVELLO PISELLO. NON PUÒ ESSERE UN VERO VIDEOGIOCO SENZA UN LIVELLO SEGRETO A FORMA DI PISELLO.
VOGLIO UN LIVELLO ANCH'IO! METTICI IL MIO NOME.
QUESTO MI DÀ UN'IDEA...

SONO RIMASTI IL LIVELLO 43 E IL 17. SONO DIECIMILA LIRE. DEBORA CON L'H O SENZA?
CHI È QUESTA DEBORAH...?
BOH. UNA DELLA 5^A B.
LALLI! DOVE VAI?
SGRUNT!
ORA TI ARROTOLO, NANETTO!
LO SAI CHI SIAMO, NO? BENE: VOGLIAMO ESSERE NEI PRIMI DIECI LIVELLI. SI PUÒ FARE?
CHE VOLEVANO, QUEI DUE?
BOH. LA GENTE SI COMPORTA IN MODO STRANO.
I NOSTRI EROI! ECCOLI LAGGIÙ! YU-UUH, RAGAZZI!
EHI! TUTTI CI CONOSCONO. SIAMO POPOLARI!
UN BRINDISI PER L'UNDERGROUND EMPIRE!
CHE FAI, VITO?
NON BRINDI?
EH? EHM, SÌ...

CHI MI DÀ UNA MANO CON IL BARBECUE?
MA GUARDA: NON È LA RAGAZZA DI IERI SERA? L'HA INVITATA!
E BRAVO VITO!
GIURO, SU MARX ED ENGELS CHE MAI RIVE-LERÒ...
MAI RIVELERÒ... IL SEGRETO DELLA ROSTICCIATA RUSSA... A UN TEXANO...
GIRARE LE MELANZANE, PRESTO!
FU UN CUOCO A FAR FILTRARE LA RICETTA DA SOTTO LA PORTA DELLA DACIA, MI GUARDAI INTOR-NO E....
TEMO DI AVER MANGIATO TROPPO...

VIENI CON ME!
DOVE?
SEI SICURA DI CONOSCERE LA STRADA?
TRANQUILLO! L'HO FATTA MILLE VOLTE, FIN DA QUANDO ERO BAMBINA.
È IL MIO POSTO SEGRETO.
È... MERAVIGLIOSO!
QUANDO VUOI, TORNIAMO.
MA SEI MATTA?
RESTIAMO!
CHE SERATA MAGNIFICA!

CORAGGIO, GEPPO!
ME NE HANNO DATE TRE!
TOCCA A NOI!
OUD
UMPHF!
MA...
GRANDE CLOUD. NEMMENO UNA MATERIA!

LIVELLO 3
SUMMER GAME

NIENTE MALE!
SEI SICURO CHE I TUOI VOTI NON LI ABBIANO SCAMBIATI CON QUELLI DI GATTI?
SMETTILA! SMETTILA! CI CREDO! CI CREDO!
RAGAZZI! A TAVOLA!
COSA NE DITE SE PER PREMIO ANDIAMO TUTTI IN VACANZA IN SARDEGNA DAGLI ZII?
YUPPIE!
NO!
VOGLIO DIRE, NO... GRAZIE. IO PREFERISCO... VOGLIO DIRE... VORREI... STARE QUI.
MA SEI IMPAZZITO?
I PAPASSINI DELLA ZIA??
LE CASADINASA, LE TZILICCASA, LE SEADAS CON IL MIELE DI CORBEZZOLO?

E PERCHÉ VUOI RESTARE QUI ANCHE D'ESTATE? HAI FATTO IL TUO DOVERE, TI MERITI UN PREMIO!
INVECE DI ANDARE IN SARDEGNA? MA SEI IMPAZZITO?
TU NON CAPISCI! RESTARE È IL PREMIO!
GIORGIO, NON ALZARE LA VOCE...
VOGLIO DISEGNARE CON IL DELUXE PAINT PER TUTTA L'ESTATE! STARE CON I MIEI AMICI! A RIVERE!
PER LA MISERIA!
CHE RAZZA DI SCIOCCHEZZE!
SI VA IN VACANZA E BASTA! E QUESTA È LA MIA ULTIMA PAROLA.
CRASH!
NON CAPITE NIENTE!

GLIEL'HO DETTO, MA NON C'È MODO DI FARGLIELO CAPIRE.
A DIRE LA VERITÀ, RAGAZZI... ANCHE IO RISCHIO DI DOVER ANDARE VIA.
IDEM. VADO IN MONTAGNA CON MIA SORELLA.
SNIFF!
QUINDI È LA FINE?
CLOUD

C'È CHI VA IN VACANZA E NON VUOLE, E CHI VUOLE E NON PUÒ. QUESTA È LA VITA.
NON CI PENSARE. VAI A DORMIRE.
'NOTTE.
VOI CHE FARESTE, EH? E SOPRATTUTTO, FARESTE QUALCOSA?
PÀ & MA
CREEEK

EHI!
MAMMA, PERCHÉ NON MI HAI SVEGLIATO? È TARDI!
MA COSA...
?!?
BUONGIORNO, TESORO. VIENI A SENTIRE LE NOVITÀ!
CIAO, RAGAZZO.

HO GIÀ PARLATO CON I TUOI, E SONO D'ACCORDO. MANCHI SOLO TU. TI VA DI VENIRE A LAVORARE DA ME, QUEST'ESTATE?
?!?
CE L'HAI UNA VALIGIA?
S-SÌ.
ALLORA VAI A FARLA.
SUBITO!
SE PENSI CHE TI PORTERÒ LE CASADINASA, SEI UN ILLUSO! ME LE MANGERÒ TUTTE!
SGRUNT!
VEDRÀ, VE LO RESTITUISCO PIÙ NUOVO DI PRIMA.
UNA BELLA FORTUNA! ANCHE IO, DA GIOVANE... CHE RICORDI! BEVEVO IL LATTE DALLE MAMMELLE DELLA MUCCA!
FATTI SENTIRE, OGNI TANTO. IL NUMERO DEGLI ZII LO SAI.
ADESSO SORRIDI. POI, APPENA GIRIAMO L'ANGOLO, SALTI DIETRO, OKAY?
DIETRO DOVE?

HAI PORTATO IL COSTUME DA BAGNO?
TISTAR!
ERA ORA. TI FACCIO VEDERE LA STANZA.
MA COME AVETE FATTO?
TA & MA
CHIEDILO A MIO NONNO. IO NON NE HO IDEA. TI PIACE?
QUESTA CELLA? È PERFETTA!
BENE. ERA LA CAMERA DEI MIEI GENITORI.
I TUOI... AH... OH... CIOÈ... SCUSA... NON SAPEVO CHE...
NON C'È NIENTE DA SAPERE. VIENI, TI FACCIO VEDERE COSA C'È DA FARE.

E QUESTA FU LA NOSTRA ESTATE: AL MATTINO, FRESCO O NON FRESCO, LAVORAVAMO NELL'ORTO.
CI MUOVIAMO? VOGLIO PRANZARE A UN'ORA DECENTE.
POI SI MANGIAVA...
LALLI! ACCOMODATI. VUOI UN'ALBICOCCA?
CIAO!
... E FINO ALLE QUATTRO, MENTRE FUORI FACEVA TROPPO CALDO PER QUALUNQUE ALTRA COSA, LAVORAVAMO, AL FRESCO DEL RIFUGIO.
TIC
TAC
TIC
TAC
TIC
TIC
PER UNA SETTIMANA, FU UN PARADISO. C'ERANO TUTTI.

E QUANDO ARRIVAVA SIMONA, ANDAVAMO AL FIUME SOTTO CASA DI LALLI.
YKES!
CHE BELLA VITA!

MA POI BUCK ARRIVÒ CON LA NOTIZIA.
DEVO ANDARE AL BRALLO.
IL BRALLO: QUEL POSTO LONTANISSIMO DOVE TI INSEGNANO TENNIS E INGLESE.
UN'ACCOPPIATA MICIDIALE!
E... RAGAZZI, MI SA CHE RAPISCONO ANCHE ME. VADO IN MONTAGNA CON MIA SORELLA.
A FARE CHE?
BOH! I MONDIALI ESTIVI DI SCI, O QUALCOSA DEL GENERE.
TI MANDERÒ UNA CARTOLINA!
CI CONTO!
STOP! EBBE UN PREVEDIBILE RALLENTAMENTO. E NOI CI OCCUPAMMO ANCHE DI ALTRE COSE.
TU NE SEI QUALCOSA DEI GENITORI DI TISTAR?
SO CHE STANNO ANCORA LITIGANDO PER LA CASA. SI SONO SEPARATI MALE E, INTANTO, ALBERTO STA CON IL NONNO.

MA GUARDA. TISTAR SI CHIAMA ALBERTO.
E TU, INVECE, CLOUD?
IO COSA?
CHE CI FA UNO COME TE TUTTA L'ESTATE A RIVERE?
IO? LAVORO E FACCIO IL BAGNO. PERCHÉ?
ZZZIP!
CLOUD?
CHE C'È?
COPRITI, ESIBIZIONISTA!
NON HAI IL COSTUME.
AAARGH!

E POI, TRE GIORNI DOPO...
THUD!
... UHM? CHE SUCCEDE?
L'HO SENTITO ANCHE IO.
MA CHI È?
BUCK?!? CHE CI FAI QUI? NON ERI AL BRALLO?
SSSST! LA PORTA DEL RIFUGIO È CHIUSA. NON HO LE CHIAVI.
SONO SCAPPATO...
... HO TAGLIATO PER IL BOSCO, POI HO PRESO UN TRENO E L'AUTOBUS. DA LÌ IN POI, MI SONO ARRANGIATO.
E NON POTEVI ANDARE A DORMIRE DAI TUOI?
NO! I MIEI NON SANNO CHE SONO QUI. E NON LO DEVONO SAPERE!

VROOOM
OVVIAMENTE I SUOI LO VENNERO A SAPERE, MA, CHISSÀ PERCHÉ, NON LO RIPORTARONO AL BRALLO, NÉ VENNERO A RIPRENDERSELO...
CAI! CAI!
CHE FACCIAMO, PÌ?
PUÒ RIMANERE DA ME. HO POSTO IN FIENILE. I RAGAZZI SONO FELICI COSÌ.
A DUE CONDIZIONI. CHE MIA MOGLIE NON POSSA PORTARGLI NESSUN ALTRO CAMBIO DI VESTITO...
E...?
... CHE TU LO FACCIA SGOBBARE!
CON MOLTO PIACERE!

CON IL RITORNO DI BUCK, LE COSE TORNARONO A GIRARE A MILLE.
CHE LIVELLO FACCIAMO OGGI?
CHE NE DITE DEL LIVELLO "VADO A CONTROLLARE I POMODORI"?
CE L'ABBIAMO LA PALLINA CUORE DI BUE?
QUELLO È UN SAN MARZANO.
CHE CARINO: "BACI E ABBRACCI, VITO"!

E CONTINUAMMO, SENZA PIÙ FERMARCI...
HO RISOLTO!
FLASH
ALLA FINE DEL MESE, AVEVAMO I PRIMI LIVELLI GIOCABILI.
♫
FUNZIONA!
E, FINALMENTE, POTEVAMO RILASSARCI.

QUESTA È LA NOTTE DI SAN LORENZO, LO SAPETE COSA SUCCEDE?
COOOSA?
CHE SI FANNO GRANDI PROMESSE.
E TU COSA PROMETTI, BUCK?
CHE FINIREMO **STOP!** PRIMA DELL'INIZIO DELLA SCUOLA!
URRÀ!

E IO PROMETTO CHE DIVENTERÒ IL CAMPIONE ITALIANO DI KICK OFF 2!
VIVA!
E IO CHE NON ME NE STARÒ CON LE MANI IN MANO.
OLÈ!
E TU, CLOUD? TU COSA PROMETTI?
IO? NON SAPREI.
EH NO, CLOUD.
ABBIAMO PROMESSO TUTTI.
ALLORA PROMETTO CHE...
... RIUSCIRÒ A CONVINCERE TISTAR A METTERE I BOGGAN ANCHE DENTRO *STOP!*
NO WAY!
AH! AH! AH! AH! AH! AH! AH! AH! AH!

PERCHÉ POI... BLA BLA... IL FILM... HOLLYWOOD...
IO DEVO PROPRIO ANDARE.
TI ACCOMPAGNO!

GRAZIE, SAI! NON C'ERA BISOGNO...
FIGURATI!
MI PIACE ACCOMPAGNARE GLI ALTRI A CASA.
MA ALLORA NON TI INTERESSANO SOLO I VIDEOGIOCHI!
EHM, NO, MA... UNA VITA SENZA VIDEOGIOCHI NON MERITA DI ESSERE VISSUTA!
PERCHÉ RIDI?
È UNA COSA SERIA.
SINCERAMENTE, NON LO PENSI ANCHE TU?
IO PENSO CHE, PRIMA DI FINIRLO, UN GIOCO VADA FATTO PROVARE A QUALCUNO.
BUONANOTTE, CLOUD!
PANE & DOLCI
EHM... BUONANOTTE!

LIVELLO 9
INSERT COIN
TUTTI, LI HO MANGIATI TUTTI! NEMMENO UNO, TE NE HO LASCIATO.
TESORO! MA HAI MANGIATO?
NOI DUE DOBBIAMO PARLARE...

VUOI CHE VENGA A GIOCARE UNA COSA A RIVERE?
E MI PAGATE?
LO SAPEVO... SANGUISUGA!
TO'!
UHM. OKAY. VEDIAMO QUESTO GIOCO.
MA QUANTO CI METTE?
EH?
SAREBBE LUI?
SÌ, È IL MIGLIOR GIOCATORE CHE IO CONOSCA.
MI RACCOMANDO, DICCI TUTTO QUELLO CHE NON VA. NON TRALASCIARE NULLA.
WOW!

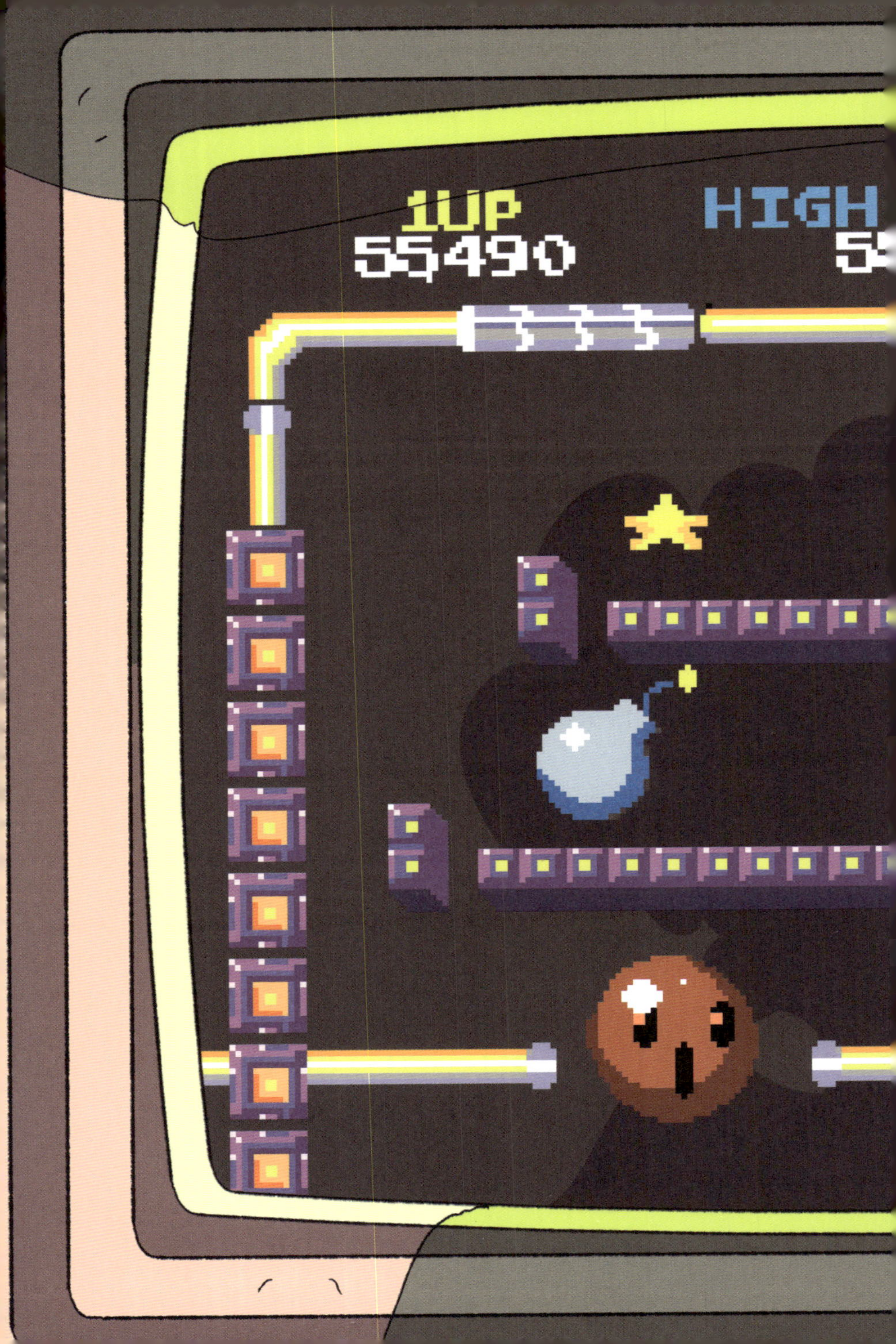
1UP
55490
HIGH

PUSH
2P

ALLORA?
MMM...
GRAN BELL'ARCADE. ORIGINALE!
MA...
LA COLLISIONE TRA LE PALLINE LASCIA MOLTO A DESIDERARE.
TROPPO PRECISA.
A VOLTE È FRUSTRANTE PERCHÉ NON TI PERMETTE IL MINIMO ERRORE.
TI SCRIVO QUI TUTTO QUELLO CHE NON VA, OKAY?
IO LO UCCIDO.
SCHERZI?
AVERCENE, COME LUI!
CHI ALTRI POSSIAMO TIRARE DENTRO?
POTETE CHIEDERE AL TIMIDO.
E CHI SAREBBE QUESTO TIMIDO?
UNO CHE NE SA. STASERA ABBIAMO APPUNTAMENTO AL TIBIDABO.

FLASH
VITO! COM'ERA LA MONTAGNA?
TIBIDABO
E TISTAR?
HA DETTO CHE AVEVA DA FARE.
EHI!
È UNA REFLEX?
FLASH
TRANQUILLO, SONO CON ME.
O-OKAY.
ALLORA, CHE VI SERVE ESATTAMENTE?
METTILA VIA! COSÌ LO SPAVENTI.
CI SERVONO DEI GIOCATORI DI VIDEOGIOCHI.
V-VA BENE.
SIETE NEL POSTO GIUSTO.

TIBIDABO

CE LE PUOI CAMBIARE?
OH, OH, SERATONA, EH?
CERCATE SOLO I MIGLIORI!
ADESSO BASTA!
È L'ULTIMA PARTITA! STUPIDO CONTROLLER!
CRACK!
OOPS!
LO DICO A TUO PADRE! QUI TU NON CI TORNI MAI PIÙ!
E MENO MALE! QUESTO POSTO È UNA FOGNA!
FLASH
ZOLFO
Nome: zolfo
Età: 11
Giochi preferiti:
Street fighter II,
Giochi di calcio
(tranne Tehkan World Cup)

UNO, DUE E...
LORO DUE!
Nome: Geordie
Età: 15
Giochi preferiti:
Out run, Turbo
Out run, Power
Drift, Lotus Esprit
Turbo Challenge
GEORDIE
WALTER
Nome: Walter
Età: 16
Giochi preferiti:
Out run, Turbo
Out run, Power
Drift, Lotus Esprit
Turbo Challenge

E POI CI SAREBBE ENZO, DETTO UNA SOLA.
PERCHÉ UNA SOLA?
QUESTA È LA SUA PRIMA PARTITA, GIUSTO?
SÌ. E ALLORA?
ASPETTA E VEDRAI.
1 UP
HIGH SCORE 287900
1 UP
HIGH SCORE 872000
RANKING BEST 5
1st ENZO_ 1922850
2nd SIUS 761050
FUORI DI QUI, O MI MANDERAI IN ROVINA!
me: Una Sola
eferiti:
tal Kombat,
Doom, Crazy Taxi
Donkey
Kong
Età:
14
UNA SOLA
ENZO
TIBIDABO
SBRANG
SIAMO AL COMPLETO!

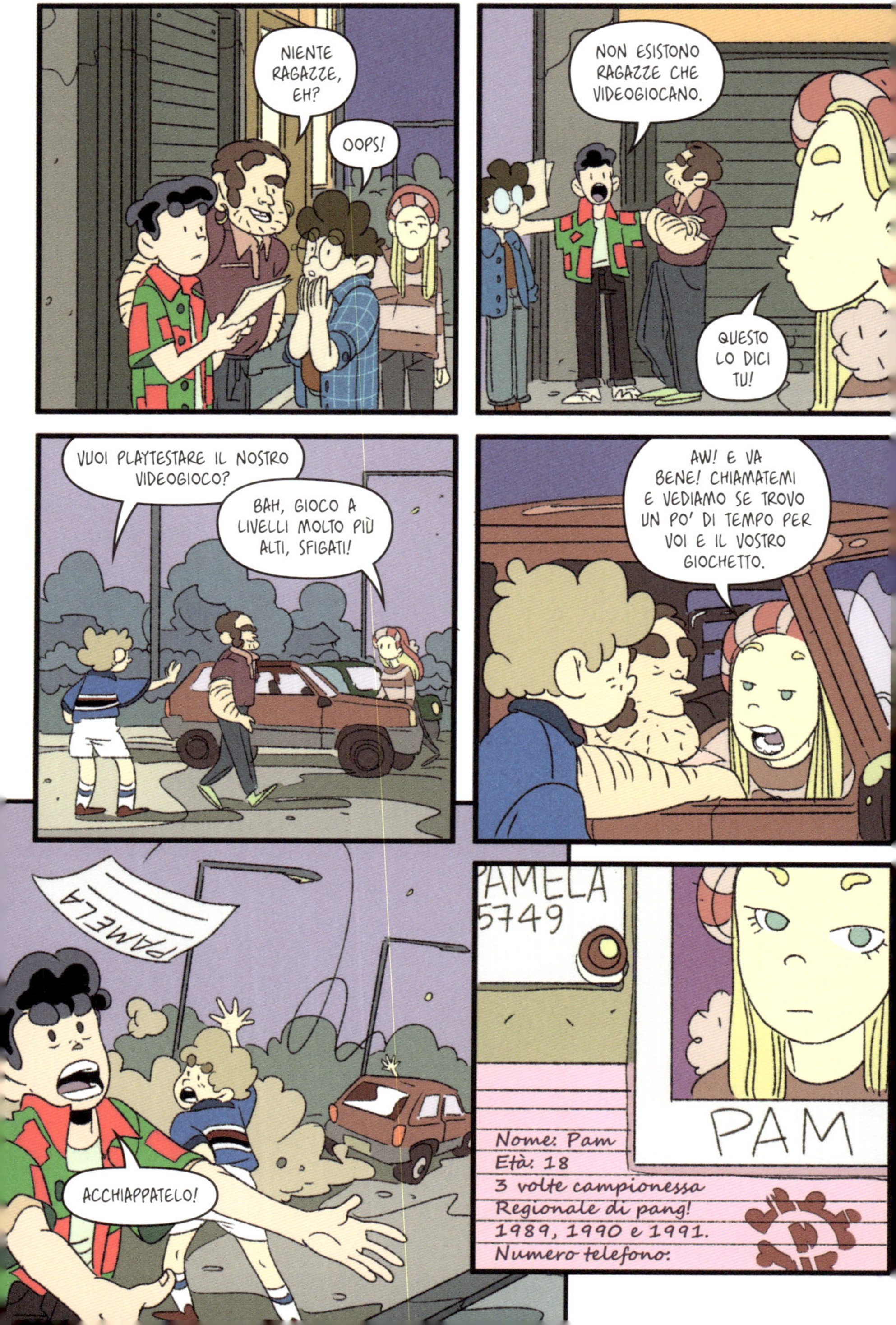
NIENTE RAGAZZE, EH?
OOPS!
NON ESISTONO RAGAZZE CHE VIDEOGIOCANO.
QUESTO LO DICI TU!
VUOI PLAYTESTARE IL NOSTRO VIDEOGIOCO?
BAH, GIOCO A LIVELLI MOLTO PIÙ ALTI, SFIGATI!
AW! E VA BENE! CHIAMATEMI E VEDIAMO SE TROVO UN PO' DI TEMPO PER VOI E IL VOSTRO GIOCHETTO.
PAMELA
ACCHIAPPATELO!
PAMELA
5749
PAM
Nome: Pam
Età: 18
3 volte campionessa
Regionale di pang!
1989, 1990 e 1991.
Numero telefono:

TIBIDABO
CI SI VEDE.
QUANTO TEMPO TI OCCORRE PER SVILUPPARE QUELLE FOTO?
LE PORTO DA FRANCO DOMATTINA, IN GIORNATA SONO PRONTE.
EHI! MA NON È *TISTAR*, QUELLO?
MA DAI, DOVE?
MA NO! SI È SBAGLIATO, NON ERA LUI. FORZA: ANDIAMO A CASA!
!!!

ZOLFO, UNA SOLA: TOCCA A VOI!
CI SONO TUTTI I MIGLIORI, POSSIAMO COMINCIARE!
CHISSÀ PERCHÉ IL TIMIDO HA RINUNCIATO.
PER FORTUNA QUEI BULLI HANNO ACCETTATO SUBITO DI RIMPIAZZARLO.
IL POSTO È TUTTO VOSTRO, MA VI SUPPLICO, LASCIATEMI ANDARE!

NON DOVETE FARE ALTRO CHE GIOCARE!
E DARCI UN PARERE SINCERO!
SINCERITÀ: QUESTA SCONOSCIUTA, EH?
COME DICI?
PRONTI? UNO, DUE E...
♫

NON SI CAPIVA CHE ERA UNA BOMBA! SEMBRAVA UNA CILIEGIA!
STAI CALMO, ZOLFO, CALMO. VEDRAI CHE LA CORREGGONO.
PERCHÉ SE PASSI ATTRAVERSO QUEL MURO APPARENTEMENTE INVALICABILE SUCCEDE QUESTO?
SONO MORTO DI NUOVO, RAZZA DI PALLINA DEL CAVOLO!
AIUTO!
CHIPS
TUTTE LE HA MANGIATE, TUTTE! NON ME NE HA LASCIATA NEMMENO UNA!
VEDO, VEDO... MA CREDO CHE ABBIAMO LA SOLUZIONE.
CIAO. SE PROVI A MANGIARMI UNA PATATINA TI APPENDO AL MURO.
CHIPS

EHI! PSST!
HO POCO TEMPO! STATEMI A SENTIRE: C'È UN BUG AL TERZO LIVELLO! SE RIMBALZI CONTRO IL MURO ROSSO PASSI DIRETTAMENTE AL 47!
EH?
HA RAGIONE.
GUARDA QUA.
SBONG!
GRAZIE A TUTTI, RAGAZZE E RAGAZZI! ABBIAMO GIÀ TROVATO UN MILIONE DI ERRORI!
VIVA!

E ORA, NON CI RESTA CHE CORREGGERE UN PO' DI COSE... TISTAR? VITO?
CORREGGETELO DA SOLI, IO MI CHIAMO FUORI!
MA CHE...
VITO! MA STAI SCHERZANDO? SENZA DI TE...
SENZA DI ME COSA? AVETE TISTAR, CHE VEDE E PROVVEDE.
IO, PER QUANTO MI RIGUARDA, NE HO ABBASTANZA.
VITO! ASPETTA.
VROOOM!
EMBÈ, CHE C'È DA GUARDARE?

È TUTTA COLPA TUA! SE NON CI AVESSI PROVATO CON SIMONA...
NON SONO AFFARI TUOI!
COME PENSI DI FARCELA, TUTTO DA SOLO?
TANTO PIÙ CHE IL PAPÀ DI VITO ORA SI RIPRENDERÀ I MONITOR E LA STAMPANTE...
PFUI! NON NE ABBIAMO BISOGNO.
VITO È L'UNICO CHE AVEVA UN PO' DI SALE IN ZUCCA. L'UNICO IN GRADO DI RIPULIRE IL CODICE DALLE TUE STRONZATE!
E TU CHE NE SAI? CREATIVO DEI MIEI STIVALI...
EHI! DATEVI UNA CALMATA...
BASTA, NE HO LE TASCHE PIENE. SAPETE CHE C'È? MI CHIAMO FUORI ANCH'IO. VIA TUTTI! CHIUDIAMO I BATTENTI!
NON PUOI DIRE SUL SERIO...
E INVECE SÌ!
SLAM!

LIVELLO 10
TEAM KILL

CI ISCRIVIAMO AL CAMPIONATO NAZIONALE DI KICK OFF 2.
E PERCHÉ?
LA FINALE È A MILANO. E IL PRIMO PREMIO È UNA VISITA ALLA FACTORY DELLA ANCO SOFTWARE, A DARTFORD, NEL KENT.
IN INGHILTERRA? FIGO!
FINALE
MILANO
IL VINCITORE POTRÀ CONOSCERE ANIL GUPTA IN PERSONA, E I SUOI PROGRAMMATORI.
CI AIUTERANNO A FINIRE *STOP!*?
STAI SCHERZANDO?
QUANDO VEDRANNO COSA SIAMO IN GRADO DI FARE, CI ASSUME-RANNO!
NON LO SO. IO DOVREI... DEVO STUDIARE, SAI? I MIEI SONO STATI CHIARI SU QUESTO PUNTO.
MICA DEVI DIR-GLIELO.
PER ANDARE NEL KENT? FORSE È IL CASO, NON CREDI?
PER ANDARE NEL KENT, PRIMA DOBBIAMO VINCERLO, QUESTO TORNEO.

Elettrodomestici
KICK OFF 2
FASI TORNEO
IL PROSSIMO!
NOME?
LASCIATEMI!
IO L'AMMAZZO!
ERA FUORIGIOCO!
CHE SUCCEDE?
HANNO PASSATO IL TURNO PER LE PROVINCIALI.
GRR...
UHM...
QUALCOSA NON VA?

CAMPIONI DI TUTTA LA PROVINCIA! IO LI CONOSCO!
BE', RAGAZZI, SE PROPRIO VI FANNO SCHIFO VENTIMILA LIRE, DATELO A ME, QUEL BUONO!
NON RIESCO A CAPIRLI: SEMBRA CHE GLI ABBIAMO UCCISO IL CANE. E TRA L'ALTRO BUCK SAREBBE CONTENTO ANCHE IN QUESTO CASO!
HAI PROVATO A PENSARE CHE FORSE SONO PREOCCUPATI?
1
E PER COSA? SONO PASSATI!
MA SONO MOLTO AMICI, VERO?
CERTO CHE SONO AMICI, E ALLORA?
ALLORA QUANTI NE VANNO IN FINALE, DALLE REGIONALI?
UNO. E ALLORA?
AH. GIÀ.
NE VA UNO SOLO. CAVOLO! COME HO FATTO A NON PENSARCI PRIMA?

ERA COSÌ SEMPLICE: AVEVANO PAURA DI TROVARSI A DOVER GIOCARE UNO CONTRO L'ALTRO, PER ANDARE ALLA FASE FINALE.
COSA POSSO FARE?
NIENTE. È UNA COSA TRA LORO, ORMAI.
E QUESTO È... IL GOLLONZO!
CHE SFORTUNA: È SALTATO PROPRIO ALL'ULTIMO SECONDO.
EVVAVAMO QVUATTVO A ZVERO...
DOVETE RIGIOCARLA, MI SPIACE.
FINALE
BACCALARIO
OLIVIERI
OH, NO!
E I DUE FINALISTI SONO...
È UN ONORE.
L'ONORE È MIO.
BE', DAI, ALLORA... CHE VINCA IL MIGLIORE, NO?

COME STA ANDANDO?
OLLIE È FORTE.
UN'AZIONE E UN GOAL PER **OLIVIERI!**
MA CHE HA? SI VERGOGNA?
HA COMINCIATO INSPIEGABILMENTE A GIOCARE MALE.
FORSE NON TANTO INSPIEGABIL-MENTE.
EVVAI! CIOÈ, SCUSA. PAREGGIO.
CHE FANNO? MELINA?
PERCHÉ NON LO ATTACCA?
NESSUNO VUOLE VINCERE.
GLOM...

ACH!
OH, CAVOLO...
GOAL DI BACCALARIO!
SCUSA.
NON... VOLEVO.
NON PREOCCUPARTI.
HO DETTO SCUSA, OLLIE!
COUGH! COUGH!
BRAAAAAA!

COME È ANDATA, RAGAZZI? SI VA A MILANO?
DOV'È OLLIE?
WEEEEE ARE THE CHAMPIONS, MY FRIENDS!
MA QUINDI SE L'È PRESA?
NAAA, NON CREDO.
NON MI IMPORTA E NON PIANGO.
NON MI IMPORTA E NON PIANGO.
NON...
BRAAAAAA!
BRAAAAAAAAAAA!
BRAAAAA!

UUUUUU!
OLLIE? CIAO. VOLEVO...
CLIC!
...
CHI ERA, A QUEST'ORA?
NESSUNO.
DRIN!
!!!

CLOUD! NON PUOI IMMAGINARE CHI MI HA CHIAMATO IERI SERA!
OLLIE?
NO, BETTA.
E CHI È BETTA?
MIA CUGINA!
PARTY
NON LA CONO-SCI. QUESTO SABATO DÀ UNA FESTA. UNA FESTA GRANDIOSA, IN ABITO NERO.
ABITO NERO?

VUOL DIRE BEN VESTITI. UNA FESTA IN UNA VILLA, CON GENTE FANTASTICA.
E A NOI COSA IMPORTA?
CHE POTREBBE ESSERE IL MODO GIUSTO PER FESTEGGIARE! TU, IO, GLI ALTRI. BETTA MI HA DETTO DI INVITARE I MIEI AMICI.
OLLIE SECONDO TE VIENE?
SE CI SIAMO TUTTI, SÌ!
AH, BE', ALLORA...
E PERÒ... A QUESTA VILLA... COME CI ANDIAMO?
L'HO CHIESTO A PAM. CI PORTA LEI, IN MACCHINA!
AH, BE', ALLORA...
ALLORA È FATTA! E RICORDATI: PUOI PORTARE CHI VUOI!
DAVVERO?
AH!
SO BENE A CHI CHIEDERLO!

IL TUO AMICO È IN RITARDO.
NON È LUI CHE GUIDA.
SST! SENTO UN RUMORE.
SKREEE!
MA CHE SUCCEDE, QUI?
E LORO CHE CI FANNO?
COME CHE CI FANNO? MI HAI DETTO CHE POTEVO PORTARE CHI VOLEVO!

MA È UN MODO DI DIRE, CLOUD, PER DIRE CHE PUOI INVITARE UNA RAGAZZA. UNA, UNA SOLA. SE ADESSO VIE-NE OLLIE NON CI STIAMO.
POSSO VIAGGIARE NEL BAGAGLIAIO. L'HO GIÀ FATTO.
E TRA L'ALTRO PENSAVO L'AVRESTI DETTO A LALLI.
A LALLI, E PERCHÉ?
SEI UN CASO DISPERATO, LO SAI?
NON POSSO DIRGLI CHE NON VENGONO. SI SONO ANCHE MESSI ELEGANTI.
CI MUOVIA-MO? DOBBIAMO ANCORA PRENDERE L'ULTIMO.
FORZA!

AVANTI, OLLIE!
DIREI CHE NON VIENE. ANDIAMO? SIAMO GIÀ IN RITARDO.
P-P-PAAAAM?
NESSUN PROBLEMA!
L'IMPORTANTE È SPARARLA GROSSA, COME HEMINGWAY. TANTO NON TI CONOSCE NESSUNO.
DICI?
MA SÌ, GUARDA.
CIAO, STEVE. NON ERI A PORTOFINO? CE LI FAI DUE COSMO CON POCO GHIACCIO?
!!!
STAMMI A SENTIRE, STRONZETTO. UNO, MI CHIAMO AGIM, SONO DI TIRANA, E DUE, HO L'ORDINE DI NON SERVIRE ALCOOL AI RAGAZZINI. LIMONATA?
O-OKAY!

E A TE COSA TI HA DATO?
DUE GIN FIZZ.
MALEDETTO AGIM!
PASSA QUI.
SECONDO VOI COSA C'È IN CIMA A QUESTA CASA?
LA SOFFITTA, CREDO.
UNA VECCHIA SOFFITTA CON FANTASMI E TRAPPOLE MORTALI?
FORZA, ANDIAMO A VEDERE! DI SICURO È PIÙ DIVERTENTE CHE STARE QUI.
FAMMI PASSARE.
EHI, CALMA!

CHE POSTO DI MERDA, RAGAZZI...
BOH? È AMICO TUO. SE NON LO SAI TU...
MA CHE HA BUCK? MICA SIAMO VENUTI QUI A SPACCARE TUTTO.
CI VUOLE ARIA, QUI DENTRO, ARIA!
OKAY, BASTA COSÌ: TORNIAMO GIÙ?
VACCI TU, DA QUEGLI ZOMBIE!
SBAM!
FINALMENTE. ORA RAGIONIAMO!
CHE VISTA, EH?
BUCK?

BUUUCK!
THUD!

WEEEO! WEEEO!
MA È MORTO?
SHHHT!
DOVREMO RACCOGLIERLO CON IL CUCCHIAINO.
EHI! MA COME SI PERMETTE? È UN MIO AMICO, QUELLO CHE È CADUTO!
"CUCCHIAINO": NOME DELLA BARELLA A CARICO LATERALE.
E RILASSATI: IL TUO AMICO È MESSO MALE. MA È VIVO.

LIVELLO 11
ZZAP!

OH, FINALMENTE! CHIUNQUE TU SIA, VAI DENTRO. BUCK STRAPARLA, MAGARI CAPISCI COSA VUOLE.
ZA... ZA... **ZZAP!**
EHM... CIAO, COME TI SENTI?
Z-Z-Z-ZAP!
INTENDI DIRE... QUESTA...?
LA FINALE... DEL TORNEO DI KICK OFF È DOMANI. DEVI... CONVINCI OLLIE A GIOCARE AL POSTO MIO. ANDATE... VOI...
PERCHÉ IO?
E PORTATI LA DEMO. NON SI SA MAI.

IO... IO NON HO NEMMENO IL NUMERO DI OLLIE! NON L'HO PIÙ VISTO DA QUANDO... QUANDO...
CIAO.
MI HANNO DETTO CHE TE LA SEI VISTA BRUTTA.
DOVRESTI VEDERE...
COM'È CONCIATO L'ALTRO!
AH! AH!
AH! AH!
AH!
STAVO DICENDO A CLOUD CHE DOVETE ANDARE AL TORNEO, DOMANI.
MA CHE DICI? HAI VINTO TU, VAI TU.
SICURO!... TRA UN PAIO DI MESI. QUANDO SARÀ FINITO. TU SEI IL SECONDO. VAI AL POSTO MIO. È NEL REGOLAMENTO!
NON POSSIAMO MOLLARE PRO-PRIO ADESSO.
...

CI...
CI DEVO
PENSARE.
CI
PARLO
IO!
PANT!
PANT! OLLIE!
ASPETTA!
OLLIE!
BUCK HA RAGIONE. ANDIAMO, SU. C'È IN PALIO UN VIAGGIO IN INGHILTERRA! LA SEDE DELLA ANCO! STOP!
LO SO.
MA...
TIENI.
E RICORDATI COME ABBIAMO INIZIATO. IO CI VADO COMUNQUE, CON LA DEMO. CHE TU CI SIA O NO.
ZAP!
KICK OFF 2

GUARDA: QUI C'È IL NOME DI BUCK!
GIÀ.
MA LUI COME STA? RIESCE A GIOCARE?
BE'... VERAMENTE NON RIESCE NEMMENO A CAMMINARE.
CHE SFORTUNA. È IL KARMA, EH?
IL CHE?
IL KARMA. BUCK HA SEMPRE AVUTO TUTTE LE FORTUNE. E PER UNA VOLTA, INVECE...
MENTRE NOI SIAMO PROTETTI DALLA MADONNINA DELL'ALTAI.
MAMMA?
COSA C'È?
E SE CI ANDASSI IO, AL POSTO DI BUCK?

IN QUESTO CASO, QUESTA SERVIRÀ A TE.
!!!
UNA SOLA COSA, PERÒ...
MAMMA!
NON DIRE NIENTE A TUO PADRE, ALTRIMENTI, COL CAVOLO CHE TI DÀ IL PERMESSO, OKAY?
O-OKAY!
E CERCA DI VINCERE, MAGARI.
CLOUD? CI VEDIAMO DOMANI ALLE SETTE, IN STAZIONE... D'ACCORDO?

ANCO
KICK OFF 2
CHE ROBA, OLLIE, C'È DA PERDERSI.
SÌ, MA È IN OSPEDALE. IO SONO IL SECONDO, VEDE?
OKAY, È TUTTO REGOLARE.
CHI È? PERCHÉ TUTTI LO INDICANO?
QUELLO È CALDIERO, IL CAMPIONE USCENTE. SPERANO DI EVITARLO.
SG PB FR BDB
RICORDO A TUTTI CHE LA FASE FINALE È A DUE TURNI, ANDATA E RITORNO. E IL GOAL FUORI CONTA DOPPIO.
FORZA, OLLIE: DA QUI IN POI SI FA SUL SERIO.
CALDIERO E AIAZZI SONO FINITI NELLO STESSO GIRONE. UNO DEI DUE NON ARRIVERÀ IN FINALE.
CHE SUCCEDE?
ED È UNA BUONA COSA?
SÌ.
CONTRARIAMENTE A QUANTO ERA SCRITTO SUL PROGRAMMA, LE PARTITE SI GIOCANO CON I TEMPI DA CINQUE MINUTI.
NON È POSSIBILE! CHE CAVOLO! IO ERO PREPARATO SULLA LUNGA DISTANZA!

OLIVIERI VECCHIO
IL GOLLONZO!
OLIVIERI ROMOLINI
3-4. VINCE OLIVIERI!
... MORTACCI TUA!
OLIVIERI GUAZZONI
SIGNORI, ABBIAMO IL PRIMO FINALISTA!
NEMMENO A FARLO APPOSTA... IL CAMPIONE USCENTE!
DAI, FORSE NON È COSÌ FORTE COME DICONO.
HA VINTO LA SEMIFINALE 7-1...
... MA IO HO QUESTO!
E ALLORA, CHE DIRE? BUONA FORTUNA, AMICO MIO!

E DATO CHE SONO QUI, TANTO VALE CHE FACCIA ANCHE IO QUALCOSA DI UTILE...
COM'È CHE SI RICONOSCE UN GIORNALISTA DI ZZAP?
STOP!
???
PB
EHI, P.B.! PAOLINA BESSER! HO LETTO TUTTI I TUOI ARTICOLI!
EHI, CIAO! MA CHI TI HA FATTO SALIRE? STOP!
PROPRIO COSÌ! COME FAI A SAPERLO?
P.B.
GOOOOOOOOOOOOOOOOA
QUESTA È LA DEMO. PROVALA. DIECI LIVELLI! DA RECENSIRE!
MA SEI SCEMO?
E C'È IL MIO NUMERO DI TELEFONO, SOPRA!

CHE TIPO DI GIOCO È?
È INDESCRIVIBILE! NON ESISTE UN GIOCO COSÌ, NESSUNO L'HA ANCORA FATTO!
QUESTO È QUELLO CHE DICONO TUTTI! ASCOLTA, CHI È IL PROTAGONISTA, COSA DEVI FARE?
BE', È UNA... PALLINA... E DEVE...
INSOMMA, È UN GIOCO DI PALLINE, TIPO MARBLE MADNESS. INCROCIATO CON SNAKE.
EHM... SÌ. PRATICAMENTE SÌ.
EHI! SU CON LA VITA. A ME NON PIACCIONO GLI ARCADE, MA, SICCOME L'HAI FATTO TU, A QUESTO CI GIOCHERÒ.
DAVVERO?
MA CERTO! E SE MI PIACE, LO RECENSISCO. PROMETTO!

FATTA.
È FATTA. E NON È STATO POI COSÌ DIFFICILE!
È IL MIO AMICO, QUELLO.
STA ANDANDO TUTTO ALLA GRANDE. ANDRÀ TUTTO ALLA GRANDE...
O ALMENO... BENE...
O ALMENO...

EHI! GUARDA UN PO' CHI SI RIVEDE.
BUONGIORNO!
BUONGIORNO, EH? DALLE VOSTRE FACCE, NON SI DIREBBE.
È UNA LUNGA STORIA...
... E COSÌ HA PERSO.
NON CAPISCO PERCHÉ! AVEVO PURE LA MADONNINA DELL'ALTAI!
PFUI! MA QUELLA NON È UNA MADONNINA DELL'ALTAI. È LA MADONNA NERA DI CRIMEA.
AH.
E QUINDI...?
... PORTA UNA SFORTUNA NERA.
PERCHÉ NON VENITE AL RIFUGIO, QUALCHE VOLTA? È UN PO' CHE MANCATE...
VOLENTIERI, MAGARI TRA UN PO'.
CERTO, CERTO! E TENETE DURO, RAGAZZI, MI RACCOMANDO.

TENERE DURO! PIÙ FACILE A DIRSI CHE A FARSI.
LO AVRANNO VISTO, IL GIOCO?
OGGI FANNO DUE MESI, E ANCHE QUI NON CE N'È TRACCIA.
DEL RESTO, A CHI INTERESSA? AVRANNO COSE PIÙ IMPORTANTI DA FARE. COME TUTTI NOI.
SPOLVERA BENE, BUCK.
CERTO, MAMMA.
CRASH!
CHE HAI? NON TI PIACE?
E LO CHIAMI CINEMA, QUESTA ROBA?
E RIECCO I PIRATI. UFF. ADDIO, CARBONE, ADDIO, METALLO...
E TU L'HAI FATTO L'UOVO, GALLINA DELL'ALTAI?
EH? L'HAI FATTO?

RRRING!
SCUSI, CHI PARLA...? MA CHI È, SCUSI, ZZAP? QUELLI DELLA LUCE? GUARDI CHE NOI SIAMO CON ENEL.
MAMMA! È PER ME!
CIAO! HAI LETTO IL NUMERO DI NATALE?
E COME? NON È ANCORA USCITO!
ALLORA QUANDO LO LEGGI DAI UN'OCCHIATA A PAGINA 34 E POI DIMMI, OKAY?
EHI! SEI ANCORA LÌ? NON HO FINITO!
L'IDEA SOFTWARE VUOLE DARE UN'OCCHIATA AL GIOCO. TI LASCIO IL NUMERO...
IDEA SOFTWARE. MA CERTO. LA CONOSCIAMO BENE. DIMMI PURE.

DRIN!
DRIN!
DRIN!
DRIN!
CAVOLI! 85%! PER UN GIOCO CHE NON È NEMMENO USCITO.
GRANDI MUSICHETTE E PROGRAMMAZIONE STELLARE...
SENTI, MI DISPIACE PER...
AVEVI RAGIONE. SONO STATO PROPRIO UNO...

NONNO! NONNO! NON CREDERAI MAI A COSA È SUCCESSO!
IN SEGUITO ALLE DIMISSIONI DEL PRESIDENTE GORBACIOV...
NONNO? È DI NUOVO ANDATA IN BLOCCO LA CALDAIA?
... SANCENDO UFFICIALMENTE LA FINE DELL'UNIONE SOVIETICA.
NONNO?

LIVELLO 12
KILL SCREEN
NON SE LO MERITAVA. NESSUNO SE LO MERITA, A PARTE I BOSS FINALI DI R-TYPE. MA QUESTA È UN'ALTRA FACCENDA.

CHE BRUTTA FINE, PER LUI!
GIÀ... UN FUNERALE RELIGIOSO! MA TI PARE?
CHE FACCIAMO, RAGAZZI??
LO SAPETE L'ULTIMA COSA CHE CI HA DETTO? A ME E OLLIE: TENETE DURO. IO DICO: FINIAMO IL LAVORO E PORTIAMO **STOP!** A MILANO, ANCHE PER LUI.
A ME HA SEMPRE DETTO: SGOBBA, RAGAZZO, E VEDRAI.
CI FOSSE ANCORA LUI, CI DIREBBE DI ANDARE A LAVORARE NEL RIFUGIO. MA, COSÌ, DOVREMMO SENTIRE TISTAR...
ECCOMI.
TISTAR, NOI...
VI HO SENTITO. HO SENTITO CLOUD. FACCIAMOGLIELA VEDERE. VI VA?

GUARDA SE È FLUIDO.
RICORDATI DI CAMBIARE L'ICONA DELLA BOMBA CON IL TESCHIO, ALTRIMENTI ZOLFO SI ARRABBIA!
LÀ!
VE LO DICO IO: PER GENNAIO È FINITO.
RAGAZZI, È PRONTA LA CENA!
E UNO ANCHE A TE.
GIUSTO: CE L'ABBIAMO IL LIVELLO NATALIZIO?
SÌ. L'87.
E QUELLO DI CAPODANNO?
... 4...
... 3...
... 2...
... 1...
BUON ANNO!

NEVICA!
NO, MAMMA, NON PUOI VENIRE A PRENDERMI! NEVICA, CAVOLO!
IL GOLLONZO!
EHI, GUARDA, HA SMESSO!
VIENI!

PALLE DI NEVE! CE L'ABBIAMO UN LIVELLO CON LE PALLE DI NEVE CHE SI SCIOLGONO?
AVEVAMO DETTO: NIENTE MODIFICHE DELL'ULTIMA ORA!

CI VEDIAMO, RAGAZZI! SIAMO TUTTI CON VOI. E... GRAZIE, ALBERTO.
NON C'È DI CHE!
TAC TAC TAC TAC
HO FINITO.
DAI, DAVVERO?
HO DETTO CHE HO FINITO.
LALLI?
BRAVISSIMO! ORMAI CI SIETE.

RONF...
I PIRATI!...
NONNO!...
AIUTO!...
CLICK!
CREACK!
VZZZ...
TAC
TAC
TAC
TAC
COSÌ DOVREBBE FUNZIONARE MEGLIO, GIUSTO, TISTAR?

TISTAR, MA SEI UN GRANDE!
MA COME HAI FATTO? È SEMPLICEMENTE GENIALE!
E SIAMO PERFETTAMENTE IN TEMPO CON IL PROGRAMMA.
TUTTI A CASA!
GEN.
CIAO, ALLORA! CI VEDIAMO DOMANI!
SI TORNA A MILANO!
A COSA PENSI?
A NIENTE... E TU?
MMM... CHE È STATO BELLO, NON TROVI?
DICI?
OH, CHE ZUCCONE!
LALLI? CHE TI PRENDE?

...
SBRAAAA
CHE FAI QUI DA SOLO, ROMEO? VUOI UN PASSAGGIO?
NO, GRAZIE!
COME VUOI.
SBRAAAAAP
CIAO, NONNO. QUESTI SONO PER TE.
STOP 2
STOP 1

CARROZZA RISERVATA. ANCHE AL RITORNO!
AVETE VISTO LALLI?
HA DETTO CHE DOVEVA STUDIARE.
TIPICO!
AH, BE', ALLORA...
SIETE EMOZIONATI, RAGAZZI?
CLOUD, TUTTO BENE?
OH, SÌ, ALLA GRANDE.

LIVELLO 13
GAME OVER

GRAZIE!
GRAZIE!
GRAZIE!
GRAZIE!
GRAZIE!
GRAZIE!
GRAZIE!
È... FANTASTICO!
NON ESAGERIAMO! SIAMO SOLO UNA PICCOLA AZIENDA, CON TRE DIPENDENTI...
ECCO... VI STAVAMO... ASPETTANDO... NON TUTTI... MA...
ANNA? CI SONO I... RAGAZZI!

CASPITA, CHE BEI DISCHETTI!
CON CHI DI VOI DEVO... PARLARE?
IL GAMEPLAY! IL GAMEPLAY È TUTTO! UN'IDEA SIMILE NON SI È MAI VISTA, E NON SI VEDRÀ PER VENT'ANNI!
LA GRAFICA È ALL'AVAN-GUARDIA!
NON HA UN DIFETTO, CAVOLO!
STOP!
CHE NE PENSI?
MA DECIDONO COSÌ?

È MOLTO CARINO!
URRRRÀ!
COSÌ, CON UNA SOLA PARTITA?
C'È SOLO UN PROBLEMA. DUE FLOPPY COSTANO TROPPO. METTETELO SU UNO, E VE LO PUBBLICHIAMO.
OKAY! SI PUÒ FARE, VERO?
NO.
COME NO?
NO.
BENE... ALLORA... NOI... ANDIAMO!
BASTA CHE LO METTIAMO SU UN FLOPPY, GIUSTO?
UNO SOLO.
SE NE SONO ANDATI?
TUTTI, SÌ.

ALLORA? PERCHÉ NON DICI NIENTE?
BE', DAI, GRANDE, NO?
DOVE SONO FINITI, GLI ALTRI?
SARANNO ANDATI A FARE SHOPPING.
SLUUURP!
NON DICO NIENTE PERCHÉ NON HO NIENTE DA DIRE.
GLI È PIACIUTO: LO VOGLIONO PUBBLICARE!
NON È VERO.
BASTA METTERLO SU UN FLOPPY SOLO!
NON SI PUÒ.
E SE LEVIAMO LE MUSICHE?
O CARICHIAMO GLI SFONDI IN MATTONELLE SEPARATE?
SENTITE, NOI NON LO SAPPIAMO FARE, OKAY?
CI VERRÀ UN'IDEA, LA RISOLVIAMO INSIEME! ALMENO CREDO.
FU ALLORA CHE, GUARDANDOLI, CAPII.

IL VIDEOGIOCO ERA SOLO UN PRETESTO.
PIXEL DOPO PIXEL, MATTONELLA DOPO MATTONELLA, SERVIVA SOLO A CEMENTARE LA NOSTRA AMICIZIA.
A RENDERCI INDISTRUTTIBILI.
È SEMPRE STATA QUESTA LA NOSTRA FORZA. NON ARRENDERSI.
INSIEME, CONCENTRATI SU UN UNICO OBIETTIVO!
SENZA DISTRARSI MAI.

EHI!
EHI!
COM'È ANDATA?
NON MOLTO BENE. LO VOGLIONO SU UN DISCHETTO SOLO, MA NON SAPPIAMO FARLO.
CAVOLO! MI DISPIACE. E QUINDI?
BE', CI VEDIAMO.
ANDREA?
MI HA DAVVERO CHIAMATO PER NOME? E PERCHÉ? COS'È VENUTA A FARE, FUORI IN STAZIONE?
!

LALLI?
COSA VUOI?
COME FACEVI A SAPERE CHE ARRIVAVO CON QUESTO TRENO?
NON LO SAPEVO. TI HO ASPETTATO E BASTA.

AH... MA...?
MA...?
QUINDI...?
QUINDI?
MAGARI...
MAGARI.
... POSSIAMO CAMMINARE INSIEME?
CERTO CHE SÌ.

VROOOOOM
EHI! MA CHE CAVOLO...

CLOUD! FINALMENTE TI HO TROVATO.
BUCK!

CIAO LALLI! COME STAI? TI RICORDI DI ME?
SCEMO!
POSSIAMO SEDERCI UN ATTIMO? HO QUALCOSA DA FARTI VEDERE.
GUARDA CHE ROBA.
NON CAPISCO.
È UN REGOLAMENTO DI GIOCHI DI RUOLO FANTASY.
E DA DOVE SALTA FUORI?
INDOVINA!

LO ABBIAMO SCRITTO NOI. CONTA! VENTI RAZZE DIVERSE, ELFI, ORCHI, MEZZELFI, MEZZORCHI...
... CINQUANTASETTE CLASSI E SOTTO-CLASSI, DAL PALADINO ALLA SPADACCINA!
TISTAR È GIÀ A BORDO. SI STA OCCUPANDO DELLE MAGIE.
E C'È ANCHE ENZO.
TISTAR? E COME STA?
CI SERVE QUALCUNO PER DISEGNARE LE MAPPE.
ESATTO: UN CARTOGRAFO! QUALCUNO DI PRECISO. E CI SIAMO DETTI: "CHI È PIÙ PRECISO DI CLOUD?". ALLORA, CHE NE DICI?
IO...
CAVOLO, NON LO SO...
ZOLFO HA DETTO CHE È UNA BOMBA. E I GEMELLI HANNO GIÀ FATTO I PERSONAGGI. DUE MAGHI, CI CREDI?
È UN GRAN PROGETTO, CLOUD. MANCHI SOLO TU. COSA NE DICI?
BE'...

STAVOLTA, CI POSSO METTERE I BOGGAN?
FINE

GLI AUTORI

PIERDOMENICO BACCALARIO

Scrittore e giornalista, ha pubblicato romanzi, libri-gioco, racconti, giochi di ruolo, progetti didattici e umanitari e articoli specialistici: nessun genere letterario lo ha mai spaventato. Le sue opere sono state tradotte in più di trenta lingue, e hanno venduto più di due milioni di copie nel mondo. Con il Castoro ha pubblicato molti titoli di successo, tra cui tutta la serie dei *Manuali delle 50* (Avventure, Missioni, Sfide e Rivoluzioni). Sempre per Il Castoro è autore e curatore dell'enciclopedia per ragazzi *Le 15 domande,* insieme a Federico Taddia, dell'albo *Storia di Goccia e Fiocco,* firmato con Alessandro Gatti e illustrato da Simona Mulazzani e del romanzo *Il grande manca*. È il fondatore dell'agenzia creativa e di storytelling "Book on a Tree".

ANDREA CANOBBIO

Ricercatore universitario ed esperto di gestione di progetti culturali e multimediali, dal 2013 affianca all'attività accademica quella di scrittore per ragazzi, collaborando con il circolo di autori Book on a Tree. Tra i suoi ultimi libri, *La nascita del computer* (EL) e *Il merlo canta libero* (Solferino), scritto a quattro mani con Alessandro Gatti.

SUSANNA MARIANI

Classe 1990, è fumettista e illustratrice. Vive e lavora a Roma, dove si è trasferita dalla provincia per portare avanti i suoi studi e il suo percorso professionale. Dopo essersi laureata in pittura presso l'Accademia di Belle Arti di Roma, si è diplomata in fumetto alla Scuola Internazionale di Comics, dove ora è insegnante di illustrazione. Come disegnatrice ha collaborato con diverse case editrici, tra cui BeccoGiallo Editore, Bugs Comics e Mondadori Electa. Da diversi anni, nella realtà de LaCOMICSkids, affianca al lavoro di fumettista quello di insegnante di fumetto per bambini e ragazzi, il pubblico che predilige per le sue storie.

Finito di stampare nel settembre 2023
presso Abograkifa d.o.o. - Slovenia

FSC
www.fsc.org
MISTO
Carta da fonti gestite
in maniera responsabile
FSC® C126477